Ferryman

Jonathon Wise

This is a work of fiction. The events and characters portrayed herein are imaginary and are not intended to refer to specific places, events or living persons. The opinions expressed in this manuscript are solely the opinions of the author and do not necessarily represent the opinions of the publisher.

Ferryman

All Rights Reserved

ISBN-13: 978-0615588582

Copyright ©2012 IFWG Publishing, Inc/Jonathon Wise

V1.0

This book may not be reproduced, transmitted, or stored in whole or in part by any means, including graphic, electronic, or mechanical without the express written consent of the publisher except in the case of brief quotations embodied in critical articles and reviews.

IFWG Publishing, Inc.
www.ifwgpublishing.com

IFWG Publishing and the IFWGP logo are trademarks belonging to IFWG Publishing, Inc

IFWG
Publishing

Chapter 1

Even the brutal heat couldn't still Clay's nervous stomach as he stood staring at the rim of the sinkhole. Others had ventured off the trail. Peter and John were trying to find the best view of the shaft by checking various spots around the rim. But Clay didn't need to look over the edge. He knew too well the abyss that waited below in the darkness. It was the bottomless pit that churned up his fears and doubts. Feelings that demanded he hold his ground. It was the same overwhelming fear that he gave into yesterday when he peered over the edge at the Cave of the Swallows. Even after he saw the parachutes open and heard the others yell victoriously as they drifted down that hellish 360 meter drop into the belly of the earth, he had been unable to bring himself to take that solitary leap of faith.

He took a deep breath and tried to picture the hillside as it would have looked before the quake hit. Yesterday he would have been staring at a simple dirt trail that zigzagged its way up the plateau to where the two Huastecan Indians grazed their cattle. But that was before last night. He would never forget the strange sensation of the ground pitching under his cot and then under his feet as he jumped up and ran out to join the others around the smoldering campfire. Almost as strange as the sensation, was how everyone reacted to it. There was no unbridled panic—only a general sense of awe. Even before they found out that the epicenter was located nearly 500 kilometers away in the coastal mountains southwest of Mexico City, no one acted as if they felt their life were in danger.

He focused again on the forty-foot wide opening. After a moment of contemplation, he pulled the bandanna from his pocket and wiped the dust-laden sweat off his face. They were too far from the epicenter for the quake to actually open up the shaft, but not too far for it to fracture a relatively thin bed of limestone over the top of it. The trail would have buckled and then given way as several hundred tons of earth plunged into the void.

He looked over his right shoulder at the two locals. The team was heading back to Aquismon when the two Indians flagged down Stein's jeep. Stein must have called Alejandro on the squawk box because a second later he ran past on his way up to the front of the convoy. Alejandro knew enough of the local Mayan vernacular to understand what the Indians were shouting, and translate it into Spanish. Stein, whose Spanish and English were muddied by his own accent, then interpreted for the team. Stein could have slapped the Indians on the back and told them good luck with the find, but then it wasn't in his nature to pass up such a rare opportunity.

Clay turned further until he could see the dirt trail descending under the lush growth of the lower canopy. Stein and Alejandro had been gone for a good twenty minutes. Normally Stein wouldn't have gone off without leaving a local guide behind. But normal protocol went out the window after the quake. It turned out that the other local guide hired for the expedition had family in Mexico City. When Felipe heard how extensive the devastation was over the radio, he jumped into one of the jeeps and headed back while it was still dark. Stein understood and took the loss in stride. Like every bump in the road that the expedition had come upon, he kept the situation in perspective. He sat the team down and informed everyone that the Mexican government would impose law to keep the airports and highways unimpeded for the relief efforts that would be coming from around the world. Until such time that the law was lifted, they would retrieve the rest of their supplies in Aquismon and then hunker down at the airport in Tampico to wait it out.

That of course was before the group abandoned the jeeps along the gravel road and followed the Indians up the trail. As soon as Stein saw the sinkhole, he swung around and told everyone to hold their ground and to maintain a safe distance of at least twenty meters. Then with a level of excitement that gave clue to the true adventurer in him, he grabbed Alejandro and the two ran down the trail toward the road.

There was no mystery to what Stein had in mind. In the same manner that no one was surprised that first day when the rugged Norwegian stood before the team at the airport in Munich and said, "You…you're not children. You're not boys and girls. There are no room for children here. You are young man and woman. You come to be challenged and prove yourself victorious over your fears." After an introductory speech like that, it was easy to figure that Stein was heading back to the jeeps to check on gear and rigging. After all, what is a high-adrenalin expedition all about if it's not one to jump at the opportunity to explore something that's possibly never been touched by another living soul.

As Clay started to turn back to the sinkhole, he spotted one of the two Indians staring at him. It was never easy to guess the age of a local Indian. Appearance was influenced way too much by the location of the village. If the village was close to an industrialized area where the locals worked in manufacturing, then it added ten years to the lines in their faces. But in the villages that were farther out, places where farming and herding were the primary way of life, the locals could easily shed ten years. Clay would have guessed this man to be in his mid-fifties, which probably meant he was around sixty-five. But it wasn't his age or the vibrant colors of his Teenek clothing that made Clay stop and stare. It was the way the man was looking at him. Not that it was threatening. In fact it was just the opposite. The Indian was looking at him the way Clay hoped his father would look at him some day. It was incredibly relaxing.

Then he heard the commotion surrounding Stein's return, but before he could look away the old man mouthed something to him. For a strange reason it felt deeply meaningful as if it were intended just for him. So much so, that even though neither spoke the other's language, Clay still found himself mouthing out the words 'The last day is coming'.

"Komm!" Stein yelled out, as he strode up the dirt path while motioning to those who had wandered off the trail.

The yell broke Clay's trance, and after a few blinks to clear his mind, he turned to see Alejandro cradling a small canister of oxygen in one arm while doing his best to keep up with Stein's long stride.

At the same time Clay felt the soft touch of Aliston's hand against his left arm, Stein exuberantly spit out in his best English, "We have enough for one! Who shall it be?"

Stein was asking for a volunteer to venture into the unknown. Peter and John ran back from the far side of the sinkhole, but then dropped to a more somber gait when they realized the gravity of the question Stein posed to the team.

Clay sucked on the inside of his mouth until he had enough spit to swallow. Then as he started to lean forward, Aliston grabbed his arm. "You don't have to do this."

There was a little shoving and jostling as everyone jokingly tried to get the one next to them to go for it. But no one was leaping at the chance to be the first to explore the sinkhole opened by the quake. Not even Peter, who up until then had been the first to volunteer for every adrenalin rush on this adventure.

Clay ignored the others and turned toward Aliston. The freckle faced Australian was the only one in the group that didn't make him feel like a coward when he refused to bungee at the Huairou's Qinglong Gorge in Beijing, or base-jump yesterday at the Sotano de las Golondrinas. Not that anyone actually said anything. And not that anyone actually looked at him any differently. But their actions couldn't hide what they were really feeling deep down. Clay had too much practice sensing that same condemnation from his dad. Aliston though was different. He looked into her blue eyes as he slid his hand over hers. "I do," drifted off his lips before he knew it. It could have been a number of different factors pushing him past his acrophobia. Part of it might have been to spite his father. Then again, it could have been that even though he didn't buy into that 'being a man' crap that his father kept shoveling on him, he still felt a need to prove that he could overcome his fears. There certainly was no shortage of reasons to explain his newfound courage. You could take your pick, though none hit the mark as good as the plain and simple truth. He just couldn't bear to take a chances that his lack of participation might dull the admiration behind those beautiful blue eyes. A second later, he turned and got Stein's attention. They had their volunteer.

The team worked like cogs in a well-oiled machine as the sun slowly inched its way to mid-sky. Alejandro, Peter, and Justin hooked on safety lines and then set about anchoring a cantilevered tripod near the edge of the rim. While they completed the work up close, others carried rigging and carted the motorized winch up the trail from the jeeps. About an hour into it, Stein took Clay to the side and walked him through what was about to take place. First he explained how to read the oxygen content by the movement in a lighter's flame. Then he drew out a scheme of simple codes that Clay could click across the two-way mike to communicate topside while wearing the oxygen mask. Foremost, he made sure Clay understood that there was only twenty minutes of oxygen in the first aid tank.

At ten to one, Clay stood in the full heat of the Mexican sun fully prepped for the motorized descent. His sweat-drenched shirt and shorts clung to his chest and thighs under the polyester straps of a full safety harness. The oxygen canister was rigged with a belt and slung around his neck to where it rested against his stomach. Stein's personal two-way headset was fitted under the lighted spelunking helmet that they borrowed from Peter. And of course there were the Bic lighters. One was still clutched in his right hand. The other was already packed in the breast pocket of his shirt. With all the preparation done, there was nothing left to do but turn around and face his fears.

After toiling in the heat for nearly two hours, the team was surprisingly full of energy as it gathered around the winch some twenty meters from the mouth of the sinkhole. Clay made his way between them and then waited while Stein tethered his harness to the end of the coiled 500-meter steel extraction line that had been threaded through the pulley on the tripod.

Peter walked over and slapped him on the back. "Hals—und Beinbruch!"

Clay looked at him, uncertain of the proper translation.

Peter smiled and repeated in broken English, "Good luck!"

There was no problem understanding John's sendoff in the Queen's English, or the meaning behind the handshakes offered by the brother and sister from San Paulo.

Clay was a little hurt when he glanced over at Aliston and saw no movement. Instead of sending him off like the others, she kept her distance a few meters off the trail. He was still staring at her when Stein grabbed him by the harness and shook him once to check the fitting. The jostle brought Clay's attention back to the matter at hand. He glanced at the harness and then started re-checking the clips as Stein began to psyche him up by going on and on about how he was going to be the first and that this would forever be burned into his mind. It didn't take long for the psychology behind Stein's ranting to prove fruitful. Clay started nodding his head. Then he pumped his fists and took two quick steps back to separate himself from the rest of the expedition. "I can do it," he huffed to himself with determination.

He remembered the challenges he had already beaten on the expedition. He had walked over hot coals and broken glass in the deep Thar Desert of Rajasthan, India. He had ridden the whitewater of the Royal Gorge in Colorado. "I can do this!" he vowed again, as he took two more steps backwards. Then he paused to look back one last time at the team standing around the winch. Instead of stopping when he saw Aliston, he kept searching until he found the old Indian standing a dozen meters behind the others. For some reason he felt that he would find courage in that fatherly face, but when he looked into the Indian's eyes, the strength and warmth were gone. All that stood before him was an old Indian.

Clay quickly swung around, preferring to face his deepest fear before he could read any meaning into what he saw. As he dropped his head and slowly began to trudge forward, he kept thinking about what the Indian mouthed to him earlier. He didn't know what the Indian meant by it, but it was something important. He was sure of it.

The words were still rattling around in his head when he heard Stein's command from twenty meters back. "Hold on! We pull in the slack." He was at the rim.

The game plan was for him to continue staring at his feet while the winch reeled in the slack. But as he listened to the pant of his breath he slowly tilted his head up and looked forward. The first thing he saw was the dirt along the edge of the rim beginning to give way under the weight of his body. With a startled gasp, he quickly shifted his attention to the different shades of limestone layered on the far side of the sinkhole. The view offered only a momentary diversion. What he really needed was to see that the shaft wasn't that deep. The midday sun brought light to even the darkest of recesses. If it could reach the floor at Sotano de las Golondrinas, it would surely show him the bottom here. He grabbed the harness and peered over the edge. His hope was to see a little circle lit up on the floor of the shaft by the sun. That's not what he found. The shaft dwindled until it was completely devoured by the bottomless pit of darkness below. He reared back to where his head fell over the centerline of his body. Then, with his pulse racing, he unclenched his fists and grabbed the front of the harness. "I'm gonna do it!" he huffed.

Stein yelled, "Good! Now you must step off. The cantilever will swing you clear."

There was no turning back. He bit down to steady his lower jaw and closed his eyes. He would do it. With his heart pounding, he stuck his right foot out over the rim and let his weight fall forward. For one horrible, weightless second there was nothing. Then the steel line snapped taut, the harness dug into his crotch and armpits, and he felt his weight swing out over the shaft.

Chapter 2

Bill moved rather quickly for a sixty-seven year old as he made his way from the kitchen to the television. Then, without a care for what his son-in-law was watching, he flipped the rotary dial over to the 5:00 news.

"What do you think you're doing? I'm watching the game!" Chuck snapped, as he reared up to the edge of the sofa.

"Another boy died this morning," Bill answered matter-of-factly while waiting on the headline story.

"So?"

"Makes three of them. All of them were down in Mexico when they had that earthquake about a month ago." Bill eased his old joints down next to Chuck and motioned with his head. "You go on now and watch the game in the kitchen with the girls."

Chuck got up and glanced at the swinging door to the kitchen. He could hear Becky and her mom laughing at the table as they recalled the worn out stories of when his wife was a little girl. There was no way he could watch the game on a nine-inch black and white amongst all that. He looked down and glared at the old, leather face of his father-in-law. But the old man was too interested in the story of some dead rich kid from North Carolina to care. "Hell with this," Chuck mumbled as he turned toward the front door.

He pushed the screen door open and stepped out on to the porch. After a fleeting thought of leaving his wife there, he grabbed the steel chain of the porch swing and sat down in the middle of the green painted slats. To be completely honest—it felt kind of good to get mad, almost exciting.

By the time the screen door popped open and Becky walked out with Bill and Gina, the staleness of his life had returned. He pushed up and walked over to his wife. "Let's go."

Becky shrugged him off. "I'm coming."

"Fine," Chuck answered with little care as he headed down the steps.

She turned back to her father and mother and gave them each a quick hug and a kiss before trotting down the steps and across the yard to where Chuck was waiting for her at the truck. "You two should never, ever, sit down and watch a baseball game together."

It was as if Chuck could feel the meat of his entire body suck in a little closer to his frame. "What game?"

Becky got in and then waited for him to get to the other side. "Weren't you guys watching the Reds?"

He pulled in behind the wheel, shut the door, and then sat there staring down at his lap. Silence was just beginning to truly set in when he slowly shook his head and mumbled, "I can't do this anymore."

He turned toward Becky, but before he could establish eye contact, it was her turn to look down. "Do what?"

"Come here…" He glanced over at her parents who were watching their exchange from the porch. Then he focused back on her. "I'm not coming here again."

Becky's stare said it all. "Fine. If you don't want to see my parents… far be it for me to make you."

"Good."

With the brief exchange out of the way, silence was the only thing that remained as Chuck put the truck in gear and backed out of the drive. Four blocks down they pulled up to the stop sign at SR 56. State Road 56, one of the many two-lane rural highways in southern Indiana, ran through Madison in the east, past Hanover and on out west to Scottsburg where it hooked up with I-65. I-65 was the main artery between Indianapolis and Louisville.

Chuck was waiting for an opening in the traffic when Becky spoke up unexpectedly. "You know I like being in the truck with you." She paused and smiled in thought of some past memory. "Remember how we used to go driving together."

He turned his attention back to the traffic and tightened his grip on the wheel of the '78 Chevy step-side. "I don't know if I'd call this driving…we'll be home in fifteen minutes." But even though he maintained a hard stare at the on-coming traffic, her statement struck a chord. He did remember when they used to pack up and go driving for a day. There was no schedule to maintain, no destination that they were aiming for. It was just an excuse to get away and spend a little quality time together.

An opening came but instead of pulling out, Chuck just sat there. The memories were good, but at the same time they were like a swift kick to the groin. They brought up the anguish he went to sleep with each night on the living room couch.

Then Becky really caught him off-guard. She slid across the worn vinyl bench seat, took his right hand off the wheel and dropped it over her shoulder as she pressed against his side. His breath snagged halfway up his throat as he turned back toward the windshield. What happened next came before he even had a chance to think about it. He pulled his arm off her and grabbed the wheel. "I can't drive like that."

"You could when we were younger."

He didn't answer. Instead he looked at the on-coming eastbound traffic. A second later an opening came and the truck shot off the side street and veered sharply onto the highway. Like a chain of falling dominos, the momentum pressed him against the door and her against his side, but as soon as the truck straightened out, she slid back across the seat to her side of the truck. In a matter of seconds, the isolation that was far too routine in their marriage once again set in.

Chuck glanced at her as he struggled to find focus through the different emotions bubbling up inside him. By the time he turned his attention back to the task of driving, they were coming up on the flashing light where State Road 62 split off of 56. 56 continued on down the bluff to the historic part of Madison along the bank of the Ohio River. 62 veered off and followed the crest of the bluff through the commercial part of town—fast food, Wal-Mart and the like. He was hoping to turn on 62 before she said anything, but it was too late. She pointed and said, "56! Take me through town."

To him, the diversion was nothing more than a waste of time and gas, but then it didn't light a big enough fire to argue either. He kept the wheel straight as they began the winding descent that ran past the two great smokestacks of the power plant. At the bottom, State Road 56 became Main Street. It wasn't that he didn't like downtown. It was quaint with its antique shops, old Victorian homes and picturesque wrought iron street posts. But he spent everyday down there at work, and besides, they lived up the hill across from the golf course. Not that he was a golfer. Twenty-three years ago they had just gotten married and needed something that they could afford. They bought the house because it was a fixer-upper and a bargain, not because of its proximity to the golf course. That being said, he saw no purpose in the detour through downtown.

Besides, he was all too familiar with the drive behind Becky's desire. It was coming up on the right side of the street. It was an old, turn of the century brick Queen Anne. His wife was obsessed with it. Every time they drove by it, she would stare out the window as if seeing it for the first time. Today was no exception. "That house is so beautiful," she stated in a wishful tone only slightly louder than a whisper.

"Why do you always insist on driving by that house? You know it'll never be for sale, and even if it did, there's no way we could ever afford it."

She ignored him and kept staring out the window.

Then for some reason, he felt the need to stress his point. He slowed the pickup to a crawl and looked at the house with her. "I bet the damn thing is a rat trap. The inside probably needs all kinds of work and there's no way I'm going to spend all my free time fixing up some old piece of shit."

"Don't worry...I couldn't imagine that you would."

Chuck reared back. "What's that suppose to mean?"

Becky didn't respond immediately, instead she slowly turned toward him and said, "It's not a rat trap...its nice...it's a home." Then she longingly turned back for one last look as he started accelerating. "The only thing it's missing is a nice flower garden. That's it, nothing else. Then it would be perfect."

He shook his head and mumbled. "Life isn't always perfect." Then without thinking he glanced her way and added, "You don't always get everything you want." As soon as the words left his lips he began to question what he meant by it. He wasn't sure if he said it to be mean, or if it was how he actually felt deep down. But in any case he felt the tension return in his jaws and shoulders.

Becky turned back toward the front as the Victorian disappeared from sight behind the truck. Neither said another word as he turned on Michigan at the light and headed back up the bluff that overlooked the river.

Chapter 3

Clay kept rolling the words 'I can do it!' over and over in his mind as he held the steel line with both hands and waited for his body to stop swinging.

"We lower you now—you good to go?" Stein asked over the headset.

Clay tried to swallow and breathe at the same time. Neither came easily. His heart was racing as he finally forced down a hard gulp and opened his eyes. "Oh shit!" He was slowly spinning like the proverbial worm on the hook as he dangled in the hot sun over the bottomless pit of darkness below.

"You okay?"

Clay clutched the line for dear life and huffed, "I'm alright," as streams of sweat trickled down his face. The limestone layered around the mouth of the sinkhole passed in front of him. Then Stein and the rest of the team swung into view and he saw Aliston clenching her hands together in front of her chest. He eased the tension in his jaws enough to gasp, "I'm good to go."

"Good. Remember lighter."

Clay didn't get the chance to acknowledge the transmission before he suddenly started descending into the pit. Except for the occasional glance below, he kept his eyes closed for the better part of the first minute of the descent.

"Watch for clearance."

Whether it was the sound of Stein's voice or simply that he was beginning to realize that the line wasn't going to snap, Clay found the courage to open his eyes. He let go of the line clutched in his right hand just long enough to flick on the lights mounted to his spelunking helmet. Then with both hands back on the line, he checked to see if his descent was clear of obstacles. The sunlight above was fading rapidly as he looked down past his chest, over each shoulder, and then behind as he slowly spun in a circle. "I can't see anything yet. No signs of the walls or bottom."

"Passing 150 meters. Breathing okay?"

Clay was inhaling deeply, but it wasn't due to a drop in the oxygen level. "Still okay." The only thing of notice so far was the drop in temperature. Top side around the winch it was close to forty degrees centigrade. It felt at least 10 degrees cooler already and he was still descending. He looked at the faint circle of light where the hole punched through the surface. "How deep now?"

Stein's voice came back across the headset. "Approaching 275 meters. Still good?"

Clay was beginning to feel a burning sensation in his lungs. He relaxed the grip of his right hand and quickly snatched one of the Bic lighters out of his shirt pocket. He wrapped his right arm around the line and flicked the lighter. The flame lit okay but was burning a bluish tint with an orange tip. "Starting to lose oxygen."

"Keep watch of flame. Passing 300 meters"

Clay kept the Bic burning but couldn't pull his eyes from the fading circle of light high above. He watched as the darkness slowly overtook the only reference he had to the mouth of the shaft and snuffed it out. By the time he looked at the flame it was burning more than a centimeter above the jet. He glanced below and to the sides. There was no light, no sound, or any sign of life. The one comforting thought in that endless descent was how this would make up for all the times his father had told him that he needed to step up and be a man. He looked at the lighter and saw the flame burning close to two centimeters over the jet. "I'm going to oxygen."

Stein's voice crackled over the headset. "Mark time. Twenty minutes and counting. Passing 350 meters."

Clay took his thumb off the lighter and pulled the mask up over his mouth and nose. As soon as it was fitted, he opened the valve on the oxygen tank draped over his stomach. He tried the lighter again, but it only flashed and wouldn't stay lit. He clicked the mike as Stein had told him to do once he had the mask on.

"Pas…425…ters."

Clay slipped the lighter back in his pocket and then wrapped both arms around the steel line as he glanced below. But this time he saw something. The lights from his helmet were reflecting off of something. Solid ground never looked so good! He keyed his mike two short dots and then held the button down. His speed slowed to half a meter per second as the cave floor came up to greet him. An iridescent display of colors followed the path of his helmet lights along the floor as he swung around to get a better view of where he was landing. He bent his knees and prepared for landing. Three meters, two, one…he let go of the mike switch as his hiking boots touched the slimy bottom between several giant cracked slabs of bedrock from the collapsed ceiling. His knees flexed and caught his weight as the steel line came to a stop.

Piles of rubble spotted the floor like celestial formations on the moon. Every exhale produced a white puff of mist that quickly dissipated. He spun around and watched the iridescent display light up the walls around him. The surface area of the floor was at least a hundred times larger than the opening above. The cave wall closest to him was probably a good thirty meters away. The cave wall opposite was closer to a hundred meters away. He looked down and saw the same rainbow of color displayed across a patch of slime on the floor.

The steel line snagged him when he tried to bend down. So he keyed the mike three times and then held the button down as Stein reeled out enough slack in the line to allow him to move around. He swiped his finger through the patch of slime on the cave floor. As he stood back up and watched the colors reflect off his finger, he exhaled and a cloud of mist swallowed up his hand. During that brief moment of obscurity, he thought he saw a brilliant orange glow radiate from the tip of his finger. When the fog cleared, the slime on his finger had completely dried to a silvery powder that flaked off when he rubbed his fingers together.

Clay bent down, pulled his mask off, and blew across the puddle. The white mist swept across the surface as the slime lit into a brilliant orange. Even though the glow didn't produce any heat, it smoked like it was on fire. The glow lasted about a second as the small area dried into a silver powder. Clay stood back up and watched the rainbow of colors dance across the floor and walls. He was wrong when he thought there was nothing alive down here. Something in the slime was alive. It was reacting to the oxygen.

Before long it would all be trampled under the adventurous feet of spelunkers and base jumpers. If only the rest of the team could see it before it's ruined. If only Aliston could see it.

"Thirteen minu...ounting."

Clay listened to the time on the headset and smiled. Stein was right. This was something that he would never forget. He was the first to go where no man had ever been before. His spirits were soaring as he stepped around a limestone boulder the size of car and saw a large patch of slime that had to be at least twenty meters across.

For a reason he couldn't quite understand, he was drawn to it. Before he knew it he was kneeling at the edge, but this time he wasn't going to exhale on it. His skin started tingling as he took his mask off. For the briefest of moments, he was taken back to his childhood when he found a rabbit that his Beagle had caught. He remembered standing over it with a shovel and the horrible feeling of knowing that he had to put the poor creature out of its misery. He felt that same guilt now as he held his mask down to the edge of the patch. The mixture straight from the tank lit the slime like a match to gasoline. The orange glow started at the edge and shot across the thirty meters like a wildfire. But it didn't stop there. It jumped across dry areas and lit other patches. It ran all the way over to the far wall. Clay swung his head up as the orange glow ran up the wall about ten meters as it spread all around the bottom of the cave. "Holy shit!" he mumbled under the confines of the mask. For nearly ten seconds the entire bottom of the cave was lit up. In the middle of the visual spectacle exploding all around him, Clay thought about the old Indian. He remembered the words mouthed to him. 'The last day is coming'.

"Ev...okay...ts...happening?"

Clay quickly braced himself as the orange glow died and the residual powder covered the cave floor like a fresh snow. He keyed the mike one long dash followed immediately by three quick dots. A second later the slack in the line was gone and he whipped up into the air.

As nervous as he had been going down, Clay was just the opposite coming up. It was like the cave emptied his emotions and drained him of any further purpose in life. The only feeling that remained, one that was growing stronger with each meter of ascent, was the overwhelming sensation that he never should have gone down.

Stein was tethered to a safety line and waiting for him when he got back to the top. "I swing you back over," Stein said as he signaled Alejandro to stop the winch. Then he pushed one end of the cantilevered tripod and caught Clay as he swung back over solid ground. "It was good time—yes?"

Clay mustered a nod while Stein switched out the winch line for a safety line. Then as Clay dropped his eyes to the ground, Stein walked him back over to where the others were eagerly waiting to congratulate him. Peter ran up and slapped on the back.

John grabbed Clay's hand and said, "Way to go!"

Hands came forward to congratulate him as did questions about what it was like, but Clay didn't have the energy for celebrating.

Aliston pushed between the brother and sister from San Paulo. "I'm glad you're back. Everyone was so worried."

"Worried about what?" Clay gasped as he took Aliston by the arm.

"We saw smoke, like there was a fire or something."

Any hope that it was nothing more than a nightmare, died with that comment. There was no denying what the others had seen. The smoke or whatever it was—came from the slime he ignited with his oxygen mask. Clay began to wrestle with his thoughts as the continued bombardment of questions slowly blended into an indistinguishable drone.

Aliston leaned closer and put her hand on his shoulder. He didn't really hear her question, but nodded just the same. The simple gesture sent her running over to the group's gear in search for a canteen. While she did that, Clay started scanning the area for the Indian. He didn't need a drink any more than he needed another slap on the back. What he needed was the strength he felt from the Indian the first time they stared at each other. He needed to know that he was forgiven.

Chapter 4

Chuck barely took his foot off the gas before he jerked the wheel in a hard turn to the right. The old Chevy swerved onto the gravel at the foot of their drive and sprayed a cloud of white dust across the weeds in the ditch. He and Becky bounced up as the tires cleared the cement rise at the foot of the driveway, and then he slammed on the brakes. The front end of the truck dipped and by the time it settled back, the bumper was less than three feet from the peeling paint of their garage door.

Neither made a move until Chuck finally straightened up, pushed his back firmly into the seat and said without looking at her, "I'm going to go get a beer."

"Fine," Becky replied in a flat, defeated tone.

Then the door opened and he heard her slip out. As he watched her walk up to their front door with her face lowered, it was like he was right there with her. He could feel the weight of each lumbering step and the quick shallow breaths that come when decisions have to be made. He leaned forward as he watched her walk up the porch steps and then he fell back against the seat and closed his eyes as the front door closed behind her. She's going to leave me if I don't give her some reason not to.

He threw the truck in park, let his head fall back over his shoulders and began to rub his face. By the time he realized that he was staring at the closed drapes, both hands were pressed palm-to-palm over his mouth as if he were praying. That's when impulse nearly took over. In a knee-jerk reaction, he slapped his hand over the keys in the ignition. The sinew in his forearm grew taunt, poised to take the next action. But the rough idle of the truck never ceased. There'd be no run in to the house. No taking Becky up into his arms. Pride has a nasty way of winning out at the worst of times. "Damn-it!" he swore as he twisted around to check out the back window of the cab. Then in one violent release, he threw the transmission in reverse and gunned the truck back out onto the street.

The best place in town for a cold beer was the Broadway Tavern. But first he would pick up his buddy Stan Jenkins. He met Stan a year before he met Becky. Their first encounter had been when they tried to beat the crap out of each other in the fifth grade. Somehow out of that fight, a friendship began that had stood the test of time. The only break in their friendship was when Chuck headed off for college. Stan wasn't the kind of guy who ever considered college an option. Instead he joined his older brother at the power plant the very week after he, Chuck and Becky graduated high school.

Chuck on the other hand was different. He had his long-term goals all planned out when he was young. He intended to get a degree in business at the university in Bloomington, marry Becky and then the two of them would get out of Madison once and for all. But those plans changed when his dad died in late February during Chuck's freshmen year. His dad was a good man, but a good businessman he was not. The little antique store he ran was in the red. Chuck intended to take it over just long enough to pay off the creditors. Then he would sell the store to pay for his tuition the following year. But like so many aspects of life, things don't always go as planned. He and Becky got married that summer and before he knew it, college was little more than a distant dream and he was the full time proprietor of the Pleasant Memories antique store on Main.

He turned onto Arlington. Then three houses down, he pulled into Stan's driveway. A few seconds later he was standing on the chipped cement porch and impatiently fingering the door bell. The door swung open with a velocity that left him teetering in its wake, as Stan, dressed in his usual blue jeans and soiled white tank top, popped out of nowhere. "Lay off the bell you son-of-a-bitch!"

Stan's chummy comment eased the tension in Chuck's posture and allowed him the chance to smile. Then with an expression as animated as his voice, he said, "Let's go get a beer."

Stan glanced back over his shoulder. "Shit…Margery's almost got supper ready."

"So…"

"You remember this—"

Margery called from the kitchen, "Who's that at the door?"

"Chuck."

"Who?"

"Chuck goddamn it!" Stan stood poised with his brows pinched, waiting for his wife to ask again. When she didn't, he turned back toward Chuck and said, "You're going to owe me one."

Chuck smiled as he tipped his chin up. "Well go on…get your shoes and for God's sake put on another shirt that doesn't smell like armpit."

Stan raised his arm and lowered his nose for a smell as he said, "Come on in."

The dark-green, shag carpet crunched under Chuck's feet as he glanced at the baseball game on the console in the corner. The window unit that he helped Stan hang in the kitchen three years ago wasn't doing much to cool the air. In fact about the only thing it was good for was pushing the aroma of fried chicken into the living room. At least he hoped it was chicken. The air in the house was so stale and full of cigarette smoke that it was actually hard to tell.

While Stan ducked down the hallway to the bedroom, Chuck waded slowly over to the kitchen and peaked around the corner. "Hey there Margery," he offered with a nod.

She prodded a floured chicken leg with her fork and then as grease spit and popped out of the pan, she glanced over her shoulder at him. "Thought that was you at the door."

He waited awkwardly for a moment, not sure whether to try and start up a conversation or not, but before the question had a chance to be answered, Stan came trotting back down the hallway. "You ready?"

Chuck smiled in relief. "Yeah!"

They made it to the side of the sofa before Margery spoke up. "Where do you think you're going?"

Stan stopped, looked back toward the kitchen and yelled at his wife. "Where do you think! I'm going to get a beer with Chuck."

"Like hell—supper's almost ready," Margery warned as she poked her head out of the kitchen.

The comment brought Stan full turn to where he was facing her. "That's fine; put the legs and a breast in the fridge for me. I'll have them tonight when I get back."

"You step out that door mister and you might as well stay the night with HIM."

Stan's smirk was followed by a laugh as he shook his head defiantly. "Calm down now, honey. Just put me some food in the fridge—that's why God made Tupperware." Then he turned toward Chuck and smiled. "I told you, you're going to owe me one after this."

Chuck slapped him on the back as he reached for the front door. "Let's go."

The Broadway was actually an old, turn-of-century inn. The upper floors were rooms for let while the ground floor was divided evenly between a bar and a restaurant. The last time Chuck had been on the restaurant side was when he and Becky celebrated their twentieth anniversary. The way things were up the hill, he wasn't sure they would make number twenty-five. But the bar side of the Broadway was a different story altogether. It was a dark, old comfortable place that had been as much a home to him over his life as any house ever was.

Stan held the heavy oak door open while Chuck took a quick glance around at the handful of regulars before walking over to the bar and easing onto a stool. Stan pulled out the stool next to him and threw his leg over it like he was mounting a horse. Then they ordered a couple of Millers and waited silently until they each had a chance to take a swig.

Stan emptied a third of his bottle before he brought up the Red's dramatic comeback against the Cubs. "You catch the end of that game?"

Chuck perked up. "I wish. Becky's dad came in during the bottom of the eighth and switched the channel to the news."

"Oh man that's fucked up!" Stan said with a chuckle. Then he took another gulp and added, "I thought you said he was a Cubs fan."

Chuck shook his head. "He is! But he was all caught up in some big stink about a couple of kids dying."

Stan set his beer down and turned to where he was facing Chuck head-on. "I heard about that. Bunch of news about these college kids on some kind of trip down in Mexico and now three of them are dead."

"So what makes that such a big deal?" Chuck asked as he started picking at the label on his bottle.

"The college kids aren't the only ones dying. They said people are also dropping dead in some of the small villages down there."

Chuck glanced at him. Then he looked back at his reflection in the mirror and shook his head. "Things are fucked up everywhere." A second later he threw his head back and tipped the bottle. After two gulps he slammed the empty down on the oak counter just as the bar keep headed over with the next round. He pulled a twenty out of his wallet, laid it down on the wet counter and said to the bar keep, "Keep the empties away Mike, we'll take care of you." Mike snapped up the twenty and gave a nod before heading off to tend to other customers. Chuck grabbed the fresh, cold bottle and held it to his forehead for a moment. Then he pulled it back and drained half in one gulp.

Chapter 5

It took Chuck well over half an hour to get home that night. Most of the delay was spent in Stan's driveway as his buddy kept wanting to tell "just one more" drunken story of their adolescent years before getting out of the truck. Chuck put up with it for a good fifteen minutes before he finally pushed his friend out the door. But as far as the rest of the time it took to get home—that was a different story.

Before Chuck knew what he was doing, the truck was idling in front of a brick ranch with a 'Sold' sign posted in the yard. He sat there behind the wheel, in the safety of his cab, unwilling or unable to commit to any further action. He wasn't even sure what he was doing there.

The 'why' though was far less ambiguous. It was Sally. At first, it appeared innocent enough when she wandered into the store last week. But about the third time she mentioned her divorce he began to pick up on it. Then when she slid her hand over his and went on and on about how exciting it was to move back to town, it left no room for misinterpretation.

He stared into the darkness behind the plate glass of her picture window as he wet his lips and swallowed. Her Impala was parked in the drive. In the midst of the decision, his attention was pulled back to his left hand in front of his chest. He was spinning his wedding band around and around his finger. An anxious smile started to pull at his lips. It was like he was a kid again and about to ask a girl out for the first time. The spark felt good. But before it could flourish and prompt action, another feeling came around. He quit spinning the gold band and let it rest firmly between the index and thumb of his right hand. It was what Becky said in the car. He began to think about the leisurely drives they used to take. The memories were dusty for sure, but not forgotten. The mental images put a different kind of smile on his face and before he knew it, he was pushing the ring into the crotch of his wedding finger.

The smile was still there as he put the truck in gear and pulled away.

When he finally made it home he found the drapes drawn and the lights out. There was no doubt in his mind that he was stinking drunk, yet it didn't feel that way as he maneuvered around the shadows in the living room. Instead of a drunken stumble, balance appeared in his gate as he headed down the hallway to the master bedroom. Balance put there by purpose.

He pulled up at the doorway and stared at the dark mound sleeping under the covers across the room. There was still silence, but this time it was a good silence. All the memories that he couldn't see during the day—were with him now. For a second he even toyed with the idea of sliding under the covers and sleeping with his wife. But in the end, he found his way back to the pillow and sheets folded next to the sofa.

Chapter 6

The first time Chuck felt the hand on his shoulder he wasn't sure if it was real or part of a dream, so he brushed it off with out really waking. But the second time left no doubt as he felt himself rocking under the force of a gentle shake. "Time to get up."

He filled his lungs and stretched out his arms. Then after a few unsuccessful tries, he opened his eyes and saw Becky kneeling next to the sofa. "What time is it?" he asked with a dry mouth.

"Just a little past eight…I would have let you sleep longer but I wanted to make you breakfast before it got too late."

She didn't have to say anything more. He could smell the hickory bacon frying in the kitchen. The aroma perked him up and got his blood flowing again. He blinked a couple of times, then while Becky took a seat on the coffee table, he propped himself up and started massaging the puffiness out of his face.

She was still sitting there when he finished—staring at him with a smile on her face. "Would you like a cup of coffee?" He started to get up, but she beat him to it. "You just wait right here…I'll get it along with the morning paper."

Chuck plopped back down on the sofa and glanced around the room. Something was different. The lamp that should have been on the end table next to the recliner was gone. He was still taking in the living room when Becky walked back over. She handed him the coffee, laid the paper down on the sofa next to him and then sat back down on the coffee table across from him. He cupped the warm mug in both hands and blew the steam rising off it before taking a sip. "What happened to the lamp on the end table?"

"You broke it last night when you came home."

"Really?"

"Don't worry about it…it was cheap and I can always pick up

another one at Wal-Mart."

He took another sip as he tried to remember what could have happened to make Becky act this way. A regretful moment later the fog cleared. He remembered the fight they had on the way home from her folks, as well as stopping in front of Sally's on his way home from the tavern. He focused back on Becky and as he did, she dropped her eyes to the floor and began to rub her hands together like she was trying to wash off some stubborn dirt. Was this it? Had he inflected too much damage on the marriage to repair?

After struggling with her thoughts, she finally looked back at him. "I'm sorry about yesterday."

Chuck froze. It was a simple gesture, one that should have been easy to acknowledge. But he found himself caught between his own selfish pride and the love for his wife.

She waited for his response with her hands clutched together on her lap. But after a few seconds of unbearable silence, she got up and headed for the kitchen. "Should be just a few more minutes. The hash browns are still cooking. You read the paper and I'll get you when breakfast is ready."

Chuck swung around and looked at her over the back of the sofa. "Hey."

Becky paused and stared at the linoleum on the kitchen floor before finally turning and looking up at him.

"I'm sorry too Baby."

There was another moment of silence as they gazed at each other. But this was a good moment. Becky began to slowly nod. "Good," she said with a smile.

Telling her that he was sorry felt really good. He matched her smile and then slowly turned back around. The front page of the paper was nothing but the typical mud slinging over the upcoming county sheriff election. He started rifling through the pages, glancing at the headlines, working his way back to the sports section where he could read about the finish of the Reds game yesterday. But then he stopped and stared at the headline midway down on the fifth page—'Third adventure youth dies in twenty-four hour span'. It immediately brought back the memory of what Stan told him last night at the bar, and in particular the statement about people dying in some of the small villages. He glanced at the by-line and saw that it was actually an associated press article picked up by the paper. Intrigued, he started reading as he grabbed his coffee and took another sip.

"Breakfast is ready, Honey."

He paused for a second and stared at the article, before looking over at Becky who was waiting for him at the end of the sofa. Then with the paper in one hand and coffee in the other, he got up and followed her to the kitchen. "Have you read the paper this morning?"

"No…I wanted to let you read it first."

He sat his cup down on the Formica tabletop and pulled out a chair. "It's got a story in here about three college kids collapsing and dying."

She was at the stove scraping the hash browns out of the frying pan. "Uh-huh."

Talking to her back, he continued, "They were on some kind of extreme adventure tour in Mexico when that big earthquake hit last month."

Becky turned and headed over to the table with two loaded plates. She sat his down and momentarily captured his attention as he took a savoring look at the eggs over easy, hash browns and bacon. He smiled as she started to sit down, but then the toaster went off and she was back up. As she retrieved their toast along with a jar of jam from the refrigerator, she asked, "Did they get hurt in the earthquake?"

Chuck looked back at the paper. "They're not sure what killed them by the sounds of it, but they didn't mention anything that sounded like it was related to the earthquake." He started scanning the article. "It says they're running toxicology on the first kid that died. He explored a cave they found after the quake; they think he might have caught something." He was about to take another sip of coffee while he scanned the article, but then he stopped and set the cup down. "It says that eleven local Indians are also dead." He looked over at Becky who was busy buttering their toasts. "Says close to a hundred others have been hospitalized and that others as far away as Mexico City are beginning to exhibit symptoms of hypoxia." He continued to read, "…a reduction in oxygen to the brain."

Becky took a seat and then reached over and set a slice of buttered toast on Chuck's plate. "You read about the finish of the game yet?"

"No…" drifted off his lips as he pulled his attention from the news to the plate of hot food in front of him. There was nothing quite as satisfying as a hot breakfast after a night of hard drinking. He grabbed his fork and mixed everything before lifting a scoop of hash browns covered in runny eggs. After the combination hit his mouth, he closed his eyes and slowly pulled the fork out with a long, drawn out pleasurable moan. He opened his eyes and snapped up a strip of beacon to add a quick bite before chewing any further. With the flavorful combination of all the flavors working as one, he set the rest of the bacon strip down and quickly rifled through the remaining paper until he came upon the recap of the game yesterday. Then he folded the paper over so that he could read the box score as he ate his breakfast.

A few lines into it, he glanced up as he reached for his bacon and saw Becky staring at him while she ate. She didn't say anything—she just smiled. He didn't say anything either. He just shoved half the bacon strip in his mouth and returned his attention to the paper.

Chapter 7

Chuck closed the antique store early the following Wednesday. It wasn't unusual for him to take in far less money during the week than he did on the weekends. His business rose and fell with the feast or famine flow of city folks coming down for a one-day taste of yesteryear. But this week it was different. It wasn't that it was slow as much as it was non-existent. Only one person came in yesterday and that was simply to get out of the sun for a spell. No one had been in today since he opened at nine—so at about a quarter to four, he closed up and flipped over the 'Open' sign hanging on the door. By five he was on his way up Michigan and by half past five he had his boots off and was leaning back in the recliner with a cold beer, aiming the remote at the television.

Timing was everything. His daily routine was synchronized to the start of the local sports wrap-up. But when the picture tube lit up, he didn't see the familiar faces of the local news team. Instead ABC was broadcasting the network feed from New York. He was about to give NBC a try, when the mention of Mexico jerked him up straight in the recliner. Something bad was happening. He could tell by the anchor's tone and posture. He kept his eyes glued to the man behind the news desk as he waited anxiously for what he feared was coming. The wait wasn't long. The anchor said something before it and after it, but the only word that mattered was "outbreak". Chuck closed his eyes, swallowed hard, and then slowly let go of the armrest clutched in his fist.

For the next several minutes every fiber of his being was fixated on the high altitude images taken over Aquismon, a small Mexican village in the Sierra Madre mountain range. A visibly shaken news anchor stated in a solemn voice that the dark spots appearing all over the screen were actually the bodies of the town's inhabitants. The anchor paused for a moment before stating that thermal imaging provided little hope of finding survivors.

He quickly flipped the channel over to the cable news network. CNN was rapidly detailing events as they unfolded on the state map of San Luis Potosi. But it was the numerous small towns highlighted in red that really had him concerned. The anchor confirmed reports of more casualties coming out of Rio Verde. Chuck forced down another hard swallow and called for his wife, "Becky! Get in here!"

As if she were being pulled away from a task of the utmost importance, Becky labored in from the hallway and stopped at the edge of the living room with a huff. "What do you want? I've got three loads of laundry to do."

"Have you seen what's going on down in Mexico?"

She pushed her hair back behind her ears and then put her hands on her hips. "Yeah, I saw it earlier today."

"This is big shit. How come you didn't call and tell me what was going on?"

"Because I've got work to do and last time I looked—it wasn't getting done by itself." Then she spun around and stomped back down the hallway.

For a moment, all he could do was stare in disbelief. His wife didn't act like that. Then he shook it off and chased after her. He found her standing next to the bed with her back to him, staring down at a pile of clothes fresh out of the dryer. When she slowly turned and raised her eyes, he could see her thoughts were somewhere else. He stepped over and pulled Becky in close. "Take a break, the laundry can wait. Come watch the news with me."

"I can't..." she whispered into his ear as he felt the moisture of a tear against his cheek.

"You can. Come sit with me. They haven't said anything about any people collapsing here in the states."

She squeezed him again as she rose up on her toes. "They did earlier in the day, while I was eating lunch. They said people were dying in California and North or South Carolina—I can't remember which."

Chuck rubbed her back as he remembered the article he read over the weekend about the adventure group. It said three kids had died. One was definitely from North Carolina. "Did they mention anything about an adventure group?"

"Yeah."

"What'd they say?"

He felt Becky's chest flutter as she took a deep breath. "The news said they were dead. All of them!"

"Fuck!" Chuck gasped, as he pulled her in tight. How could it go from three kids to all this in a matter of a few days? After a much needed moment to steady his own nerves, he said, "Let's go see if this is anything that we need to be concerned with." Then arm in arm, they headed back for the living room.

He sat her down first before taking a spot on the sofa next to her. CNN was trying to pull in a live feed from a hospital in San Luis Potosi. But for the first few seconds all you could see were images of mass chaos. The hospital was overrun. Doctors raced by the camera in biohazard suits while the strong arm of the military tried to maintain order. Then the camera swung around and settled on a field reporter who was interviewing a member from one of the medical units of our National Disaster Medical System. The detail along the bottom of the screen indicated that he was a doctor from Philadelphia and that his unit had been one of the first on the scene after the earthquake. It was a live feed shown through picture-in-picture, but apparently the information had already been cleared for broadcast because as the doctor started reviewing the known symptoms, CNN already had the detail in graphic form. The doctor said, "Those infected first exhibit signs of exhaustion followed by disorientation. We have conflicting reports, but based on the majority of data seen so far, this period may last between six and twenty-fours before complete incapacitation and death."

The reporter asked, "Has a source or cause been identified yet?"

The doctor started to answer, but then jumped back against the brick wall of the corridor as the camera feed bounced and jarred while a stream of on-duty hospital staff rapidly wheeled a train of five or six gurneys between the doctor and the camera crew. After they passed, he stepped away from the wall and repositioned his headset. Then as the picture stabilized on him he said, "Based on the timing of the first fatalities, and our investigation of the area surrounding the initial outbreak at Aquismon, we think that we may have located the origin point of the outbreak." The doctor stopped and stared at the ground like he was waiting in concentration for the next question.

The reporter asked, "Can you elaborate on the origin point?"

Without looking up he said, "At this point in time we haven't been able to collect conclusive evidence to support our assumptions—as soon as we have that information it will be made available."

"What is causing the deaths?"

Two more gurneys wheeled by the doctor and this time he followed their passing with his eyes before turning back to the camera. "Field autopsies have provided evidence that the loss of life is due to an unknown airborne pathogen which results in hypemic hypoxia for the host."

"Can you comment on the reports we've heard that the loss of life has crossed over to include livestock and domesticated animals?"

"Yes Jim…the pathogen has been found in livestock. It is not restricted to human hosts."

"I see you're needed, but please one last question. Do you believe the outbreak is contained?"

"The efforts expended by both the governments of the United States and that of Mexico have successfully quarantined the affected regions, both here and along the coasts of the United States. There is no reason to believe that as tragic as this has been already, we will not be able to put a quick resolve to the situation."

"Thank you Dr. Robinson for taking the time to speak with us. Please pass on our prayers for our good friends to the south."

The doctor nodded once then looked back in the camera and said, "I'd like to pass on my love to my wife, Kelly, and my son Jonathon. I love you!" Then they lost the feed and split screen.

The shot of the CNN anchor expanded to full picture as he said, "Once again as Dr. Robinson emphasized, the outbreak has been contained. We have to break for a moment, but our extended coverage of this most tragic of days will continue after this."

Chuck was still caught in an open-mouth stare when an advertisement for the Wall Street Journal came up on screen. He slowly fell back against the sofa with his wife. He wasn't sure that he actually believed it, but he said it anyway. "See, everything is going to be alright." He pulled back to where he could see Becky's face. She was still worried. He brushed her hair back with his hand and said, "Come on now, CNN said we we're going to be alright."

She lifted her face and exposed the pain in her eyes. "When they showed it over lunch…they showed an entire town dead."

"Aquismon. I saw it too."

"Aquismon? No, they showed pictures of some small town in

North Carolina. Rocky Mountain or something like that."

Chuck's heart skipped a beat.

"They were showing pictures of dead dogs and cats…" her voice started to shake, "…and they showed pictures of people lying dead on the streets." Her eyes started to gloss over and root out in red veins. "It was horrible!"

He wrapped his arms around her and asked, "Was everybody dead?"

Becky started to whimper but still managed to say, "I don't know."

As he started to think about the implications of an entire town dying, he found it difficult to swallow—so much so that when he finally did it was audible. The sound announced the anxiety growing in his stomach that would quickly make it impossible to sit still. "Come on, we can't keep sitting here. It's not doing us any good to think about it any longer." He pulled away again, but this time he grabbed her upper arms and shook her mildly. "Come on, were getting up." He stood, pulling her up with him, and then supported her while they walked around to the kitchen. "You need to get your mind off this."

She glanced up as the life started to return in her face.

"That's it." He let go of her arms and started rubbing her shoulders as he looked into her eyes. "It's contained! No more people are going to die."

She looked down and started to nod in half-hearted agreement. "No more people are going to die." She looked up, met his stare and then said again, but with more confidence this time, "No more people are going to die."

"That's right." He forced a smile and said, "Now why don't you finish up your laundry and then get started on supper." He let go of her shoulders and started to leave.

She immediately reached out to him. "Where are you going?"

He paused with his back to her. "I've got to go back down to the store and stock the shelves." He turned. "Remember…we're fine. I've got work to do and I'm going to go do it. Why don't you push supper back to around eight—I'll be home by then. Okay?"

He waited for Becky to nod. Then he headed for the door. Truth was that he had to get out. He needed to feel the numbing effects of alcohol in a friendly environment—someplace where he could take his mind off of what he just saw and heard. Someplace where he wouldn't see or have to deal with the fear he saw in her eyes. The place for that was Stan's. As he stepped out the door, he took a quick glance back to the kitchen and saw her still standing in the same spot—still staring at him. For a second the flush of shame overcame him and he felt his hand start to shake on the doorknob. Then he closed his eyes, tightened his grip, and pushed on out the door.

Chapter 8

Margery caught Chuck off guard when she opened the door. It wasn't so much that it was her and not Stan who answered, as it was the lack of expression across her face. Margery never tried to hide the fact that she didn't care for Chuck. In fact she gave him the distinct feeling that she blamed him for anything and everything that went wrong in her marriage. If Stan forgot to set out the garbage—it must have been Chuck's fault. If Stan wanted to go out drinking—it was that worthless Chuck that put the idea in his head. Over the years he had grown accustomed to the stone look of contempt that she always directed his way. That's why it felt so peculiar when she answered the door with that soft, lost look on her face.

"Stan around?" Chuck asked cautiously.

Margery stepped aside and let him in as she motioned once with her head. "He's in the basement." Then without another word, she turned and slowly walked back to the kitchen.

Chuck closed the door and shadowed her through the living room. When she stopped to open up the refrigerator, he veered around her and slipped through the door to the basement.

Stan's basement wasn't finished, but that didn't keep it from being the perfect hangout. Over the years the two of them had wasted countless afternoons getting drunk and shooting pool below ground. It served the same function that a tree house would for a child—it was a place for them to escape. Besides, it wasn't that bad. They painted the cement floor a dark gray to contrast with the off-white paint on the concrete block walls. Simple bulbs with pull chains hung from the floor joist at the corners of the basement and provided the necessary light, while a couple of worn lawn chairs provided seating. The pool table was at the far end, away from the foot of the stairs and the piles of storage boxes. This wasn't done just to ensure an added moment of privacy should Margery suddenly come down unannounced—it was also the only place far enough away from the metal stands that supported the floor joists, to allow sufficient room to maneuver one's pool cue.

Chuck plodded down the stairs into the dim light of the basement. As usual, the only bulb on was the one over the pool table. He walked over, glanced at the billiard balls scattered across the felt and Stan's lucky cue resting upright against the edge of the table, then at his friend. Stan was sitting in a lawn chair, holding a beer and staring through the dark at the cinder blocks along the far wall. "Hey buddy."

Stan looked at him for a long second before any recognition set in. Then he jumped up. "Hey Chuck. What brings you over?"

Chuck didn't respond. Instead he wandered over to the end of the pool table and grabbed the orange, number five ball. He squeezed it and then started rubbing it against the felt as if he were trying to work a stain off of it. Stan walked into the light, took a drink of beer and then supported himself against the table as he stared at the felt between his hands. There was no need for Chuck to ask—he could tell by Stan's face that he had seen the latest news of the outbreak. He rolled the orange ball down the length of the table and watched it drop into the far corner pocket. "Any more beers?"

Stan kept his eyes on the table as he raised the half empty in his hand and pointed to the dorm size refrigerator between the two lawn chairs. Chuck grabbed a cold Miller from the stash, twisted the top off and took a long, soothing drink.

Stan spoke up as Chuck leaned back against the table, "Have you been to Wal-Mart today?"

Chuck wiped his mouth and said, "I try to stay away from the stores and let Becky do the shopping."

Stan looked up from the felt and met his eyes, "You wouldn't have believed it...it was a mad house. I mean people were buying supplies like they were gearing up for a winter storm. And I'm not just talking about food...they were buying up all the batteries and camping equipment they could get their hands on." He paused and walked around the corner of the table to where he was within arm's reach of Chuck. "They were buying up the shotguns too."

Chuck didn't even realize that he had started shaking his head. "I can't believe this is actually happening."

Stan drained his beer and while he walked over to the refrigerator for another, he said, "You see on the news where some of those guys in the biohazard suits are dying? Even ones that had been wearing them since the get go!"

Chuck started to shake his head, but then jumped as a heavy crash hit the floor upstairs.

Stan looked calmly up at the floor joists while he motioned for Chuck to hold his ground. After a moment of silent stare, he gently shook his head and whispered his wife's name. "Either they don't know shit or they aren't telling us shit. One or the other!"

"You want to check on her?"

"Nah, she's dealing with it in her own way."

"You sure?"

"Yeah."

Chuck let his concern drift away as he glanced up at the joists again before slowly taking a seat in one of the lawn chairs. After a drink he asked, "Do you think it's really contained?"

Stan plopped down in the other chair and took a quick sip. "I don't know. I'd like to think so. It's one thing taking out the spics south of the border or the niggers in North Carolina, but those guys dying in the biohazard suits are white." He took another sip. "This ain't the Lord's doing."

Chuck stared at the floor and held his tongue. A second later he looked back at his friend. "Becky is taking it pretty hard too."

"I bet! Anything like Marge?"

"No, not yet anyway, but I still had to get out of there," Chuck said with an air of remorse as he pictured Becky staring at him from the kitchen. After a moment of reflection, he drained his bottle, sat the empty on the floor and grabbed a fresh one out of the refrigerator. "What about you, are you doing anything…you know, just in case?"

Stan perked up and nearly boiled over as he leaned toward Chuck. "Hell yes. That's why I went to Wal-Mart in the first place. It was a scramble but I made sure that I got everything I thought we'd need. Some son-of-a-bitch thought he had the last twelve-gauge—that is until I jerked the sucker right out of his hands." Stan spouted a devilish grin and added, "I could tell he was one of those guys who never owned a gun. He started to call out for the department manager, but I smacked him in the jaw with the stock—sent him flying over the counter."

"You hit some guy?" Chuck asked, as his thoughts shot to the two hunting rifles back home in the closet, as well as the shotgun he kept behind the counter in the store.

Stan took the mindless question with a grain of salt. "Shit man I told you it was a mad house. It wasn't just me—there were fights breaking out everywhere. I almost got to see two broads go at it over a few cans of stew, but then some guy yelled that there was more food in the storage racks back around the dock." Stan suddenly pushed out of the chair and motioned with his head. "Come on over here."

Chuck followed him over to the shadows under the stairs and waited while Stan fumbled around in the dark. A second later the light came on and he found himself surrounded by boxes of canned food and five-gallon jugs of water. Stan pointed to the shotgun resting up against one of the stair risers and grinned. Then he stepped over a couple of boxes and pulled off a tarp. "Bought car batteries too." He threw the tarp back over the batteries and started picking up boxes one at a time. "I've got a CB radio, two cases of twelve gauge shells, first aid kit…"

Stan continued to gloat over his bounty as Chuck slowly began to feel overwhelmed by an empty nauseous sensation. He and Becky were grossly unprepared if matters took a turn for the worse. His stomach started to knot up as he pictured the empty shelves at the Wal-Mart. It would be like that everywhere. Without realizing it he started creeping back out from under the stairs.

Stan broke from his recital when he saw Chuck leaving. "Hey buddy, where are you going?"

Chuck didn't know how he got there, but he was at the stair railing. Then before he could answer his friend, he was stepping up the stairs. "I've got to go." He was halfway up before he turned and looked down at Stan staring up from the foot of the stairs. With a face lost in thought and deep concentration he said, "You take care of yourself and that wife of yours."

Stan raised his hand and said, "You too!"

Chuck opened the door to the kitchen and saw Margery sipping iced tea while staring out the window over the sink. "You take care of yourself, Margery."

She glanced over just long enough for him to notice the puffiness around her eyes and see the trails of dried tears on her cheeks. Then she took another sip of tea and turned back toward the window without saying a word.

He suddenly felt like he couldn't get out of there fast enough. He shuttled around Margery, but then his next step hit standing water and he almost slipped. The entire kitchen floor was wet, all the way over to the carpet. He grabbed the counter and scanned the linoleum. The scattered pieces of broken glass weren't hard to find. It was Margery's sun tea jar. That's what he heard in the basement. He looked back at her. "Margery?"

This time she didn't budge. She maintained her frozen stare at whatever it was in the backyard as she took another sip of tea. Denial was her way of dealing with it.

Chuck shook his head and headed for the surefooted crunch of the living room carpet. A second later he was catching his breath behind the wheel of the truck. In that surreal chain of events, the hard vinyl of the bench seat felt like a safe haven to him. He was going to get out of there, but he wasn't going home. Not yet anyway. He needed to see what was happening in the rest of Madison. So he took a left on Michigan and headed downtown.

It was an eye opener. The farther he drove the more alone he felt. He hit Main, took a right and while he drove along the deserted street he noted how many of the stores were closed. They should have been open for another half hour. As he started to drive by his antique store, he saw the 'Closed' sign hanging on the door and slowed down. He was as guilty as anyone. Finding Main Street deserted shouldn't have been a surprise for him. He pushed back down on the gas and hung a U-turn at Broadway as he shot a quick glance over to the bar he and Stan frequented. It was closed too.

As he swung the truck around, the high altitude images of the dead bodies in Aquismon flashed through his mind and shot his pulse through the roof. It wasn't much of a stretch to imagine the same thing happening in Madison. The Chevy's right front tire jumped the curb as the truth hit him like a brick wall. "They're lying." He pictured Becky standing in the bedroom and staring at the pile of clothes. Instead of veering back onto the street, he bit down and accelerated down the road with the right side of his truck cocked up on the sidewalk. "It's not contained!" He hunched over the wheel and screamed, "Goddamn it!" as he aimed the truck at the newspaper machine on the corner. But as he pressed his foot to the floor, an image flashed through his mind that he couldn't explain. He saw himself—staring out a window at the distant glow of a town burning in the dark of night. Before he could question it, the right side of the bumper caught the newspaper machine and sent it flying into the air.

The truck bounced as all four tires landed on the asphalt and he found himself shooting through the intersection. It took another block before he was able to let the tension go and yank his foot off the gas. After straightening it out, he eased his grip on the steering wheel and let the truck coast. Becky couldn't see him like this. He had to calm down. After a few deep breaths, his heart rate started to return to normal. Two blocks later he put his foot back on the accelerator and started driving again.

He kept his speed under the limit as he drove back past Michigan. But then he purposely drove through the stoplight at 421 while it was red. Somebody had to still be around. If you ever wanted a cop in Madison, the one place you could be sure and find one was at that intersection. The police loved to sit along the adjacent curb and nab the ignorant driver who didn't realize the speed limit suddenly dropped down from 45 to 30. But as he looked in his rear view mirror and started to brake, he realized that today was going to be the day that speed limit offenders would go unnoticed. Downtown was dead. He hung another U-turn and headed back for Michigan.

He glanced down the side streets as he maneuvered the truck up the winding road. The first few streets he didn't see anyone outside. But then halfway up, he saw a man loading up his car with boxes and sleeping bags while his family waited impatiently in the grass.

He was still looking down the street when a Grand Am came out of nowhere and almost hit him head-on. Chuck jerked the wheel and hit the brakes as the car sped past him on the left. On any other day the Grand Am would have gotten a rise out of him, but with what seemed to be happening, the event passed right through him without any lingering thought. He glanced in the rear view mirror to see if any other cars were coming before giving the Chevy some gas and resuming his steady rise up the hill.

A few blocks before his street, he passed an older couple lifting suit cases into the trunk of their Lincoln. But what really made the bile rise up in his throat were the cheap paper-masks they were breathing through. "No…no…"

His skin was beginning to crawl as he turned on his street and then popped up onto their cement drive. He got out, stood in the twilight and listened to the silence. Most of his neighbors appeared to be home. Their lights were on and he could see movement around the windows through the drapes. He could even see a couple of televisions on. But he couldn't hear anything. As the sound of a dog barking several blocks away broke the silence, he thought of the old couple wearing the masks. He looked across the street at the activity of his neighbors behind the drapes and realized that they were probably throwing blankets down at the foot of the exterior doors and taping up crevices around the windows—trying to seal off any openings where outside air could seep in.

With the realization of how unprepared they were gnawing at his stomach, he ran inside and called out for Becky.

Chapter 9

Chuck sat Becky down on the sofa shortly after midnight and showed her how to handle a rifle. Ten minutes later he jumped in his truck and headed out to search for supplies. He took a right on SR 62, drove past the shopping center with the Marsh grocery store, then pulled into Wal-Mart parking lot and parked along the curb right in front of the store. Under normal circumstances, Wal-Mart was open twenty-four hours a day—but not tonight. The lot was empty, the doors were closed and the lights were off. Just as well. From what Stan told him, there were too many fights over too little food.

He grabbed the tire iron from behind the seat as he got out. With a long forceful stride, he walked over to the plate glass windows at the entrance to the store. He reared the iron back over his head and was about to strike the glass when he saw the reflection of the Marsh sign in the window. Disbelief spread across his face as he turned around and looked at the sign. Habit was hard to break. He had driven right past a real grocery store without even thinking about it. But it probably didn't matter which one he hit first. The chance of finding much food at either was slim at best.

He turned back around, raised an arm to protect his face, and then struck the glass with the tire iron. The first attempt ended in surprise as the iron bounced back without cracking the glass. The second was a different story. The glass fractured and set off the store's alarm. The rapid, high-pitch metal clang of the bell had no affect on his effort. Chuck continued to break out the glass until he had an opening big enough to walk through.

The store would have been pitch-black inside if it weren't for the emergency lighting. It was dim, but there was enough light for him to see where he was going. He grabbed a shopping cart and then started making his way down each and every aisle. The place was in a shambles.

This was a small town, free of big city crime, but as he wheeled down the cluttered aisles, the store looked like it had been looted in a riot.

Nearly everything that anyone could fathom a use for had already been taken. But he did lay his hands on a few cases of baby food. And surprisingly, it didn't look like anyone even bothered with the candy displays at the checkouts. He threw what he found into the cart. Twenty minutes later he barely noticed the alarm still ringing as he calmly pushed the cart out through the broken glass and dumped everything onto the passenger floorboard of his truck.

Then he drove over to the Marsh store. After breaking the glass and finding little inside, he searched the dumpsters out back and found two cases of Hormel chili. The dates were still good—probably hidden there by one of the employees who planned on retrieving the bounty sometime in the morning.

Finally, a little over an hour after he started, he headed back down 62 with the passenger floorboard full of supplies. As Michigan Road came into view, he saw a semi-truck and two government-issued Ford LTD's idling with their lights on under the canopy at the corner gas station. Were they waiting there to arrest him?

He killed the lights and eased the Chevy to a stop along the gravel shoulder. If they wanted him, they would have to come and get him. He wasn't going to drive over and turn himself in. *They know I'm here, they had to see me pull off. What are they waiting for?* The tension peaked when a county patrol car pulled up next to the two Fords, only to fall off moments later. Everyone got out and shook hands. Chuck was too far away to hear anything and it was too dark for him to read what was on the side of the semi, but he could see the men gesturing like they were discussing something. Whatever it was, the deputy felt it was more important than responding to the security alarms still ringing back at the stores.

The deputy walked a few feet out into the intersection and pointed down 62 in the opposite direction before walking back and joining the other men. Then after the deputy shook hands with one of the Feds, they all got back into their cars. It looked like the Fed who shook the deputy's hand talked to someone on the radio, and then he flashed his lights at the patrol car. The patrol car pulled out onto 62 and then waited as the two Fords and the semi-truck pulled out of the station. When the semi cleared the canopy, the moon provided enough light for Chuck to see that it wasn't any normal commercial semi. The side of it read, 'NDMS—TM unit C61'. From what was going on and what he had seen on television, he was pretty sure that the first four letters stood for National Disaster Medical System. But he had no idea what the TM stood for.

He waited for the taillights of the convoy to blend into the night before he turned his lights back on and headed home. A few minutes later he was tapping the front door with his foot while balancing a heavy load of Hormel Chili in his arms.

"Chuck?" Becky was doing as he asked—staying away from the drapes and not letting anyone know that she was there by herself.

"Yeah, hurry let me in." He was happy to see her still holding the rifle when she opened the door. He looked her in the eyes, and for a second a feeling he couldn't explain came over him. At first it was a jumble of emotions—fear, love, anger, and even regret, that somehow, inexplicably, culminated in the most satisfying sense of belonging that he had felt in quite some time. He caressed her arm and asked, "Anything new on CNN?"

For a second her eyes locked on his strength, then she shook it off, blinked once, and looked over at the television before turning back and saying, "Oh yeah! There's been a survivor!"

He dumped the cans of chili on the floor, locked the front door, and joined her on the sofa. Becky slid her hand across the cushion to him. He saw it and immediately wove his fingers between hers and took her hand. Instead of looking at the broadcast, he looked into her eyes. He knew every feature and expression of her face. He remembered the story she told him on their second date about how she got the scar under her right cheek bone. He could describe every hair style she had ever tried. And he remembered the first time those lips whispered that she loved him. Most of all, he knew the expression in her eyes. He would never forget the joy he saw when he proposed, or the pain they shared when the doctor told them that they could never have children. When he looked into them now—he saw hope. After a lingering gaze, he asked, "Where'd they find the survivor?"

She responded with a whisper. "Suburb just outside Atlanta."

He reared back. "Atlanta?"

Becky confirmed it with a straightforward yes, a simple response with grave implications. The outbreak was spreading. Then she squeezed his hand and pointed to the television, "Here it is."

They both watched an attractive, professional looking lady behind the CNN anchor desk announce, "Once again it has been confirmed that at least one individual has survived the illness associated with the outbreak. We're taking you live to Dr. Brett Williams, the head physician of the NDMS response team in Atlanta, Georgia."

The station signal flickered once, and then a room full of murmuring reporters, doctors and military personnel filled the screen. The room suddenly grew quiet as an elderly man with a neatly trimmed full beard and mustache took the podium without any introduction. He retrieved a pair of glasses from the breast pocket of his lab coat, put them on, and began to read straight from his notes. "We have confirmed a survivor to the outbreak. Her name is being withheld until any extended family can be contacted through proper channels. We can say that she survives her immediate family, but I can't give you any more details than that. Her condition is stable, but the attending physician has stated that she will not be in any condition to provide any insight to her survival for at least several days." He looked up from his notes, took his glasses off, and slid them back in his pocket. "I'll take orderly questions."

From somewhere in the crowd, "Dr. Williams, do you have any theories about why she survived?"

"We've concluded that the outbreak is caused by the introduction of a spirochete shaped, previously undocumented bacteria. It infects the upper respiratory tract and after a short incubation period, it causes nitrates in the body to bind with the host hemoglobin. We have generalized that the incubation period is roughly four weeks. As you know, this affliction quickly triggers a rapid progression of events that ultimately leads to death. So far our efforts to thwart the progression have been unsuccessful. The pathogen itself is highly resistant to natural control measures such as temperature. Understand, the problem is not in getting oxygen to the blood, but in getting the blood to carry the oxygen to the organs. This is a complex issue…but we have the world's resources as all countries are uniting in battle of this common foe. So to answer your specific question as to my thoughts, this is speculation on my part…but nature has a way of ensuring survival. I suspect that we'll soon find an anomaly in this woman's hemoglobin that will allow us to formulate a viable biocide."

Another question from the crowd, "What kind of anomaly?"

"At this time it's hard to be any more specific. But I think the evidence points to an anomaly at the genetic level. There are real world examples of this phenomena occurring naturally. Take the incidence of Sickle-Cell Anemia in our African American population. This is a genetic disorder that poses a severe health risk to those carrying the defective gene. But this same defective gene that represents a health risk today, at one time represented a primary benefit to people of certain geographical ancestry. Those with the defective gene were less susceptible to malaria, which as you know was a leading cause of death in those regions. The defective gene actually allowed specific branches of a people to survive and multiply. It is my current belief that a similar factor is at work here."

"But didn't you say that she survived her immediate family?"

"Yes, but genetics is a game of numbers. Her survival, if indeed resulting from a genetic disorder, could be tied to a recessive trait."

"Have there been other survivors?"

"Some of the other countries are reporting—"

Chuck felt a heavy weight pressing against his chest as he turned to his wife. "They're talking as if it has spread all over the world."

She wrapped her arms around him and buried her face against the side of his neck. "Tell me that we're going to be okay."

He squeezed her and put his lips to her ear. "We'll be okay. I'm not going to let anything happen to you." But he couldn't muster much confidence in his words. Not while he was thinking about the semi-truck he saw driving down 62. He couldn't imagine what those last two letters on the side of the truck stood for—but he had an awful feeling that it wasn't good.

He pushed back from her. "I've got to get the rest of the stuff out of the truck."

"Leave it, I want you here with me."

He pulled from her clutch and stood. "I've got to or you can bet it won't be there in the morning. It'll just be a second." He held her gaze until he thought she would be okay for a few seconds. Then he ran back to their bedroom closet and dumped the dirty clothes out of the plastic basket.

A moment later he was back in the house carting a basket full of baby food and candy. He set it down next to the chili, locked the door and then rejoined his wife on the sofa. As they both leaned back, he asked, "Has the President been on at all?"

"A couple of times earlier, but you know he didn't say anything meaningful. I wish they'd just keep the coverage on the doctors."

"Yeah, me too," Chuck huffed, as he settled back in the sofa to watch the coverage with his wife. There was a deep comfort in holding her—a feeling of warmth in his heart that he couldn't ignore. As she rested her head on his shoulder, he let his guard down and asked, "Why haven't you left me?"

There was no surprise in Becky. It was as if she felt the question coming. She started rubbing his chest and without lifting her head from his shoulder, she said, "I asked myself that same question after our fight the other night. In fact I laid awake most of the night thinking about it. And the longer I thought about it, the more I realized that I was as much to blame as you for letting our marriage get away from us. There was really only one thing to decide." She paused and patted his chest. "Give up on us, or fight for our marriage."

Chuck rubbed her outside arm. "Did you decide?"

"I wasn't sure until I woke you that morning."

Chuck remembered her sitting on the coffee table and struggling with what she wanted to say.

"I was all ready to give up. But then you did something that surprised me." She pulled her head off his shoulder and looked at him. "You told me that you were sorry. And when I looked into your eyes, I could tell that you meant it. That was enough to give me hope that we could save our marriage."

Chuck looked at her as a warm sensation began to flow over his skin. Then a smile spread across his face that was quickly equaled by one on hers. "I want to fight for it too."

Becky smiled as she closed her eyes and laid her head back on his shoulder.

~~~

The heat against his face forced him to back peddle onto the street as he watched the flames shoot up through the roof of their house. Then a sudden flinch sent his foot kicking against the bottom of the coffee table. He jerked awake, started to close his eyes again, then pulled his face out of his wife's hair and reached up to his cheek. But his face wasn't hot and their house hadn't burned to the ground. It was just a dream. He was spooning his wife on the sofa—where they fell asleep watching the news.

He took a few, deep calming breaths and then quietly eased his arm out from under Becky's head. He got up, being careful not to wake her, and stretched as he glanced at the television. CNN was still carrying coverage of the events as they continued to unfold. He looked over at the light coming in through the drapes and glanced at his watch—8:17.

He took a few seconds to admire the beauty of his wife stirring on the sofa. Then while she began to stretch and wake up, he headed for the kitchen to get the coffee going. A moment later, when he was grabbing a mug out of the cupboard, daylight suddenly flooded the kitchen. He spun around and saw Becky pulling the drapes open. "What are you doing?" he gasped, as he motioned for her to stop.

Becky was still half asleep when she turned toward him. "Letting some light in—"

He walked over with the mug in his hand and started to cut her off, "We can't take a chance on anyone looking in here and seeing what we—" when suddenly a dark object fell outside the picture window and stopped him in mid-sentence. It was nothing more than a flicker in his peripheral vision, but it was enough to steal his train of thought. His mouth dropped open as he stopped a few feet from the window.

Becky froze solid. "What is it?"

He heard her, but he was too busy running possible explanations through his mind to answer. He was praying that it was an illusion or just a coincidence and that it had nothing to do with the outbreak. That hope ended when he saw another bird hit the roof across the street. The mug slipped through his fingers, fell to the floor and slung coffee across the carpet.

Panic hit Becky as she glanced back out the window and demanded, "What is it?"

Chuck swallowed hard. He didn't know how to answer her. They were just beginning to work out their marriage. How could he destroy that hope by telling her that the outbreak was in Madison? But he knew that he had no choice. They had to be prepared for the worst. After a moment of deliberation, he tried to convey the dire implications of what she was about to see in the subtle shake of his head as he took her hand. The air of the moment already had her trembling as she followed him out the front door and onto the porch.

He squeezed her shoulder and whispered, "There," as he pointed to two doves flapping their wings in the tall grass of their weed filled lawn. Then in as calm a tone as he could muster, he said, "They're dying," as he pulled her next to his side.

She looked across the street and pointed at a small, lifeless lump of feathers on the gray-shingled roof. In a shaky voice she said, "Honey…" It was the same bird Chuck saw fall just moments ago.

A soft thud hit behind them and then a black bird rolled off their roof and fell to the sidewalk. Then they heard a more familiar sound— that of a door opening. A neighbor three houses down on the right stepped outside. A second later another door opened. "Baby, I want you to go back in and gather my rifles and bring them along with all the shells to the living room."

She searched his eyes for answers. "Why?"

He had to wet his lips and swallow before he could talk. Then he lowered his face, and whispered, "When people start seeing the birds fall from the sky, they know the end is coming. There won't be any more rules or laws…from here on out we're on our own."

Becky hurried inside without saying another word. He turned back toward the street and took a hard look at the two neighbors who had come outside. As he stared at the men, he started wishing that he had taken the time to drive by the store last night and grab the shotgun he kept behind the counter.

Chapter 10

Under normal circumstances, the modest ranch home on the north side of Indianapolis would have been brimming with joy and hope as the day of the young couple's marriage drew closer. Unfortunately other matters had come to the forefront. Jason pulled his fiancée against his side as they stared at the horrible images of bodies littering the streets of downtown Los Angeles.

Leslie cringed and asked, "Can this really be happening, with all our doctors and all our medicine?"

Jason was unable to answer. He'd spent half his life wondering whatever happened to her and whether he would still feel that same warm feeling in his chest if he ever got the chance to see her again. For this to happen less than a year after finding her again—it wasn't fair. He looked into her eyes and said, "We're going to be alright." A warm feeling surged through his chest, just like it did when he rescued her from that awful teasing in the school cafeteria when they were twelve. And just like then, she looked at him with admiration in her heart. It was no different now. He would always be there to protect her.

He kissed her softly and asked, "Will you be okay for a little bit? I don't think Mrs. Conner has done anything to prepare and I doubt her kids are going to help. Not that she's really going to need anything—but just in case—it'll make her feel better." They had only known Mrs. Conner since moving in last winter, but that was plenty of time for Jason and Leslie to build a close relationship with her. He was always helping her out, doing whatever needed to be done. He had shoveled snow, raked leaves, mowed her lawn, and carried in groceries. Jason never thought of it as any big deal. It was just who he was. Whenever he saw anyone in need, he was always the first to jump in and help.

Leslie knew how uncomfortable he was with compliments, so she never told Jason how proud she was of his giving, even though it was one of the reasons why she had never forgotten about him in all those years. With that understanding, she kept the alarm in her voice under control as she said, "You go on honey and help her out. I'll stay and watch the news—see if there are any updates."

Her bravery brought a proud smile to his face. "I may have to run to the store to get her some additional supplies, but I should be home before dark."

"Be careful!" she said, as her weight shifted to her toes.

He smiled, said that he would with a nod, and started to leave, but before he opened the door she asked, "Will there still be enough time for us to get the food and supplies we need?"

Jason smiled and nodded. "Oh yeah. You'll be surprised by how everyone pulls together at a time like this. We'll be okay."

Chapter 11

Except for the distraught voice of the local news anchor on the television, the house was fairly quiet. Becky was filling up Tupperware and plastic jugs at the kitchen sink. A simple distraction meant to keep her mind off what was happening. While she bottled up water, Chuck sat on the edge of the sofa and cleaned his rifles. It was a chore made so routine over the years that it left him time to reflect. Surprisingly, his thoughts weren't on their current situation. Instead the smooth feel of the steel barrel and the warmth of the wood stock, made him think about the day his father brought home the rifles.

Like most boys in town, Chuck started going to the woods to shoot as soon as he was big enough to carry a rifle. Sometimes he went with Stan or some of his other friends, but mostly he went by himself. But up until the day his dad brought home the two matching Winchesters, he had never actually hunted anything.

It was an early Saturday morning in mid-January that his father walked him through a fresh snow into the deep woods. His dad despised tree stands—said that any damn fool could setup in a tree and wait for a deer to come to him. Real hunting was about being on the same level, tracking a deer through the brush and being quiet enough not to spook him before you got the shot.

That day he and his dad tracked a buck to a sheltered patch of tall grass and brush. They approached downwind under the cover of a sycamore that had fallen along a creek near the patch. His dad would take the shot, or at least that's what he figured until his dad motioned that it was time for him to become a man. He could still remember the chill he felt when he lined up the buck in his crosshairs. Chuck pulled the wire brush from the rifle barrel he was cleaning, and took a second to rub his thumb against the tip of his right index finger. He could still remember the feel of the trigger against his finger. He remembered how nervous he was until his dad whispered, "Make it clean. You don't want the creature to suffer."

He pulled back to the present and started to inspect the barrel he just finished. That was when the first shot echoed up from the distance.

Becky ran out from the kitchen. "What was that!"

He looked at her without as much as a flinch. "It's starting."

"What's starting?"

He lowered the rifle to his lap and made room for her on the sofa. "Sit with me." She hurried over and sat down next to him, still holding a two-quart Tupperware container and the dishtowel she was cleaning it with. He took her hand, and then in a soft, calm tone he said, "It might get pretty bad, and if it does we're probably going to hear some things that we're not used to hearing."

"Like what?"

He nodded toward the window. "Like that gun shot." Becky was scared. He could see it in her eyes and sense it in her posture. He squeezed her hand and said, "We'll be fine in here. We've got enough food and water, we've got guns and plenty of ammo. We'll just sit it out. They'll have this outbreak under control in a few days and then folks will start calming down. Things will return to normal. After it does, then you and I can get started on making up for all the time we lost." He smiled as he paused to rub the back of her hand. "I'm looking forward to that." After a moment to let that thought sink in, he continued, "You mentioned the other day about how we used to go driving. You remember that?"

Becky nodded as she bit down to settle the quiver in her jaw.

"I tell you that sounds pretty good right now. Why don't you start putting together a list of all the places you'd like to drive to before it gets too cold out. Can you do that?"

She nodded and forced a smile. A moment later she began to relax her grip on his hand as she rose off the sofa, but then they heard another gunshot and she clutched his fingers. This shot sounded closer. Too close in proximity and coming too quickly after the first shot to be from the same gun.

He squeezed her hand once and said, "Go on, fill up anything else you can find. And start putting that list together."

She let go and drifted on back to the kitchen with her head hung low.

He waited until he heard the sound of the faucet before he

finished cleaning the rifle. He was setting it back down on the floor as the female anchor at the CBS affiliate out of Indianapolis broke away from her coverage on the national front to get a live feed from one of the local reporters out on the street. With dark circles showing through the makeup around her eyes, she sighed once and said, "We've got Jim Hanson reporting from the street outside Circle Center Mall." She waited for a second, and then prompted, "Jim…Jim are you there?"

"Marie, we're having some problems with the video feed."

"Go ahead, the audio is okay, but speak up—there's a lot of background noise."

"I'm standing here just outside what used to be the commercial heart of downtown. I say used to be because now it looks more like a war zone. Looting has been going on for several hours. There's no sign of it letting up or that the local police have the manpower to put an end to it."

"Can you describe the atmosphere—what do the people—" She paused and tilted her head to the side, then said, "Hold on…we've got video now." The broadcast flicked away from the stable picture of the exhausted anchor to a shaky view of the field reporter's back as he stood and watched a small mob bust out a storefront window a half block away. "Jim, is this going on everywhere?"

He turned toward the camera. "I don't believe so Marie. It appears to be localized in a few small pockets around the city. Most people are leaving. I don't know if we can get a shot from our live eye in the sky, but the interstates should be interesting right about now."

"Are people just looting or is it worse?"

The reporter cupped his hand to his ear, as the rioting in the background grew louder. "I'm sorry Marie, could you repeat that?"

"Is it more than just looting?"

"Ahh…" the reporter stammered for a second, "…yes, before we tied in we did see a fight break out and—"

Marie broke in as a car suddenly shot around the intersection behind the mob. "Here comes a car—are they letting vehicles through?"

The camera swung over and focused on a Buick as it veered toward the mob. "Oh shit," Chuck mumbled, as he watched the car ride up onto the sidewalk. A few dove out of its path. But the majority never saw it coming. Chuck pushed back against the sofa as a man smashed against the windshield and flipped over the Buick's roof while another body disappeared beneath the undercarriage. For a horrifying second he could see a man being crushed and dragged under the rear axle. Then the Buick sideswiped a brick building, veered back off the sidewalk, and crashed into a light pole.

The reporter gasped, "Jesus Christ!" as he started to run over to the wreck. Thirty feet from the Buick, the driver's door popped open and the shaky image of a man who looked to be in his mid-twenties stumbled out. The reporter sounded less like a professional newsman and more like a regular guy who just witnessed a vehicular manslaughter, when he pulled up and yelled, "Hey! Where are you going?"

The image stabilized as the driver slowly hobbled along the fender toward the front of the smashed hood and then stared at the camera crew with the blank look of a lost child. Chuck leaned toward the screen and watched as the man teetered like a drunk and screamed, "Help me!" Then he managed one last wobbly step before he stumbled backwards and fell out of view.

The image bounced up and down again as the cameraman and reporter raced over to the wreck ahead of the mob. There was a blur as the view swung past a brick wall to the sidewalk behind the Buick. Then Chuck caught a quick flash of the driver going into convulsions before the image jumped as the mob rushed in. A torn shirt flashed across the television right before the lens crashed against the sidewalk and the screen went blank. The video feed was gone but he could still hear the audio. And what Chuck heard caused his breath to stall. It was the sound of the reporter pleading as he was being bludgeoned to death. "It wasn't me! It was him!" Chuck pulled back from the television as a thud came over the speakers. Then there was nothing but static.

Chuck was still staring in disbelief when the broadcast switched back to Marie in the newsroom. The anchor crumpled up a fistful of bulletins and started shaking her head. Then without looking up at the camera she said, "Fuck this bullshit!" and yanked out her earpiece. She threw her chair back, got up and walked off screen.

For over a minute the only thing being broadcast was silence and an empty desk. Then a young kid who couldn't have been but a year out of college, dressed in blue jeans and a Colts T-shirt, walked around the desk, sat down and took the earpiece. With a shaky voice, and fighting to be heard over the emotional release of others in the background, he snatched up one of the bulletins and began to read. "From yesterday…

the Center for Disease Control has confirmed that the first contact with the pathogen was a student from the University of North Carolina. As a member of an Extreme Adventures group touring San Luis Potosi, he came into contact with the pathogen while exploring a vertical pit, newly created by the earthquake which devastated that region May fourteenth." He paused and looked through the pile of bulletins, grabbed another and then read, "The office of the President has announced on his behalf, that the deployment and use of temporary morgues by the Nation Disaster Medical System has been authorized."

While the boy shuffled through more bulletins, a tingle washed over Chuck's skin as he made the connection between the last announcement and that semi-truck he saw. Temporary morgues—TM unit C61, the CDC was sitting up a temporary morgue in town. A prolonged silence drew Chuck's attention back to the broadcast. The boy was digging through the bulletins and by the way he kept cupping his hand to his head, it looked like he was being directed by the voice from his earpiece to find a particular sheet in the pile.

He watched the frustration build in the boy's face until the broadcast suddenly switched over to what looked like a live feed from Florida. An older voice simultaneously broadcast that this was a tape from yesterday. A distinguished looking man strolled toward the camera with a backdrop of high-rise condos to his rear, and said, "Florida, sandy beaches and fun in the sun. Well not today. Not here in Palm Beach, not anywhere." The feed switched to a camera angle 180 degrees from the first, to where the crashing surf replaced the condos as the backdrop behind the reporter. At first it looked like seaweed washing up around the reporter's feet. Then slowly, Chuck's mouth started to drop open as the camera tightened in on the debris. It wasn't seaweed. Dead fish were washing up on the sand. The gray-haired reporter looked down as he walked along the fish and said in a solemn voice that truly sounded genuine, "It appears that the oceans are dying too." The picture froze with the reporter staring down at the loss of life. Then the words appeared across the bottom of the screen, 'In memory of William "Bill" Tourney'.

The screen went black and Chuck started shaking his head. These guys were still trying to do their job while the world around them was dying. The broadcast suddenly popped back on and he jerked back toward the television. That's when it hit him—a sudden, dull pain between his eyes. He winced and muffled a low moan as he shut his eyes and grabbed his head.

"Honey! Are you okay?" Becky asked, as she ran in from the kitchen.

When he first looked up she was nothing but a blur. But after a couple of quick flexes of his face, his eyes finally focused on the crisp lines of his wife's body. "Yeah baby…I'm okay…just watching the news. You cooking supper?"

She studied him for a second, then smiled and said, "No silly, I'm filling jugs with water just like you told me." She paused to study him for a second and then disappeared back into the kitchen.

He glanced down at the rifle resting on the sofa next to him. The casual glance turned into a stare for several seconds before he finally looked around the room at the boxes of shells and canned food. What am I doing? He lowered his head for a moment and it suddenly came back to him. "Yeah!" he said with an air of discovery and a hard nod. He was cleaning his rifles.

He looked back at the television screen and saw another frozen image. This one was a young, pretty female reporter standing in front of several thousand dead cows at what looked to be one of those bigger-than-life ranches in Texas. The bottom of the screen read, 'Leslie Anne Wilson, you will be missed'.

Chuck sat there and stared at the poor girl's face. She was young and full of ambition. She had her whole life ahead of her. And now she was dead. He felt himself sink down into the sofa as his eyes started to water up. There was an unfamiliar pull on his heart as he started thinking about the children playing on the sidewalk in front of his store, the ones that he always chased off. But those pleasant mental pictures quickly turned into the horrible images of them dead. He closed his eyes and tried to push the images away, but they persisted. He saw the soft, peaceful face of the little blond haired boy that called him a mean, old man last week. His innocent face pretending to be asleep, but it was a sleep that he would never wake from. Chuck doubled over and buried his face in his hands.

It was too much. He suddenly pushed off the sofa and yelled, "No!" But as soon as he stood he felt the blood rush out of his head.

Becky ran back in from the kitchen, "Honey—" Before he knew it, she was there with her arms around him.

A cool flush filled his temples that made his eyes feel like lead weights about to roll back. "No! No!" he stammered, as his head fell backwards.

Becky caught his weight as he started to collapse. "Come on honey!" she screamed, as she shoved her shoulder under his arm.

His head rolled forward as he started panting for air.

"You can't die on me!" she cried, as she propped him up against her body.

Then his entire body jerked once as he sucked air into his lungs and raised his chin from his chest. After a moment, his vision returned and he saw his wife's face.

She looked at him through a steady flow of tears as she put a hand to each side of his face and cried, "Can you see me?"

He grabbed her shoulders to keep the room from rocking like a ship at sea. Then as things started to steady, he swallowed and said, "I…I'm okay…I just stood up too fast…that's all."

She slid her hands down around his back and pulled in tight to his body. "I'm here for you."

Chuck closed his eyes and squeezed his wife as he took several deep breaths. Then he pushed her back. "I'm okay. Really." He followed up the statement with a smile and then waited for her to return it before he said, "I better get down to the shop."

The smile left her face and a questioning look came over her. "What do you mean?"

"What?"

"You remember what's going on, don't you?"

Unwilling to admit his uncertainty, he stared at her for a second and then forced out a laugh. "Of course I do baby, don't you?" But it was all bluff. He was operating on instinct. Something was scaring him, but he couldn't quite remember what it was. The only clear thought in his head was that he needed to get the shotgun from the store.

She grabbed his face again and said, "You remember the plague don't you?"

"Of course I do." But it was only as the words came out of his mouth that he actually began to remember. While still facing her, he shifted his eyes to the supplies boxed up on the floor and he remembered breaking into Wal-Mart last night. "Yeah baby, you know with all that food and the way things are, I thought I better go to the shop and get my sawed off."

She continued to search his eyes. After a few seconds she seemed to be satisfied with what she saw and let go of his face.

He took a step away from her as bits and pieces of his mind came back on line. "Seriously, we can use another gun for protection."

"We've got both your hunting rifles and plenty of shells—isn't that enough?"

"Those are great if they're not right on top of you." A few more circuits flicked back on line. "But if someone is breaking in through the door I'd rather have something that has a little more scatter power to it." He took another step back and found the keys in his pocket. "I won't be gone long." He blew her a kiss and then started to turn.

"Wait! You're going to take a rifle aren't you?"

He tried to act like he was embarrassed about forgetting it. But truth of the matter was that he wasn't sure why he would need a rifle. Then he remembered the images of the mob up in Indianapolis and what happened to that poor reporter. He smiled and nodded as he walked back past her and grabbed the rifle and a few shells off the sofa. That was why he needed to get the shotgun.

As he walked back by her she grabbed his arm. "You sure we need it?"

He smiled and placed his hand over hers. "Yeah…I won't be gone long. Just do like you did last night and keep the other rifle at your side." There's one in the chamber and three in the magazine. Anyone other than me try to come through that door, you shoot first and ask questions later. You got that?"

She smiled and said, "Yeah."

As soon as he stepped through the door he knew that it would be the last time they ventured outside. The yards in the neighborhood were littered with the still bodies of fallen birds. Scattered among them were several dead dogs and cats, pets that had been left out to die by owners who were fearful that they might bring the plague in with them. There were a couple of thick columns of black smoke rising up somewhere to the west of his house. Surprisingly, he didn't hear as much distant gunfire as he heard earlier.

After another momentary lapse, he found himself sitting in the middle of the street with the truck running. He gave it a little gas and then hit the brakes as the truck went backwards. He put the transmission in drive, looked over to make sure that Becky wasn't watching from behind the drapes, and then slowly gave it some gas. He passed the open front door to an abandoned house two yards down from his. Then at the stop sign on Michigan, he looked over at the house on the corner and saw the front door kicked in. Across the street from it, there were two open suitcases and a week's worth of clothes scattered across the yard.

He looked both ways and then forgot where he was going. A second later he slapped his palm against the steering wheel as he remembered. With a nod and a smile, he turned right and began the winding descent to downtown. Main Street brought a truer picture of what had been going on over the last twenty-four hours. Many of the storefront windows were broken along the street. He could even see the taillights of a late sixties Impala several feet inside the pharmacy where it had come to rest after crashing through the front wall. He smiled as he thought about how somebody must have taken the pharmacy's advertised drive-thru pickup a little too literally.

But the smile vanished quickly when he saw the first body. Until then he had only seen dead animals in Madison. With all the talk and hype about a plague sweeping over the world, he had not yet seen any human casualties in Madison. That blissful ignorance was now over. He stopped and fought down a hard swallow as he stared at the body of an older man slumped across the curb of the sidewalk. Further down the street there was another body—perhaps someone he knew. He started shaking his head as the reason why he hadn't seen any bodies until now finally dawned on him. It was because most people were dying in their homes with their families. The realization sent a shiver up his back as he pictured someone finding him and Becky dead on their sofa.

It wasn't an image that he wanted to dwell on. He pushed away the thought and gave the truck some gas. Movement at the next intersection caught his attention and he glanced over at a man and a woman fighting. He drove on past, but as he started to slow down in front of his store, his mind made the connection about what he actually saw. He didn't see a man and woman fighting. As he stopped in front of his store, he realized that what he saw was a man raping a woman. He sat there for a moment, squeezing the wheel as he looked at his shop. Not too surprisingly his store was one of the few not broken into. That's the thing about antiques—in a time of crisis, they're not a priority with anyone.

As he stared at the 'Closed' sign hanging in the front door, he picked up the rifle, loaded it and chambered the first round. Then he got out and walked back to the intersection. The man had the woman pinned down on the other side of the street, but was having trouble undoing his pants and keeping her under control at the same time. Chuck steadied himself and raised the rifle to where the guy could see it. "Hey! You! Get off her!" The impact of yelling was felt immediately. His head dipped and rolled, and he had to grab on to the parking meter to keep his balance.

The man across the street paid no attention to the warning. But the woman heard Chuck and started screaming for help.

Chuck licked his lips, pushed away from the parking meter, and fired a round at one of the oversize terracotta pots that served as giant planters underneath the streetlights. Half the pot shattered and fell to the sidewalk. But the assailant didn't even flinch.

Chuck's head started to swim as he sucked in a deep breath and chambered the next round. Then he slumped up against the parking meter and used it to steady his aim as the shrill of her screams pulled at his nerves. But as he tried to stay calm and hold the sights on the man's head, he started to lose the feeling in his index finger. At the same time the back of the man's head started to blur. Chuck closed his eyes for a second and then took aim again. He slowly exhaled as the numb belly of his finger settled in on the trigger. Then in that second of calm, he squeezed off the shot.

A white puff kicked off the asphalt a half block past the man as the shot echoed through downtown. The man had the woman's hands pinned behind her head and was driving freely into her as Chuck quickly chambered another round. Chuck half mumbled and half slurred in disbelief, "How could I miss him?" as he settled back on the parking meter. Then he found the man's head in the crosshairs again, but this time the disbelief of missing the first time helped steady his aim and took away the shock of actually shooting another human being. A second later he gently squeezed the trigger. At the same instant that the shot echoed out, he saw the man's head lurch forward and his blood splatter across the asphalt behind him.

Chuck wanted to run over and help, but he couldn't even maintain a straight line as he walked over. She was still screaming when he stumbled up to her. In fact it seemed like it had been one continuous scream since he shot the man. As soon as she saw Chuck bending over, she started pushing and kicking in a desperate attempt to roll the dead weight off her. She was still hysterical even after Chuck pulled the body off. Like a mouse exposed by a young boy who turns over an empty crate, she looked up with the wide eyes and pale, clammy face of someone near shock. Then while shaking uncontrollably, she started inching back away from him on her ass and elbows.

He looked at her and yelled like a drunken idiot as he swayed back and forth. "What are you doing down here, you trying to get yourself raped?" He waited for the stars to clear in his vision, and then he lurched at her. "Now go on, get out of here and find yourself someplace safe to stay."

A glimmer of gratitude broke through the look of fear on the woman's face. Then she pushed up to her feet and took off running.

As he zigzagged his way back across the street to his store, his field of vision started to constrict while his other senses began to deaden. He saw the broken glass from the looted stores on the sidewalk as he plopped one foot down in front of the other. He knew that it had to be crunching and snapping under the weight of his boot. He didn't hear it or feel it. A moment later he slammed into the door of his store. Exhausted and not even sure what he was doing, he dug the keys out of his pocket and started fumbling with the lock.

He swallowed and his entire body mimicked the movement. He opened his eyes and saw the sawed-off twelve-gauge on the seat of his pickup. "What…" he slurred out in wonder of where he was and how he got there. He jerked at something hard in his left hand and almost hit the sidewalk. It was the door handle of his truck, and it was the only thing that kept him from falling. He bent over and put his nose to within inches of the chrome handle as he tried to focus on it through eyes that he could barely hold open. While threads of spit drooled from his mouth he began to giggle as he climbed back behind the wheel.

Chapter 12

Infrastructures around the world quickly crumbled as the plague took its victims. Communication systems were left unmanned. Ships, railcars and tractor-trailers loaded with food and supplies were left to spoil when crew, linemen and drivers fell dead. Rumors spread like wildfire and ignited a mass hysteria across the country. Everyone's fear was that if you survived the plague, you would likely starve to death because so much of the available food would be locked away and rotting in the house of someone who didn't.

In the local fight against pillaging and stockpiling, the Mayor enlisted the National Guard to patrol the network of food distribution centers that had been setup overnight around Indianapolis. Their sole purpose was to ensure that everyone had an equal chance at a ration of food. Each household was allowed one hand-basket and given ten minutes to shop as entire neighborhoods were cycled through the makeshift supermarkets. While one group searched the half-empty shelves for staples, the next group waited their turn outside under armed guard. It was society's last hope for order in a growing state of chaos.

Jason grabbed Leslie's arm and froze at the sound of the first gunshot. Then several plate glass windows along the front of the makeshift supermarket shattered and he heard the screams outside. In a sudden gasp, he yanked his fiancée to the floor and shielded her with his body as he watched one of the guardsmen run past the end of the aisle and open fire.

Everything happened so fast. They covered up and flinched as the exchange of gunfire sounded all around them. A guard stumbled back against the shelves at the end of the aisle and dragged down several cans of food as he slumped to the floor. Jason was nearly in shock as he stared at the guard's blood pooling on the tile floor. And that's when he noticed it. For several seconds there was no noise at all. No screams, no gunshots, no murmurs of panic or anguish. The store was completely silent. He looked down at Leslie and for one fearful heartbeat, their eyes shared the terror of the unknown.

They heard a man several aisles over bark out orders. "Quick! We don't have much time!"

A second later they heard other voices along with the sounds of grocery carts racing up and down aisles. They were ransacking the place.

Jason looked under his arm at Leslie. She had her eyes shut and face pressed against the floor. While she maintained her clutch of his hand, he glanced up and down the aisle. No one was going to do anything. He whispered, "They're going to take everything!" Then when he saw a mother shielding her two children against the floor twenty feet back, he knew what he had to do. He pushed up on one elbow and looked at the pistol resting in the dead guard's hand. "I can't let that happen."

Leslie squeezed his hand and pleaded, "Don't! Don't go—stay here with me."

"Somebody has to stop them."

"No Jason! Please...not you!"

Her nails dug into the skin of his arm. A heartbeat later, he pulled away and started crawling cautiously toward the dead guard at the end of the aisle. Another gunshot sounded from a few aisles over—somewhere near the bottled water and pop. He glanced back and saw Leslie shaking her head and urging him to stop. But everyone deserved a share of the food and water.

He was almost there when he heard a man yell for someone to get the guard's gun. In a mad panic, he scrambled over and lunged at the dead guard just as a man with a rifle appeared from behind a display of crackers. Their eyes met and for a split second they both froze in a moment of shock. Then Jason grabbed for the guard's pistol.

His fiancée's scream was cut short by the rifle shot as a can of tomatoes exploded on the shelf behind Jason's head. He yanked the pistol out of the guard's hand, swung it around to where the tip of the barrel nearly clanged off the steel barrel of the man's rifle, and pulled the trigger. He felt the tingle of adrenaline and the kick from the 45 caliber at the same time he saw blood splatter across the display of crackers behind the man. The man paused and blinked once—like he didn't understand what just happened. Then he began to reel as he struggled to hold the rifle steady.

Jason jerked back against the shelf as the barrel wavered in front of his face. Then at the last second, the impulse from his brain hit his hand and he yanked the barrel to the side just before it discharged. A can exploded and soaked the side of his face in tomato puree as the man finally collapsed and fell backward.

Barely audible above the ringing in his ears, Jason heard one of the other men yell, "Frankie...Frankie!" Dazed and feeling like the whole ordeal was a nightmare that he would soon wake up from, he climbed to his feet and stepped out into the open in front of aisle seven. An older man with a shotgun was running toward him while screaming and crying. Jason glanced down and saw that the man he shot was barely more than a kid. But that fact had no impact on him. He felt nothing. A heartbeat later, he found himself staring at the charging man, as if trying to understand what the man was screaming. He watched the man raise the shotgun and fire in mid-stride. As he heard the muffled blast, he felt the pull of the searing air blow by his left side.

Jason was operating on blind instinct as he raised the pistol and pulled the trigger again. The charging man looked like he slipped on a patch of ice—one foot slipped out from under him and he spun around and went down. Then as if his ears were stuffed with cotton, he heard a muffled thump and a box of crackers exploded to his right. His entire body was tingling as he turned and watched the box flip in the air. Everything was happening so slowly. It was amazing. Then he saw his fiancée. She was screaming something at him. She was pointing behind him. She wanted him to turn around.

Something stung the side of his right arm as two more boxes exploded. His mind was so in tune with the moment that he could see individual crackers breaking apart in the air. Then for a reason he couldn't explain, he turned and fired the pistol again. He felt the kick from the discharge against his shoulder and arm an instant before a man crash into him. He buckled, and together they flipped over the display onto the next aisle.

Numb to everything, all emotions, all sounds, all feelings, he stood with a dazed look on his face. The man who crashed into him struggled for a second to get up, then fell face first onto the floor. A jar of jelly popped beside him. He stared at the broken jar for a second and then followed the line of fire back to the checkout registers. A woman was screaming and charging, and with every stride she took he saw a flash.

He heard the soft, muffled sounds of raindrops hitting a tin roof behind him as more jelly jars popped. But the sound died after he raised the pistol and pulled the trigger.

He still had the gun raised when he heard a sound to his rear. He spun and with a pale, blank look on his face, squeezed the trigger again. For a timeless moment, the only thing he saw was her eyes as the spent casing ejected between them. They were the eyes he would love his entire life. Then just as he started to smile, he saw the smoke drifting up in front of her face. He watched as shock and despair displaced the life in her eyes. Then as he saw the cringe in her face, he slowly started shaking his head as all the emotions that had been absent during the gunfight, suddenly came rushing back in. "No…No…No…" he whispered as the pistol slipped from his hand. His lips started trembling as the love of his life reached one last time for his shoulder. "No!" he cried out as his fiancée fell into his arms.

He grabbed her and crumpled to the floor. "No! Dear God… anything but this!"

Barely able to see through his tears, he held her as she reached up to touch his face. "Somebody! Help me!" he cried out. "Get a doctor!" Then as he started sobbing uncontrollably; he cradled her head and whispered, "We're going to get married…you and me…we'll be together forever." He sobbed as a tear ran from her eye while she smiled one last time. Then just like that—everything that he'd ever hoped for was suddenly stolen from him. A quiver washed over his body that climaxed in a pain-ridden wail as he closed his eyes and rocked her back in his arms.

Shaking and heaving with each gasping moan, he jerked around and looked for someone to tell him that it was just a bad dream and that he would soon wake up to find her sleeping by his side. But no one came to help. No one cared. With the gunmen dead, everyone was busy scooping up canned goods and bottled water into shopping carts. It was a free-for-all.

He looked at the people jumping over the checkout counters, and screamed, "Help me! Somebody!" But as no one paid any attention to him, he turned back to the precious weight in his arms. He pulled her face to his chest and then began to rock with her on the floor. As the pain of his loss quickly boiled up in him, the tears of remorse started to make way for something much darker. He turned back and glared at those running past him with their cans of stolen food. With his face full of tension he screamed at the top of his lungs, "Why didn't one of you stop me before I did this!"

Chapter 13

Chuck pounded on the door. He wasn't sure where he was or how he got there, but there was something instinctual driving him; a deep rooted feel of belonging on the other side of the door. As his vision started to fade out again, his weight slumped against the door and he professed in one final garbled cry, "Let me in, damn it!"

The door popped open and he fell into the slender arms of a woman. His weight shifted again and just as he was about to fall over backwards, she reeled him in and kept him upright. Even in his bemused state of mind there was an immediate recognition of something familiar about her. "I know…you…" he gasped. Before she could reply, the room began to spin and his legs buckled. A second later he toppled over the sofa with her in tow.

~~

His eyes darted aimlessly about the room until they locked onto the woman straddling his midsection. As she held his face between her hands and screamed, he used every ounce of life that remained in his soul to distinguish the meaning in her words. "You've…gone…all day…where's…truck…gun?"

His eyes rolled back and then he felt her shake his head. He came back around and cried out, "Becky!"

His exhausted state gave him a brief moment of peace before his stomach suddenly constricted and sent him cringing in pain. He doubled over as a bile taste burned his throat and erupted over his face and shirt. In the midst of it all, he lashed out at the body on top of him and coughed, "I've…got to get back to…Becky…"

As if the outburst were his last gasp, he fell back flat on the sofa and felt the life leaving his body as every muscle in him went limp. Then something pulled open one of his eyelids. He couldn't distinguish anything in the blurring movement of light and darkness. The eyelid fell back closed, and suddenly he popped back up to his feet. "Got to go...home." He felt something holding him back, something trying to keep him there. He pulled free and for a second he felt himself standing. Then everything spun around as he felt himself succumb to gravity and crumple through the grasping arms that were trying to hold him up. His body came to a crashing stop, but he felt no pain. He just felt himself falling asleep.

~~~

Something cold and wet touched his forehead that lit him up like an electrical jolt. His back arched up high off the floor and he gasped. Then just as quickly, he felt a soothing sensation as cold streams trickled down both sides of his face. The small of his back touched the floor once more and then his head started shaking. He fought through the confusion and slowly opened his eyes. As his vision pulsed on a round shape in front of a dark background, a voice broke through the confusion and dispelled his fear. "Don't go...don't leave me."

There was something deeply comforting about it that made him smile. Then he felt his head shaking again and he opened his eyes once more. The round object over his face grew larger and darker. When it was all that he could see, he felt something soft press against his lips while little wet drops fell against his cheeks. He smiled and said, "Love... you..."

Then everything went dark.

~~~

His eyes popped open as he jerked and tried to cry out in pain. He felt the muscles of his chest and back flexing all at once, fighting against each other, pulling at his ribs and spine, trying to snap his bones. He couldn't scream; he couldn't breathe. He felt the terror of nothing in his lungs, no substance to produce a sound. For a brief moment he recognized the ceiling of his living room and felt the sorrow of the dark figure holding his hand. Then flashes started going off and his vision was nothing but bursts of light followed by halos as he felt himself starting to bounce and pop off the floor. Again he tried to scream out as he felt the sharp, cold pain of knives plunge into his hands and feet. His mouth made the horrible movement but produced no sound as he felt the constriction of their blades dragging up through his limbs toward his heart—filleting him like a fish as the stars overhead closed in around him. His head jerked from side-to-side and he started kicking his feet against the floor. Then all thought and feeling left him.

Chapter 14

Jason wasn't sure how long he had been sitting on the floor with his back against the foot of the sofa. Time had slipped through his fingers like sand through an hour glass. He couldn't remember if the shoot out at the supermarket happened earlier that day or if it was two days ago. He looked over his shoulder at the object of his sorrow, laid out across the cushions behind him. How he got Leslie home was forever lost to him. So too was why he still had the gun. Like an indecisive twitch, he slowly rubbed the hard steel barrel of the pistol up and down his thigh.

Only a few things stood out clear in the horror of what happened. The police never came—no one ever helped him—they all left him there with the body of his dead fiancée. If anybody else had jumped up to help, his Leslie would still be alive. The only other thing he remembered was dumping the guns and rifles from the four he killed into the back seat of his car.

He held the pistol a few inches from his face and studied it as if the answer were buried deep within it. Then he slowly closed his eyes and winced in pain. In a fight of emotions, he gasped and rammed his back against the sofa. A heartbeat later he pulled forward and did it again. She couldn't be gone! He threw his face to the ceiling and screamed, "Dear God, take me from this pain!" He waited and stared. Then in a wince of defiance, he swung the pistol to his head and pressed the tip of the barrel to his temple.

There was no point in living without her. No reason to go on living with this pain. He clamped his teeth together, and with the cool steel of the trigger resting against the soft belly of his finger—he pulled.

Jason flinched as the hammer clicked, but there was no discharge. He immediately broke down crying and began to shake uncontrollably as he turned to look at his Leslie. "I'm so sorry!" he wailed. He dropped his arm under the weight of the gun and when the pistol hit the floor, it unexpectedly went off. The kick nearly sprung his wrist as the slug slapped against the drywall and blew a hole through the vinyl siding on the exterior of the house.

Jason fell into a moment of shock. He stared at the wall, then at the pistol for several seconds. Then all of a sudden he broke into delirious laughter as the uncontrolled mixture of emotions boiled out of him. He threw his head back and stared at the ceiling again. "What do you want of me?"

That's when he started thinking about all those people who could have stopped him, but didn't. All they had to do was grab him. If they had, Leslie would still be alive. The more he thought about it the more the anger built up in him. These were the same people that he had gone out of his way to help every day of his life. Help without ever expecting anything in return. He had given everyone the best he had to offer his entire life and this is how they repaid him.

He turned around and climbed up to his knees so that he could kiss Leslie goodbye. Then he pushed off the floor, but when he stood everything started spinning and a warm feeling filled the back of his head. He grinned as he latched onto the sofa to keep his balance. They refused to stop him before he shot his fiancée. He was going to see if they would stop him now, because with God as his witness, he was going to shoot every last mother fucker he saw until someone did.

Then, as if a sign from Heaven, a beautiful halo started to appear around everything he looked at. As far as he was concerned, it was proof that he was on the path of righteousness. He let go of the sofa and stumbled toward the door. Out in the back seat of his car, vengeance waited for him with a debt of love still to be paid for.

Chapter 15

Chuck stared at the ceiling for several minutes after waking. It wasn't the first time he opened his eyes, but it was the first time he had been able to keep them open longer than a few seconds. His muscles were sore, his back was stiff and the heels of his feet were tender to the touch. But those pains were only an afterthought given the difficulty he had in breathing. His throat was so dry and swollen that every exhale produced a weird rasping sound.

He rolled his head to the side and saw the body of his wife less than a foot away. But it wasn't an image that his mind was ready to accept. Even the dull, lifeless reflection in her eyes couldn't elicit any emotion in him. For all practical purposes, Becky might as well have been a piece of furniture.

After another painful inhale, he rose up on one elbow and then used the stiffness of her body to push up to his hands and knees. A loud moan rolled up through the dry skin of his throat as he arched his back like a cat and stretched out his sore muscles. The pain was evident in his face as he bit down and started pushing himself off the floor—a feat that on any normal day wouldn't be worth mentioning. Today, though, was about as far away from normal as you could get. He found himself so weak that he had to grab the arm of the sofa to catch a second wind before pushing up the rest of the way. In fact he felt so beaten down that his first thought was that he had been in a car crash. That thought stayed with him as he hobbled his way toward the kitchen, pausing once to rub his lower back.

There were several jugs of water lining the counter top, but he passed them up. Instead he opened up the cupboard, grabbed a glass and filled it under the sink. He slowly sipped the first glass down in one continuous drink. The second glass he paused periodically and took the water down in gulps. He held the glass under the faucet and was about to go for a third, when his stomach suddenly cramped up. He flinched and dropped the glass. A second flinch doubled him over. Then in a blind grab to keep from falling, he pulled off several jugs of water before he fell and hit the floor.

He woke again—this time on the wet linoleum in the middle of the kitchen. As he slowly pulled his head up he saw a couple of Tupperware containers and an old plastic milk jug lying on the floor just out of his reach. That was as far as he got before he fully understood just how sore his stomach was. Slowly and gingerly, he rose up to where he was sitting. He slid backward on his rear to where he could rest against the bottom cabinets. He let out a few slow, deep breaths, this time without the rasping sound, and then reached up over his head and pulled one of the jugs of water over the edge. But as soon as the half-gallon jug pulled free of the counter, his arm crumpled under the weight and he dropped it. The plastic jug crashed to the floor and splashed water everywhere.

After a moment of anguish, he wet his hand in the standing water and patted down the taunt, dry skin of his face. That was when he realized how much effort it took just to lift his own arm. He rested for a minute, and when he reached up to the counter the second time, he used both hands.

This time he slowly sipped the water and avoided the debilitating stomach cramps. When he was confident that he could stand again, he clutched the counter and pulled himself up. With his thirst satisfied he went to work on hunger. He angled over to the pantry and grabbed a bag of chips. Then with a small pitcher of water in hand, he made his way back into the living room, edged his way between the body of his wife and the sofa, and plopped down in front of the television.

He sat the pitcher on the seat next to him and tore into the bag of chips so savagely that half the contents flew out over the floor and surrounding cushions. But he didn't care. Satisfying his need for a salty, greasy potato chip was all that mattered. He plunged his hand down into the foil bag and pulled out a fistful. Then as he sat and catatonically stared at the static on the television, he shoveled the chips into his mouth, pausing only long enough to wash mouthfuls down with a splashy gulp of water.

Midway into the feast, he scraped a handful of crumbs off his shirt and dropped them in his mouth. But he tasted the difference as soon as they hit his tongue. The pile of tempting morsels weren't all potato chips. His shirt was covered in a crusty layer of flakes. He peeled off a large one and stuck it in his mouth. The flake dissolved into a bitter flavor that made his face cringe. It was the same acidic taste that burned his mouth when he had to visit the porcelain god after a night of hard drinking…it was dried vomit. He voiced a subdued, "Oh," of discovery as he began to brush the flakes off his shirt. Following a few half-hearted swipes, his hand was back in the bag and his concentration back on the static of the television.

He continued in that state until he reached the greasy bottom of the bag. After the chips were gone, he stood up and brushed the crumbs and remaining flakes off his shirt. Then with a little bit of food in him, he decided it was time for a walk. He stepped over Becky's body and turned the television off. But before he walked out the door, he turned, looked at his wife on the floor and said, "I'm going to go for a walk." He waited for a second, then nodded and stepped out.

It was a beautiful day outside. Sunny enough that he had to squint and shield off some of the light, yet breezy enough that he didn't have to worry about sweating like a pig. He walked down the middle of the driveway and in a matter of minutes he was standing at the end of his street. He took a right on Michigan and his stride grew as he started working his way down the hill. A few blocks into it he came across his truck abandoned in the ditch. He looked at it for a second, then opened the door and saw his rifle and shotgun on the seat. The keys were still in the ignition, and after a second of thought, that's where he left them. He slammed the door and started walking again. The truck wasn't stuck and it still had gas. But it was just too beautiful of a day to drive—he felt like walking.

Fifteen minutes later he was a few blocks from the river and approaching Main Street. Out of habit, he took a right and started walking over to his antique store. A beautiful day like this would bring several folk out—maybe even some shoppers from the city. He would open up and rake in the money.

He stepped over the broken glass and maneuvered around the discarded store merchandise that littered the sidewalk. Every once in a while a piece of trash or clothing would get snagged on a piece of broken wood or bent metal and flap in the wind. Most of it blew around like tumbleweeds in the breeze as he stepped over a body. A few stores farther down he came upon his antique shop.

The windows were broken out and the displays tipped over. Most of the glass antiques were shattered on the floor. The old farm tools hadn't been touched, but most of the antique mantle clocks that he picked up at the local estate auctions were in pieces. But none of that had any affect. As if it were an everyday occurrence, he slowly stepped through the mess and grabbed the broom from behind the counter.

Then he went to work. First he set the large display cabinets upright and filled their shelves with the smaller stuff. Next up was sweeping. As he pushed the growing pile of dust and debris from the rear of the store forward, he began to work faster. People would be coming any minute—he had to hurry. He had to be ready to open when they got there. His breathing continued to increase until he was sweeping the mess out the front door with such ferocity that he looked like a frantic golfer trying to swing his way out of a sand trap. For a reason he didn't understand it seemed that no matter how fast he swept the floor—it wasn't fast enough. Then he felt his jaw start to quiver and his throat start to swell up. In a fit, he swung the broom and let go. A cloud of dust rose up around him as the broom sailed out to the middle of the street. For the next minute, he stood there at the threshold of his store, panting and staring out the door with a wild look in his eyes.

His consciousness was fighting so desperately to cling to what no longer existed. He spun around and looked at what remained of the store he inherited from his father. A heartbeat later he shot out the door to the middle of Main. He stopped, and with a frightened gasp, looked up and down both sides of the street. Every store was in shambles just like his store. He peered at the sidewalks. They were covered in glass and broken debris. As the crack in his denial opened up a little more, he started seeing the bodies. There was a black man stretched out on the cement a few shops down from his. There was another body farther down crumpled over on the sidewalk.

His breathing picked up as his stomach started to lift out of place. Not everything littering the street was trash. Several small mounds were covered in fur. Small, fist size clumps of feathers tumbled in the wind along with the other debris. He swallowed hard as the whites of his eyes opened up. Then without any warning and before he could stop it—he screamed. He bent over at the waist and wailed the way a mother would over the dead body of her only child.

As his pent up emotions started erupting, he did the only thing he could do. He ran. He sprinted down one of the side streets and ran up the sidewalk to the front door of the first house he came to—a little brick bungalow. He didn't bother ringing the bell. He just started pounding on the door. "Help! Help me! Somebody. Please help me!" He sobbed openly and loudly as he beat the door until the meat of his fist was numb. Then in a huff, he stepped back, reared up his right foot and rammed the heel of his boot against the door. The wood jamb inside the house gave way as the door burst open and swung into the wall. Before his heart sounded the next beat, Chuck was in the living room. He stopped dead center in the shadows, cupped his hands to his mouth and screamed for help. But when he turned, he discovered that no help would be coming. There, sitting side-by-side on the sofa were the bodies of the elderly owners. They had died in each other's arms.

He clutched the front of his shirt with both hands and started shaking his head back and forth. "No! No! No goddamn it...this can't be happening!" He sprinted out the door and ran to the house across the street. This time he didn't bother knocking. As soon as he found it locked, he kicked the front door open. He quickly searched all the rooms as if he were looking for an escaped prisoner. When he found that house empty he ran out and broke into the next house. As soon as he kicked the door open, he tripped over the bloated body of a Basset hound and fell face first against the fat belly of a dead middle-aged man wearing nothing but boxer shorts and a T-shirt. The sour smell of dead, rotting flesh hit him like a slap to the face. It was the heat in the house that made it so bad. The air conditioner—if it had one—wasn't on, and all the windows were closed up and taped over.

The repulsive shock of landing on rotten flesh was enough to stop his crying. He jumped up and staggered backwards until he bumped against a recliner. Even then, his wide-eyed stare lingered for a few seconds before he cupped his hand over his nose and mouth and continued to look around. But the half-hearted search ended just seconds later when the smell became too much for him. He quickly yelled once to make sure there wasn't anyone alive in the house, then after an excruciatingly long pause he ran for the door. He stopped on the porch and filled his lungs with clean air as he wiped the half-dried tears from his face.

That was when a dreadful sense of knowing began to overwhelm him. "It can't be," he said out loud, as he cautiously walked down the sidewalk to the street. As he looked at one house after another, an undeniable panic began to grow. He was alone.

He sprinted back out to the middle of Main and started yelling at the top of his lungs. "Is anybody there? Hey! I'm on Main Street!" After waiting for a few seconds and hearing nothing but the blowing wind, he started walking down the middle of Main. "This can't be happening… Jesus fucking Christ…this can't be real." He glanced from side to side in disbelief as he passed the looted stores.

He saw the black man on the sidewalk. He walked over and kneeled down to check for a pulse. It was while holding the stiff arm of the dead man that he started to have the strangest sense that he was forgetting something. He remembered feeling something just like the man's wrist earlier. He remembered pressing his hands down on something unnaturally cool to the touch that had the texture of hard wax. He had used it to push up off a floor somewhere. But what was it and where was it? By the time he was walking down the middle of the street again, the question was nagging him to the point where he couldn't let it go.

He started rubbing his hands together in thought. He pictured the elderly couple that died together at the first house and his pace picked up to a fast walk. Then he remembered walking down to Main Street. His pace picked up to a slow trot. He had come down here from his house. The trot became a jog as he searched the empty space in front of him for answers. Where was Becky? A shiver ran up his back foretelling of a memory better left in the dark. With each pound of his foot against the pavement, more light was shed on what he refused to see. His mouth dropped open and he began to mumble, 'No…' over and over as he started to realize that he hadn't been alone up at the house. His eyes took on the distant look of a scared child as he broke into an all-out run and screamed, "Becky!" Heart pounding and adrenaline pumping, he sprinted around the corner onto Michigan.

Chapter 16

Chuck's feverish sprint up Michigan Road broke when the lack of nutrition finally caught up to him. He was running as fast as he could when his legs suddenly locked up and sent him crashing face first against the sun drenched asphalt.

He flopped over onto his back and sucked in several deep breaths as beads of sweat trickled down his face and burned his eyes. The muscles in his legs were quivering and on the verge of cramping up, yet he couldn't stop. Not with every ounce of his being praying that he was wrong—that he didn't remember her lying on the floor of their house. He had to find out. If she wasn't there—he had to see it. If she was, even though it would rip his heart out, he had to see that too.

He rolled back over onto his hands and knees and grunted as he pushed off the hot, tacky road. After teetering on his heels for a second, he leaned into the grade of the street and started walking as fast as he could.

Sweat was still beading on his flushed face when he rounded the corner and saw his Chevy in the ditch. A brief spark gave him the energy to run. He hit the side panel of the truck, opened the driver's door, and saw the keys still in the ignition. A few seconds later the Chevy flew over the last rise on Michigan as he barreled down the middle of the street. The truck fishtailed out of the turn onto his street and then flew up his driveway. He locked up the brakes, and skidded into the garage door.

His heart was pounding as he threw the front door open and looked in. For a second he lost his ability to breathe as his face trembled and his lips contorted like they had a life of their own. Just as his knees were about to give, he dropped to the floor and scooped his wife up in his arms. He closed his eyes and held her to his chest as he rocked back and forth and cried. Nothing in his life could have prepared him for that moment.

He remembered staring into her eyes the night of their first date. How he saw nothing but her beautiful face. How warm and comfortable he felt as they shared a private moment in the crowded restaurant. He remembered the feel of her breath against his ear the night she whispered that she loved him in the back seat of his Barracuda. Then he remembered how good it felt to hold her hand the other night as they watched the news coverage. She didn't say it, but he knew it was a comfort to her, just like it was for him. Holding hands told them that they weren't going it alone. But best of all was when he woke up next to her on the sofa the following morning.

Chuck nodded as he squeezed her body. We were going to make it work. When he opened his eyes and looked upon the face of the woman he loved more than anything else in life, those wonderful memories dissolved away. As the tears ran down his face, all he could think about were all the times he wanted to tell her that he loved her and didn't. Like just a few days ago when they got home from her father's birthday. He saw the pain in her face as she stared at the ground and walked past the truck into the house. Did he stop her and tell her that he was sorry? No! Did he run in after her, take her in his arms and tell her that he loved her? No! Instead he sat in the truck like an idiot.

He closed his eyes and slammed his fist against the floor. "What was I doing?" A gritty moment of intense anguish was followed by another punch to the floor. He tried to fight it, tried to push them away, but the awful memories of how bad he had been to her kept coming. The worst of them happened just the other day when he came home drunk. There was no forgetting the terrible things he said to her that night.

The memories and regret continued to rip away at his heart. Until finally the emotional scars of pain and remorse etched their way across his face and he cried out, "Oh God!" He jerked up straight, and with her stiff body still clutched to his chest, he raised his face to the ceiling and began to wail, "Why Lord?"

Chapter 17

Jason stumbled down the steps of his house with the pistol that killed Leslie. The other guns were waiting for him in the car parked along the street. There was enough there to make everyone pay—and that was exactly what he intended to do. As he started to fumble with the keys a woman sprinted around the sidewalk on the other side of Mrs. Conner's house and screamed for help.

He turned and teetered on his heels as the crazed woman ran up to him.

"You've got to help me!" she cried out as she clutched his arm. "Some black guys are going to kill my husband and his brother!"

Jason stared at the halo around her head but never once mistook it for anything heavenly. And even though he knew it was another woman, he couldn't see past the mother who was protecting her children back at the supermarket. The same mother who didn't lift a finger to stop him before it was too late.

His expression turned to a scowl as he squeezed the rubber grip of the pistol. "What did you say?"

"You have to help me! Hurry! They're going to kill him!" she screamed, as she tried to yank him toward the direction she came from.

Jason felt the trigger of the pistol with his finger. "Where are they?"

The woman was so frantic that her words couldn't keep pace with her actions. She threw an arm out and pointed as she tugged on him. "Parking lot…next block…Hurry!"

"I'll take care of it," Jason said, as he reached up and pulled her hand off his arm. "You wait here. I'll get them."

"Oh dear God…thank you…thank you!"

Jason took a couple of steps before he turned back toward her. Then without the slightest hesitation or any sign of feeling, he raised the pistol and calmly said, "Here's your help." The woman glanced up in time to see the flash. Vengeance would be his.

A second later he heard a gunshot come from where the woman pointed. He picked up his pace to a fast jog and ran around the corner. The parking lot was empty except for an old four-door Impala. A few feet from the car, three black guys were working up a real sweat as they tried to beat a big redheaded white guy to death. One of them was going to town with a baseball bat while the other two were putting their weight behind four to five foot lengths of chain.

The big redhead was doing his best to fight them off. His face was all bloodied and he was swinging blindly, but he sure wasn't giving up. He grabbed one of the chains as it broke the skin across his back and gave it a hard yank. The black guy that was anchored at the other end flew over next to him like he was being reeled on to a boat. The redhead wrapped his meaty paw around the guy's throat and got in one roundhouse right before one of the other black guys brought a bat down across his forearm. Truth of the matter was that it was actually a pretty fair fight. If it had been hand-to-hand the big redhead would have easily overpowered the three black guys.

While the three danced that fight, another black guy was standing with a gas can over the body of the redhead's brother. He was so busy demeaning and spitting on the remains that he never saw Jason walking up behind him as he doused the corpse in gasoline and set it on fire.

Fifty feet away Jason yelled, "Hey!" as he raised the pistol.

The guy turned around. "What you want you white motherfu—" A 45 caliber shell blew the lower half of his face off before he could finish the sentence.

Jason spun around toward the others but lost his balance and went down on one knee. Everything was beginning to spin. He saw the other three black guys break from the big redhead and run back to the Impala. At first he thought they were going to drive off. But as he pushed off the asphalt and stood, he realized that they were actually going for the guns in the trunk.

He raised his pistol and started walking towards them. He was within thirty feet when one of the guys stepped out from behind the trunk and opened up with an automatic assault rifle. Jason heard the roar and saw the flame as thirty rounds perforated the asphalt next to him.

A second later the other two jumped in. One had a double-barrel shotgun and the other a pistol. The guy with the pistol yelled, "Kill that mother-fucker, Avon!"

Jason steadily closed to within two car lengths and took out the man with the pistol with one shot. Avon slapped in another clip as the other man fired the shot gun. Pellets sprayed across the front passenger fender as Avon squeezed off another clip. Jason fired once and struck the assault rifle. The next shot struck Avon in the shoulder and spun him around. Avon managed to keep his feet under him and tried to make a run for it, but the next shot struck him in the leg and put him down.

The last man was fumbling with a box of twelve gauge shells in the trunk as he tried to reload. He slipped two in and started to snap the shotgun shut when Jason walked around the fender and pressed the barrel of the pistol to his head.

The man shrunk back at first, but then pushed out his chest and said with a stiff jaw, "What you waiting on motherfucker."

Jason motioned toward the big redhead who had managed to crawl over to the dead body and put out the fire. "Why them?"

"Been the white man's nigger long enough. Don't get no whiter than them two." Then he pumped his chin at Jason and said with a sneer, "Payback's a bitch isn't it."

"Shoot that son-of-a-bitch!"

Jason looked over at the redhead. Then he glanced at the black guy that he shot in the shoulder and leg. "That man kin of yours?"

The black man spit out defiantly, "I ain't telling you shit!"

"Kill him!" the redhead cried out as he slumped over the burnt body of his brother.

Jason swung around to the redhead. "Shut up!" Then he turned back to the black man and grabbed his jacket with his free hand. As he rubbed the canvas collar of the man's duster between his thumb and finger he said, "Nice dusters. I'm guessing you and your buddies stole them."

"Fuck you!"

Jason said, "No matter," as he shrugged his shoulders once and pulled the trigger. The hammer of the pistol clicked once, twice and then a third time as Jason kept squeezing the trigger.

"Out of bullets mother-fucker," the black guy said with a grin as he stepped back and snapped the shotgun closed. "Guess you won't be killing me or my brother now will ya."

Jason shifted his weight back to his heels as the redhead yelled.

Then there was a sudden blink and he jumped. But even before the shotgun backfired and exploded, he knew that he wasn't going to die. He was on the righteous path. That was the only explanation. It had to be. There was no way a guy could squeeze off two full clips from an assault rifle and not hit a man standing out in the open less than twenty feet away.

Before the barrel and stock exploded, Avon's brother was standing behind the open trunk with the shotgun braced against his hip. Afterwards he was stretched out over the bumper, halfway in the trunk with most of his stomach and hip blown out.

Jason dropped his head and huffed out a giggle as he grabbed the rear fender for support. The clean lines of the world around him were starting to blur and fade. But that wasn't going to stop him. He staggered over and scooped up the pistol the one man dropped a few feet from the car. He checked the clip. A weary moment later he rolled Avon over on to his back and was about to shoot him in the face.

"Wait!" the big redhead yelled. Jason glanced over as the redhead climbed to his feet and grabbed the can of gasoline. "I want to burn that son-of-a-bitch."

Avon wasn't conscious, but he was alive. Every few seconds he would twist at the waist and moan in pain. It wasn't much, but it was enough. It told the world that he could still feel pain. As Jason swayed, the redhead poured gasoline all over Avon. A second later the blaze sucked in the surrounding air as the man's shrill scream echoed through the streets. It was the only one he got out.

As if the fire sucked out what little life Jason had left, he stumbled backwards and fell on his ass. The big redhead ran over and squatted next to him. "Mr. I sure am thankful for what you did. I don't know how you made it through all those bullets, but I sure am glad you did." He extended a hand and said, "I'm Mark."

Jason tipped back and smacked his head against the asphalt. Then as Mark bent over him, Jason raised the pistol and pressed it against Mark's stomach. The redhead would be his last victim. But before he could pull the trigger, Mark pulled the gun from his hand and said, "I'll wait here with you to the end."

Jason closed his eyes, and as he began to see the brilliant bursts of light he cried out, "Why didn't you stop me?"

"You talking to me?"

Jason swore as the life started to leave his body, "This isn't over. We're not square by a long way."

"I'm right here by your side," Mark said, as he shook Jason lightly. "Did you see a woman on your way over here? My brother's wife…she went looking…"

Chapter 18

The shadows of sunset made their way across the room as Chuck sat against the bottom of the sofa, lost in an endless stare at the floor while he held the lifeless body of his wife. His only movement during those hours came from the occasional kiss he placed on the marbleized skin of her forehead.

Then darkness fell and the only illumination in the house came courtesy of the streetlights outside. It was time. He slid out from under her body and laid her down gently on the carpet. After he got up, he shut the front door and turned on the lights. He paused to look at her one last time and then headed for the bathroom in the hallway.

For several minutes he stood under the light above the sink and stared at the blank features of the reflection in the mirror. Who was that man in the mirror? It wasn't until he slowly began the chore of undressing that he took notice of his appearance. The dried vomit on his shirt was no surprise. But the dried crap caked in his boxers did raise an eyebrow.

He threw the soiled clothes in the corner and stepped under the cold spray of the shower. Other than the goose bumps along his arms and thighs there was no sign that the chill bothered him at all. There wasn't even the slightest shiver as he stood there watching the water take on a brownish tinge as it washed away the dried clumps from his midsection. As the spray began to warm up, he grabbed the shampoo and started washing his hair just like he would any other day.

He didn't sense anything peculiar about the situation until he was rinsing off. The hot water was beating against his back when he slowly looked up at the bathroom light on the ceiling. The water continued to run as he stepped out onto the rug and stared at the ventilation fan. He reached over to the switch and flicked it on. A second later he heard the initial clanking sound of metal against metal quickly followed by the gradual buildup of a hum as the blades started turning.

There still wasn't any visible expression on his face as he turned off the shower and went to the bedroom for some fresh clothes. After he got dressed, he turned on all the lights in the house before heading out the door. All the streetlights were on. So too were the lights in several of the houses. He could even see the glow of the television through some of his neighbors' drapes. For the first time since he found his wife, expression broke the cast numbness of his face. His lips parted and a slight pinch formed between his brows. He walked out to the middle of the street and yelled, "Is anyone there?"

Before his echo had a chance to die, he headed across the street to Bill and Rena's house where it looked like the television was on. He and Becky had never put forth much effort to socialize with the neighbors, but this was different. They would understand him coming over at a time like this. He glanced through the drapes as he crossed the sidewalk to the front door. They were both on the sofa watching the television. He knocked on the door. "Bill…it's Chuck from across the street." After a few seconds he knocked again. "Come-on Bill…This is important." He rang the doorbell and as the chimes finished their short musical score he tried the knob—it was locked. He jumped off the porch and pressed his face against the picture window. "Hey man! Let me in!"

When they still refused to budge, he resorted to banging on the picture window with his fist. "Goddamn it I'm not going to ask—" His hand broke through the glass before he could finish. He jumped back as the entire panel slid out in several large pieces and shattered on the landscaping stone next to the house. After a quick glance at the cuts around his knuckles, he stepped over the broken glass and popped his head between the drapes as they began to ripple in the night breeze.

A moment later he walked back across the street with his head hung low. He pushed a section of the broken garage door off the hood of his Chevy, climbed in, threw the truck in reverse and backed out of the garage. Even though the front bumper dragged out the lower section of the metal door, he was in no mood to stop. He gave the truck a little gas, and after a few sparks and scrapes, the section pulled free halfway down the cracked cement of the drive.

He pulled onto Michigan and stopped right in the middle of the road. He was going somewhere, he just didn't know where yet. He rolled both windows down and started a slow, easy descent down the hill toward the historic district. Halfway down he rounded a curve and had to stop. There were so many lights on. He climbed out and walked over to a spot on the shoulder for a better look. At first, downtown looked the same as it always did. Streetlights were on, roughly a third of the old houses clustered around Main had their lights on, and even some of the stores were lit up. It was only as he continued to scan the streets that he noted the difference. There weren't any cars driving around. His head dropped and his chest sank. After a dry swallow, he climbed back behind the wheel and continued down the hill.

The stark reality that he couldn't see from above was readily evident once down on Main. Nothing had changed. The bodies of the three men were still lying on the street. The wind pushed and rolled debris from the looted stores along the sidewalk and out into the street. Broken and discarded merchandise, fixtures and displays were scattered on the ground in front of several vandalized stores.

He drove all the way down to the gas station at the far end of town and pulled in to fill up. While the dollars rang up on the pump, he started scanning the area for any signs of life. At first glance he swept right past the smoke bellowing from the power plant. It wasn't until he started to come back around that a slight ray of hope perked up the corners of his mouth. He stepped away from the truck for a better look at the smoke churning up toward the sky. There was a chance. He topped off the tank and headed for the two towering smokestacks at the power plant.

There were at least a dozen cars behind the locked gate, but he didn't bother to honk. He eased the bumper up to where it was touching the gate, and then gave the truck just enough gas to snap the chain. He parked at the foot of the stairs to the main office and ran up to the steel door. It was locked so he peered in through the wire mesh, reinforced window. There were two technicians slumped over in their chairs next to a long panel full of lights and gauges. Knocking would be a waste of time and he knew he couldn't break out the window, so he walked around and looked for another way in. Unfortunately every exterior door to the facility was either solid steel or if it had a window, it was the same kind of window as the door to the main office. There was no way for him to get in. As he trudged back to the Chevy he knew it didn't matter. No one was alive inside anyway. The place was running on automation—at least for the time being.

On the way back to town he had to stop again. It was just too unbelievable. Everything looked so normal from a distance. Before he realized it, he was slowly weaving up and down each side street, honking his horn and yelling out the window, "Is anybody there?" Somebody else had to still be alive. Surely he couldn't be the only one.

By the time he reached Michigan he was beginning to wonder. He turned around and instead of taking Michigan back up the hill—he drove down to Highway 7 and took it up. He stopped at the state mental hospital near the crest of the hill, broke through the gate, and checked it out before continuing on. He continued to weave in and out of each street along 7, honking and yelling just like he did downtown. But just like downtown, there was never any response.

He took a right on State Road 62 on his way back over to Michigan. There amongst the stores, hotels and fast food restaurants was the semi-truck he saw at the gas station the other night—the TM unit C61 truck. It was sitting under the bright lights in the high school parking lot. As soon as he pulled in he sensed a horrible presence of death.

The scene at the high school was completely different than what he saw elsewhere in Madison. The parking lot was over half full—and most of the cars weren't empty. Many had more than one lifeless occupant. He grabbed an old napkin off the floorboard to hold over his nose and got out. Every car he passed, as he zigzagged his way over to the semi-truck parked at the edge of the lot, had a body in it. Some were laid out across the back seat while others were slumped over on the passenger side up front. He knew what they were. They were drop offs. Their loved ones brought them there to die.

The closer he got to the semi, the more his senses were assaulted. Not only was the smell of death penetrating the napkin, but a droning hum was also beginning to echo in his ears. It was the hum that set him on edge. Not because it was the first real noise he had heard all day, but because he recognized it for what it was. He had seen too many carcasses while hunting in the deep woods not to know.

The droning sound grew louder as he slipped quietly between the cars. He saw the half dozen thirty-foot trash dumpsters lined up, side-by-side behind the semi and put it all together. He walked a few steps past the trailer and there they were. At a quick glance, they looked like small puffs of smoke drifting over each dumpster. But he knew better. They were actually swarms of flies, hovering over the rotting contents in the depositories. He walked over and was about to inspect one of the metal bins, when better judgment beat out curiosity. "No...no way."

Instead, he climbed up the metal stairs attached to the semi-trailer and pushed open the outer door to an air lock. That was as far as he got. When he hit the button to release the inner glass door nothing happened. Since the room on the other side of the glass was dark, it was reasonable to conclude that the trailer wasn't getting any power. That meant he wasn't getting in. So he pressed up against the door and cupped his hands to the glass for a look. It didn't take long for him to realize that he didn't need to get in. He could see the dark lumps of three bodies lying dead on the floor in biohazard suits.

A few minutes later he was back in his truck. Hope of finding anyone else alive was fading quickly. He continued his weave in and out of the first two streets along Michigan. After finding no one, he decided to go for broke. He skipped the rest of the streets and drove on down to where Stan lived. Surely his best friend wouldn't abandon him. He parked in front of the dark house, climbed out and then methodically walked up to the porch. But once at the door he couldn't bring himself to knock or ring the bell. He stood there and stared at the bottom of his friend's front door for almost a minute. In the end, he walked back to the truck and slid behind the wheel. After a long, drawn-out sigh, he raised his head and turned the key.

Chapter 19

Chuck headed straight for bed when he got home. It wasn't the late hour that drove him to seek the comfort of his sheets—it was the hope that once he closed his eyes he would forget everything he had seen. He shed his clothes between the door and the bed and then withdrew from the world under the security of the sheets.

That's where he stayed as daylight came and went. What was the point of getting up? What was the point of living? Everything and everyone was gone. Even the smell from his wife's body couldn't pull him from the depression. It simply drove him further under the covers.

He wasn't sure how many days had gone by, but one night when he got up to go to the toilet—he flicked the light switch in the bathroom and nothing happened. As he flicked it again he became aware of how dark the house was. There wasn't any light coming in from the streetlight outside. He ran over to the window. The neighbors' houses were dark too. He immediately began to fumble his way through the dark shadows to try every light switch in the house. Wearing nothing but his boxer shorts, he walked out to the middle of the street and looked around the neighborhood at the dark shapes under the starlit sky. For nearly a minute he stood staring at the ground while slowly shaking his head. Things were changing whether he liked it or not.

It was that awareness that pulled him out of bed at the break of dawn the next morning. Whether he was ready or not, he needed to take proper care of his wife. After he got dressed he opened all the drapes in the house and then grabbed Becky's favorite quilt out of the linen closet. It was the one her grandmother made. Becky's mom handed it down to her several years ago. It was old and soft with age, but still withstood the test of time due to the skill and artistry of its maker. He spread the quilt out on the floor next to his wife. Then with a sigh and a pain deep in his chest, he rolled her onto it. He grabbed a corner of the quilt and was about to pull it over her face, but paused to stare into her eyes one last time. Even in the dull reflection he saw the love and life she once had. While fighting the uncertainty and regret erupting within him, he slowly lowered the flap over her face. After a solemn moment, he bent over and gently kissed the quilt before rolling her up in the possession she prized most.

As he slowly rose to his feet, his soul was caught by the sight of his life mate wrapped in a cocoon of sewn linen and fill. The finality of it was more than he could bear. Everything drained from his body as he fell back on the sofa and began to sob.

He sat with his face buried in his hands for the better part of the morning. Emotional outbursts came and went, and then came again. It wasn't until he was finally able to breathe without his chest fluttering, that he wiped the tears off his face and went out to the garage to fetch some rope. He tied the rope around the foot of the cocoon and then started wrapping it around her as he worked his way toward her head. He stopped around the shoulder and tied the rope off. Before he could agonize any further about it, he lifted her up and carried her out to the bed of the truck.

As he made his way down the hill, he rounded an outside turn and caught a glimpse of the smokestacks at the power plant. The grand cement pillars in the sky were silent—their steam-driven generators at a loss of heat to drive them. Two blocks before Main, he took a right off Michigan and headed for the hospital a half block down. What he saw there was similar to what he saw at the high school, but with fewer cars and no dumpsters. Drivers were slumped over the wheel in several cars while others were abandoned with their back seat doors open. As he drove past one of the cars, he pictured a hysterical husband lifting his wife out of the back seat and rushing her in to the hospital for help. What the poor guy didn't realize was that he was bringing his wife there to lay her to rest—just as Chuck was doing.

He pulled into the circular drive at the emergency entrance and parked alongside the line of abandoned cars. He got out and gingerly picked up his wife and carried her to the entrance. Out of habit he waited a second for the glass doors to open, then remembered the smoke stacks and kicked the doors open.

Halfway to the reception counter he stopped. *What am I doing here?* He looked at the dead bodies lying against the walls of the tiled corridor. He then glanced over at the waiting area and stared at the wives and husbands and fathers and mothers who came there out of hope, but who deep down knew the inevitability of what was going to happen.

He lowered his head. I can't leave you like this. He turned around and carried her back out to the truck. Five blocks later he parked along the curb of First Street on the bank of the Ohio River. He closed his eyes and let the cool morning breeze wash over him in the cab. For a second he lost himself in the memory of the wild time he and Stan had on this very street last summer during the regatta. But when he opened his eyes, it wasn't a jubilant crowd that he saw—it was something else. At first he thought they were logs floating down river, like the kind that get caught in the current after a good storm. Yet it hadn't stormed in several weeks. He got out and scrambled down the steep bank for a better look. They were bodies.

He glanced up river past the bridge over to Kentucky, and saw more floating down. The flow was sparse and inconsistent. For a few minutes dozens of bodies would float by, and then there would be a gap before the next cluster. It was as if they were dumped one truckload at a time up river.

He climbed back up the embankment and stood next to the truck for a moment of thought. A few seconds later he spotted the boat ramp two blocks up river and climbed back behind the wheel.

He parked the truck parallel to the water at the bottom of the ramp and carefully laid the body of his wife on the cement and positioned her to where the left side of the bound quilt was sitting in an inch of water. As he kneeled on his knees next to her, he smoothed out the quilt over her chest and stroked the flap over her head as if it were her hair. With his eyes growing redder by the second, and his nose beginning to run, he fought through the swelling in the back of his throat and said, "I'm so sorry for letting us drift apart. And for not being there when you needed me." He rubbed his eyes. "I love you with all my heart…everything there is in me. You were my one true love." Tears started trickling down his cheeks. With his face and hands trembling, he pushed her into the river. "Please be at rest my love…please forgive me…"

He continued to watch as the current grabbed hold of her burial cocoon and carried her down river. The rolled quilt soaked up the murky waters and sank until only the very top of it was visible above the rippling water. Like the current flowing to the ocean to become a part of something much larger than itself, so too did his wife.

As he watched her disappear behind the shimmer of the reflecting sun, other bodies began to break into his peripheral vision and something instinctual took over. Without a word or pause, he climbed back in his truck and drove to the house he broke into several days ago—the house where the husband and wife died in each other's arms on the sofa. He carefully placed them in the bed of his truck, and drove back to the boat ramp and provided them as respectful of a burial as he could. As soon as they floated off, he drove back to the house where he saw the fat man and the dog. Man and animal alike, he gave them both a proper burial.

Sweating profusely in the summer heat, he climbed in the truck and turned on the air conditioner. While he relaxed under the refreshing breeze, he prepared himself for who he owed the next burial to. A few minutes later he was up the hill and taking a left on Arlington. Everything looked just as it did the other night when he dropped by but didn't knock. The drapes were still closed and when he tried the door he found it locked.

The second hard thrust of his foot against the door sent the deadbolt bursting through the jamb. As soon as he was in he headed straight for the basement. Stan had told him that he would shoot anyone that came in uninvited, so Chuck yelled down the stairs just to be safe. "Hey buddy…it's me…Chuck." He took a few cautious steps down and yelled again, "Hey don't go shooting your only friend." After no answer, he continued down as he yelled once more, "Coming down!"

Stan's basement had three small windows along the back of the house and two along the side opposite the garage. Together they provided enough light during the day to see most everything except for the very corners of the room. Out of habit, Chuck took a few steps toward the pool table, half expecting Stan to be standing there with a grin on his face, a cue in one hand, and a Miller in the other. But he wasn't. The area around the pool table was cleared. The lawn chairs were gone and so was the little refrigerator. His skin began to tingle as he closed his eyes and slowly turned to look under the stairs.

A felt blanket nailed to the outside runner of the stairs, stood between Chuck and what he would find behind it. After a moment of hesitation, he walked over and slowly pulled it back. Twenty minutes later he was headed back down to the boat ramp with Stan, Margery and two room temperature Millers. He sent Margery off first with a nice prayer and an apology for not getting to know her better. When it came time to say goodbye to his lifelong friend, he said a prayer and then twisted the cap off one of the beers. He drained it under the heat of the sun and then flung the empty into the river. Then he took the other bottle and held it against Stan's chest for a second before flinging it unopened out into the river. He smiled as he kneeled next to his friend and pushed him into the water. "You won old buddy."

After he took his sweat-drenched shirt off and wiped his face, he got back in the truck and headed for the body of a man he saw a block down from his store. This man was different than the rest. He didn't commit suicide or die from the plague; someone blew the back of his head off. An uneasy feeling started to come over him as he got out of the truck and walked over to where the ants were working feverishly on the remains. Something about the man or the way he died raised the hairs on the back of Chuck's neck. "Who shot you? Why?" For a reason he couldn't remember, he started to reach down to touch the asphalt next to the man, when he stopped and looked over at the parking meter across the street. That was as much as he wanted to think about it. He scooped the man up and carried him over to the truck.

He continued the burial process as the sun swept across the sky. After a few more individual trips, he started picking up as many households as he could fit in the truck. There were so many to seeing too. He labored under the physical strain of loading adults in his truck as well as the mental strain of caring to the bodies of children and infants.

The plague wasn't the only cause of death. There were also those who thought it was better to end life on their own terms. Evidence in one home pointed to a mother drowning her children in the bathtub and then laying their bodies out on the bed before taking her own life.

However life came to an end, everyone deserved a proper burial—or at least as proper as he could give. He continued to work until he started stumbling over furniture in the dark. With his stomach growling he called it a day and headed back up the hill. He was about to pass Arlington when he locked up the brakes and skidded to a stop in the middle of Michigan. The shine of his high-beams over the dark road reminded him that he didn't have anything at home to see by. Thankfully his old buddy Stan did down in his basement. He backed up, turned down Stan's street, and a minute later he was fumbling his way through the dark in Stan's house heading for the basement. He found the soft touch of the felt blanket, pulled it back and tried to remember where he had seen everything in the day. After a few fumbled stabs in the dark he found one of the flashlights.

Stan had done a good job preparing for the worst, even better than what he had shown Chuck the other day. But that was Stan—he never did anything half-ass. Besides the canned goods, bottled water, and pump shotgun that Chuck knew about, Stan also had two lanterns with plenty of kerosene, and best of all—a brand new generator from the local Sears.

After he got the lanterns going, he kept one in the basement and set the other on the kitchen table where it lit up both the kitchen and the living room. He backed the Chevy up to the front porch and started loading supplies. The generator was the heaviest so it was the last to load. It would have been a strain for two men to carry up the stairs and was nearly impossible for him alone. But he did.

Since the garage door at his home was broken he wouldn't have to worry about carbon monoxide building up in the house. That made it the natural choice for the generator. He dragged it over to the patio door at the rear of the garage, and then ran an extension cord from it through the kitchen door to the refrigerator.

After a quick read of the instructions, he primed the motor and set the choke. He hit the start button. Nothing happened. He tried again and then checked to make sure the cap was firmly seated on the spark plug. After another try and failure, it dawned on him. He unscrewed the gas cap and looked in the tank. "Shit!" Luckily there was still a gallon left in the can for the lawn mower, so he dumped that in the tank and on the second try the generator kicked over and started up.

Like an excited child, he ran into the kitchen and swung the refrigerator door open. There was light. A quick smell of the milk told him that he had saved the food from spoiling. But he needed more gas. He threw the empty one-gallon can in the front seat and headed for the gas station at the corner of 62 and Michigan.

For a few seconds he did nothing as he held the gas nozzle in the small can with the trigger squeezed. He heard nothing, he felt nothing coming out, but still he stood. As if he were afraid that gas would suddenly start shooting out, he slowly pulled the nozzle out of the can and looked at it. He tried resetting the pump, squeezing the trigger, and strangling the nozzle with both hands, and still nothing worked. That's when it hit him. No electricity to power the pump meant there would be no gas to power the generator. "Damn it!" He slammed the nozzle into the pump slot and thought. A second later a grin flashed across his face and he jumped back in the truck.

There was a hardware store a couple of blocks down 62 on the left. He broke through the plate glass door and started rummaging through the dark shelves with his flashlight. After a few minutes he hit pay dirt—a hand operated pump. He grabbed two of them and found the largest crowbar and bolt cutter in the store. On his way to throw them in the truck he spotted the display of five-gallon gas cans. He grabbed four before heading back to the gas station.

Access to the buried tank wasn't going to be easy but with the possibility of ten thousand gallons of gasoline waiting for him, he wasn't going to be deprived. He put all his weight into the crowbar, and after a long, strenuous pull, the locked cap finally snapped off. A few minutes later gasoline was being drawn up through the hose and pumped into one of the cans. The process, while simple enough, was laborious to perform. The repetitive motion of turning the crank on the pump was getting to him by the time he topped off the first five gallon can. Nonetheless he kept at it until all four cans were full.

After he filled the tank on the generator, he ran back to the hardware store and got enough electrical cable to wire the generator to the main service panel in the garage. The generator probably couldn't support the water heater, but it would give him enough power to keep the refrigerator going as well as light most of the house.

Chapter 20

Chuck was back at it the next day. Hours turned into days and days into weeks as he spent most of the daylight hours taking those he could find down to the river. It was exhausting, yet it occupied his thoughts and that was what he needed most.

When it was too dark to care for the departed properly, he collected supplies and cleaned the house. Water wasn't an immediate issue. The public water tower could be seen above the tree line on the other side of Michigan just a few blocks down. He didn't know how full it was, but at least he didn't have to worry about how to get the water out. The tower used gravity and pressure buildup through pipe reduction to supply water to over half the houses in town, including his. So as long as there was water in the tower, his faucets would work just fine.

After a few frustrating days of continuously running back up to the gas station to refill the 5-gallon cans, he set his mind to finding a solution. Using a gasoline powered transfer pump he took from the Public Works office, he was able to quickly fill several 55-gallon drums he found in one of the local plants. A forklift made it possible to transport the drums down Michigan to his garage. After some rather imaginative plumbing and a little tinkering, he ended up with six drums hooked up in a series that provided the generator a 330-gallon reservoir. That meant it could go for weeks unmanned.

As soon as he finished improving his fuel storage, he turned his attention to the potential buildup of exhaust gases. He replaced one of the window panes in the patio door with a piece of plywood. Once that was secure, he cut a four-inch round hole and ran a flexible dryer vent hose from that to an insulated coupling he put on the generator's exhaust port. That would take care of the exhaust gases as long as he didn't open any of the windows on the back of the house. The only other thing left to do was replace the garage door panels.

Even though most of the stores were ransacked prior to the mass death, everything he needed could be found in the houses around town. Most homes had a cache of supplies similar to what he found in Stan's basement. There was enough chili, beef stew, tuna, soup, peanut butter and the like to last a couple of years if it didn't go bad first. To minimize the potential of that happening, he sorted the food by expiration date and began to plan his meals around which expired first.

The only real problem he had was in finding a long-term supply of drinking water. He had counted well over one hundred cases of bottled water and almost a hundred 5-gallon jugs in various locations around town. But he was still concerned because he had no idea how much water remained in the tower. He could always climb the ladder on the side of the tower and cut off the access lock. But the thought of dangling seventy-five feet above ground kept that option in the 'when hell freezes over' category. In any case, he knew the supply wouldn't last forever. He needed to do two things. First was to conserve water. This meant fewer, more efficient showers and perhaps even a few baths replaced by a dip in one of the neighbor's swimming pools. The second was that he needed to find a way to increase his potable water supply. That could mean collecting rainwater, finding a farmhouse with a well, learning how to distill water, or even building a purification system. He chose to carefully consider them all.

The library down on Main was a wealth of information. He read books, magazines and manuals, anything that would help him understand how to do what needed to be done. Hours were spent perusing the Popular Mechanics and Science periodicals. He read how to use windmills for power generation and how batteries stored electricity. He read about water purification and techniques for collecting condensation. He also read up on farming. Crops that were most tolerant to climatic conditions and infestation were of particular interest.

It occurred to him that he'd never really taken the time to read before, at least not if he could find anything on television. Since that was no longer an option, reading was the only thing left to keep his mind off being alone. He would take what he learned in the library and then tinker with an idea in his garage. Along with collecting supplies he also managed to build up quite a collection of tools and machining equipment. He had all the basic woodworking and mechanics tools, as well as an acetylene torch and electrical spot welder.

The hours just after sunset were used for keeping up the condition of their house. Each time he cleaned something he would stand back and take a look at it. He would squint and evaluate what he had done through her eyes—would it have been clean enough for his Becky. If he shook his head no, he would get back to it and do it all over again. This newfound desire in maintaining the appearance of their house wasn't limited to just the inside. He set some of the daylight hours aside for keeping the grass mowed and touching up any places where the paint was starting to peel. As the days and weeks continued to pass, the neighbor's yards grew into a gangly mess of knee high grass and weeds. It wasn't long before his house started to look more like it was planted smack-dab in the middle of a field than in a residential neighborhood. But that didn't bother him. As long as he had a street to park his recently acquired Corvettes, SUVs, Cadillacs, and his Harley on, he didn't care.

One day while he was raking autumn leaves in the front yard he heard a thundering boom in the distance. He froze and listened to the dissipating echo. It might have been thunder, but it sounded more like an explosion. He threw the rake down and sprinted into the house with his heart pounding. A second later he burst out the door and jumped off the porch with the keys to his Harley, his hunting rifle, and a pistol. In one seamless movement, he straddled the bike, started it up and kicked up the gravel around the drive as he shot out toward Michigan. With a look of panic on his face, he took a left on 421 and then buried the needle of the speedometer as he sped north toward Versailles.

He left in such a hurry that he didn't bother to grab his backpack. It was his lifeline. It held a hand pump, necessary tools and crowbar for popping off locked caps, a flashlight and flares, binoculars, compass, matches and a small revolver with a box of shells. Besides the hunting rifle, it was the one thing he never intended to leave home without.

A few hours later he motored back into town at half the posted speed limit. The features of his face appeared hard as he stared straight ahead with his lips pressed together. He went with the hope that the sound would lead him to another survivor. But the trip netted nothing. He never found the source of the sound or saw another living soul. All it did was reinforce his belief that he was the only man left alive on the planet.

He turned down his street unable to shake the heavy weight of dejection. As he hit the end of his driveway, he gave the bike some gas and slid off the back. The Harley squirreled on the gravel shoulder for twenty feet, then flipped over onto its side and slid into the ditch. Chuck didn't look—didn't care. In fact at that very moment he didn't care much about anything as he trudged up the driveway and went inside.

He stomped through the living room and pulled up in the kitchen. For over a minute he stared at the clean shelves and tidy stacks of canned food. Everything was so damn neat. Everything was so damn clean. A person wouldn't even realize that everyone was dead by the looks of his house. Chuck knew different. A quick glance out the window to the overgrown weeds in the neighborhood was quick proof that indeed—everyone else was dead.

A panic started to creep up from the pit of stomach as his nostrils began to flare. He had to get out of there. He snatched the keys to the Cadillac off the table. A few heavy strides later the front door slammed against the wall.

There was only one place he could go. He needed a friendly environment where he could relax and get numb. He hadn't even thought about drinking, let alone setting foot in the Broadway Tavern since it all came to an end. But that was no longer the case. The Cadillac fish-tailed onto Main and then accelerated to sixty-five within two blocks before squealing to a stop in the middle of Broadway. That's where Chuck left it as he jumped out and kicked the tavern door open.

Once inside, he spotted the salvation he came for. They were the 750ml bottles behind the bar. He grabbed a bottle of Jack off the shelf and a shot glass off the counter. He plopped down on his regular stool and hurriedly poured a shot of whisky. His fingers eased around the wet glass, but before he could throw his head back and slam down the drink, he looked at his lone reflection in the mirror. The place was dark and lifeless. Stan wasn't there. The regulars that had become friends over the years weren't there either. No one was.

Chuck lowered his eyes as he pictured the river.

He pushed back from the shot of whisky as he remembered the countless bodies he carried in the bed of his truck. He remembered the woman who committed suicide in the garage. After her husband and daughter died, she climbed into her car, closed the garage door, started it up, and went to sleep. And he would never forget the painful shock of finding the little boy curled up on his side in the backyard tree house. The mother and father were dead in the house. His only prayer was that the parents didn't die first and leave the little boy to die alone—scared and crying.

Chuck looked back at his reflection in the mirror. There were so many who suffered so much. He glanced at the amber colored liquid in the glass and slowly started shaking his head. "This isn't right."

The shot glass was still full and sitting on the counter after Chuck walked out the door.

Chapter 21

Jason's people had their fun. After spending the night in the Holiday Inn, they ransacked the place and set it on fire. Actually it was an injustice to his influence in saying they were just his people. Under his charge, they had turned into a warring tribe hell-bent on hunting down every last survivor in Indianapolis. Captures were given the choice of joining the tribe or burning to death in the ritual cleansing.

Jason draped the duster over his arm as he stared toward the thick column of black smoke billowing up from the hotel into the morning sky. But it wasn't the foul stench of burning plastic and polyester that held his thoughts. It was something much deeper and darker that he was just beginning to struggle with. He sat down on the curb.

"Anything wrong sir?" Mark asked, as he walked over and took a seat next to him.

Jason stared at the decaying remains of a body across the street as he voiced his concern in a soft whisper. "Are we doing the right thing?"

"Burning the hotel...that's no big deal."

Jason turned toward the big redhead. "No...not the hotel. I mean what we're doing...killing all these people." He turned back toward the apocalyptic imagery of the street before him. "It was what I wanted at first, but now I don't know. It seems that no matter how many people I kill, or how much I make them suffer, it does nothing for the pain I feel."

Mark put his hand on Jason's shoulder. "You've been chosen to bare the pain of the people. That's what God put you here for. And that's a fact."

Jason started shaking his head. "How do you know?"

"I knew it as soon as those niggers unloaded everything they had on you." Mark paused as he shook his head, "and you didn't even get a scratch. Then the shotgun exploded in that son-of-a-bitch's face. That wasn't natural...none of it was. Only God can grace someone with that kind of power—and only God can take it away."

Jason shrugged Mark's hand off his shoulder. "That's what I thought at first too, but this just can't be right."

"If it wasn't God's work then at least one of those bullets would have hit you. But none did. So for the time being—you're just going to have to face up to the responsibility of bearing that pain. Maybe down the road when you've done His Will, He'll send someone to put an end to it for you."

Jason reached over to the big redhead's shoulder. "What if He already has? Maybe that's why these men and women follow me. They're supposed to help me find him."

Mark stared at Jason long enough to make him feel uncomfortable. It was like the big redhead was disappointed with what Jason said. "Perhaps," Mark said to the morning breeze as he pumped his chin and gazed out to the street.

"Sir."

Jason looked over his shoulder as his best scout walked up. "Yeah Mike."

"Do you want me to search anywhere in particular today?"

Mark covered his mouth and mumbled, "There's talk of a couple kids scavenging for food just inside the loop on the south side."

Jason looked past Mike at the rest of the tribe collecting along the sidewalk. He could tell that some of them lacked the heart for what they were doing. Others had a hunger for more death and destruction. Somewhere between the two was his original intention. He thought about the kids Mark mentioned and then about the old man the tribe cleansed the other night. "I want you to take a car and look around Lebanon."

Mark grabbed Jason's arm, but before he could disagree with the directive that would send Mike in the opposite direction, a man broke from the rest of the tribe and yelled, "No more hunting, Jason!"

The man pushed Mike aside and stopped a few feet from them.

Mark climbed to his feet and clenched his fists. "You better watch that shit you're spitting out!"

"Hold on," Jason said, as he pushed off the curb and grabbed Mark by the shoulder. "Let the man speak his mind." Jason walked over to him. "You joined us a few weeks ago didn't you?"

"Yeah," the man answered, as he took a step backwards and crossed his arms over his chest.

"If I remember right, you had the chance to voice your opposition and you had nothing to say."

"Nothing to say! Are you kidding me? I know who you are. I know what happens to anyone who has an opinion that's different from yours. You burn 'em!" The man shook his head as his determination grew. He walked right up next to Jason and said, "I watched you burn that old man the other night." His chest started heaving as he stared at the ground with his hands on his hips. "This is a new day and we're going to start fresh." Then he grabbed Jason by the collar. "This madness has got to stop!"

Mark was on him in an instant. He yanked the man's hands off of Jason and backhanded him across the jaw. The man sailed off the curb and tumbled halfway across the street. But that didn't stop him. He scrambled up to his hands and knees, and after a pause to shake the cobwebs out he pushed back up to his feet. His mouth and nose were bleeding as he spit out, "You're not God. And this isn't God's work." Then he pointed at Mark and said, "The only reason the others do what you say is because they're afraid of him" He barely got it out before Mark stepped off the curb and sent the man cowering back with both arms in front of his face.

"Hold on Mark!" Jason commanded with a raise of his hand. "You don't think we're doing God's work here?"

The man lowered his arms and looked at the others watching from the sidewalk. "We know about your fiancée and how you accidentally shot her. Everybody knows that you're on some kind of vendetta." He glanced at his feet and swallowed. "I know how you feel. We all know how you feel. We've all lost loved ones. But that animal," he huffed as he pointed to Mark, "has you mistaking blind luck as heavenly intervention. You're just like the rest of us. You can be shot. You can be killed."

Jason lowered his head and dropped his shoulders.

"Don't listen to his bullshit!" Mark snorted from the side.

The man took a step closer and opened his arms. "Did you ever think that it was just time for your fiancée to die?"

Jason's chin jerked up off his chest as his right arm pulled back and his jaws clamped down tight.

"You should be thankful that she didn't have to suffer like

everyone—"

The scream of a madman cut him off as Jason tackled him in an explosion of violence.

Jason cried out as he ripped handfuls of hair from the man's head. What was happening could never be considered a fight. It was an erupting fury of clawing, biting, punching and kicking. Mark backed off in shock as Jason ripped the man's ear off and ground it against his face. He clawed through the man's shirt and dug gouges across his chest. Then he started punching the man in the mouth, breaking teeth and plowing his fist in farther with each blow. He yanked his fist back out and grabbed the man by the throat with both hands. But before he could crush all life, he saw the desperation in the man's eyes. Then just as abruptly as he attacked, Jason stopped and let go. His chest began to quiver. A second later he rolled off the man and started crying.

Mark stepped over and cautiously helped their leader to his feet while the man clutched his throat and gasped for air. "You want me to kill him?"

Jason snatched the Colt 45 out of Mark's jeans and shoved the big redhead back. Tears were flowing and his arm was shaking as he pointed the gun at the man rolling on the ground. "It wasn't her turn to die! And she wouldn't have if any…" he closed his eyes and started sobbing again, "…if any of those ungracious mother-fuckers would have stopped me." He opened his eyes and looked down at the stark face staring up at him through the blood.

For a few seconds neither moved. The man winced in pain but didn't try to get up. Jason stood over him with the pistol aimed at his head, but didn't pull the trigger.

After a tense moment, Jason dropped the gun on the man's chest and stepped back. "If what you say is true…then shoot me dead right here and now."

"What are you doing?" Mark gasped, as he jumped over in front of Jason.

"Out of my way!" Jason screamed as he tried to push Mark out of the way. "If I'm doing what I'm supposed to be doing then this man can't kill me. If I'm not then he's the one to end my pain." He grabbed Mark by the shoulders and looked him in the eyes. "I know you're trying to look out for me…but I need you to step back."

Mark shook his head a couple of times and then reluctantly gave up his position.

Jason pointed at the man. "Pick up the gun and get up!"

The man raised his head but refused to go any further.

"Do it!" Jason screamed.

The man left the gun lying on the asphalt and slowly stood empty handed. Before he said anything, he took a few seconds to spit out blood and teeth. After he wiped his mouth, he gently touched the remains of his ear and pressed his hand over the wounds on his chest. "There's been enough killing. It ends today."

Jason huffed and walked over to within five feet of the man. "It's only going to end today if you kill me. Now pick up the gun!"

The man hobbled as he fought to keep his balance, but didn't move for the gun.

"Do you know how many women and children I'm going to burn alive if you don't stop me?"

The man shook his head in defiance as he painfully bent over and picked up the gun. "I don't want to do this."

"Desire has nothing to do with it. If you believe in what you said then you'll kill me."

The man gasped, "I can't."

"You can!" Jason screamed at the top of his lungs.

In a defensive reflex, the man jerked the gun up and pointed it at Jason's head.

"Do it," Jason said softly while the others cleared out of harm's way behind him.

The man started crying. "You're crazy."

"Are you the one I've been searching for? Are you the one who will stop me? Think of the lives you can save."

Tears were cutting clear channels through the blood on the man's face as his trembling hand finally found a steady pulse. "I am—"

A shot rang out at the same time a glass window shattered across the street in the Holiday Inn. Jason flinched and rocked back on his heels, but never lost sight of the man holding the gun.

The man gasped in shock. "It can't be!" The tremble returned to his arm and a second later the gun fell like dead weight to his side.

Mark immediately stepped over, grabbed the gun and yelled out for everyone to hear, "I told you we're doing God's work. Jason IS the Hand of God."

Jason dropped his head and closed his eyes. Anyone else would have been on an adrenaline high after a moment like that—but not him. His pulse was slow and steady. The only thing he felt was disappointment. It would have been nice if the man had ended his pain. After a moment of contemplation, he pulled himself up and began to scan the solemn faces of the men, women and children standing in front of the burning hotel. They were all scared. But now he understood what he had to do. He would keep pushing until fear turned to anger. He would force someone else to step up and try. That was a day to look forward to.

Mark asked, "Do you want me to kill him?"

Jason walked over to the duster he left laying on the curb, and as he picked it up and slipped it on, he said, "No…I have something else in mind for him."

Chapter 22

Chuck had been staring at the ceiling for hours when the alarm finally went off at six. He kept picturing the mothers and fathers and children that he set adrift in the river. Their faces came to him at the tavern yesterday—and stayed with him all through the night. They consumed his thoughts to such an extent that even the cool morning breeze that was blowing through the drapes and raising goose bumps across his arms and shoulders had no effect. Any other time the draft would have been enough to drive him under the warmth of the blanket. That wasn't going to happen today. Finally at seven minutes past the hour, he reached over and shut off the alarm.

He lethargically made his way to the shower, slipped his boxers off and climbed in before the propane water heater in the garage had a chance to do its job. It didn't matter. Hot or cold, it all felt the same to him. As the shower beat against his back, he remembered moving the coffee table off the man on the floor. The man's wife was positioned on the sofa with her hands clasped together over her lap. He must have set her there as he waited for his turn to die. Chuck remembered looking over and seeing the stuffed toy in the hallway as he bent down to scoop the man up. It was a monkey with long yellow hair and a pink face. That's when he realized that a child had gotten scared and hidden somewhere in the house. He spotted the green frog next to the hallway closet and reluctantly walked over. It was homemade, old, probably passed down from the mother. It had green felt for skin and two brown buttons sewn on for eyes. After a moment of hesitation, he pushed it to the side with his boot. With a heavy thumping in his chest, he slid his fingers around the door knob. He didn't want to open the closet, but he couldn't bare the thought of leaving her in there.

He leaned forward against the tiled wall and lowered his head into the warm spray of the shower. The water soaked his hair, ran down his face and trickled off in streams from his nose, chin, ears and lips. He stood there watching it splash on the porcelain around his feet, wishing that it could take the memories of what he had seen down the drain with it.

After getting dressed, he doused a large bowl of Cheerios in clumpy instant milk and sat down at the kitchen table—more out of habit than anything else, because his appetite sure wasn't there. No matter where he looked he kept seeing the blanket nailed to the stairs in Stan's basement. Why did he have to pull it open? He slipped a spoonful of cereal in his mouth, but the image of his best friend slumped against the cinder block wall kept him from chewing. It looked like Stan had pulled Margery's lifeless body over to his lap before he went into convulsions. Chuck opened his mouth and let the milk and cereal spill out into the bowl as he slowly set the spoon down on the table. All he could manage was a sip of Tang.

He had scheduled a search for supplies in the neighborhood across the street from the north entrance to Clifty Falls State Park. But he just couldn't get up for it. Instead, he spent the morning in the garage tinkering with his tools. He wasn't building anything and he wasn't cleaning anything. He would simply pick up a tool, look at it for a bit, then put it down and pick up another one. Eventually he wound up in the corner on a folding metal chair next to the acetylene torch. He turned on the gas and sparked the tip. He sat staring at the white and blue tip of the flame as he thought about the man he found shot downtown across from his store. He swiped the torch once, flame down, a foot and a half over his knees as he remembered leaning against the parking meter across the street from the man. He stared into the flame and saw his hunting rifle. He swiped the torch over his knees again—this time close enough that he felt the heat press against his jeans like a hot poker. But like a paraplegic with no feelings in his legs, he didn't flinch. He brought the torch up in front of his face and held his breath. Just like he remembered doing before squeezing the trigger. As he stared into the flame he remembered sighting the man's head in the crosshairs of his rifle. "Oh my God…It was me." He nearly choked on his own swallow as he dropped the torch and jumped up. After a quick pace back and forth, he took a few long strides into the kitchen and grabbed a cold soda from the refrigerator.

He fell back onto the sofa as his thoughts shifted to Becky. When he looked up, he saw her in the rearview mirror, standing in the dust on the shoulder of the road. It was two years ago in the middle of an argument. He told her to get out and walk home. He gasped and muttered, "How could I have done that?" His emotions were already beginning to swell when he remembered the hurtful things he said to her the night before the world ended. A tear ran down his cheek, as he relived her sitting down on the coffee table the following morning and saying that she was sorry. He remembered the look on her face as she sat there with her hands in her lap, waiting for him to say something. Chuck let the pop slip through his fingers as he jerked around to the kitchen just like he did that morning. "I'm so sorry, baby!"

It took a second for the spill to register, but when it did, his emotions came un-bottled. There was a quick gasp, like someone yanked a dagger from his heart. He jumped up and cried, "Oh my God!" as he ran into the kitchen for a paper towel. A second later, his knees thudded against the carpet as he dropped down and started dabbing up the spilt soda. "I'm so sorry!" he panted, "I can get it all up!" As his frantic dabbing continued, it became less and less controlled until he was eventually punching the floor with the paper towel. "Everything will be alright!" When the soaked paper towel shredded against the carpet, he jumped up and ran back into the kitchen for more. He yanked the last sheet so hard the entire roll flew off the holder and hit the wall. "Goddamn it!" he cried out. He grabbed the roll off the floor, ran back into the living room and dropped down on the mushy carpet.

He slammed the entire roll of paper towels on the floor with both hands, but as he raised it above his head for the next swing—he stopped. For the span of two heartbeats he didn't move or even blink. That stillness gave way by the third pound in his chest when he began to shake so uncontrollably that he lost his grip on the towels. He clamped his eyes shut and began to pull in each deep breath through his nose. With each breath he gained a little more control over the jerky movements of his arms and head, until there was barely a quiver by the fourth. He opened his eyes—and that's when everything exploded.

He jumped up in a fury, snatched a cushion from the sofa and started beating the stain on the carpet with it. After the third swing he started pummeling everything within arm's reach. He took out the ceiling light with one overhead swipe. Without warning, he ran to the television and in one continuous motion took out the tube with one out-of-the-park swing. He spun on his toes and threw the heavy cushion through their picture window. But the sound and sight of the shattering glass only acted to intensify his release. He kicked the recliner over. He grabbed one end of the sofa and with a surge of adrenaline powering his muscles, he screamed like an animal and flipped it over against the wall.

After destroying the living room he moved on to the kitchen. The refrigerator went down first. He ripped off the oven door and started beating the counter top and cupboards with it. After an explosive minute, the adrenaline finally gave out. He took one last half-hearted swing with the oven door and dropped it on the linoleum as sweat rolled off his face.

After glancing around at the damage all around him, he dropped his chin and stared at the floor while the rapid rise and fall of his chest slowly returned to normal. All expressions of pain or remorse or anger were finally gone. The only thing left was the empty feeling of someone who had given up all hope.

It took a while, but he finally found his key ring in the mess on the living room floor. He took the time to slip off the keys to the Cadillac, Chevy Suburban, and the Harley that was laid out in the ditch. Those keys joined the clutter on the floor. All he wanted was his truck. The only other thing he needed was the backpack, but habit was hard to break so he ended up carrying his rifle out to the truck as well.

He calmly walked back into the garage and went straight for his twenty-pound sledgehammer. He took a batter's stance next to the first 55-gallon drum of gasoline hooked up in the series to the generator, and with one effortless swing, he knocked off the coupling that hooked into the fuel line to the generator. Gasoline started pouring out as the reservoir began to empty.

He walked over to his store of five-gallon gas cans in the corner of the garage. He opened the spout on one, positioned it on his shoulder so that it poured out behind him, and walked in through the kitchen door to the rest of the house. He doused a trail of gasoline through the house that he and Becky had spent the last twenty-three years trying to pay off. When he made it back to the door to the garage, he turned around and inspected what he had done with a critical eye. Everything was covered. With a nod to himself, he stepped into the garage.

There was almost an inch of gasoline on the garage floor and the driveway was soaked down to the street. Gas was filling in the ditch around the Harley and beginning to seep under the Cadillac and Suburban. He backed the Chevy a safe distance down the road and walked back to where he was standing in the middle of the street in front of their house. In a calm and steady manner, he bent over and sparked one of the flares off the street. For a minute he just stood there, holding the flare and looking at their house as gasoline continued to pour out through the first drum. The very next second it didn't even feel like he was the one throwing the flare into the garage. He heard the dragon draw in its breath as a blue fire rolled down the driveway like a wave washing up on the beach. That was the last thing he saw before the explosion knocked him on his back.

He clambered to his feet as burning insulation slowly drifted over the fire. The Harley had but a few seconds as it was charring quickly in a pool of fire. Chuck knew it was going to explode—knew that he needed to run, yet he was held there by the strangest feeling that he had watched his house burn before. It was just like the dream he had the morning he woke up on the sofa with Becky.

He snapped out of it and took off running right before the tank on the bike exploded. The Suburban followed within a few seconds. By the time he jumped behind the wheel of the Chevy a half block away, the dried out grass and weeds in his neighbor's yards were ablaze and the sky was already beginning to fill with smoke. It wasn't until sitting there behind the wheel and staring at his creation through the windshield that he realized the whole neighborhood might go up. Even that knowledge didn't elicit any expression in his face.

He started up the truck and headed for Michigan Road. There was a place about ninety miles north on interstate 65 calling his name—Indianapolis. He had always wanted to get out of Madison. The dream back in high school was for him and Becky to get married and move to the city. There was nothing he could do about that anymore. In fact there was only one thing that he still had control over. He could choose where to die. He pulled the backpack across the seat to his lap, opened the flap and pulled out the pistol as he turned off SR 62 and headed west on 256. Austin and the interstate were only a half-hour away. As long as he didn't come across any wrecks blocking the road, he should be inside the city limits of Indianapolis with plenty of daylight left. That's where he would put an end to this godforsaken pain in his heart.

Chapter 23

Chuck had ventured out of Madison more than once since the world ended. He had driven up to Versailles and spent a couple of days in Columbus. In fact he had visited several surrounding areas on both the Indiana and Kentucky side of the river. All the trips were to relatively small towns. If he had gone to one of the larger cities it might have prepared him better for what he was about to see. It wasn't until he was north of Columbus that it started getting really bad. Then it continued to build all the way up to the Franklin and Greenwood areas on the south side of Indianapolis. That was where he first laid eyes on the ghostly trail of death—a logjam of southbound traffic clogging up both sides of the interstate. It was a lasting tribute to the mass exodus from Indianapolis several months back.

He swerved around a southbound Dodge sitting in the middle of the northbound corridor with its doors open. The weathered remains of the passenger lay strung out on the asphalt under one door. Beneath the driver's side door there was nothing more than the faded marks of a blood trail. Vehicles backing up behind the Dodge must have hit the driver and dragged him in their desperate attempt to escape the bug.

Chuck had to slow down to a crawl as he wove his way around car after car and body after body. In some places the graveyard of metal and flesh was so dense that it forced him onto the shoulder, and in a few places that wasn't even far enough. But as bad as it was on the northbound side, the southbound corridor was worse. There were dozens of pileups where someone must have died at the wheel and started a chain reaction of screeching tires and bodies flying through windshields. He saw cars sitting in fields and ravines several hundred feet off the interstate. Some of them were probably cases where the driver felt it was his only way to avoid a potential pile up, while others probably occurred because the driver simply lost consciousness and veered off the road. In either case their death was more peaceful than most of those who stayed on the road.

He had to stop in the midst of all the death when he saw a family of four in a Mazda. They couldn't have all died at exactly the same time, yet they were all there. Their shriveled, desiccated bodies were still sitting as if they were ready to go for a Sunday drive in the country. He wondered if they stopped because the driver died, or because they gave up the fight against the inevitable.

He lived his entire life with the illusion that everything would have been better if he and Becky could have gotten out of Madison. That illusion made him feel trapped and stole any chance of being satisfied with his life. It might have even been partly to blame for the troubles in his marriage. And it was definitely the driving force behind his trip today. Yet as he looked at the death on the highway, he realized it for what it truly was—only an illusion. The dead on the highway had been no better off than him. They were scared during their final days. They mourned the loss of their loved ones just like him. Their marriages had trouble just like his. It was too late to be of any benefit, but he finally realized that it wasn't Madison holding him back. That had been his own doing.

After breaking his stare from the family in the Mazda he pulled his pistol out and studied it. *It's still the right thing to do.* He couldn't take being alone any longer. *But this isn't the proper place.* He slipped the pistol inside the backpack and gave the truck some gas.

The median was jammed with cars at Southport and started to thin back out as he drove over the bypass that circled the city. That was his first opportunity to take his eyes off the obstacles in the road and study the approaching skyline. At first it didn't seem that much different than it did when he drove up to buy items to sell in his antique store. But the closer he got and the longer he looked, the more he was able to see that it was different. He nearly scraped the side of the truck along the guardrails of more than one overpass as he slowed along each exit ramp for a better view. When he finally hit downtown, he had to stop and get out.

He bumped the guardrail with his knees as he stood in a daze and stared at the city streets. "Dear God," he mumbled in shock as he looked at all the bodies. There weren't that many cars littering the streets, but of the ones he could see, most were burnt out. Same held true for many of the smaller office buildings and warehouses. If arson hadn't claimed it, then the windows were broken out. But looting had nothing to do with the broken windows near the top of some buildings. Chuck didn't have to see the jumper smashed against the sidewalk to know what had happened there.

He stood and stared in disbelief for several minutes before finally pulling himself back to the truck. The thought of walking out to the fifty-yard line on the football field and ending his life under the dome first crossed his mind back at Southport. Though not as strong as it was, the thought was still there as he took the Market Street exit and headed for the stadium. He slowed to ten miles per hour as he started driving over shattered glass and pieces of broken metal and wood. He passed a burnt out car and noticed the remains of a woman on the sidewalk. He didn't know what it was, but something about her kept his eye for a second as he drove by. When he finally turned back around, the desire to end the pain was no longer the only thing on his mind. Three blocks later he came up on the steps to the stadium and parked.

The lone sound in the city was the wind blowing between the buildings. It made an eerie whistling sound that kept him on edge as he cautiously walked over to look at the bodies strewn over the steps to the main gate. The first thing he noticed was the differences among them. He could still see signs of the bluish tint on some of them—in their lips and eyelids, and along the tips of their fingers. But there were some that didn't show any signs. It might have been because of the state of decomposition, but his gut was telling him different. There was a revolver clutched in one man's hand. Apparently some of them must have ended their life on their own terms. He nodded. Given the situation, there wasn't any shame in that. *Hell, that's what I came to do.*

After seeing all the bodies on the steps, he began to wonder how bad it would be inside. It would be easier to forget about the fifty-yard line and just do it on the steps. Chuck sat down next to the man with the revolver and pried the gun out of his hand. Initial inspection didn't show the revolver in too bad of shape, but when he checked the cylinder—all the shells were spent. *Maybe the man didn't end his life on his own terms?* Chuck pushed off the cement step and was headed over to the truck to get the pistol out of his backpack, when something about the partially burnt out car at the next intersection looked out of place. He headed for it, and the closer he got the more he couldn't believe what he was seeing.

It was the charred remains of a man, slumped over the scored asphalt outside the driver's door. He stopped in front of the body and looked at the rest of the car. Only the driver's side of the car was burnt. The rest of it didn't look too bad—so it wasn't the tank that exploded. He bent over and poked his head partially through the door where the window had been. Something about it wasn't right. As he started to pull back he noticed something hanging just inside the door. He glanced down at the burnt body and then slowly jerked the door open. As he did, something small fell from the liner down to the half-melted driver's seat. It looked like a melted piece of nylon rope. He picked it up, shut the door and looked at the man on the ground.

Why didn't he run? You would think that a man on fire would run off screaming in pain. But not this guy. He studied the side of the car and the scorched mark on the road. The fire was contained to such a small area. Why didn't he try to get out of it? Chuck squatted and watched the burnt skin flake off the corpse as he poked it. He slid his hand around the neck of the corpse and pulled him forward. He was heavier than he should have been. This man hadn't been dead near as long as the others. He let the head fall back against the door as he began to get an idea of what happened. He grabbed the man's left hand and looked at it. He rubbed his thumb along the burnt forearm and watched the skin flake off. The same thing happened when he rubbed the back of the man's hand. But when he rubbed the man's wrist, nothing flaked off. It had a completely different texture, hard and waxy. He rubbed the piece of rope between his fingers. It was the same.

Chuck dropped the rope and stood as he cupped his hand over his mouth. Someone had tied him to the car and then set him on fire—and not that long ago. He backed up a couple of steps and quickly scanned the area for any recent signs of life. As he hurried back to the truck, he looked at his watch. It was just past five. There was still a good hour of daylight left. He could look around, see if he could find who did this. There was no confusing this with thunder—he wasn't the only one that survived the end. He felt the spark of hope light again in his heart as he retrieved the rifle and backpack from the front seat and headed out on foot.

He worked his way around burnt-out cars and trash along the sidewalk, being careful to keep as close to the storefronts as possible so that he wasn't exposed for any significant amount of time. As he slowly inched his way along, it was strange how much it reminded him of deer hunting. The real difference wasn't the environment. It didn't matter to him that the trees and bush were replaced by broken glass, mangled cars and bodies. What did feel different, what kept him alert and his heart pounding quicker than normal, was the distinct feeling that there was more than one hunter and more than one hunted. He could feel himself cast in both roles. Strangely, for a man who had come there to die, he had no intentions of going out like the man tied to the burnt car.

The sun continued to set as he made a zigzagging sweep through the heart of downtown. He passed in front of a bagel shop and had to stop to stare at the floor. It was so loaded with roaches and ants that it looked like it was moving. Apparently looters didn't clear out all the flour and sugar in the store.

He was tempted to call out a couple of times, but then thought wiser. Before he let anyone know he was there, he wanted to see them first. If he thought they were the ones responsible for setting the man on fire, he would slip away unannounced. Not that he was judging what they did. It wasn't his place. After all he had taken a life too. He wished that he could remember why. As it stood, he had nothing more than a prayer that there was a just reason for what he did. Perhaps the man back at the burnt car deserved to die. Just the same, he no longer felt like today was a good day for him to bid his final goodbye. Not with other survivors around.

As the presence of the once mighty towers fell victim to the dusk of night, he suddenly heard a sound that he didn't think he'd ever hear again. He caught his breath, froze and listened. It echoed across the night air like a beacon of hope cast out between the failing giants of concrete and steel. It was the murmurs and rumbling of people—several people, a group…a mob. With that sound, everything that he'd finally come to accept—changed. He sprinted to the next cross-street and the wonders continued. This time it was visual. At the intersection four blocks to his right, shadows flickered across derelict cars and shattered storefront windows. This was no hallucination. There was no mistake. Actual living people were gathered somewhere around that corner. Part of him, which came from that deep need to grasp and clutch another living soul, wanted to breakout in a headstrong, glorious rush and dive into the crowd the way a rock star leaps off the stage. Yet the wiser part of him, knew it best not to dive headfirst into an unknown situation.

Like a hunter stalking prey, his run down the middle of the street quickly slowed to a steady and deliberate approach under the cover of whatever ruins the city had to offer. He pressed against the brick at the corner building, stepped over a weathered body that looked like an old woman, and peeked around the wall to his right. There were several bonfires burning and movement from dozens of people in the street three blocks down.

He crouched low to the curb and shuffled over to the rear of an abandoned car parked along the street. As he slowly rose to spy over the trunk, his heart jumped at the wonderful sight of those survivors. He started shifting his weight from one foot to the other, urges and desire sparring with planning and caution.

They were too far off for him to clearly understand what they were saying, even the mumbles sounded like fine music to his ears. He snatched the binoculars out of the backpack and got a better look. There were three men standing in front of the flickering flames of a burning car. He quickly focused on the clump that was burning on the ground in front of the driver's door. Just as quickly he pulled the binoculars away and told himself that it could be anything. It could have been a pile of clothes they used to get the fire going.

He quickly scanned the area around the three men. There were several others standing further away from the flames that were somewhat lost in the shadows. Some appeared to be women and a few looked like children. He couldn't make out their features or faces, but they all were looking at the three men. He focused the binoculars back on the men. Two of them were standing in attention to the third. The lenses weren't powerful enough to see any real detail of the third man, but it was easy to see that he was the one barking out orders. It looked like he had long, shoulder length hair and unless the shadows and flickering fire were playing tricks on his eyes—the man was wearing a long, canvas duster like the gunslingers wore in the old westerns. Then Chuck saw him point at something. He followed Duster's gesture over to the other side of the street and saw a woman standing next to a sedan with her arms spread to the sides. As soon as he adjusted the focus of the binoculars his breath caught midway in his throat. The woman was tied to the door. Her head lurched forward and a split second later he heard her scream. "Please… just let us leave!"

Chuck swung the binoculars back over and saw Duster holding a bottle with a rag stuck in the top. That wasn't from any old western—it was a Molotov cocktail. Chuck heard more screams from the woman but kept the binoculars on the man. He saw Duster mumble something as the other two men forced a fourth guy over to him at gun point. As he watched, Duster handed the Molotov cocktail to the guy and drew a pistol on him.

It was like some morbid nightmare. Duster turned toward the woman and yelled, "Are you the one that will stop me?"

The woman shook her head and sobbed that she wasn't. For a second it looked like it might be over. Duster dropped his face to the ground like he was disappointed. He pulled out a lighter and lit the Molotov cocktail. As soon as the rag caught fire, the fourth guy started pleading for mercy as he backed away with the lit bottle. The other two men jumped in and prodded him back over to Duster with their rifles. There was no escape. The guy was either going to throw it at the woman, or they would kill him and throw it themselves. Chuck heard her scream, "Throw it Sam; just throw it and get out of here while you can!"

They know each other. Chuck slung the rifle off his shoulder and tried to find Duster in the crosshairs. But with the fire flickering in the background, he couldn't line up the shot. He tried to line up the other two men—they were standing too close to that damn fire. In a panic, he brought the binoculars back up as Duster pressed the barrel of the pistol to Sam's head. Chuck shared in the gut-wrenching anguish as Sam drew back a shaky arm. For a reason he couldn't explain, Chuck dropped the binoculars and swung the rifle back on the woman. As soon as he lined her up in the scope—he flinched and drew back. *She's staring at me! She knows I'm here!* He quickly put his eye back to the scope and saw her mouth something to him. For a second, he was back in the woods with his dad, taking aim on the buck from behind the sycamore. His dad's voice drifted past his ears. "Make it clean." Before he could stop himself, he pulled the trigger.

The shot echoed through the dark, silent caverns between the giant steel and concrete structures. Chuck kept his eye to the scope only long enough to see the woman slam back against the car and then start to slide to the ground. A frenzy of screams and commotion erupted from those cheated of the moment. He yanked the rifle back and ducked behind the car. He couldn't stop shaking. *What have I done?* He bit down and started hitting himself in the thigh as he cursed himself.

A voice echoed up through the streets. "You! You out there with the gun…show yourself."

Chuck swallowed as he peeked around the fender at Duster. He was standing next to the fire with his arms raised and turning as he addressed all the streets coming into the intersection. He wasn't sure without the scope or binoculars, but it looked like Sam was on his knees, crying a few feet away.

Duster lowered his arms, walked over to Sam and pointed at him. Chuck saw the flash and heard a pop like a firecracker as Sam slumped to his knees and fell over face first. Before he even hit the ground, Duster was back addressing his people. He shook his fists in the air and worked them into a fury. At the end, he turned a circle and pointed to the surrounding buildings.

Chuck ducked behind the car as the mob started to disperse and spread out in all directions. He heard the loud, banging thumps of the mob hitting everything they came across with bats and pipes. Like the tigers of India, he was being driven toward the hunter. He pushed off the bumper and shot back over to the corner of the building. Once behind the cover of the storefront he ran as fast as he could back toward the truck. They were searching slow and meticulous; he was running as fast as he could—they wouldn't catch him. Or so he thought before he heard the sound of car engines turning over. For the first time in his life, he knew the taste of real fear.

The Chevy was eight blocks away, sitting out like a sore thumb among the burnt out and mangled cars around the stadium. If they got there first they would know it was his and wait in the shadows for him to return. He knew they would do that because it's exactly what he would do. He sprinted and dove into the cover of several decaying corpses as a truck sped through the next intersection. He would make it back—today was not going to be the day he died.

Chapter 24

Chuck barely took his eyes off the rear view mirror as he weaved his way down the interstate toward Madison. A couple of times he thought he saw headlights coming up behind him, but then a cloud passed overhead and the lights died. It was only the moonlight reflecting off one of the wrecks on the interstate. Between the fearful glances in the mirror and trying to navigate his way through the nightmare of mangled cars in front of him, he kept seeing flashes of the woman he shot. Each time he did, he told himself that it was the only option he had. That it was the only chance for at least one of them to live. How was he to know that they would still shoot the man after she was dead? Besides, he had the feeling that she wanted him to shoot, or at least he thought he did. He saw it in her eyes—right before she said. What did she say? He could almost remember mouthing the words with her. Then he pulled the trigger and they were gone. For some strange reason he felt the words were still with him, sleeping deep inside his soul, waiting for the day when he would speak life into them.

In all the times that he prayed to find other survivors, he never imagined that he might stumble on such merciless behavior. What did the couple do to deserve that kind of death? What did the man in the duster mean when he yelled, "Are you the one that will stop me?" He felt the agony and remorse of the guy kneeling and crying. They had known each other. It could have been that they were husband and wife, brother and sister, or maybe just two survivors who finally found a reason to go on living. He could picture the guy looking up as the man in the duster drew the gun on him, and in his mind he knew the guy just closed his eyes and gave in to the end.

He eased the white-knuckled grip he had on the steering wheel, pulled his right hand free, and held it in front of his chest. He didn't need the dim light from the dash to know he was still shaking. He used the hard plastic surface of the steering wheel to anchor his hand again and whispered once more, "What have I done?"

He continued to second-guess himself all the way back to Madison. It wasn't until he turned onto Michigan that he even remembered that he no longer had a house to go to. It didn't stop him from turning on his street and driving up to where his house used to be. He parked along the shallow ditch on the opposite side of the street and got out. Only a partial brick shell stood on the burnt lot where his house used to be. The memory of carrying Becky over the threshold swept over him. He remembered the laughter and the love. It was their first home—meant only as a starter before they could afford something better—yet it was home nonetheless. He let out a deep sigh as he turned from the charred remnants that were once his walls, ceiling and roof, and climbed back behind the wheel.

The next morning, he woke up on his side, spread across the bench seat of the Chevy. After taking a moment to moan and acknowledge the pain of a sore back and stiff neck, he opened the door, slid out, and raised his arms and stretched so hard that his hands shook. He rubbed the life back in his eyes and the blood back in his face as he pulled in the morning air. The smell of smoke took him back to the days of burning raked leaves as a child. Not too bad of a memory by itself, but unfortunately it also reminded him that he no longer had a place to stay. He walked to the ditch, unzipped the fly of his jeans and starting urinating on the weeds as he looked at the other houses in his neighborhood.

There was Bill and Rena's place. Like any other home in the neighborhood, that would mean seeing the remains of their old house every day. Then it came to him. There was really only one choice. He zipped up, jumped back in the truck and headed for downtown.

He took a right on Main Street and drove past his antique store and further on to where the homes began. He parked in front of the old brick Queen Anne on the left side of the street and walked through the wrought iron gate. Midway to the front door he stopped and looked at the front façade. The house was completely brick except for the covered porches on the front and west sides. The wood was painted and accented in keeping with the tradition of proper Victorian architecture. The house had two full floors and judging by the steep pitch of the roof, a good amount of usable attic space above. A big beautiful elm shaded the front yard, and beneath the thriving weeds and grass he could feel closely fit stones which made up the walkway to the gate. Becky was right, this place was beautiful—or at least it was on the outside.

He remembered not finding anyone in the house when he was gathering the dead. Beyond that, he couldn't remember a single detail about what the house looked like on the inside. That was answered when he walked through the nine-foot oak and beveled glass front door. It still smelled like old people inside—that wasn't all bad. It made it feel like it could have been his grandmother's house. He inspected the floors, the trim and the grand staircase. He made his way to each room and tried the faucets in the bathrooms. There was still water pressure. It could be that the roof leaked like a sieve, but he wasn't going to inspect that now. No…other than the smell of mothballs and a fair coating of dust, the place is actually in pretty good shape. He walked into the parlor and sat on the antique sofa. His rear didn't sink into it like the one they had back in their house, but he could always swap out furniture—hell, he had an entire town to choose from.

He started nodding in recognition of the possibilities as he walked out onto the covered porch. There was even a porch swing. He made himself comfortable on the weathered oak slats as his thoughts shifted to how much this house would have cost before the end. The numbers that came to mind made him smile and shake his head in disbelief. He leaned back in the swing and stretched his arms out as he looked at the magnificent houses on the other side of Main. This was nice…he could get used to it. He was just beginning to relax when it suddenly dawned on him that he hadn't seen a garage. He left the swing rocking as he made his way around the side of the house. As expected with the architectural period, there wasn't a garage to be found. Instead, there was a small carriage house at the rear of the property.

He rubbed his chin as he thought about the difficulty in running a line from a generator in the carriage house to the main house. It wouldn't be that bad. Besides it would mean he wouldn't have to worry about carbon monoxide collecting as he slept. Although it could mean a couple of frigid, late night treks in the snow if the generator stopped during the winter. He took a moment to think about it. Most of the supplies like gas, tools and food were more prevalent up the hill in the commercial part of town. Still, there was something to be said about this place. Besides, it was Becky's dream house. He dropped his head as he thought about how excited his wife would have been.

He walked to the middle of the front yard and looked at the house towering over him. "For you Becky—this will be our new house."

Chapter 25

As the deep scarlet leaves fell from the elm in the front yard, Chuck readied the old Victorian for winter. Two bedrooms were stocked as pantries while the third was used as a large walk-in closet. The extra clothes allowed him to minimize the water needed for washing. The oil furnace still had a partial tank of fuel, but most of the heat would come from an old wood stove and a couple of base-board units. The generator was hooked up and the carriage house was stocked with gasoline and batteries. To make sure that he wouldn't get stuck if the snow really came down, he had a slightly used Ford Bronco parked out on the street and a Suzuki ATV parked in the carriage house.

With all the preparation done that could be done, he made one last trip to the library to round up some books before it got too cold. Then it was time to settle in for the solitude of winter. His favorite books were those that detailed the mechanical workings of pumps, generators and diesel engines. He started off reading and scribbling ideas down on paper. Working solutions to the problems that were months or even years down the road was good for him. It helped keep his mind occupied during the daylight hours. Though as the winter dragged on, it still left plenty of idle time to think about Becky.

He began to mimic the way she did things, whether it was the way she would organize the dishes or the odd way she would hold the spoon when she stirred the soup. All the little idiosyncrasies that made up his wife came alive in his actions as he started to live for them both. They were the treasures that kept him connected to her.

One night while he was wrapped in a blanket and reading a romance novel on the sofa, he said, "This is pretty good sweetie, I can see why you like it so much."

He set the book down and before he realized what he was doing, he responded for his late wife. "When did you take up reading? I thought that unless it was on the boob tube you remained clueless."

He grinned and said, "No...you'd be proud of me. I've actually been doing a lot of reading lately."

"Great...you wait till I'm dead before you take up something that we'd have in common."

He looked at the empty cushion to his side as the grin left his face. "I wish I had taken it up sooner." He got up and walked to the picture window to stare at the darkness outside as he sucked on his gums. "There's nothing wrong with talking to yourself. It keeps up your knowledge of the English language. In fact I'd be surprised if talking to yourself isn't prescribed in the survival manuals that deal with prolonged isolation." For a second he thought about the survivors he saw in Indianapolis. He wondered if they would make it through the winter. It would be worse there. The average snow for Madison was nothing compared to what usually fell in Indianapolis. And if he hadn't been prepared, he didn't know if he could have survived.

He turned away from the window and started nodding. "Talking to yourself is good...means that I'm not alone in all this."

One restless night in bed Becky asked, "Do you remember the day we had that argument on the way home from my folks?"

"Sure"

"Well, when I got out of the truck and walked in by myself, I wanted you to come after me. Why didn't you?"

"I wanted to."

"Then why didn't you?"

"I guess I was just scared."

"Scared of me? Don't be silly."

"No, not you. I don't know how to explain it."

"If you really loved me then you should have at least tried."

"I could feel us drifting apart...and I just...I...didn't..." Before he could finish he began to cry. There was so much more that he needed to say, but the words to express what he wanted to tell her were lost to him. There was no taking back what was in the past, no forgiving for not saying what should have been said. He pulled the blankets up around his neck and prayed that closing his eyes would stop the flood of emotions he felt.

Even though a chill in the air could still be felt now and then, the winds were coming up from the south more often than not. Winter had lost its life and spring was starting to be born. That meant he was getting out more. There were the runs necessary to restock his pantries, hunts to find more clothes that fit him, and of course trips to the library to catch up on his reading. One damp spring morning he ended up at the foot of the cement boat ramp on the river. It didn't really surprise him. He knew he was walking that way—he just hadn't done it intentionally. As it was every spring, the river was a little more turbulent and murkier than it was the rest of the year. The color was brought about by the mud washing in from the feeder streams. Along with the mud came sticks and trash and the occasional log.

He spotted a clump of sticks drifting in the middle of the current. If they didn't get caught on anything they might eventually end up in the gulf. He was watching them roll and bob in the murky water, when he began to picture the dead. The past residents of Madison he set adrift from the boat ramp. They were all there. He saw the pale, bloated face of his best friend break the surface and then slowly sink back down. Then he saw something else. There was no confusion in the small patch of material. He knew it for what it was—it was part of Becky's favorite quilt. It was his wife. His heart sank as he pictured her there with the others, yet alone in her isolation. She was the only one he set adrift wrapped in anything. The others had the company of one another, but not his Becky...she was the one that none of them could see.

He toyed with the thought of taking the pistol out of his backpack and sticking it in his mouth. It wasn't bad enough that he abandoned her in life; he also had to do it in death. He slung the backpack off his shoulder and clutched it to his chest. He closed his eyes and as he slowly opened them, he took two steps into the cold water of the Ohio River and opened the flap of the canvas bag.

He stood staring at the shimmer on the water. If he was going to do it—it wouldn't be out of a panic-stricken moment of despair. It would be calculated and done with the forethought that there was no reason not to. He took another step and felt the icy chill of the murky water creep up his leg to just below the knees. He reached into the bag and pulled out the pistol. He glanced at the weapon and then closed his eyes and pulled in a deep calming breath. A second later it was all business as he began his inspection of the gun. He checked the barrel. It was clean and clear. He popped out the clip. It was full. He ejected the chambered round, slapped the clip back in and loaded a fresh round.

With his heart pounding, he prayed for a reason to keep on going—any reason to prolong his loneliness or give hope that he could ever add value to this godforsaken land.

He was about to take another step into the river when he started to think about the woman he shot in Indianapolis. He also remembered what the man in the duster yelled at her. He asked her if she were the one that would stop him. In the same way that he would never forget watching her mouth those few unknown words to him, he would never forget the sound of that question, nor the context in which it was asked. What did the man in the duster want her to stop him from doing? Why didn't she just say that she was?

He remembered how duster shot the other man in the head, and how he worked the others into a frenzy before turning them loose. He could still picture him standing in front of the fire with that duster blowing in the wind.

Chuck rolled his wrist and looked at both sides of the pistol. After a moment of thought, he flicked the safety back on and slipped the gun in the bag. He had his reason to continue living.

Chapter 26

Chuck ground his teeth as he thought about the man in the duster. "Let him ask me if I'm the one who came to stop him." His nostrils flared as he nodded and then weaved around a car on the interstate. "I've got his answer."

He relaxed his grip on the wheel every few seconds. "Stay loose... keep cool, need to stay focused and get done what needs to be done." His thoughts shifted to the woman he shot. "I'll make it up to you and your friend—that's a promise."

By the time he crossed over the bypass, he had been on the road for almost three hours and dusk was falling across the skyline. At no time during that span did he ever start to lose the courage to go through with it. For him, his extended existence was ordained for the singular purpose of putting an end to the life of the man in the duster. To do that, he would have to track him down and get in close enough for a clean shot.

He killed the lights and coasted down the Market Street exit. The incident with the woman occurred somewhere in the vicinity of Michigan and Senate. But of course that was nearly a year ago. If the mob survived the winter and were still in Indianapolis, they could be anywhere now. With that in mind, he pulled into an alley two blocks from the ramp and killed the engine.

He pulled the backpack, loaded with extra shells and his sawed-off twelve-gauge, and slung it over his shoulder. He buckled a holstered revolver around his waist and slipped his favorite pistol under the belt behind his back. Short of war, he was ready. After one final check, he grabbed his rifle and headed out on foot.

The first thing he noticed as he crept along the shattered glass and broken doors that lined the street, was how much difference a year made. The overwhelming smell from last fall was gone. He no longer stepped across the shriveled, dried out bodies of the dead. Time, weather and a feast of insects had taken care of that. All that remained were bones, picked clean by nature.

He was approaching monument circle when a distant shot echoed softly between the surrounding buildings. He stopped to listen to the dying echo. The last reverberation came from the buildings to the south, so he headed north. A block into it he picked up his pursuit to a light jog. It was fast enough to make better time, but slow enough that he never lost touch with what was going on around him.

He headed north on Illinois and as he closed in on 10th street he began to hear the laughter and mumble of a mob. The question of whether or not they made it through winter had been answered. He moved off the street and back to the ruins along the sidewalk as he pulled the bolt back on his rifle and chambered a round. Like a thief in the night, he slipped through the darkness toward 11th.

He slowly maneuvered his way along the brick facades and narrow alleys until he came to a vacant lot. The lot presented a span of sixty feet that offered nothing more than dirt and rubble for cover. He stopped at the edge of the building and listened to the ruckus of the mob while he scanned the area. There was a vacant lot two buildings up on the other side. Every path he could see had at least one exposure to it. He tightened his grip on the rifle and briefly closed his eyes. His next step would be his first into the open. He kept it slow and even as he felt his way through a scattering of old brick.

He was halfway across the lot when a pickup rolled into the intersection two blocks away. Chuck froze. The truck stopped and a guy with a rifle slung over his shoulder jumped up in the bed and started searching the area with a flashlight. Luckily the batteries were low, so even though it lit up a nice circle on the building closest to the truck, it lacked the power to illuminate anything more than a block away. Chuck watched the beam wash along the storefronts on its way toward him. No movement, not a blink, not the rise of his chest or the fog of his breath—and they wouldn't notice him. A soft illumination fell on his jeans and then stopped as the man in the truck held the flashlight on him and squinted.

The pounding in Chuck's chest was the only visible movement in his body. If he had to, he could get off the first shot before the man with the flashlight could even ready his rifle. If the driver didn't floor it immediately, he could probably take him out as well. The only problem was that he had no idea how many others were in the area. For all he knew, there could be men searching the area all around him. One shot would bring hell down on him.

Chuck slowly moved his thumb over to the safety on the rifle and flicked it off as he watched the man in the back of the truck stretch his neck out for a better look. He was about to swing the rifle up and shoot when he heard the exhaust rumble of another vehicle speeding down from the north. He held his position as the sound grew louder and started to veer to his right. From the corner of his eye, he saw the car's headlights one street over as it passed the opening of the vacant lot across the street. As the rumble faded to his rear, the dim beam of the flashlight finally moved off him and onto the buildings across the street. Seemingly satisfied, the man standing in the back of the truck flicked off the light and started to turn back toward the cab. Chuck blinked and was about to let out the breath he had been holding, when the man suddenly turned back to take one last look in his direction. A second later the man banged his fist on the metal roof of the cab and the truck lurched forward, most likely to perform the same search at the next intersection.

Chuck relaxed his grip on the rifle. It could have been a nightly routine, but it looked like they were searching for someone. He quietly made his way to the corner of the next building and crouched under the cover of some taller weeds at the edge of the vacant lot. That was when he noticed that the street wasn't as dark as it was a few minutes earlier. He looked up to the night sky. The clouds were still clustered in front of the moon. It wasn't his eyes; they had already adjusted to the dark. Something was going on. He peeked around the front of the building and saw a soft glow flickering on the face of a shop across the street one block up. His first thoughts were that they were either burning another car, or they had started another bonfire like the one he remembered Duster standing in front of. But that didn't make sense. He pulled around and looked through the vacant lot to the back of the buildings one block over. There was a faint light falling between them too. Either the source of the light was moving or there were multiple sources. As he struggled to understand what it meant, he heard the horrible sounds of bats and pipes banging against metal and brick. They were driving someone toward capture or death.

He was about to move in for a closer look when he heard a man yell out, "Cindy! Don't make us hunt you down—it will only make it worse.

You know that!"

Even though Chuck was full of confidence and determination, that voice still sent a chill through him. It was the same voice that yelled for him to come forward after he shot the woman. It was the voice of the man he came to kill. Duster was looking for a girl named Cindy.

Chuck slipped inside the building and surveyed the storefronts at the next intersection through the broken glass of the front window. A few seconds later he spotted a guy with a torch a block beyond the intersection. He drew his rifle and caught the figure in the crosshairs of his scope. It wasn't Duster—it was a teenage boy. The boy stuck the torch through the broken window of a storefront, quickly scanned it for the girl they were chasing, and moved on to the next. He continued in that fashion as he worked his way toward the intersection. They were probably doing the same thing on every street in the area. Whoever the girl was—they wanted her pretty bad.

As the boy popped his head in through another broken window, Chuck saw movement at the intersection between them. He focused the scope on the corner storefront across the street. When the boy pulled the torch out of the building he was searching, Chuck caught the reflection of a black girl's face in his scope. She had to be Cindy.

Chuck continued to watch as the boy ducked in to search the next building. That was the girl's opportunity to run. All she had to do was take it. But she didn't and moments later, the boy pulled back out and continued on to the next one, just four buildings from her position. Chuck could see the fear in the girl's face as the boy stuck the torch in the next building.

"Now! Go damn it—do it now…" Chuck huffed in a whisper, as the kid poked his head in the window three buildings away. A few seconds later the features of his face tensed up as the boy popped back out—another opportunity missed. He thought about the woman he shot and the terrible and painful death she would have endured if he hadn't. He didn't let it happen then, and he couldn't let it happen now. As soon as the boy poked his head through the storefront two buildings from her position, Chuck ran out of the building and ducked behind an abandoned car across the street from the girl.

Chuck quickly peeked over the fender and saw the girl withdraw further into the store. The boy pulled back out of the window and the torch lit up the area like a streetlight. It was a matter of timing. As soon as the light dimmed again, Chuck shot across the street to the car parked along the curb just outside the girl's window.

He had to take a chance. He slowly peered around the front bumper as the boy's torch lit up the storefront. He didn't see the girl, but that didn't matter. As soon as the boy stuck the torch in, Chuck drew his rifle back and jumped up from behind the car. With the clanging of bats and pipes echoing in the street, the boy never even heard him. Chuck turned him off like a light with a quick pop to the back of the head. The boy dropped the torch and started to fall, but Chuck grabbed him before he hit the jagged edges of the broken store window. He laid the boy down on the sidewalk and snatched the torch lying inside the broken window. "You still in there?" he whispered.

No answer came. He glanced up the street to make sure no one else was coming, and then he ran around to the door and went inside. The torch lit up a junkyard of tipped over display cases, clothes racks, boxes and other debris. "I'm not going to hurt you…if we hurry…we can still make it out of here." He swung the torch in a sweep of the store and caught the girl crouching behind a wooden display. Keeping his distance and being careful not to scare her any more than she already was, he calmly said, "I'm not with them. If you want, I can help get you out of here and take you to a place that's safe."

The girl raised her head and peered over the display. In a voice that didn't sound as young as he would have expected, she asked, "How do I know you're telling the truth? How do I know I can trust you?"

He lowered the torch so that she could get a good look at his face. "Listen, I don't know what to tell you. You know I'm not with them…I didn't give away where you were hiding, did I?"

"No, but that doesn't mean anything. How do I know you don't want to rape me?"

For a reason that made absolutely no sense, he put his own life on the line. He took the revolver out of the holster around his waist, showed her that it was loaded and then inched a little closer and laid it down on the floor. He slowly backed away and said, "We can't stay here any longer. I'm leaving. You can come with me or go on your own. Either way, you'll have a loaded gun to defend yourself." He turned his back to her. After a moment of hesitation he walked over to the door and stopped. If she came, he would take her back to Madison where she would be safe. If she didn't, he would continue with his plan to kill

Duster.

He was about to step outside when she huffed, "Wait!"

Chapter 27

Chuck waited until they were outside city limits before turning the headlights on. When the dash lit up, he got his first real look at the girl sitting with her back against the door on the passenger side. They hadn't spoken one word to each other since she followed him out of the trashed remains of the store. He led, and although she kept fairly close to him, he wasn't sure who she was more afraid of—the mob looking for her, or him. Whichever was the case, she made sure that he knew where the revolver was pointed during the slow, tedious trek back to the truck. Just as it was now.

When he first saw her crouched behind the storefront window he thought she was a kid, but now that he could really see her, she looked to be in her late teens or early twenties. He wasn't too good at guessing age. When you reach your mid-forties, everyone under twenty-five looks like they're still in high school. He studied her face and then met her unwavering stare back at him. There was a look of confidence in her eyes that told him she wasn't one to back down. He broke his stare first and shifted his gaze to her hair. Although it was dirty and tangled, it didn't look dry and coarse like he was used to seeing on black women. It hung all the way down to the middle of her back and looked like it would have been soft and straight if she were cleaned up. He followed her hair to her arms, down to the scraped knuckles on her hands, until finally he ended up back at the revolver pointed at him.

"Where are you taking me?"

The accusation in her voice pushed his attention away from her and back to the burnout cars coming up in front of the truck. "We're going to Madison. You know where that is?"

With a little less tension, she said, "Down south of Columbus—right?"

"Yeah...it's on the Ohio River."

"Why are you taking me there?"

"It's where I live."

"Bull shit...If you lived down there—why would you come all the way up here?"

After a second of silence, he lied. "I was looking for supplies."

"In the city! You're not as smart as you look."

"Maybe not, but I saved your ass."

She took her eyes off him for the first time and quickly scanned the darkness around the interstate. "Hey I'm appreciative and all, but you can let me out here."

"Fine," he said softly as he slowed the truck to a stop. She opened the door and dropped one foot to the pavement, stopping short of getting out as she looked over the graveyard of derelict cars under the moonlit sky.

He looked over as she sat poised on the edge of the seat, but instead of seeing Cindy—he saw his wife. It was Becky all over again. He was about to leave this poor girl on the side of road just like he did his wife that day. It was definitely a time of uncertainty, but one thing stood out clear as day. He wasn't about to let that happen again. His hand shot over to her in a startled reflex. "Wait..." Cindy glanced down at the hand on her shoulder and then looked back out into the darkness. "Please don't go."

Without turning to look at him, she asked, "You really live in Madison?"

He let out a thankful sigh. "Yeah I do."

"And you have food there."

"Enough to last for years."

"I thought you said you were up here looking for supplies?"

Chuck glanced away. "Forget about what I said...it's not important. I'm offering you a safe place to live where you don't have to worry about the assholes that were after you. What do you say?"

She turned and looked him over. "Why would you do that?"

Chuck had gone to Indianapolis, willing to die in order to kill a man. That was the only response that came to him when he prayed at the river for a reason to keep on living. Now as he looked at the girl who was about to get out of his truck, and tried to imagine all the hardship she had been through over the last year, he found another reason. "Hope."

"What are you talking about?"

"Hope that tomorrow may be better than today. Hope that people still care." Chuck held out both hands, palm up over his lap and emphasized one last time. "Hope!"

After a moment of study, she pulled her foot back in the truck and closed the door. He gave the truck some gas and as they headed down the interstate, she asked, "You're not crazy are you?" in a manner that made it difficult to tell if she was joking or serious.

Chuck smiled as he thought of all the conversations he had with himself over the winter. "No, I'm not crazy." As he wheeled the truck around a Volvo he asked, "Why were they chasing you—you are Cindy, right?"

"Yeah, who are you?"

"Chuck…well that's what I answer to, my name is Charles Bain. And you, is it Cindy or is that short for Cynthia?"

"It's plain old Cindy. Cindy McKay"

"Well Cindy, we've got another two or three hours on the road. Why don't you tell me what was going on back there."

She slowly shook her head as she stared through the window. For a moment he didn't think she was going to answer, but then in a steady voice of reflection she said, "Jason wanted to kill me."

That perked up his attention. "Is Jason the leader?"

"Yes."

"Is he the guy with the long hair who wears the duster?"

"Yeah, that's him."

Knowing the man's name gave him some satisfaction. He settled back down and asked, "Why did he want to kill you?"

"They burned my baby…and I wouldn't stop saying that what they did was wrong."

"You had a baby?"

Her face twitched, as she turned toward him while trying to hold her lower lip firm. "No I lost him back when it was still cold out…still birth." She addressed her runny nose and then confided, "I don't think anyone has actually given birth to a live baby since the coming."

The corner of Chuck's mouth pulled up in a questioned snarl. "Coming…you mean the End?"

"End…Coming…whatever, that's just what Jason called it."

"So why did he burn your baby—was he afraid of disease?"

"No. That's just what he does." She took a deep breath as if she needed it to continue. "He likes to burn people."

"That's fucking crazy!" Chuck exclaimed, as he tightened his grip on the wheel. "Why in the hell would he do something like that?"

"I don't know. If you don't agree with him…power trip…you name the reason—any is as good as the next."

"So he was going to burn you because you said it was wrong to burn your dead baby."

"Yeah, I think so. I wanted my baby buried," she said wishfully as she dipped her head. "I didn't want to see him thrown in the pile with the rest of them. You can understand that can't you?"

Chuck nodded in silence.

"And I guess I just couldn't keep my mouth shut afterward. I knew I was walking on thin ice…had been for several weeks. I just didn't care." She raised her face. "That is until he sent them for me…then I guess I did care. I mean since I ran and all."

"And no one would stand up for you?"

"Most of them believe in what he says so they do it without question. And the ones who have tried to stand up to him…" she lowered her face again and shook her head, "…they didn't make it."

"What does he say, you know, to get the others to follow him?"

"He tells them that all this is God's way of finding out who's worthy. That he's the hand of God and that God told him to burn—or cleanse as he puts it—all those who would not follow the word of God."

Chuck's jaws tensed up. "Why is it that whenever anything good or bad happens, some asshole tries to make it religious." He pinched his lips together. "Is that what you think?"

She reared back. "Hey I'm here with you aren't I? No one can tell me that God didn't want us to ever have babies again. But the stories I've heard…"

"What stories?"

"Some people say that Jason can't be killed."

Chuck took his eyes off the road and looked at her. "What are you talking about?"

"Just what I've heard. He'll give anyone a chance who wants to take it."

Chuck thought of the woman he shot and the words that Jason yelled to her 'Are you the one that will stop me'. "Has anyone taken him up on it?"

"They say some men have tried."

"What happened to them?"

"They're dead."

Chuck looked back at the dark path ahead of them and shook his head. "How many survived up there?"

"There's probably been a couple of dozen under Jason at different times. And then I don't know. We find heathens every once in a while." Cindy gave a queer smile and shook her head. "I mean stragglers; you know, folks by themselves, hiding around the city."

"All ages?"

"All ages, both sexes, some who were once rich and others who have always been poor. Besides me there were two other women who had gotten pregnant since the…the End. One was older and the other was about the same age as me."

"Have you been with Jason and the others the entire time?"

"Pretty much…they found me wandering around late last summer and took me in. They gave me food and water and a warm place to stay."

The image of the woman he shot popped back in his head. That must have been about that same time last year. He kept his eyes on the dark road ahead of them as he remembered the small crowd standing in the shadows around Jason that night. None of them lifted a finger to stop the tragedy. He was about to ask if she was there, but then thought better of it—what would be gained by knowing. Instead, he asked, "Was it one of them that got you pregnant?"

"No…it was like a week or so after I woke up—" she paused and looked at Chuck as he nodded that he knew what she meant. "I don't know who it was. I was searching for food and then the next thing I know I'm on my back and some white guy is on top of me." Her eyes took on a distant look. "I didn't even try to fight him off. It didn't matter. Back then there wasn't anything that he could have done to me that would have mattered. Fact was, I was happy to feel the company of someone. I would have done anything he wanted if he would have stayed."

Chuck nodded once and said, "I know what you mean."

"What about you, how many others are alive in Madison?"

Suddenly he felt embarrassed about being the only survivor. "No others—just me."

She perked up and gave him her full attention. "Just you?"

He turned his eyes from her. "Yeah."

"My God, all this time by yourself?"

A thankful sigh escaped as he realized the situation was about to change. "Yeah."

"Were you married?"

Chuck turned his attention back to the road as he softly confided, "My wife didn't make it."

"Your children didn't make it either?"

Chuck simply said, "No…"

His answer seemed to pull the life from his passenger. The air left her lungs and she fell back against the seat in a stupor.

"What about you?" he asked quickly. "What were you doing before it happened?"

Cindy was still distant when she said, "I was about to get my education degree. I always wanted to teach grade school." She pulled herself from the memories of what was once to be and added, "I was about to graduate from IUPUI." She smiled painfully, and after a lingering moment said, "I was from Lawrence Township on the east side. My family didn't make it either. My little brother and my mother, I mean." She paused to rub her face. "My father died several years ago." She started shaking her head. "I…always regretted that he wasn't going to get to see me graduate from college…it would have made him proud."

There was a long awkward silence as neither knew what to say. They passed the congestion around Greenwood and Franklin and then hit several miles where the interstate was barely cluttered. Cindy cleared her throat, and while making enough commotion to ensure that Chuck saw her, she set the revolver down on the seat between them and returned her gaze out the windshield. It was a nice gesture that actually made him smile. A moment later they caught each other glancing and they both smiled.

A few miles farther down, Cindy broke the silence. "Are you originally from Madison?"

"Yeah, I grew up there."

"After everything ended, you were never tempted to leave?"

Before everyone died—before he knew better, his answer would have been quick and simple. It would have been an ecstatic 'You bet I have!' As it turned out his answer was equally as simple after it all ended. "No, it's my home. Besides it has everything I need as far as food, water and shelter goes. And I know you probably don't believe this, but being the only one there does have some advantages…I don't have to worry about some lunatic trying to burn me alive."

Cindy smiled and conceded his point with a nod. "I bet you used to be a cop."

"What makes you think that?"

"Back there, the way you snuck up on Justin and took him out." She tilted her head. "But you didn't kill him. And the way you approached me. It seemed like you had done that kind of thing before."

Chuck grinned. "No, I'm not a cop." He smiled to the point of laughing. "I own an antique store."

Chapter 28

Chuck and Cindy traded yawns the last hour of the drive. Finally at a little past two in the morning they pulled up in front of the Victorian in Madison. Cindy plopped down on the sofa in the parlor and was already asleep by the time Chuck got back with a blanket from the bedroom. He threw it over her and then hit the sack himself.

He woke earlier than normal the next day and decided to treat his guest to a special breakfast—his very own recipe that he affectionately referred to as 'egg slop'. It was a combination of instant eggs, powdered potatoes and imitation bacon bits all stirred together and cooked on his propane stove.

He was spooning it on the plates as Cindy walked in the kitchen and stretched. "What time is it?"

He glanced at his watch and was about to tell her when she started to laugh. The time of day was an invention of the past that had very little meaning in the present. There were no schedules to keep, jobs to get too or television shows to watch. "Get out of here," he smarted back with a grin as he set the plates down on the table. He brought two glasses of tang over from the counter and they sat down together. The anticipation was killing him as he glanced at the meal and then looked across the table at her. "Well…what do you think?"

She had a perplexed look on her face as she stared at the plate and asked, "What's it supposed to be?"

"Its egg slop…you know…eggs, potatoes, bacon and—"before he could finish, he remembered the cheese. In a matter of seconds he was peeling the metal lid off a can of cheese dip he retrieved from the cupboard. He scooped out a spoonful of the creamy, orange gel and plopped it in the middle of her egg slop the way one would top a dessert with whip cream.

She reared back. "You are kidding I hope?"

At first he thought she was joking, but as he quickly recognized the look on her face as real disgust, his rear sank back in the chair. He popped up and grabbed her plate. "Fine! Don't eat. I couldn't care less."

He was halfway to the garbage can when she blurted out, "Wait! Let me try it."

He held the plate over the trash can for a moment as he turned and looked at her.

"Really...let me try it."

He sucked on his gums in a moment of deliberation before finally walking back over and putting the plate in front of her. He sat down and set about watching her tentatively poke his pride and joy meal with her fork. Just as he was about to retrieve it again, she finally took a bite.

The first couple of chews were slow and cautious, but then the tension left her face and she dug her fork back in for a heartier bite. Two bites later she was really going at it—silently moaning her enjoyment after each swallow. As he watched her dig in, he pulled his plate closer to himself and positioned his arms around it. "My God woman—you eat like a pig!"

The comment didn't break her stride. She continued to shovel forkful after forkful into her mouth even as she started laughing. Food fell from her mouth as she coughed out, "Mister you sure can cook. I mean it may look like shit, but it's damn good."

Five minutes later Cindy pushed back from the table and stretched out in her chair while Chuck finished his plate. In between a bite, he asked, "You guys were eating up there weren't you?"

Cindy smiled and relaxed. "Yeah we ate, but nothing as flavorful as this. And I love food...always have." She pushed up in her chair and announced to the world, "I used to be so fat...Now look at me, I can tell where my tits end!" Like an explosion, she burst out laughing almost before she finished the sentence.

It caught Chuck off guard. He coughed out the spoonful of slop that was halfway down his throat and started laughing too. It was his first real release of tension in some time, and after a few seconds he was laughing so hard he started tearing up. Then his back began to quiver behind the laughter. Before long his hands joined in, and his lips started quivering. Without realizing it, he had gone full swing from laughter to sobbing, and for the life of him, he couldn't stop. He glanced over and saw the look of concern on her face.

As the sobs grew more emotional and less controllable, he got up and turned his back to her. He walked over and stood at the sink, still sobbing for no apparent reason. A quick peek over his shoulder confirmed that she was still at the table, eyes lowered to her lap and allowing him his space. He was at a loss for words to explain this sudden outbreak. Bobbing his head and crying, he turned back to her and said, "I'm sorry…just give me a few minutes…"

Later that day, he showed her where everything was in the main house and then introduced her to the carriage house out back. "This little baby is my generator."

"So that's what's been making that constant noise. I honestly don't know how you ever get any sleep."

"You get use to it," he replied as he pumped his shoulders. He pointed out the series of 55-gallon drums. "There's enough gas in these eight drums to keep the generator going non-stop for several weeks." It was stated as fact, although he actually had no idea. They continued over to the other side of the carriage house and he displayed the shelves loaded down with 12-volt batteries and propane tanks. "As you can see we're pretty well stocked."

Cindy gestured to the pile of copper tubing, steel tanks and screens in the corner. "What's this stuff for?"

"I was thinking about building a water purification system."

"You know how to do that?"

Chuck smiled and said, "Sure, the library's got a few books on it."

"I'm not keeping you from it am I?"

"No…no…I haven't done anything on it for a while," Chuck answered as he stared at the pile of junk. It was true—he hadn't done anything with it in quite a while. That got him wondering what he had been doing all winter and spring.

"If you want to tell me what to do, I'd be more than happy to help."

Without thinking about it, he reached over and put his hand on her shoulder. "I appreciate the offer, but—" They both looked at his hand on her shoulder at the same time. His weight shifted to his toes and as his face started to flush, he quickly pulled his hand back and said, "I'm sorry…I didn't mean to touch you."

Cindy shot him a queer look as she tried to understand. "You don't have to apologize for putting your hand on my shoulder." She took a step toward him and when that sent Chuck back a step in retreat, she sunk down heavy on her heels in a moment of disbelief.

As she looked up, the pain and resentment in her eyes slowly vanished into the distant look of a blank face. She had misinterpreted his action. Life had conditioned her to read what he did as prejudice. She thought he pulled away because of the color of her skin.

The truth was that for close to a year he hadn't felt the warmth of another living creature—let alone another person. To finally feel it again, stirred up a feeling in him that aside from his wife, he hadn't felt for a woman since his days in high school. He felt that same warmth surge through his chest that made his heart pound with renewed life. No, there wasn't any prejudice behind his retreat—it was guilt. He felt like he was being unfaithful to Becky.

Not knowing what else to do, he took a jerky step toward her and asked, "Would you like to walk through town with me?"

She held her ground and asked defiantly, "Why…what's the point in that?"

"I do it everyday. I go out to a different area and search around, see if there's anything I can use. Besides, I thought it might be nice to get a little fresh air."

He felt like he was being studied as she scanned him from head to foot and back again. Then without answering, she turned, and headed for the door. Right before going out, she called over her shoulder, "You coming?"

He joined her and together they walked out to the curb, and then took a left on Main Street to stay in the residential section. Neither said a word for the first three blocks. Chuck finally broke the silence when he pointed across the intersection and said, "We'll turn here and search the homes a few blocks in."

Cindy appeared a little tense as she kept her eyes on the houses across the street. "Don't all the remains freak you out?"

"No, there aren't any around here."

"What do you mean?"

"I took care of them." Cindy continued her questioning stare, so he explained, "I spent the first several weeks taking their bodies…" he motioned with his eyes and a nod of his head to the surrounding homes, "…down to the river. I got the idea when I saw other bodies floating down stream. I know it's not really a proper burial, but I thought it was better than nothing." As he finished the explanation, he was happy to see that she appeared to be taking down the wall that had sprung up between them back in the carriage house. She was letting her emotion show again. Her look was somewhat hard to decipher—it could have been respect, or it could have been curiosity. But when it came to her smile, it didn't really matter to him where it came from.

He led her along the sidewalk and into a house. She stood in the living room not sure of what to do, while he made a quick search of the cupboards in the kitchen. When he walked back into the living room, she asked, "Do you remember if you found the owners in here?"

"I'm not sure…" he paused and took a sweeping glance around the room for any signs that the owners had died there. "I think they were gone. I'd say about ten or fifteen percent of the folks left town as things started going to hell." He looked back at her and started nodding. "These guys were gone."

"You were looking for food in the kitchen?"

"Yeah, but they didn't have anything that was still good. Besides food and water, I'll look for clothes and furniture—things like that." As he answered, he got the sense that she had never done anything like this. "While you were up in Indy with Jason and those guys, didn't you ever go out searching for supplies?"

"Not really."

"What did you do for food and water…and lights and heat…" the rest of his question died into a whisper as he waited for an answer.

"We didn't have it like you have it here. I mean Jason sent out certain guys for food and water, but the girls…our job was to reward the guys. And we never had electricity…at least not that I know about. I'm not sure if he didn't know how to rig up a generator like you do, or if he just didn't want it, but our light came from torches and lanterns. " She shook her head, "And I'm astonished that you have running water…we didn't. It was a lot different. You look like you've been in that same house for quite a while. We kept on the move during the day. When night came we'd just find some hotel or house big enough to sleep in." She looked at him for understanding. "Your breakfast was the first hot meal I can remember eating since it all ended."

Until he heard that, he thought he understood how hard her life had been. But the hardship was more than simply living under the atrocious reign of a madman. It was also the daily struggle just to survive. "My guess is that you probably didn't have running water because the water company up in Indy needed pumps to generate the pressure. Down here the pressure is provided by gravity's pull on the water from the tower." He paused as he organized the rest of what she said and made sense of any implications. Then a smile suddenly broke across his face. "Did you have hot showers?"

Her mouth dropped open and she took a step toward him. "A hot shower!"

His smile grew. "I not only have running water—I have hot running water."

"Don't be messing with me!"

"I'm not…I didn't even think about mentioning it…figured it was no big deal. But yeah, you can take a hot shower as soon as we get back."

Cindy started giggling as she trailed him out, but before shutting the door behind her, she paused to look inside one last time. "Can you show me where you took them?"

"You mean the bodies…I took them to the boat ramp."

"Do you mind?"

"No problem," he replied with a shrug of his shoulders. They walked back across Main Street and as they stepped around a section of the sidewalk pushed up by the roots of a shade tree, Cindy caught her first glimpse of the river three blocks away.

They crossed River Street and headed north along the brick paved sidewalk that ran along the bank of the river. A few hundred feet up river, they walked down the boat ramp to a piece of driftwood, rocking along the edge of the water. "I brought them all here," he stated as he looked out to the middle of the river.

"Your wife too?"

He nodded as she took a stance next to him and then matched his gaze out to the river. After a moment of silence, he respectfully said, "We've got plenty of supplies, why don't we head on back and you can take that hot shower."

"You sure? I can wait."

"No…let's go on back."

Chapter 29

Chuck was surprised by how much more energetic he felt when he woke the next morning. Right out of bed he walked around to the parlor to check in on Cindy. When he saw her sleeping peacefully on the sofa, he smiled. He didn't know why at first, but as he continued to look at her it came to him. It was because he felt responsible for taking care of her. It was something he desperately needed. It made him feel good about himself, giving him a purpose for living.

That night they opened a bottle of wine to go with their dinner of macaroni and cheese. Halfway into it, he found himself sitting there watching her eat, captivated by the differences between how she and his wife handled the fork and chewed their food. As his thoughts drifted to how Becky would never look up from her plate until after she swallowed each bite, he smiled and watched Cindy take a sip of wine. "What was your family like?"

She rolled the wine around on her tongue and studied him. "What?"

After she swallowed, she covered her mouth and said, "Nothing… I'm just surprised. Most people don't talk about the past anymore."

"I understand if it's too personal," Chuck said, as he raised his hand in apology. "I was just wondering. I can only imagine how difficult this had to be for someone your age."

Cindy looked down at her plate but stopped short of taking her next bite of macaroni. "When I was younger…Bracey, my little brother…we used to fight all the time." She smiled as she thought back. "But it was amazing watching him grow up. He had just turned thirteen…" She took a bite, followed that up with a sip of wine, and while holding the next bite in front of her face, she continued, "I think he was the main reason I wanted to get into teaching. Mom always made me help him with his math and spelling as he came up through grade school." She paused and then smiled. "The way he looked at me when he finally understood how to multiply or sound out the spelling of a word was incredible. I saw so much pride in his eyes." She took her bite and nodded as she chewed. "Yeah...that was my little brother...that's why I wanted to be a teacher."

She had Chuck's full attention. "So your family was pretty close?"

"Yeah."

"Did your mom ever think about remarrying?"

"No...I don't think so. I think my dad was her one true love and that was all she needed. Besides, she always had me and Bracey."

"What about you. Did you have a boyfriend or anyone?"

"Yeah, Marshall and I started dating my junior year. We were pretty close...don't know if we would have gotten married. But we loved each other."

"How'd you two meet?"

Cindy paused and looked at him with a slight smile.

Chuck held out his hands. "I mean unless you don't want to talk about it. I'm just curious."

Cindy's smile broadened as she nodded. "No, its okay—but you really want to know?"

"Yeah, I'd like to hear about it."

They finished the bottle of wine as Cindy told him about how she and Marshall met and fell in love: from their first date through their last night together. From there she told him about the other guys she dated and about growing up in Indianapolis. She had just started talking about family get-togethers and Christmas celebrations when the wine and late hour of the night began to take their toll.

Chuck yawned as Cindy folded her arms on top of the table and laid her head down. He looked at her for a second and then reached over and shook her arm. "Hey...if you want to...instead of sleeping on the sofa, you can sleep with me." She opened her eyes and looked at him inquisitively. "I'm not talking about sex...just thought that it might be nice to know that someone is there with you. I've got a king—"

"I'd like that," she interrupted. "That would be nice."

Without saying another word, they got up and retrieved her pillow from the sofa and headed for the bedroom. Drunk and sleepy, neither hesitated as they undressed and climbed into the same bed.

~~~

The dogwoods and perennials came into bloom and then turned a solid green as the heat of summer set in. Each night they continued their pleasant dinner conversation and she told him a little more about her life. He seemed really interested in listening to her, but he hadn't told her anything yet about his life. It wasn't until the hottest part of the year that he finally opened up. That was when their supply of drinking water from the public tower went dry.

They were ready for it. Chuck had a 250-gallon plastic tank strapped to a flatbed for transporting water from one of the wells just outside of town. It was on their way back with their first load of sloshing water that Cindy observed, "You know in the long haul it might be easier if we move to the farm house."

Chuck shifted the flatbed into second as he turned on Main Street and shook his head. "I can't."

She watched him maintain his stare straight ahead. "Why not?"

After a second of thought he said, "Let's go for a short drive after we drop off the water…then you'll understand."

They parked the flatbed at the side of the house, jumped into his Chevy, and headed out again. Neither said anything until they were turning off Michigan. Chuck pointed across the street to a flowing field of grass and trees. "That used to be the golf course."

Halfway down the side street he stopped and put the truck in park. He got out and by the time she caught up to him, he was standing at the head of a cracked driveway and looking out over an overgrown lot between two fire-damaged homes. Without looking at her, he said, "This was our house."

As she matched his gaze of the weeds, she thought about asking what happened. But then he stirred and pointed. "My wife died right over there."

When she looked back at him, his eyes were red and his lower lip was beginning to tremble. Out of nowhere her lips started to tremble as well. With a pull on her heart, she slid her hand across his shoulder and said, "I'm here if you want to talk about it."

Chuck lowered his head and covered his eyes with his hand. "I was so mean to her," he confided, as he started shaking his head. "And the worst part is that I don't really know why. I loved her…more than anything else in the world." He pulled in a shaky breath. "Like the way you said your mom loved your dad. But I let us drift apart…I guess it was my pride. I don't know." He paused and rubbed his face as the redness continued to grow in his eyes. "The bug hit me first and put me down…she died while I was out of it. You know where she died?" he asked rhetorically. "She died down on the floor by my side, holding my hand."

Cindy slid her hand down to his waist, "I know…I know…"

He added, "For all she knew I was already dead. She could have gone someplace where she wouldn't have had to die alone, but she didn't—she stayed right by my side."

Cindy slid her other arm around him and pulled him closer. "Maybe in her mind she wasn't alone."

Tears were trickling down his cheeks as he wrapped his arms around her. By the time he mumbled, "I hope so," he was already crying.

She put her hand on the back of his head, and guided his face down to her shoulder as she also began to cry. While she comforted him, he told her about giving up hope and burning down his old house. As she rubbed his back he confided that the night he found her in Indianapolis, he had gone up there to die.

Silence filled the truck for most of the drive down Michigan. It wasn't the uncomfortable silence where you feel prompted to speak. This was the silence between two people that didn't need the verbal communication to maintain the bond. They were almost to Main Street before Chuck collected himself and said, "The house you and I are in… that was Becky's favorite house in town. It was the home she always dreamed about. That's why I moved there. I wanted it to be her home."

Cindy nodded. "I understand…we'll stay right here."

That was the start. With that hurdle out of the way, he started opening up to her and the relationship became more balanced. Frequently their excursions to find supplies turned into leisurely walks where their only finds were deeper understanding of one another. At first, they talked about the past. Chuck loved to compare their times in high school, and they would laugh about how things had changed from one generation to the next. She told him about her friends growing up and he told her about his adventures with Stan. As the days started getting shorter again, they began to talk about the future—their future.

Chapter 30

By the time the elm had gone through its leaves again, their water problem was solved. For a long as Chuck could remember, the city supplied the drinking water to the homes in town. So it never occurred to him to check the old Victorian for a well. Not that he would have known where to look if it had. But that was one of the side benefits to having searched all the country homes for wells—they learned their natural placement and where to look. One thing led to another and by the time they were on their second 250-gallon tank of water he was tearing up the wood floor in the back mud room. That's where he found the metal plate covering the old well. It hadn't been used in fifty years. Even so, when they dropped a garden hose down and hooked up a transfer pump—water came up. Of course the hardest part was that one of them had to taste it. After holding a glass of the well water between them for almost a minute, Chuck pinched his nose and tentatively took a swallow.

Finding a source of drinking water right there in the house fueled their ingenuity. Their very next project was a small windmill to pump water up to an elevated storage tank based on designs they found in the library. One windmill led to another and before long they had built four. The latter three were used to generate electricity. Those came just in time, as more and more of the stores of gasoline they depended on were beginning to take on the viscosity of varnish.

They retired to the parlor after dinner one chilly, autumn night and sat on the floor in front of the wood stove with a bottle of wine. Chuck was pouring their second glass when Cindy finally brought out what she had been hiding all night. With a grin matched only by the brightness of her eyes, she said, "Look what I found today," and pulled a five-inch, plastic bottle shaped like a bear out of her sweater pocket.

Chuck's mouth fell open as he leaned toward her with guarded enthusiasm. "Honey?"

"Yep!"

"Oh my Lord," drifted off his lips as he stared at the golden liquid showing through the clear plastic. After a hard swallow, he asked, "It wasn't covered in ants was it?"

"No. I couldn't believe it either," she answered as she handed it to him. "I had given up hope of ever tasting sugar or chocolate or anything like that again."

A second later Chuck was hurrying back from the kitchen after cutting the tip off.

"How is it?" she asked.

"Your find, you get the first try," he said as he handed it back to her.

She tilted her head back and squeezed the plastic bear as a thin, golden string dribbled down on her tongue. For the next ten seconds, Chuck heard moans and witnessed a slithering movement that he hadn't seen for some years. The sight and sounds of which were not without affect. When she brought her head back down and giggled, it took him a second to close his mouth.

Even though he was sure that she didn't mean it that way, when she looked at him and asked, "So…do you want some," it came across flirtatiously.

He gasped, "Oh…yeah," and held out his hand.

She was about to pass him the bear, but then pulled it back at the last second. "No…you'll squeeze it all into your mouth."

"No I won't."

She looked at him coyly, squeezed the bear across her finger, and laid a line of honey down on her skin. "Here…you can have this much."

He was unsure what she meant for a second. That is until she held her finger up to his mouth and he saw the line of honey glistening on the black skin of her finger. With her moans still lingering heavily in his thoughts, the line of honey only held his attention for a split second. His eyes quickly wandered from her finger to the smooth skin of her palm. Before his admiration could flow up her arm, she slowly started pulling her hand back. He met her eyes, and again he saw that she had misinterpreted his lack of action as having something to do with the color of her skin. "No, that's not it!" he spit out as he grabbed her hand.

She passively resisted before quickly giving in and allowing him to slide her finger into his mouth. For the sensual moment that followed, he battled to keep his natural instincts and arousal in check as his tongue shamefully took in the texture of her skin as much as the taste of the honey.

A long, delicious second later, she whipped her finger out of his mouth and said, "That's all we get tonight. I want this to last."

He licked his lips and smiled with the hope that she wouldn't suspect the true source of his enjoyment. After a pleasurable sigh, he turned back to the fire and finished his second glass of wine.

~~~

It was a colder winter than usual in Madison. The baseboard heaters and wood stoves were working overtime just to keep them from seeing their breath. There was a blanket of snow four inches deep outside and a layer of quilts almost as thick on the bed that night. He and Cindy had grown very comfortable with their sleeping arrangement. On more than one occasion, each woke to find themselves in the comfort of the other's warmth. Such was the case that night. They were sleeping peacefully until she gently nestled her rear against his crotch. The second such nudge caused him to swell. He woke and immediately rolled onto his back out of guilt.

She stirred again, and he thought she was going to follow his retreat and roll over next to him. But she didn't. Then a quiver rolled through her, and the fear that something might be wrong woke him completely. A few seconds later he heard her mumble something and then she quivered again. This time it was followed by a soft moan. Cindy was having an erotic dream. After a moment of mental debate, he gave in and started to lift up the quilts in hope of seeing her hips in action. As he did, the cold air in the room rushed in under the sheets and woke her up.

He closed his eyes and pretended to be asleep while she tossed and turned and continued to fidget under the blankets. He heard her quietly ease out of bed. A few seconds later he slowly opened his eyes as the door to the hallway bathroom shut.

It was winter, there was snow on the ground, and if anything was going to stir, he was going to hear it. He listened and imagined.

When she finally opened the bathroom door ten minutes later, he was about to explode. Somehow he managed to remain quiet and still as she climbed back in bed—definitely looking more relaxed than she had when she left. He swallowed and asked, "You okay?"

"Oh...yeah I'm fine...I'm sorry for waking you."

"No problem...I've got to use the bathroom too."

That night he had a strange but pleasant dream. Cindy was standing at the edge of a cliff of sheer white, rock that dropped a hundred feet straight down to the thundering crash of the swelling ocean. He didn't sense any fear or danger from her. Instead he felt a sense of pride as she gazed out across the ocean at the setting sun. Behind her a mixture of grass and stones rolled into a panoramic landscape of valleys and knolls.

The next morning a light pressure and nudge brought him out of his sleep. He opened his eyes and saw Cindy sitting on the edge of the bed next to him. After a quick stretch, he slid his hand over hers and said, "Good morning...what time is it?"

Already dressed, she smiled and said, "A little past eight. I wanted to let you sleep."

He expected her to get up, but she didn't. She continued to sit there with her hand on his chest, looking at him and smiling. Confused he asked, "What's going on?"

She rubbed his chest the way one might rub a dog's back and said, "I made you breakfast."

He popped up onto one elbow. "Really!"

She grinned and stood. "I do know how to cook you know." She started to walk out of the room, but midway to the door she turned back toward him and said with a warm smile, "You've always made me breakfast...this morning I wanted to make it for you."

As the bitter cold of winter continued its grip on Madison, they ventured out of the house less and less. One comfortable routine they had fallen into was reading together on the sofa in front of the wood stove. This was their personal time; time to be alone, lose their thoughts in a good story, and not worry about where they would find their next meal or gallon of good gasoline. Normally, they would each take a corner of the sofa and curl up under a quilt to enjoy their read. But one night when Chuck settled in before Cindy got there—things changed and an even more comfortable routine came into play. Cindy walked in with the romance novel that she started the day before, and instead of taking her corner, she slid under the quilt on his side and pressed her back up against him. Without realizing it or taking his attention from the horror novel he was reading, he simply repositioned himself to where his arm draped over her shoulder and his hand rested against her stomach. She slid her hand on top of his and they both continued reading.

Chapter 31

Jason stared into the darkness. Like a man on stage caught in the tight circle of a spotlight, he was blind to everything but himself. He spun around, only to find that darkness surrounded him. It progressed from the shadowed light of dusk just beyond his reach, to a solid curtain of pitch black less than fifteen feet away. Then he understood—there was nothing else, only him. He was alone. He was trapped with no way out. Panic started to mount as the sound of each heartbeat pounded in his head. There was something dreadful about this place!

His skin crawled as a chill slowly crept over from the darkness. From out of the black void, the outline of an object started to come into view. First there was a straight edge, then a sharp corner. He stretched out his neck and stared. It was a small box. As his focus adapted, he spotted another shadowed box underneath it, and then others around it. A few feet over something else started to come into view. At first it was simply cylindrical—then it was a small can. It set chest high in the dark, it was in a row of other cans.

More items came into view and he began to whimper. His breathing became more sporadic as he spun around and saw other items piled in similar columns around him. "No." This was the place that tormented him in his nightmares. "No!" It was where Leslie died. He stood helplessly in their center, while grocery aisles branched out from him in all directions like spokes of a wheel.

His jaws quivered as he sensed the presence finally coming to end his misery. He stared down the void of each aisle. One after another, he continued until he lost himself. Void upon void, the next looked the same as the last. He would never find it. Just as time started to lose meaning, he came to an abrupt stop and his heart jumped. Staring down the endless abyss of darkness, he could feel it…it was with him.

His weight shifted to his toes as he slowly reached out to welcome it. As his hand pushed through the darkness, he had the fearful sense that a mirror stood before him, and that behind the darkness, it was his own reflection reaching back for him. He caught his breath as he lost sight of his hand. The desire to end his pain pushed him further as he stretched out his fingers and turned his fear to a plea, "Please…stop me!"

No answer came. He bit down to silence the chatter of his teeth as the whimpers began to echo through his head again. In a desperate moment of need, he screamed, "No!" and lunged forward, leaving the light behind. As he did, he felt the dark presence retreat and pull the cold winds of death back with it.

Jason flinched and kicked out of instinct as he pushed the hand off his shoulder.

"Jason…you okay?" asked the burly man crouched over the bed in a low, raspy voice.

It took a second for Jason to clam down enough to recognize Mark. Once he had his bearings, he demanded in a defensive tone, "Yeah—what do you want?"

"I just heard you…" the man stumbled for a second to find the right words, "…it sounded like I better wake you."

"Well you have. Now get the fuck out of here!" Mark started to leave, but just as he got to the door, Jason barked out, "Did we find anyone today!"

"No sir—not today."

Jason glared at Mark before closing his eyes and pulling in a deep, calming breath. When he opened his eyes he addressed his first in command with more restraint. "Get the men out looking…scour over everything." After Mark left he started nodding as he mumbled to himself, "He's out there…I can feel him."

Chapter 32

Spring was the perfect time of year in Madison. Temperatures were extremely comfortable, the flowers were beginning to bloom and everything seemed cleaner than it did at any other time of year.

Their gasoline stores had degraded to the point that if they ran the generator continuously it would have required cleaning every other day. To minimize the gum and varnish buildup in the jets and filters, they limited generator use to the night when electrical demand was the greatest. During the day they depended solely on the electrical output from the windmills. But that wasn't really an inconvenience. In fact it turned out to have a truly wonderful unexpected benefit. Without the sound of their generator running, the town was so quiet and peaceful that if they stood and listened, they could hear the ripple of the Ohio River flowing along its banks four blocks away. Without the mechanical sounds of civilization, they could close their eyes, hold out their hands and imagine that they were standing in the middle of a field of waist high grass swaying under a gentle breeze. It was truly a peaceful state that reminded them that they were a part of something much bigger.

That same peace was echoed in the relaxed silence of their work. They could walk for blocks without feeling the awkwardness of not speaking. That's how it was late one afternoon after a nice rain. They were walking leisurely down Main, holding hands and smelling the clean, fresh air as they headed out in search of new clothes. Without breaking stride or the swing of their hands, Chuck led her over to the right side of the street. "We should check out Amacker's…they have a good selection of jeans."

Cindy voiced her agreement through a soft squeeze of his hand and a smile. Two buildings down they turned into the store with the fluid gracefulness of one person knowing exactly where he was going. Once inside they split as Cindy made her way to the ladies clothing scattered on the floor to the left, and Chuck went for the jeans interwoven with shattered glass, broken wood displays and tangled hangers to the right.

He was searching for his size in a pile of relaxed-fit Lees when Cindy called for him. She was back by the dressing rooms, standing in front of an unbroken, full length mirror mounted on the wall. She smiled and held out her hand. "Come on over here and stand with me." He complied and stepped over to her side. "What do you see?"

Chuck shot her a questioning glance, but when she pinched her brows and gave a slight nod toward their reflection, he looked back at the mirror. "I see an old...I mean I see a middle age man...standing with a young woman in front of a ransacked clothing store."

"Is that all you see?"

He looked at their reflection. He saw his hand in hers and looked up and saw her reflection smiling back at him. "I see two people who despite all odds have found the good that remains."

"You don't see a white man holding hands with a black woman?"

"I don't see you that way. I see you as a beautiful woman." He waited for her to return his smile before he said, "Tell me what you see."

As they turned back to the mirror, his anticipation was suddenly overwhelmed by the tension of seeing something different in the reflection. Something had changed. Something was there that wasn't there a moment ago. He continued to scan the mirror, but he wasn't looking at their reflection. He was searching for signs of movement in the reflection of the background behind them.

Cindy was unaware of what was going on as she started to say, "I see a man and a woman who are too afraid to admit that they—"

But then he saw it—the blink of an eye. In one flowing motion, he swung around and un-shouldered his rifle as he pulled Cindy behind him and chambered a round. "You," he yelled, "step out in the open!"

Cindy didn't question his action. She stopped mid-sentence and stood perfectly still behind him.

Chuck kept the rifle aimed at a pile of wooden display racks, broken glass and clothes heaped against the front counter of the store. In a loud, but controlled voice, he yelled, "I'm not going to say it again—step out in the open."

There was a crisp sound like glass snapping under the weight of someone's foot. A couple of packaged dress shirts slid off the pile.

Chuck readied himself. A moment later a young boy tentatively rose from behind the counter. With his hands held out to his sides, he slowly moved to a clearing in the aisle and pleaded, "Please don't shoot me!"

Chuck let the tension ease out as he lowered the rifle. "I won't shoot you if you don't move—deal?"

"You got it mister."

Cindy came around from behind Chuck. "Brandt…is that you?"

The boy searched his memory for a second and then asked, "Cindy?"

She pushed past Chuck, ran to the boy and threw her arms around him. Chuck eased his posture while he slung the rifle back over his shoulder. "I take it you two know each other."

Cindy turned back toward him with a smile larger than life. "This is Brandt…he was with Jason too." Chuck started to bring his rifle around again, but Cindy stopped him, "No…it's okay…he was like me. He wanted to get away."

Chuck slung the rifle back over his shoulder. "That right boy? Are you running from Jason?"

"Yes sir," the boy answered without hesitation.

"Anyone else with you…do we need to worry about finding others waiting for us outside?"

"No sir, I came down by myself."

Chuck walked over to the two. "We're a long way from Indy…I didn't hear any car. How'd you get down here?"

"Rode my bike, sir," Brandt answered, as Cindy started rubbing his shoulder.

"Rode your bike?" Chuck questioned as he squinted at the boy. "That's a long ride. Did you know Cindy was down here? And don't call me sir anymore…call me Chuck."

"No, we all thought that Cindy was dead. I'm glad to see we were wrong."

"So what brought you down here?"

"You…the ferryman…I wanted—"

Cindy cut him off and said, "It doesn't matter," as she pulled Brandt over to her side. "Main thing is that you weren't followed…right?"

"No one followed me. I left in the morning while everyone was still asleep. Besides, they wouldn't have missed me until it came time for scouting."

Chuck furrowed his brows. "How long did it take you to get down here?"

"It took me a couple of nights."

Chuck looked down his nose and studied the boy. "That's amazing." He watched him a few more seconds before he asked, "How old are you?" But the blank look on the boy's face told him that the boy didn't know for sure.

Cindy broke in with, "I think Brandt's in his early teens."

The boy squared his shoulders and spoke up with pride, "I've got crackers and a canteen of water in my back pack along with a map." He nodded to the front of the store. "They're around the side of the building. You know I'm not a kid. I can take care of myself."

Chuck reared back with both surprise and respect. "I'm sure you can." The boy's moxie took him back for a second. "How about a hot meal to temper down that spit and vinegar?" he asked with a grin, as he glanced at Cindy.

Chuck made spaghetti on the propane stove while Cindy and Brandt sat at the table talking. She spit out names and as the boy gazed around the kitchen, he would tell her if they were still alive. From what Chuck heard it sounded like two thirds of the people she knew were no longer living.

Chuck set three servings of hot spaghetti and three glasses of tea on the table, retrieved another folding chair, and joined them. As the boy shoveled the hot food in his mouth, Chuck asked, "So you wanted to get away from Jason?"

The boy barely glanced up from the plate as he answered between swallows. "Yeah...a few wanted to get away. But they were too scared to come with me. Told them I wasn't scared and that I was going."

"You weren't afraid that Jason would hunt you down?"

"Have to find me first, and he wouldn't look this way."

"Why do you say that?"

"Because you're down this way."

Cindy interrupted, "Let the boy eat his meal." She avoided Chuck's gaze.

After a moment of thought, Chuck said, "Okay...then why don't you tell me. What's the boy talking about?"

Cindy laid her fork down on the table and slowly shook her head. She had the look of someone about to say something that they wished they didn't have to. "It's just a bunch of bullshit—"

"Well if it's bullshit—then there's no reason not to tell me."

Cindy stared at her plate and said, "Jason tells everyone that the south is off limits. He calls you the ferryman, you know from mythology. The ferryman is the tormented soul whose eternal task is to ferry the dead across the river Styx to Hades."

Chuck pulled back as he tried to understand what mythology had to do with him.

"One of Jason's scouts saw you down here." She paused and when no reprise came, she reluctantly continued, "He saw you taking the dead to the river and setting them adrift."

Chuck didn't know what to say or how to respond. He suddenly felt violated. His one time of innocence and open vulnerability, the one time when he tried to do what he thought was right, now seemed ugly and perverse. With his mouth open and the look of remembering something painful, he asked, "How long—"

"He was up on the hill with binoculars. He said that he camped out and watched you for days on end. He said you never stopped—not even to eat or sleep." She gave him a moment to absorb what he just heard, and then she finished with, "Jason tells everyone that you're the walking dead, and that your job is to take care of all the sinners who died."

Chuck stared at her for several seconds. Then he asked, "You knew about this when I found you?"

"I didn't know it was you, not until you told me that we were going to Madison. Then I figured it out."

"Why didn't you tell me?"

"Why would I? It's just a stupid story that Jason uses to help keep people under control."

"What do you mean?"

"You're the boogeyman story that he tells the children. He tells them that if they don't do what he says, that the ferryman will come for them and take them back to eternal hell."

Brandt stopped eating long enough to pipe in with, "I didn't believe it. I know there's no such thing as the boogeyman. That's why I wasn't scared."

Chuck forced a smile before looking back at Cindy. "Is there anything else?"

"Mike, that's the scout who saw you, well he saw you a couple of other times too. I don't know if Jason told him to go back and watch you or not but he did. I don't know when, but he said that he searched your house."

"That's impossible."

Cindy lowered her eyes again. "Mike told everyone that he set off a stick of dynamite outside of town and that you took off on your motorcycle. Do you remember that?" She looked up at him, but when he didn't answer she continued. "He told Jason that you were still living the old way, you know, electricity and stuff like that."

Chuck had a blank look on his face. "Were there any other times?"

"Only one other time he told us about. He said he watched you burn down your house."

Brandt added enthusiastically, "Jason also says that it was you who took..." he paused for a moment as he tested his memory, "...I don't remember her name but she was an old woman. Jason says that you took her soul back to Hades before he could cleanse it."

Chuck dropped his head as his entire body began to tingle. Brandt was talking about the woman tied to the car that he shot. The woman that he made the promise to—the promise to kill Jason.

Cindy came around the table and squatted next to Chuck. Then as she slid her arms around him and rested her head against his arm, she softly said, "I'm so sorry."

For a long minute the only sound in the kitchen was Brandt scraping his plate clean and slurping down his tea. The boy then broke the silence, "Are you going to help the others get away?"

Chuck asked the boy, "You mean the others staying up there with Jason?"

"Them too...but there's still others hiding in the city."

Cindy nodded as Chuck glanced at her. "That's what Jason does. He hunts down survivors and then gives them the choice of either joining him or burning. I think he's looking for someone."

Chuck lowered his eyes for a second and asked the boy, "You think we should help them?"

"Of course...why wouldn't we?"

Chuck lost himself in thought, before asking, "Would you like to take a hot shower?"

The boy's eyes lit up. "Are you kidding!"

"Take your plate over to the sink...then I'll show you the bathroom."

A few minutes later Chuck rejoined Cindy at the kitchen table. She reached over and slid her hand on top of his. "I think we should go up for the others. You know Jason treats the children like slaves and pimps out the women to keep the men in line."

Chuck didn't know how to respond. "I feel bad for them…but you know we don't have enough supplies. If we try to save everyone, we could all end up starving. To be truthful, I don't know if we even have enough for that boy to stay with us."

"We can't just leave them up there."

Chuck stared at her in silence for several seconds. Trying to understand where she was coming from, he cocked his head and asked, "Is it the boy? Is he making you feel guilty or something?"

Cindy's mouth dropped open. "Why would you say that?"

"It's just that you've never mentioned wanting to save anyone else until now. I know this boy makes you feel like you have an obligation… but believe me, you don't."

She pressed up against the table. "It's not the boy and it's not guilt. I've always wanted to go back and try to help the others."

He didn't say a word.

"Besides…what if it is…does that make it wrong? You saw him. You saw how starved he was. We have so much and they don't have anything. How can we live with ourselves if we don't try?"

Chuck settled into his chair. "Now let me get this straight. You're saying that you're willing to share your food with someone you don't even know?"

"Yeah…if it means saving the life of some poor kid, I'll share my food. You would too. And don't tell me you wouldn't because you did with me. You didn't know me yet you brought me in and shared your food and bed with me. You gave Brandt food and a hot shower…and I'll tell you that means a hell of a lot to that kid." While Chuck reflected on what she said, she ended with, "We can do it. We can make a difference."

Chuck sighed again as he settled further into his seat. "Well, I guess that water won't be an issue—"

"And we can plant more crops and expand our search for food," she quickly added.

"What about electricity, heat and gasoline; what if we don't have enough."

She squeezed his hand. "You'll figure something out, I know you will. And I'll be right beside you to help. Besides, anybody who wants to stay with us will have to work too. We're not offering a free ride—only a chance at something better."

Chuck rubbed the back of her hand with his thumb. "What if Jason finds out…you know…off limits or not, I'm sure we'll have that crazy fucker to deal with."

"Well, we won't take them all at once. If we take just a few at a time…maybe he'll think that they just ran off."

He pondered the concept. After a moment he tested the sound of what he was thinking, "Okay," he glanced in the direction of the shower, "if we're going to do this…let's get started. We'll leave Brandt here and go up and take a look around tomorrow." As he began to work over the strategy of how they would do it in his mind, she squeezed his hand and he knew that they were doing the right thing.

That night he had the dream of Cindy standing strong at the edge of the cliff again. Only this time he felt more a part of it. He could feel the tension in her muscles as she held her stance against the misty chill blowing in off the ocean.

Chapter 33

Chuck dropped his breakfast plate off at the sink. Without saying a word, he grabbed a baseball bat out of the hall closet and walked out the front door. Cindy and Brandt were still eating and didn't give his actions much thought until they heard the front door close.

Chuck was already at the pickup and preparing for the first swing when Cindy yelled, "What are you doing?"

He noticed Brandt pushing between her and the door. The boy jumped off the porch like he was chasing an ice cream truck and pulled up to watch halfway down the stone walkway. Something about little boys and tearing up stuff—they can smell it coming for miles. Brandt was no exception. Chuck shot him a devilish grin as he shifted his weight. "If we're going to go up to Indy…we need to blend in." With a grunt, he brought the hickory bat down across the hood of his old Chevy as hard as he could. A dull clang echoed through the street as the sheet metal gave in and bowed under the force of the blow.

Cindy yelled, "Wait a second!" and ran out to the street. "What do you think you're doing?"

Chuck leaned against the truck while shouldering the bat. "I'm going to give the old girl some good dents, shatter the windshield, spray some graffiti on it and then torch part of it."

Cindy wasn't as quick to jump on board as Brandt. She shook her head and raised her shoulders. "I don't understand?"

Chuck looked his Chevy over. "You know how cars look up there. They've been abused and abandoned. The truck needs to look just like them, like it belongs up there. We need to blend in. That'll go just as far to saving our hides as any gun will."

She thought…and nodded. "You're right. Is there anything I can do?"

He stepped away from the truck and raised the bat over his head.

"Why don't you get a gallon of gas from the carriage house and find a blanket or something that we can use to put the fire out with." He grunted again and threw his weight into denting the left front fender.

Brandt stopped him before his next swing. "You're crazy, aren't you mister?"

Chuck teased the boy by raising his eyebrows and pretending to ponder the question for a second. "Sometimes I wonder about that very question myself."

~~~

They parked the Chevy among the derelict cars a few blocks inside the bypass around Indianapolis and proceeded on foot. Chuck kept them close to the buildings and out of the streets as they pushed slowly into downtown. The fact that it was eerily quiet heightened their tension. They knew the slightest miscue could give away their position.

Half an hour in, he showed her through a broken entry door and guided her to the shadows at the rear of the building. In a soft whisper he asked, "Now you're confident that if you see someone you know, you'll be able to get them to come to us without giving us away?"

"I think so…"

"You sure? We can always turn back if you want to."

She squeezed his hand.

"Okay…okay…just stay behind me and keep quiet. We'll head up to where I found you."

He saw her nod through the dark. They left the building as quietly as they came in.

Chuck came to an abrupt stop two blocks up and quickly, and calmly, pressed himself and Cindy up against the brick face of the building. He put his finger to his lips and motioned for her to be quiet. For over five minutes they were one with the wall. Cindy found an object to focus on while she concentrated on breathing calmly.

When he finally took his hand off her stomach, he gave her a quick nod for her effort and they started moving again. As they crept past the broken brick façade two buildings down, he discreetly grabbed a piece of mortar about the size of a golf ball. With it clenched in his fist, they made it one more block before he stopped again and pressed up against the wall. This time he whispered, "We're being followed."

Cindy stayed calm as she mouthed, "Where?"

Chuck slowly motioned across the street to a spot a half a block back. He whispered again. "Only one I think…been with us for the last three blocks."

She slowly turned her head and looked to where he indicated. There was a rusted out car and a pile of rubbish along the corner of a building where the brick had broken free. "I don't see anybody."

"Left side of the brick pile next to the pipe sticking up. Keep looking. You'll see him when he moves."

She located the pipes and splintered wood protruding from one of the brick piles. About three minutes later she spotted the eyes staring at them through the pile of rubbish when they blinked. She squeezed Chuck's hand.

He asked, "Can you tell who he is?"

"No."

"Get ready. Keep your eyes on him and be ready to run if we have to." He put his hand on her stomach and held her there as he turned his eyes from the stalker and slowly edged along the building again. Then he quickly spun around and fired the chunk of mortar at the pile of rubble. The stalker shot off running as soon as Chuck spun around. He hurdled over two piles of brick, slid across the hood of a burnt out car and disappeared among the buildings a block ahead of them. It happened so fast they barely got a chance to see him. Chuck spun to Cindy and pressed her back up against the storefront. "Did you recognize him?"

"I don't know…he moved so fast. But I don't think so."

Chuck grimaced as he thought of the blown opportunity.

"What do you think he was doing?"

"He was just watching, probably trying to get a feel for whether we were friends or enemies."

"What do we do now?"

"We're going to show him that we're friends." She gave him an uneasy look; he nodded and mouthed that it would be alright as he unshouldered his rifle. He scanned the street in both directions and quietly stepped over to the curb, laying the rifle on the road a few feet out from the sidewalk. When he was done, he retraced his steps back to her side, and they both stood and waited while holding each other's hand.

Their palms were getting sweaty and their backs beginning to cramp when Cindy gave in and asked, "How long are we going to wait?"

He scanned the area again. "I'm sure he's watching us…just a few more minutes." Chuck wanted to give it every chance he could, but he also didn't like the thought of being so far away from his rifle. Not that he felt they were in any danger from the stalker. Whoever it was seemed to be more curious than harmful. Based on how fast the man sprinted through the debris, he could have charged the two of them before Chuck could have drawn his rifle. No...the figure was only checking them out. But Jason and his followers were a different matter. Even though he and Cindy hadn't heard any sounds of riot, gunfire or squealing tires, that didn't mean that Jason and his mob weren't out there, ready to speed down the street at any second. The thought of that happening made him mighty uneasy about being so far away from his rifle.

The tension kept mounting until Chuck bit down on his lip and finally shook his head. "That's it," he gasped softly. He saw the relief in her face as he let go of her hand and quietly stepped away from the storefront. He reached down and picked up his rifle. As he started to turn around, he froze with his body half-twisted. The stalker was standing in the shadows right behind Cindy, holding a three-foot section of steel pipe and quietly slapping it down into his open palm. Only a cracked plate glass window stood between them. Somehow the stalker had gotten behind them and found a back entrance to the store.

As soon as Cindy saw Chuck's face, she started trembling. Chuck forced himself to think quickly as he stared eye-to-eye with the young man. Cindy wouldn't hold still much longer. The twitches in her face made her look on the verge of exploding. He could yell at her to move and swing the rifle around and probably get off a shot before the young man could react. That was what his instincts were telling him to do.

But they weren't there to kill anyone. He forced down a swallow. He slowly bent over and laid the rifle on the sidewalk while maintaining his stare on the young man. Cindy closed her eyes and started shaking as Chuck backed up without their protection. By the time his weight was back on his heels the man behind the glass had moved to the door. Chuck flinched at his instinct to grab the gun. He didn't and in a matter of seconds the man was on the sidewalk with them.

That's when Chuck got his first clear look. The young man stood without a shirt, wearing only jeans and tennis shoes as he kept the steel pipe reared back past his long, black hair. He was lean and sinewy, with the tanned skin of someone always in the sun. Although he probably wasn't much more than a boy, he had the strong facial features of a man.

His brown eyes were clear and focused, and set within a long face that carried a strong jaw line and a sharp-ridged nose. The boy's chest rose as he demanded, "Who are you?"

Chuck held his ground, and quickly glanced at Cindy to make sure she was okay before he answered. "We've come here to offer a safe place to stay for those who want it."

"Then what's with the rifle?"

Chuck thought before answering. Was he sure this young man wasn't part of Jason's mob? He could be a scout. Chuck glanced back at Cindy. Her shoulders were pulled forward and her arms pinched close to her sides out of fear, nonetheless she was still observing the man. It didn't look like she thought he was part of Jason's gang. Chucked cleared his throat and said, "To protect ourselves."

The young man pumped his chin and prompted, "From who?"

"From Jason and the mob that follows him."

The young man continued to stare at him like he was sizing him up—getting a feel for whether Chuck was telling the truth or not.

Chuck added, "Jason ties people to cars and then sets them on fire."

The young man looked down and swallowed. "I don't believe in what Jason preaches." He looked over at Cindy cowering against the window and asked, "What's your story?"

Cindy had trouble voicing a response through the tension in her face, but managed to sputter out, "Like he says…we want to help."

The man turned back to Chuck and, with the pipe still reared back, he walked over to within arms reach and stood face-to-face with him. Chuck held his ground and onto his hope that the young man didn't mean any harm. A second later the man slowly kneeled down while keeping his eyes on him, and picked up the rifle. He rose back up just as slowly. He then did the unexpected—he handed the rifle back to Chuck. As surprising as that was, he topped it a moment later when he turned his back and walked halfway over to the front of the store. He stopped, dropped the pipe and just stood there with his back to Chuck.

Chuck opened up his arms as Cindy ran over to him. They both understood what the man was doing. He was tired of hiding and was giving his trust to them. Still they needed a moment to themselves. Chuck cradled her face against his chest and breathed a sigh of relief. After she nodded that she was okay, he shouldered the rifle and then walked over to the man. "I'm Chuck Bain…she's Cindy McKay…and we are here to help."

The young man let out his own sigh of relief as he dropped his shoulders. "Thank God…" He swallowed and while struggling to force a smile, he said, "I'm Andy Jones."

Chuck offered his hand and said, "Nice to meet you Andy. How long have you been here?"

Cindy joined them as Andy said, "Since it happened…I was a senior at Chatard one day…next day I was alone."

She asked, "You know about Jason?"

Andy stopped her with his hand. "Let's get out of the open." After all three disappeared into the shadowed safety of the store, Andy said, "Yeah…I know who you're talking about." He dropped his head and stared at the floor. "I've seen what that son-of-a-bitch does. What they all do." He filled his chest with fresh air. "Where's the place you're talking about…place where we'll all be safe?"

"We'll take you there if you want to go." Chuck wasn't going to disclose the location until they were on the road—just in case.

"Hey I can't live like this any longer. If you're offering, I'm accepting."

"Good!" Chuck said as he started to make his way back to the door.

"Aren't you guys going to look for any others?"

Chuck looked over at Cindy. It was easy to tell that she had taken all she could for one day. "Not today," he answered. "I think we've had enough excitement for now. We'll see how things go…then maybe. But I'm not making any promises."

Andy strutted after them and said, "I hope we do! I can't think of anything I'd like more than saving some kids from that mother-fucker."

A moment later they slipped out of the store and worked their way back toward the truck. As Andy brought up the rear he asked, "Hey… how'd you see me?"

Chuck motioned with his head, "Back there…"

"Yeah."

"You moved."

"No I didn't"

"Yes…you did…enough for me to see you."

"How?"

"Years of hunting…staring at the bush…waiting for a deer to flinch and give away its position."

"Is that something you can teach me?"

"Sure. And maybe you can show me how you got around us without being seen…that was really something. There's probably a lot we can learn from each other."

A few minutes later Chuck heard Andy ask, "You're him aren't you…the one they call the ferryman?"

He ignored the question and kept moving.

Chapter 34

Each morning after breakfast Andy would ask Chuck if they were going back to look for more survivors. After the first few days it became more of an urging than asking. Brandt quickly jumped onboard and added his own pleas. Cindy got hers in at night after they went to bed. At the darkness as he started to fall asleep, it was the last thing Cindy asked him. Their pleas didn't fall on deaf ears, though Chuck thought it best to see how they adapted to the additional demands on their food and water supply before jumping into any rash decisions. If someone up there needed saving today, they would surely still need saving in a few weeks. But after five straight days of hearing it from everyone, Chuck finally gave in. He and Andy drove to Indianapolis.

They found Teresa and her younger brother Robby that first trip. She was in her last year of elementary school when it happened, and since then she had been taking care of her little brother as best she could.

Andy spotted the pair scavenging for food a few blocks inside the loop. They didn't want to scare the children, so they trailed them on foot back to an apartment building a few blocks farther in. Once they had the right apartment, it took them nearly an hour to convince the girl to unlock the door to the only home she had ever known. When she finally let them in—it was hard to believe that the two kids had survived. The remains of their mother and father were still in the bedroom where they died in each other's arms. That room looked untouched, but the remainder of the unit was in a shambles. Food wrappers, covered with ants and roaches were discarded about the place. The floors and walls were soiled. Planted right in the middle of it all, like a small oasis surrounded with trash and human waste, was a tent the children made by pushing two couches close together and draping a sleeping bag over the gap. That's where they had slept since the End—in a pile of sleeping bags, quilts and blankets.

Chuck scooped up the scared little girl and was shocked by how light she felt in his arms. Her eyes were set in deep, dark sockets and when he raised her torn shirt he could see every rib. He closed his eyes and dropped to the sofa while she weakly clutched to the life he offered. His lips were trembling and his eyes watering when Andy walked over with the boy in his arms and asked, "Chuck…you okay?"

Chuck raised his head and saw the small helpless boy resting in Andy's arms. He swallowed hard and mumbled, "These poor children…I can't imagine…" The back of his throat started to swell. "…I can't believe they survived all by themselves."

"Well…I don't think they would have made it through the summer," Andy said, as he instinctively bounced the boy in his arms while he lost himself in thought. Then he shook it off and said, "And I can't believe that Jason never found out about them."

Cindy watched the father come out in Chuck during the days that followed. She witnessed a softer side in him that until then, he had only shown to her. She saw the smile on his face as he watched the kids wolf down their first real meals since the End. That first night after she finished the dishes, she was on her way to read with Chuck in the parlor, when she heard the children giggling. She peaked around the corner and saw Chuck leaning against the wall next to the bathroom door at the end of the hall. He was listening to the playful sounds of Teresa and Robby in the shower. She couldn't help but match his smile as she whispered, "What are you doing?"

He raised a finger to keep her quiet and then whispered back, "Come here…you've gotta listen to them laugh."

~~~

The next morning before they got started on their chores, Chuck asked Cindy to sit with him on the porch swing and watch the children play with Brandt in the yard. She could feel his warmth as he watched with the wonderment of a child. Every once in a while he would nudge her and point to the children as one of them did something cute. It didn't matter if it were Teresa, Robby or Brandt. He found joy in each of them.

Cindy didn't mean to stare, but she couldn't pull her eyes from

Chuck. In fact she spent more time looking at him than she did watching the children. As her stomach filled with butterflies, she wanted to kiss him and tell him that she was in love with him. He made her feel safe. He made her feel loved. She had spent many nights imagining what it would be like to feel the heat of his body as they made love. She wanted to tell him. She reached up and caressed his face.

He turned to her with a warm smile. "Yeah?"

She bit her lip as she stared into his eyes. After a long second, she watched the children and said, "It's wonderful to see such life isn't it."

He turned back to the kids and said with a sense of fulfillment, "Oh yeah…it sure is." He squeezed her and added, "I'm so glad we went back. It feels good…it feels like we did the right thing." A smile of appreciation spread across his face. "Thank you."

"For what?"

"For pushing me."

She smiled and watched the ongoing display of joy and life with equal enthusiasm as she rested her head against his shoulder.

~~~

After Chuck was confident that Teresa and Robby would be okay, he and Andy headed north to search for others. This time he didn't need any urging. He wanted to go. Brandt wanted to go too, but Chuck told him that he had to stay and look out for the women and young Robby. Brandt took his appointed job seriously and helped Cindy with the more physical chores while still doing his own. He even found the time to show Teresa and Robby how to do the chores Cindy handed down to them.

It shouldn't have been a surprise to anyone how quickly the bonds started forming. When you take individuals who have endured the kind of isolation they had for that long of time, and then suddenly throw them back into any resemblance of community or family, their psychological needs quickly led them to establish bonds similar to those that were lost. The effect was readily evident in the children within the first two days. The way they followed Brandt around and how they jumped on Chuck's lap after they finished playing. Chuck recognized what was happening because he felt it too. Brandt and the kids were starting to feel like his children, Andy like a younger brother, and Cindy—well, she had captured his heart long ago.

Chuck and Andy worked the second trip differently from the first. Instead of parking and both proceeding on foot, Chuck remained in the truck and slowly trailed Andy as he scouted the area a few blocks ahead. In that fashion, Andy provided the eyes for finding those who wished to remain hidden, Chuck maintained the means for a quick get away, and together they would listen for any noises that could indicate trouble. As they cautiously made their way along the street, Chuck kept observing Andy. He watched the young man in total amazement. Andy always appeared calm and cool. He stayed close to the buildings and kept his movements precise and deliberate. Even more compelling was the courage and confidence the young man had in himself. But what Chuck truly respected was the unending compassion the young man showed for others.

Andy signaled that it was safe to proceed. As Chuck watched him return to his methodical advance of the street, he knew that he was looking at a natural born leader. Before him was a man who others would follow. Including himself.

Andy suddenly stopped, threw his right hand up and made a fist. Chuck killed the engine and ducked to where he could barely see over the dash as Andy dropped behind the cover of a derelict car. A second later he heard the low exhaust rumble of an approaching vehicle. Suddenly a blue pickup shot out from the cross street two blocks up. Chuck saw a blur of blue metal and sparks as the truck's undercarriage bounced off the rise in the middle of the intersection. No sooner was it gone than a Monte Carlo shot through in hot pursuit.

They waited for the echoes to fade out before Andy stood back up and waved him on. That night they arrived back in Madison safe, but empty handed.

They found Bill hiding on the roof of an eastside convenience store the next trip. He was a divorced businessman from Cincinnati. When the End was imminent, he had tried to make it to Terre Haute to see his ex-wife and grown children one last time. He never got the chance. The bug caught up to him just outside Indianapolis and he crashed into the guardrail on I-74.

Bill wasn't the most agile survivor they found, but he also didn't back down when something needed to be done. The following weeks went by and two more trips netted Jim Sinclair and Sara Jennings.

Chuck and Andy were about to head back up for another search when Brandt ran up to the Chevy and panted, "One of the windmills is making a grinding noise!"

They jumped out and followed him over to the side of the house. It was one of the power generation windmills.

"What is it?"

Chuck pulled a lever and the grinding noise stopped.

"Did you fix it?"

Chuck bent over and started inspecting the gears and shaft. "No, I just uncoupled the drive." He stood up and addressed Andy. "We're going to have to put off Indy today."

"No," Andy said with a shake of his head. "You stay here and fix this and I'll go up."

"Not by yourself—you won't!"

Andy thought for a second. "What about Bill? I think he wants to go."

"You sure?"

"Yeah…I think he feels that he needs to…you know, to make things right."

Chuck bought a few seconds by opening the cover to the windmill's gear assembly and pretended to assess the damage. "Alright…you go on up with Bill." As he started toward the carriage house to grab some tools, he looked back at Andy and yelled, "But take it easy…play it safe up there."

From that point on Bill made the runs with Andy instead of Chuck. That left Chuck to keep things running at home. But he didn't stop with mechanical issues. He realized the need to train folk so that if something ever happened to him, they would know what to do.

He also knew that he wasn't the only one that brought value to the table. With that in mind, his first task was to find out what the others were good at. Some were mechanically gifted. They could teach others how to maintain and rebuild the group's vehicles, and work on new ways to generate electricity and purify water. Others were better with nature. He put their expertise to work in planting crops and maintaining the properties. Still others were best with people. He felt they were the most valuable resource of all. Their job was to teach the young and explain why they couldn't give up—why they had to go on. Once he understood and structured the exercise of one's competency for the benefit of all, he made sure that everyone started to be cross-trained.

By the time the searing heat of mid-summer arrived, they had outgrown the old Victorian and were boarding new arrivals in the houses on both sides of it. They took down the wrought iron fences that divided the lots and before long the three adjacent houses took on the flavor of a small community. As their numbers continued to grow, so did the foot traffic and play of the children. Within weeks the grass was run to bare dirt. But that didn't matter. What they were striving for was more functional than aesthetic. They dug a large fire pit roughly one foot deep by ten feet in diameter in the front yard between the main house and its neighbor to the west. The pit was an instant hit with everyone and quickly led to a group campfire each night where they would discuss the day and any issues that arose. That also happened to be the perfect time to formally introduce new survivors to the rest of the group. It was the one meeting that Chuck thought too important for anyone to miss, not just because of the introductions, but because it gave everyone a chance to keep in touch with what was going on outside of Madison.

Andy and the new arrivals would describe what they saw and how things were changing to the north. Through it all, they were beginning to realize that the few souls that lived through the End were drawn to the cities like moths to light. In some cases it made perfect sense. The canned and freeze-dried food found in the city meant living for another day. In other instances there was no apparent thought given to it. People simply found themselves migrating to the cities. Unfortunately, based on the stories passed from one survivor to the next, it didn't sound like venturing to the cities was the best idea. It appeared that Jason wasn't unique in his behavior. There were similar mobs in Chicago and rumors of violence in most of the other major cities. Not that all violence was spawned by the same ideology as Jason's. Some people were just scared. Lashing out was one way of overcoming that fear. Others were simply driven crazy by the massive loss of life and the isolation that followed. But then there were those like Jason, who by all accounts tied the pending extinction of mankind to God's biblical wrath. Jason kept his followers in line by stating that he was the right hand of God. He told them that if he wasn't doing God's will—then someone would have stepped up and stopped him. In either case the best path to surviving in the city was for you to keep to yourself. But with that said, some would wonder what was the point of living.

One afternoon while making their rounds, Chuck and Cindy stopped at the library to see how the children were doing with their reading assignments. It was a routine born out of necessity. They usually found at least one child sleeping, playing or reading something outside their assignment. That day was no different. Kyle was reading on the floor with his back to a bookshelf and noticed Chuck and Cindy as soon as they eased the door open. He glanced up from the manual on gasoline engines as Chuck smiled and motioned for him to keep quiet. Julie and Cathy were busy reading at one table, but Teresa—she was another story. She was at a table over by the windows looking through a magazine. Chuck smiled and motioned for Cindy to stay by the door while he quietly walked over behind Teresa. She was scanning through the worn pages of Vogue when he appeared at her side and said, "Hi."

She was the keepsake image of childhood guilt as she looked up. "Hi Chuck."

There were a few giggles and smiles from the younger children, but they came from the playful innocence of a child and weren't meant to cause Teresa any embarrassment. Even so, they quickly stopped when Chuck glanced up from the table.

He knelt down next to her and pulled the magazine over in front of him. After thumbing through a few pages he came to a full-page advertisement showing a model enamored with the delicious taste of a diet candy bar. "She's pretty, isn't she?"

Teresa scooted over next to Chuck for a better look. "She's beautiful."

He pulled back and glanced at Teresa with a smile. "To tell you the truth though…I can't take my eyes off that candy bar…can you?"

She grinned, "No…it looks awfully good." Her expression quickly changed and asked, "Am I in trouble?"

"Why do you ask that?"

"I'm supposed to be reading about first aid."

Chuck puckered his lips and nodded for a few seconds like he was thinking. "Why do you think you should be reading about first aid?"

"In case somebody gets hurt, I'll know what to do."

"But don't we have other folks that would know what to do?"

"Yes…but if they get hurt then the rest of us have to know how to take care of them."

Chuck nodded. "You know you're a pretty smart girl."

They smiled at each other and then she asked, "Do I have to go get the book I'm supposed to read right now?"

He rubbed the back of her head and said, "It can wait a few minutes if you want to finish the magazine first."

She smiled with excitement and said, "Thanks Chuck!"

He started to stand up, then stopped. "Everything else okay… you're happy aren't you?"

"I wish my mommy and daddy were here…that would make it best. I miss them…but I have Robby and you…" she looked over at Cindy standing by the door, "…and Cindy. We don't ever want to go back home."

Chuck leaned over and gave her a kiss on her forehead before standing up. He pumped his brows once as he shot a glance over to Cindy. She walked over with a smile and slid her arm around him. Then together they walked around and checked on the others.

As they were heading back down Main toward the house, Jim Sinclair yelled from the middle of the street two blocks over and waved them down. It was his day to work the crops planted in the vacant lots down along the river. He was covered in dirt and sweat, wearing only a hat and a pair of ripped, blue jean shorts to go with his work boots. They were about to wave when Sara Jennings came storming out of the field and stopped in a mad huff at Jim's side. She was dressed in similar fashion to Jim, with a T-shirt covering her top. With a sigh of both humor and frustration, Chuck looked at Cindy, took her hand and said, "Here we go again."

Jim stood his ground and waited for them to get close enough to hear without yelling. While Sara nervously tapped her foot on the ground he said, "You guys have got to find me somebody else to work with."

Cindy spoke first, "Why's that?"

"Look at what—"

Sara interrupted, "My work is every bit as good—"

"No way…look at it…it looks like shit!" Jim shot back at Sara.

Chuck observed Jim as he expressed his frustration. What he saw was that even though Jim was complaining about Sara's work in the field, he never took his eyes off the sweat soaked T-shirt clinging to her front. "Hold on…is this really something you guys want us to decide?" Before they had a chance to answer, he pointed at Sara and said, "Come on over here for a second." When she walked up, he turned around and continued with her a few more yards. Then with his arm around her and his back to Jim, he said, "You know what's got him all riled up don't you?"

"He says my work sucks!"

Chuck smiled and said, "You do good work."

"Then what is it?"

He grinned and said coyly, "You really don't know?"

She criss-crossed her hands to indicate she had no idea.

"Sara…you're a young woman…a beautiful young woman…" he continued, even though he could tell she was starting to understand, "your top." She lowered her head and then raised her eyebrows as she saw what he was talking about. "I might be wrong, but I think Jim is acting like an ass because he likes you, and seeing you like this is really hard on him…if you know what I mean."

She glanced over her shoulder at Jim. "You really think so?"

"That's my guess." He squeezed her shoulder and said, "Now, I can break you two up if that's what you want, or, if you like, I can tell Jim that my hands are tied and that I can't do anything with the schedules for a couple of weeks. That way if you want to see—"

"Let's do that…okay?"

He nodded and they walked back to where Jim and Cindy were talking about crop yields. "I'm sorry Jim." He looked at Cindy and when she nodded, he couldn't help but crack a slight smile. "I can't do anything with the work schedules until next week at the earliest. Until then, you guys are going to have to work it out on your own."

Jim tried to raise an objection, but Chuck stopped him with a hand and said, "That's it, you two are adults. Work it out." Before either could say another word, Chuck took Cindy's hand and led her toward Main Street. Once they were out of hearing distance, Chuck said, "You know it's so obvious to us what's going on. I can't believe that neither of them has picked up on the chemistry they share."

Cindy met his eyes with a queer look. "I know, it's truly unbelievable."

When they got back to the main house, Cindy followed him to the small wooden platform at the foot of the porch. Brandt built the platform and mounted a bell on top of a post next to it so that whenever Chuck wanted to address everyone he could do it properly. At that moment, it wasn't being used to address the others. It was simply a good place for he and Cindy to take a quick break and look out over what they had created before they went back to work.

Appearing before them was a vast, vacant, stretch of dirt yard. The grass might have been gone, but that didn't mean they were lacking in other areas. Windmills now numbered eight, two for each of the additional houses to go with the four for the main house. The other houses were plumbed into the well in the main house. They had one crude, wood-fired boiler to heat water for hot showers in a new shack outside the main house. Each day everyone had the opportunity to take a hot shower in the main house. Probably most important of all, was the fire pit with the scattering of lawn chairs and comfortable logs standing on end around it.

What they didn't see was any one of the other thirteen people who helped them build it. But that was as expected. Andy and Bill were in Indianapolis looking for other survivors. Hopefully, Robby wasn't getting too much of an eyeful as he helped Jim and Sara with the crops. The day's schedule had Mike helping Brandt with vehicle maintenance. The children were reading in the library, and Jeff was helping Lori with her household chores. In fact he and Cindy were the only two not doing anything at that very moment—a matter quickly solved. Chuck smiled as he squeezed her hand and said, "Time to search for supplies."

That night everyone gathered around the fire pit for the formal introduction of the new arrival that Andy and Bill found earlier that day. Most had already met him, but the fire pit was a standing tradition. Brandt and Mike had a nice fire going. Not so big as to be too hot for that time of year, but big enough that it made for good atmosphere in the dark of night. Chuck and Cindy walked over with a man in his mid-twenties and joined the assembly at the fire pit. While Cindy sat down, Chuck put a hand on the man's shoulder and said, "Now I'm sure that most of you met Mike before supper. Some of you probably knew Mike even before that." Chuck glanced around the fire and nodded as he called out names. "Jeff, Julie...Brandt and Cindy...you all probably remember Mike Cameron as one of Jason's scouts." There was a murmur around the fire and a few soft greetings as the group continued to listen. Chuck looked at Mike as he held him at arm's length by the shoulder. "Mike and I, we sort of met a couple of times ourselves. Mike is the scout who saw me long ago and gave birth to that crap about the ferryman." He gave Mike a nod and let go of his shoulder.

Mike rubbed his chin and stepped forward as he addressed the group. "As Chuck said I'm Mike Cameron and until just a couple of days ago I was still running with Jason."

Cathy Ferguson voiced her skepticism. "What made you decide to leave?"

Mike cocked his head once to the side as he swallowed, and said, "Well…I'd been meaning to leave for quite a while. I didn't believe in Jason's bullshit any more than the rest of you…but as some of you know…you just don't get up and tell Jason you're leaving."

"So why now?" Jim Sinclair questioned.

"Well…I'd been noticing that people were suddenly disappearing. Sometimes it was somebody from the tribe…and sometimes it was somebody that I'd seen in the city. But it always seemed to happen four or five days apart." He opened up his hands and gestured. "Pretty simple to figure out that someone was coming in and taking them. Didn't know for sure that it was Chuck or that you guys had a good size camp down here. But figured that whoever it was they couldn't be any worse than Jason. So over the last three weeks or so, I'd tell Jason that I was going out scouting. But what I was really doing was looking for you guys. Today I lucked out and Andy," he paused to find where Andy was sitting, then looked at him and smiled, "well…I'm glad he found me."

Chuck stepped back up next to Mike. "Well guys…what do you say? Do we welcome Mike into the group?"

Andy spoke up. "What do you say Chuck?"

Chuck said, "I know every time we offer sanctuary to someone that ran with Jason, it feels kind of scary. That's only natural. But you look at those I named earlier and to the last one, we're all better off by their presence here tonight. We all need to remember that the problem up in Indy is pretty much the cause of one man. Many of those up there are just doing what they have to do to stay alive. Mike and I talked over supper and for what it's worth…I think he's sincere about wanting to be free of that life."

Cindy immediately voiced her support of Chuck's opinion. "I say let him stay."

Chuck started making eye contact with each person sitting around the fire as they nodded their agreement.

Lori Wilson, the oldest woman in the camp said, "Chuck, you've given me a life with hope. I didn't know if I…" She stopped herself as she started to get emotional. "I say let him stay."

"Thanks!" Chuck said with an appreciative nod before looking on to the next person.

When he got to young Mike Donaldson, the teenage boy said, "We'll have two Mikes. How are you going to tell us apart?"

"Well, we can call you little Mike—for now I mean. A couple of years and we'll have to find another way to distinguish you two because you'll probably be bigger than him."

Little Mike smiled as Chuck continued on through the rest of the folks sitting around the fire. "I guess its unanimous then," he said, as he offered his hand to the man standing next to him. "Welcome to Madison." They shook hands and then Chuck offered Mike one of the logs standing on end. They sat down and joined the others around the fire. "Why don't you tell us how things are going up in Indy?"

Mike stared at the flames and confided, "They're not very good. Food and water are pretty damn scarce and they don't have any electricity like you guys. The only good thing I can say is that Jason isn't killing as often as he used to."

Someone asked, "How many people are with Jason now?"

Mike let out a big sigh as he thought for a second. "Must be about thirty. But it's not really growing any more. He hasn't found any other survivors in the city for at least three or four weeks. I think that's why he's kind of mellowed out on killing—replacements are getting scarce." He took on a dead serious look as he added, "And don't think that rescuing people every week hasn't been noticed. If he figures out that it's..." his sentence died off as he pictured the unthinkable.

One of the younger boys asked, "Why is Jason the way he is? Why can't he live in peace like we do?"

Chuck saw the uncertainty on Mike's face and spoke up. "That's Kyle Thomson."

Mike nodded and smiled. "I don't know, Kyle. But I'd say he's just crazy. Somehow he's convinced that what happened is God's way of dealing with the damned. Hell...you know."

Sara asked, "But who's the damned? Those who died or those who lived?"

Chuck broke in before Mike could answer. "That's enough of that. We're not going to make this into something that it's not. God had nothing to do with what happened."

Julie McAllister stared into the fire and added, "I remember one night up there, a bunch of us started talking about what happened. I don't know why this guy said it or how he knew, but he said that right before we lost everyone…that some scientists were on TV talking about how they might have been wrong about what killed the dinosaurs."

Chuck saw Cathy Ferguson lower her head. Jim Sinclair did likewise. They were beginning to relate what Julie said to the extinction of the human race.

"Okay!" Chuck said loud enough to get everyone's attention as he stood up. "Let's not get too concerned about what might have happened way back when…or even what happened to our world. That's the past, nothing we can do to change it, so let's just let it be. The important thing for you to keep in mind is that the world didn't end…life continues on." He looked around the group and tried to instill as much confidence as he could. "Look at us! We're still living. I promise you that life will go on. We may not have the details yet—but believe me it will."

"But why…why did we live?" Brandt asked from across the fire.

Chuck replied, "Before the End they were talking about a genetic defect in some people. My guess is that's why we made it."

"If we all have this defect, then how come none of our babies are living?" Sara asked.

There was a lengthy silence until Chuck spoke up. "Someday… one of you will spot a bird flying overhead…or see a fish swimming in the water. Or maybe it will be a squirrel or a chipmunk or something. Animals that we all thought we'd never see again—we'll be surprised. And take my word for it—just as we'll see that, sooner or later we'll also hear about a baby living. That's the day we're all working for. That's the day that brings us the fruit of our hope." He stood there and looked around the fire until he was sure they weren't giving up. He got Andy's attention. "Go ahead and lead the discussions about the day and let everyone know their work assignments for tomorrow." He waited to make sure that everyone was participating in the discussion before he and Cindy headed back to the main house. It was vital to the survival of the group that they not dwell on Sara's question. Yet that very question was still on his mind when he shed his clothes and climbed into bed.

That night his recurring dream took on a new aspect. Cindy no longer stood alone at the edge of the cliff. A young boy was holding her hand and pointing over the ocean waters to the sun setting on the horizon. Chuck could still feel the chill and push of the ocean breeze, but now there was more to smell than simply the ocean. He could smell the grass and flowers, and something else that he couldn't quite put his finger on. It was a fresh, woodsy aroma. In fact it was so pure and exhilarating that when he woke the next morning the lingering memory left him in particularly high spirits.

Chapter 35

Two nights later Andy and Mike Cameron caught up to Chuck and Cindy as they were walking up the steps to the porch after the nightly meeting around the fire pit. "Chuck! Can we talk to you for a minute?"

"Sure...come on up and have a seat."

Andy and Mike picked out a comfortable spot along the railing while Cindy and Chuck took the swing.

Andy said, "Mike wants to go with me tomorrow."

Chuck looked at Mike. "You sure about that...you've only been here a few days. Are you that anxious to go back up there and put your life on the line?"

"No, not really. But I know what it's like to live in fear under Jason. I still have friends up there living with that fear and I can't turn my back on them." He then looked for understanding in Chuck before he finished with, "Let me go."

Chuck turned to the others for their read on the situation. Cindy dipped her head and raised her shoulders. She was on the fence. Andy gave a nod of approval for letting him go. When Chuck looked back at Mike, he could see the sincerity in his eyes. He raised his shoulders and said, "Alright...you can take Bill's place tomorrow."

Andy quickly responded, "Actually we'd like to take two trucks."

Chuck straightened himself in the seat. "What?"

"Since Jason is getting suspicious about people disappearing, we thought that we'd go up one last time and use two search trucks to make a quick sweep of the city. We'll find as many as we can and then call it quits."

Initially, Chuck reared back at the thought of something so brazen, but as he let the idea set in, he became a little more comfortable with it. "Who else would you take?"

"Jim Sinclair has been itching for the chance," Andy answered. "I thought I could scout with him in one truck, and Mike could go out with Bill in another."

Chuck leaned back in the swing and gave it a slight push as he rubbed his tongue over the front of his teeth and considered the proposition. "You're sure about this?"

"Yeah…let's do it."

"You know Jason will be out for blood after something like this."

"Nothing new in that!" Mike stated.

"You don't think this will bring him down here?"

Mike replied, "He's suspicious. He believes someone is gathering the people, but no one has mentioned you or Madison beyond the scope of that stupid boogieman story. So I'm pretty sure that he believes it's someone up there doing it."

Chuck stopped the swing and bent over to where he was resting with his forearms on his thighs. While staring at the weathered wood planks of the porch floor, he said, "Okay…Tomorrow night at the pit, after we introduce whoever you find…we'll tell everyone that we've decided not to chance taking any more trips up to Indy." He nodded to himself as he thought over what he just said. "Okay…keep it fast and safe."

~~~

Cindy and Sara were busy in the kitchen preparing supper for everyone after a full day of chores. Kyle and Julie were lined up in the hallway outside the bathroom waiting their turn for a hot shower. Teresa, Robby and Brandt were playing tag around the fire pit in the front yard. And Chuck was resting on the porch swing, one Chapter further into the romance novel he started a week ago, when the sound of squealing tires jerked him out of his seat. He jumped off the porch and made it to the sidewalk in time to see the Chevy fishtailing as it cleared the turn off Michigan. It was Andy and Jim coming back from Indianapolis. There was someone else in the cab with them, but finding another survivor wouldn't make Andy drive that way. Nothing positive was ever expressed like that.

Chuck threw his hand up like a mechanic on a pit crew waving a driver in as Andy locked up the brakes. The truck skidded along the curb and Andy shot out the door before the truck even finished rocking from the sudden stop. "They got them!" he panted, as he ran up and grabbed Chuck by the arms.

Chuck glanced down the street for the other truck, and then pulled Andy in front of him. "Bill and Mike?"

Andy nodded vehemently as he tried to wet his lips.

Cindy stepped out on the porch while the others ran toward the truck to see what the commotion was about. Chuck walked Andy farther into the street to where the Chevy fell between them and the gathering crowd. He put his arm over his shoulder like a father consoling his son and asked, "What happened?"

Andy swallowed and said, "We picked up Jamie." He glanced over his shoulder at the man standing with Jim. As the tears began to roll down his cheeks and drip off his trembling lips, he gasped, "And we were on our way to find Bill and Mike..." He stopped abruptly and looked away as the emotions became too much for him.

Chuck rubbed his back. "It's okay, they knew it was dangerous."

Andy faced him again as the tears silently ran down his face. "It was my fault. I never should have let them go."

"You didn't let them go—I did. You guys asked me remember. And I misjudged the danger—not you. I'm so sorry...I just thank God that you and Jim made it back. Now tell me exactly what you saw."

Andy was still shaking as he said, "I was out in front of the Chevy, heading in their direction when we heard the shots." He paused and stared at the cracks in the asphalt fingering out from under his right foot as he took a deep breath. "We were going to make a run toward the sound but then heard the trucks coming our way. I never saw Mike—he was scouting on foot—but Bill...the Dodge shot through the intersection a couple blocks up from us." He started shaking his head as he said, "The mother fuckers were hot on his ass. A car and a truck, loaded with guys—and they all had rifles. We waited for a while..." Andy's thoughts drifted as he started shaking his head again. "I should have gone after him. But instead I ran to the truck and we shot back here like a bunch of pussies."

"I doubt we'd be talking right now if you had chased after him. As hard as it may be to understand, you did the right thing. I've seen you in action, and believe me there's not a soul here that would ever consider you a pussy. You're the bravest man among us—bar none." He squeezed the back of Andy's neck. "You were thinking of Jim and the new guy, you were thinking about their safety. That's why you didn't chase after Bill—you didn't want to gamble with someone else's life."

"If I did the right thing then why does it hurt so much?"

"I know…I know. Putting others before yourself is what makes you such a great leader."

"You're our leader!"

Chuck swallowed hard. No one had actually ever come out and said it like that. "Maybe now I am…but you will be. And they'll follow you. It's a grave responsibility that sometimes will force you to make difficult decisions. Like today. But you have to know that what you did was best for the entire group."

"How's that?"

"Well consider what you told me. It sounds like Jason was waiting on you—expecting someone to make a rescue attempt."

Andy's face took on a sense of calm as he listened. A moment later he made the connection. His pupils constricted as he voiced his thoughts out loud. "You mean it was an ambush!"

"Yeah, basically. Remember Mike said he thought Jason was starting to suspect something."

Andy nodded, "Yeah…it all happened so fast…I didn't hear any cars before the gun shots…it was like they were hiding and waiting on us to show."

Chuck suddenly let go of Andy's neck and took a step back from the situation. He needed to think. His original intentions were simply to relieve any guilt that Andy might have—but it was beginning to look like they might have a much bigger problem than just Andy's guilt. They could be in real trouble. He looked over his shoulder at the crowd waiting with Jim and Jamie on the other side of the truck. They needed to know. "Come with me," he said, as he led Andy around the truck and through the crowd toward the main house. He left Andy at the foot of the porch while he stepped up on the platform

Cindy walked over and stood silently by his side as he started ringing the bell. As soon as they were sure that everyone was there, Chuck raised his hands to quiet the crowd. "Folks…how's everyone doing today?" He paused as several looked up with questions on their face. "Take a look around," and swept his hand in a display of the dirt yards in front of the three houses. "Six months ago this part of the street looked just like any other abandoned section—no sign of life, no sign of hope. But you came down here and changed all that. Think about all you've done in such a short amount of time. Most of you have tilled the soil and planted crops. Most of you have picked up a wrench and worked on an engine—some of you can even rebuild one now. You've all learned what it takes to generate electricity and where to find good water." There were nods of pride in the crowd. "You've learned how to do all of this in a very short time. That's a lot of change. And even more impressive is that you've done all of it in a group setting." He paused and held his hands out in recognition of everyone. "And still you managed to get along. There have been no fights, no ridicule or harassment. You guys have gotten along and in some cases, have done more than just gotten along." He looked at Sara standing hand-in-hand with Jim. "That's something to be proud of, something to base our hope on."

He squeezed Cindy's hand as he continued with what he was preparing the group to hear. "Now we MAY have one more challenge." He paused until he had everyone's attention. "As you know only one truck came back from the run today, and I don't think the other truck is coming back."

"What about Mr. Campbell and the fellow that just joined us?" Lori Wilson asked.

"Bill was last seen running from some of Jason's men. And Mike Cameron, well we don't rightly know. Gun shots were heard though."

A soft mumble of shock started in the crowd that quickly grew into a fury of fear, remorse and revenge. Chuck raised his hands again. "Folks! Folks! Let me finish. I feel the loss as much as any of you do and I take full responsibility for it. Mike had told us that Jason was starting to wonder what was going on; well it appears that he might have anticipated the run up there today."

"What exactly are you saying Chuck?" Sara asked.

"I'm saying that we may have one last challenge to overcome." He paused and looked in Cindy's eyes. It was there that he found the strength to continue. "Let me start off by saying that we're not going to make any more runs for survivors, at least not to Indy. I think we have to be prepared for the possibility that Jason knows we're down here. I mean…I would expect that Jason will try to find out where Bill and Mike came from and if there are any others."

Kyle asked, "What do you mean, 'try to find out?'"

Chuck shook his head. He didn't want to have to say it out loud.

Andy helped him out. "We mean that Jason may torture them if they're still alive."

"I've seen him torture people," Julie McAllister said with a numb look. "And I pray that I never see anything like that again."

Chuck broke in before the speculation got out of control. "So! We need to be prepared to defend ourselves. We can do it," Chuck said as he tried to muster confidence with a nod.

Jim asked, "What about going up there and hitting first, gain the element of surprise?"

After a moment of consideration, Chuck said, "Not a bad tactic, but no. That's the kind of behavior that we're trying to stay away from. Defend ourselves—yes, but go up there and murder others, no, that's not the way. Besides, we don't know for sure if they even know we're down here. And if they do we don't know for sure that they'll attack."

"Sorry."

"Don't be. It was a good idea and it shows that you're thinking. Now all we have to do is turn that mind of yours around into figuring out how best to defend ourselves."

Jim smiled and nodded. "Will do, Chuck!"

Chuck looked at the new man standing next to the platform and offered his hand. Jamie took it and joined Cindy and him on the platform. "Everyone, this is Jamie…"

"Jamie Ross," the man finished.

"Can you add anything to the situation?" Chuck asked.

"Well, I think you're right about them waiting on you guys. Andy pulled me out of there. I was part of Jason's tribe, had been since around the start of summer. He didn't trust me too much yet so I can't say for sure, but the last couple of weeks he seemed to be talking a lot with Mark and a few of the other guys. Jason's got this small group of guys that he keeps close to him at all times. Mark leads them and is like Jason's right hand man. He's a real big, mean son-of-a-bitch. But anyway…they'd all been doing a lot of whispering lately, like they were planning something."

Chuck interrupted, "How many of them are hard core followers? How many will do what he tells them to do without question?"

Jamie pumped his shoulders once. "I don't know…twenty maybe. But there are at least four in his tribe that we don't have to worry about.

That is unless there's a gun to their heads. They're friends of mine. Like me, Jason found them and they had no choice. It was join his tribe or burn."

Cindy and a few of the others indicated they knew what Jamie was talking about.

"Anything else?" Chuck asked.

"Yeah. Based on what Andy and Jim told me about this place, and from looking at all of you, you look healthier and better prepared to fight than they are. But that doesn't mean you don't have anything to worry about. Those guys up there are mean mother-fuckers. You guys have electricity and wells and...I mean look around, you guys are actually living. They don't have any of that shit. Jason has them held up in the old Radisson on Ohio Street. No electricity or running water... very little food. They see by torch light at night and most are on the verge of starvation." Jamie paused to look at Chuck and then around at the others. "In a fair fight—hand to hand—you guys would win. But that's not the way Jason does things. He works his men up to a boil and then turns them loose. Christ, I've seen them nearly rip a man apart with their bare hands. You guys...I mean we...we need to be ready in case they do come down."

Chuck slapped Jamie on the back and told him thanks as he sent him back to stand with the others. Chuck started to talk but stopped when he saw the desperation on the faces of those looking to him for reassurance. He had seen that look before in individuals, but never collectively in the entire group. To see it like that—stole his thoughts.

A silence settled over the group as the sun continued its descent to the west. Sara and Lori's flocks caught the sunlight and burned a brilliant red, as did Robby's, while they stood and waited for Chuck's wisdom. Chuck's gaze diffused as he started to think about the dream of Cindy and the boy at the edge of the cliff. Within it, he found the strength and confidence to face everyone and say, "Okay...there we have it. You all eat a good supper tonight and while you rest and wait for the start of tomorrow, I want each of you to think about what we can do to defend ourselves. It needs to be something that we can live with, that we don't have to worry about the children getting hurt on, but at the same time will make Jason and his men think twice about continuing on. We'll get together around the pit tomorrow after everyone's had a chance to eat breakfast. Normal chores are put on hold until we figure out what we're going to do. Any questions?"

Cathy Ferguson asked, "Are you scared, Chuck?"

Chuck knew how delicate the question was as a few nervous laughs broke out. "Yeah, I am a little scared. That's only natural in a situation like this. But when I look out and see all of you, when I think about what we've done and what we're capable of, then I'm not so scared anymore." He gave a reassuring smile and finished with, "We're going to be okay. You know what I mean?"

Cathy smiled and nodded.

"Anything else?" Chuck gave them a few seconds and then said, "Alright. Everyone eat a good supper and get a good night sleep. We'll talk tomorrow. Oh, and by the way, the hot shower is still open."

That night he and Cindy lay awake in bed. Partly because of what the day brought, but also because of how warm the temperature remained well into the night. The windows were open and a gentle breeze was blowing through, but any movement brought trickles of sweat. The only comfortable position was sprawled out on their backs on top of the sheets.

Cindy whispered, "Do you really think we'll be okay?"

He found her forearm and gave it a gentle squeeze. "Yeah, we're going to be alright."

He heard the sounds of her rolling onto her side and then felt her breath against the side of his face. "You're always so confident and calm."

It was too dark to see her, but he could sense her lips within inches of his. "I get a lot of that confidence from you."

Then he felt the smooth warmth of her thigh slide up and across his midsection as she asked, "What do you mean you get it from me?"

"I see it in you…there's a—" Cindy cut him off as she pressed her lips to his and slipped her tongue into his mouth. Even though this was something that he had thought about for a long time, he did nothing at first. There was still Becky to think about. How could he cheat on her? But the night he heard Cindy in the bathroom came rushing back to him. That was all it took. He slid his fingers down her back. That night was a sweaty one—their first.

Chapter 36

The harsh sting of smelling salts brought Mike Cameron back into the conscious world. The shock snapped his head like a whip and drove him back against a hard surface. That split second of tension gave him the illusion of having some control over his body. Then it passed just as abruptly and he turned to dead weight. As he started to slump forward, something coarse snagged his wrists and jerked him to a stop with a painful grunt. He rolled his head to the right and after a moment of grogginess, he saw his hand tied to the front pillar of a car. After a wince, he checked his left and saw it tied to the frame of the rear door. He was bound to a car with his hands out to the sides.

He rolled his head back to the front as a man walking away slowly came into focus. He then saw the others, including some he recognized, milling around the street. His look for familiar faces stopped when he saw the man sitting in the leather wingback chair directly across the street, slowly nodding and staring at him. It was Jason. He sat like a self-proclaimed King in his royal leather chair on the sidewalk—completely out of place in all minds except his own.

Mike felt the pain and swelling of the various bruises all over his body as he tested the strength of the rope. He could remember being surrounded and then rushed. He remembered the Dodge and Bill. That's when he saw the unconscious man tied to another car twenty feet to his right. It was Bill.

"Mike…Mike…You disappoint me," Jason said, as he stood and strolled over. "I always thought of you as my second in command after Mark. And here I find you running with this man, trying to take the very people that we're trying to save—right out from under my nose."

"You're not trying to save anyone!" Mike spit out as Jason came to within arm's reach.

Jason shook his head as he leaned against the car to whisper in

Mike's ear. "You're right. I really don't give a shit about any of these people. I'm going to make them suffer and then kill every last one of them unless someone stops me." He pulled back and took a moment to study each individual feature of Mike's face. When he finally settled on Mike's eyes he dipped his head and whispered, "Is it you? Are you the one that will stop me?"

Mike tensed up. "You're fucking crazy! If you're going to kill me, then kill me."

Jason stepped back and glanced over his shoulder as if someone were behind him. Then with a grin that would make the devil back down, he looked over at Bill before returning his gaze to Mike. "Plenty of time for that. First I want to know where the others are."

"What makes you think there are any others?"

"Simple. Unless you have the ability to be in more than one place at one time," he motioned with his head toward Bill, "then someone else was helping that man find survivors." He paused for a moment and looked at Mike like he was admiring him. "Come now, you know what I'm capable of, you know I won't hesitate to do something really delicious to you." He grinned and added, "Or perhaps to your friend over there. Shall I take my time with him?"

Mike looked past Jason to the others who were watching. Some were friends, but when he made eye contact with them they quickly looked away. They were scared—too scared to help, and he understood the reason for their lack of action. "There is no one else. The guy was just lucky to be able to do it before I hooked up with him."

Jason's grin grew and then he bit his lower lip. "Good. I'm glad you've chosen to do it this way." He swung around and put his back to Mike as he yelled across the street. He told them to get Mark. Then a second later he yelled, "And have him bring a saw."

"What are you doing, Jason? I told you there is no one else."

Jason looked at him with a stare that stole his breath. It was the look of someone beyond insanity—the look of someone who recognizes no life other than his own. "True enough, he could have been lucky before you came along. But then what happened to all those people he found? Did they just disappear?"

Mike started to panic as he watched Mark running down the street toward them. "Jason!"

Jason stepped back over toward him.

"He let the people go! They left for the safety of the country, up toward Pendleton I think."

Jason smiled and nodded. He didn't care if Mike was telling the truth or not.

Chapter 37

Chuck saw the jagged white face of the cliff and heard the thundering boom of the ocean crashing against the rock a hundred feet below. He saw the grasses in the knolls and valleys sway and roll like green waves as the chill of the ocean breeze pushed across them. He saw the boulders that spotted the land as if they were pebbles dropped from the hand of God. In the distant horizon the sun was setting over the ocean. What he didn't see was Cindy or the boy.

Chuck woke with a sudden flinch, and then immediately pulled out from under Cindy's arm as he sat up on the edge of the bed.

The sudden movement brought her upright. She clutched his arm and gasped, "Is it Jason…Is he here?"

He patted the back of her hand and whispered, "No. We're okay."

Cindy blew out a sigh of relief as she slumped back to the comfort of the mattress.

Chuck remained on the edge of the bed. He stared at the early morning display of light outside the window and organized his thoughts. Before Cindy could fall back asleep, he asked, "I'm guessing that as a teacher you're probably pretty good with geography."

Cindy struggled with the question as she propped herself back up on one elbow. "It's not my strongest subject, but yeah."

Chuck pictured the landscape of his dream. "It's a place on the ocean with rocky cliffs, white rocky cliffs. There are green rolling hills next to the cliffs with lots of rocks and boulders everywhere." Deep down he knew the answer himself, but he wanted the additional confirmation that came from Cindy.

"Could be Scotland or Ireland."

Chuck smiled. "I think I know why we lived and the others didn't!"

"Why?"

He jumped up. "We've got to wake the others!" As he scrambled to throw his clothes on, he said, "I can't believe it. It's been staring me in the face the entire time."

"What?"

"A reason to keep hope alive. Get up and get dressed. I want everyone to hear it at the same time."

Cindy jumped out of bed and started throwing her clothes on as if her life depended on it, almost falling to the floor as she tried to drive her foot through the leg of her shorts. It was a panic, the kind of urgent rush associated with being late for an appointment.

Chuck started clanging the bell on the platform as fast as he could.

Andy was the first to show. He slung himself out of the house next door while balancing the hunting rifle that Chuck gave him in one hand and trying to pull on his left shoe with the other. He tripped going down the steps and lost the rifle just as he hit the dirt. One dusty roll later his athleticism brought him back under control. He snapped the rifle off the ground as he sprang to his feet and then sprinted over to Chuck. "Where are they?" he panted.

Chuck raised his hands and said, "Its okay, it's not Jason. I have news for everyone."

Andy bent over and grabbed his knees while Chuck signaled for the others to stay calm. With the initial fear that they were under attack quenched, everyone proceeded to gather around the platform in an orderly fashion. As their numbers began to grow, so did their curiosity about what was going on.

Chuck raised his hands and the murmur of questions and concern died out. First off he said, "Jason and his men are not attacking." He followed that with a smile that couldn't be contained any longer, "I think I know why we survived. The genetic defect that the scientists talked about." He looked across their faces as a sudden hush fell across the fourteen souls gathered around him.

Cindy stood with the others around the platform, but there was no look of curiosity on her face, only a smile. A smile meant to convey more than just excitement over what he was about to say. Last night she told him that she loved him. He held her and kissed her, but hadn't told her what should have been said—that he loved her too.

Chuck glanced over at Lori and Kyle with an eye of discovery. He found Sara standing with Jim Sinclair, and down in front he saw young Robby—held still by his sister who was standing behind him. There were four redheads in a group of fifteen. He looked at the others. Brandt Watson, Julie McAllister, little Mike Donaldson, Cathy Ferguson and the rest. His grin kept growing. Finally he said, "This is really important…so I want you to think before you answer. How many of you know where your ancestors came from?"

A few raised their hands right off. Others were slower to respond, but after a couple of seconds almost a third of the hands were showing.

Chuck held his hands out and then spread them apart. "I want you guys to separate—hands in the air to the left, others to the right."

Jeff Neilson asked, "What is it Chuck? What are you looking for?"

"You guys still remember when everyone was dying, after the first one pulled through the doctors speculated that it was because of some genetic defect the woman had." He saw a few nods in the crowd. "I remember the comparison they used to explain it. They talked about how people in some part of Africa had this genetic defect in their blood that caused Sickle-Cell Anemia, but that the same defect also made them less susceptible to malaria. What if we lived because of something like that?"

The crowd started looking around at one another. Chuck pointed to the group on the left, "Where'd your ancestors come from?"

The new arrival Jamie Ross, spoke up first, "My father always claimed we were Scottish."

Julie glanced at Jamie before looking back at Chuck. "I'm part Scottish or Irish…don't know for sure which one."

Teresa was still holding Robby to keep him from wandering. She said, "We used to go to the Scottish festival at Military Park every year. My dad said that we should be proud of where we came from."

Chuck met Kyle Thomson's eyes and a nod told him all he needed. He looked at those standing to the right, Cindy among them. "Ms. McKay," he said with a smile. Like he was taking a headcount, he pointed at each individual standing to the right and announced their surnames to the group. "There may be no way to tell for sure, but I think it's a safe bet that we all share a common tie. Maybe not full blood—but at least some part of all our family trees came from Scotland. Enough of it anyway that we all carry the same genetic defect. The same genetic defect that enabled us to survive the bug and the End."

Cindy was the first to voice the obvious challenge to his logic. With a look of question on her face, she asked, "Why did I lose my family then?"

Lori Wilson echoed the same question about her brother.

Chuck raised his hands for silence again as the group started to get restless. "The doctors didn't say anything about being immune. They only talked about being less susceptible. If we were immune we probably wouldn't have gone through the same symptoms as everyone else." Chuck pointed to Andy and asked, "Did you go down with the convulsions and then pass out?"

"Of course I did."

"Didn't we all go down with the symptoms? Didn't our parents, our brothers and our sisters all go down with the same symptoms?"

There were nods and solemn confirmations to Chuck's question as some started thinking about the last days before the End.

"It may be like how a cold or flu hits some of us harder than others. Luck had a play in it. By chance you survived where your brother or sister didn't quite make it."

Chuck watched as the group finally started taking hold of what he was saying. First there were subdued nods of thoughtful acceptance. Then a few smiles and hugs between friends. It continued to build as laughter of both surprise and acceptance broke out. The giant burden of guilt everyone felt was being lifted from their shoulders. They finally had a reason for why they survived when their friends and loved ones didn't.

Cindy looked up at Chuck and held out her hand. In an instant he was on the ground with her, holding her in his arms. But their private moment was short lived as others came around and started slapping Chuck on the back, or wrapping their arms around the both of them in one giant hug. A moment later, Chuck and Cindy were mingling and rejoicing with the rest. It was the most uplifting time in their lives since it happened.

After several minutes of joyful ruckus and play, Chuck made his way through the others back to the platform. He stepped up barely able to contain his own joy. Without wasting any time in trying to still the group with his hands, he rang the bell and after few seconds they all took control of their emotions. Sharing their excitement and about to burst himself, he yelled out, "Do you know what this means?"

A hush came over everyone as they looked up at Chuck, unable to follow the path he was laying before them. Julie spoke up. "What…what do you mean?"

Chuck was a little surprised that he had to say it. "It means that we could find civilization in Scotland. Now there's no guarantee, but logic would suggest that the number of survivors may be much greater there. And if that's true, there may still be civilization close to what it was like before the End." The reaction wasn't what he expected. He stood and watched as strange looks and questionable glances were exchanged between most of those standing before the platform. "Don't you guys understand?"

"But Chuck," Jeff seemed to speak for everyone, "why would we even try to go to Scotland? We have everything we need right here."

Chuck shook his head in frustration. "You're right…you have what you need to live—the necessities anyway. But what you don't have is a future. Obstacles are going to come up that we don't have the numbers or the knowledge to overcome. I probably use the library more than any of you, but it can only help us so much. No matter how much we read we're never going to be doctors or engineers. We can't just think about the here and now." He paused long enough to make eye contact with all the adults. "Can any of you honestly tell me that you've spent any time thinking about what the future holds for these kids…or the future of the world?" With a scowl, he continued, "We survived by the grace of some genetic anomaly, but are we to be the end of it? Is Mankind destined to die out with us? Are we just going to sit back and accept that we can't have any children?" He drove in the thought with a pause and discerning look. "Not me! And I can't believe that you folks would accept it either. In fact I won't!" he barked out. "We've been through too much to simply give up on a future."

Cathy Ferguson raised her head and said, "But no one has had a baby that lived."

"I know, I know, but that doesn't mean we won't or can't. I KNOW that someday a child will be born—a baby will live. And our burden isn't just the genetic anomaly that allowed us to live. Our burden, our purpose is to ensure that when it happens, that there will still be a world for that child to grow up in. It's our responsibility to start over, not to give up. If we can't dream of a future, how can we ever expect those who come after us to? I know that we could all use a sign, something to base our hope in." Chuck paused as he pictured the boy standing with Cindy in his vision. "It will come. But while we wait, we need to take the next step." With a heart-felt stare, he shared his strength and conviction with each individual until they slowly started nodding with him. "The next step is going to a place where there's enough people to overcome any obstacles thrown at us."

Chuck had done what he could. The only thing left to do was to give them the time to decide. He waited on the platform as several simultaneous discussions broke out in the gathering. After several minutes he was about to head over for the comfort of the porch swing when the discussions broke long enough for Kyle to speak up. "Suppose you're right. We find more survivors there and together we learn how to overcome the obstacles you're talking about. Then what?"

Chuck dipped his head and put some thought into his answer. "Then you take what you've learned and go back out to the rest of the world and save as many as you can. You bring hope back to those who've lost it."

Discussion picked up again for several minutes. It was only natural that he was nervous as he watched his friends slowly make up their minds and turn back to the platform. He trusted his instincts and he trusted his belief in the dream. But when it came down to it, the only thing that truly mattered at that moment was whether they trusted him. With that decision at hand, he yelled one more time. "Now do you know what this means?"

Andy pumped his fist into the air and answered in an equally loud and determined yell that was meant to instill a like belief in the others, "We're going to Scotland!"

Someone else yelled Scotland. Chuck smiled and pumped his fist into the air, "Scotland!"

Sara joined in and proclaimed, "I'm not going to give up!"

"None of us are!" erupted someone anonymously in the crowd as the momentum continued to build.

A question asked in a soft voice broke through the growing enthusiasm. "But how will we get there?" It was Teresa.

Silence fell over the crowd again as all eyes turned to Chuck. This time he saw something different in the faces that awaited his response. Gone was the look of giving up. In its place was something else—a look he could embrace. They all shared the familiar face of a child who has just had a present dangled before his face and now wants it more than anything else in the world. It was the look of hope. He yelled out,

218

"Does anyone know how to sail?" A hand slowly rose in the middle of the crowd. Chuck pointed to the individual and announced, "Everyone, I give you Mr. Jim Sinclair!" and the crowd erupted into celebration.

Chuck jumped down and made his way through the joyful hugs, handshakes and backslaps until he found Cindy. There, in a sea of commotion, he wrapped his arms around her, looked into her eyes and said, "I love you."

She let out a whimper of joy and excitement in return as she clutched him in her arms and feverishly kissed his face.

Chapter 38

Mike prayed that Bill would remain unconscious this time. He had already endured Bill coming to three times, and each time it was the same horrific experience. While Bill was still groggy there would be the low, drawn-out, incoherent moans of pain that would give Mike a chance to prepare himself. Then Bill would once again realize that his left hand had been sawn off just above the wrist and those godforsaken screams of hysteria would start. Short shrills at the top of Bill's lungs followed by quick, sobbing, gasps for breath that cut off as quickly as they started by more nerve shattering shrills.

Mike tensed up like a board each time. Still tied to the car and unable to help, all he could do was shut his eyes and try to block the horrible sounds from his mind. When that didn't help, he would try to drown out Bill's cries by screaming so loud himself that he could feel the vibrations in his skull. Then not more than two or three seconds later the cries of pain would stop as Bill would pass out again. Mike's stomach would ease back down and he would wait, unable to sleep, preparing himself for the next time Bill woke. That's how the first night went.

Mike woke early the next day when Jason, Mark and a few others emerged from the hotel across the street. The light of predawn gave the whole ordeal a nightmarish quality. The sight of the small, square-bladed saw in Mark's hand forced Mike to remember that the nightmare was all too real. As they walked past him on their way toward Bill, Mike yelled, "Jason, come on, how fucking sick is this."

As if he were expecting it, Jason paused and slowly turned around. Mark stayed with him as the others walked on over to prepare Bill. Jason smiled and said, "Good morning! Hope the night wasn't too harsh."

"Don't hurt him anymore."

"Hey, if you want me to end his pain, all you have to do is tell me where the others are?"

"I told you. It was just me and him. The others left for the country."

"Very well. Let's hope your friend never needs to pick up anything," Jason said with a grin before heading on over to Bill with Mark.

"Goddamn it Jason! You're a fucking lunatic!"

Jason stopped again but kept his back to Mike.

"You're always fucking with people, asking them if they're the one that will stop you. Well ask me again you fucking bastard! I'll give you the answer you're looking for!"

Mark flared out his chest and started for Mike in a fit of anger, but Jason stopped him with a simple hand gesture. "Okay…" drawing out its pronunciation to where its meaning was more ominous than a simple reply. He turned around and Mike saw the most unnatural stare as he walked over. He stopped three feet away and asked in a calm and steady voice, "Are you the one that will stop me?"

Mike's thoughts started swimming in confusion and doubt as he was suddenly given the opportunity. If he ever wanted to kill a man, it was no more than now. The suffering had to end. But was he the one that could accomplish what others couldn't? He had seen so much since the End, and some of what he had seen was unbelievable. Jason had an unnatural hold on his men. They believe that Jason was enforcing the will of God and that until God's wrath is complete—no harm can come to him. They had all stood witness to events that supported that belief as truth, including himself. Could he stop Jason? His fear was founded in doubt. Like a seed starting to germinate, he sensed a feeling from deep within that he was not the one. In that same sense there was a reassuring thought that he knew who was. Still, he had to try. He pushed his chin out and said defiantly, "You're damn right I am!"

The three men that were preparing Bill heard the challenge and came running over to watch. Jason said, "You know the deal. You kill me and my men will let you and that poor cripple go free. But you only get one try, anything else and we'll make sure that crip never forgets that you're the reason we wouldn't let him die."

Mike pushed out his jaw and said, "Cut me lose you fucking asshole!"

One of the men stepped over, whipped out a knife and cut the ropes holding Mike to the car.

Mike's legs were so stiff and lethargic that as soon as he lost the support of the ropes around his wrist, his weight almost pulled him crashing down to the asphalt. At the last second he caught himself and slowly managed to stand. Swaying under the push of the gentlest of breezes, he fought to steady himself as he rubbed the burn marks around his wrists. He would only have one shot, so he couldn't afford to miss. He studied the weapon each man was holding and then pointed to the man standing to the right of Mark. "I'll take his shotgun."

Jason looked at the man and nodded. The man walked over to Mike and pumped all five shells out of his Browning 12 gauge. He gathered up the shells and laid them on the ground at Mike's feet along with the shotgun. Mike took his eyes off Jason and the others as he kneeled down and inspected each of the shells. He picked out the one that looked like a winner, grabbed the shotgun and stood up. The others stepped out of the line of fire as he loaded the one shell.

While Mike pumped the shotgun, Mark pointed at him with his burly finger and spit out, "You who stand in the path of God's wrath shall fail!" While the others in the tribe started running over, he swung his finger toward Jason and announced for all to hear, "For he is the hand of God!"

Jason pushed his chest out and clapped his hands behind his back. As Mike aimed the shotgun at him he yelled, "Are you the one that will stop me!"

Fatigue had taken its toll on Mike and it was hard enough holding the shotgun steady without thinking about what would happen next. He had watched this from the other side of the fence once before. Out of all the times Jason asked that question, he had only seen one other man stand up and say yes. It was shortly after the End. Jason was gathering his people when one of the men tried to challenge his authority. To get a rise out of him, the man made an unsavory comment about how Jason's fiancée died. That was all it took. Jason was on him like a wild-man. In his entire life, Mike had never seen such a savage attack on another human being. But the scariest part was that right in the middle of the beating—Jason stopped and climbed off. While the man slowly pushed back up to his feet, Jason started crying and threw the man his gun. He told the man to stop him. In fact he begged the man to stop him. And the man tried. The man fired a 45 caliber Colt at Jason's head from less than fifteen feet away, but somehow missed. Mike found it difficult to swallow as he remembered what Jason did to that man.

He started glancing at the faces in the growing crowd. A few were pointing and yelling at him while others stood and watched in silence. One man that he considered to be a friend pumped his fists and urged him to take the shot. Standing next to that man was the oldest woman in the tribe. She met his stare for a second. She then lowered her eyes and shook her head. It was as if she knew that he wasn't the one. He was still looking at her when his well left him and he lowered the gun.

Mark snickered and shifted his weight as he called Mike a pussy-faggot. Then the three men standing next to Mark joined in and also began to heckle him.

Jason then did the oddest thing. With his hands still clapped behind his back, he lowered his chin and addressed Mike with the soft voice of a friend in need. "Please...you can do it."

Mike stared at the ground as he thought about the pain Bill was enduring. He remembered the horrible cries of pain and pleas for help when Mark took his sweet time in cutting off Bill's hand yesterday. He could picture that dull saw blade, bloodied and slowly grading against the bone in Bill's other wrist. That was something he couldn't let happen again. Something he wouldn't let happen. Mike flexed his jaws and turned back around with the shotgun. As he raised the barrel once more, he saw the hope of an innocent child in Jason's face. He wouldn't let that unnerve him. He told himself that he was not going to fail. He would kill Jason. He took another breath and steadied his arms as best he could. He looked down the barrel at Jason's head as he took three steps closer to where the tip of the shotgun was less than a foot from its target. "I am the one," he said with determination as he pulled the trigger.

Mike was anticipating the kick of the 12 gauge so much that he jerked his shoulder back even though the action of the hammer produced nothing more than a soft-click. For a second he couldn't believe that the shotgun had misfired. He continued to stand there waiting for Jason to fall. As reality began to take hold, Mark tackled him and pinned him against the asphalt. "The fucking gun doesn't work!" Mike screamed in panic as Jason slowly walked over with his head lowered and a tear trickling down his cheek

Mark handed the gun to Jason. Jason pumped out the shell, looked at it, then loaded it back in the gun and pumped it once. After a pause to wipe his bloodshot eyes, he lowered the barrel over Mike's face and said, "You don't think it works?" He swirled the barrel over Mike's head and then said, "You're right handed if I remember correctly."

Tension grabbed Mike by the heart as his worst fear was about to unfold. In a panic of preparation, he filled his lungs with air and held it as he watched the barrel swing away from his face. He heard Jason say, "Hold his left hand out for me," as he clamped his eyes shut. No sooner did his world go black than his entire body jerked from the blast.

Just as suddenly as the blast, the release of tension overwhelmed him. He almost started screaming for joy as the relief of still having his hand surged through him. It was a miracle. He had never known Jason to bluff. But this time, a spark of electricity touched the nerve endings deep in the muscles of his shoulder and he jerked. The thought of a miraculous miss left him as his arm suddenly began to feel warm. He swallowed and stared up at the clouds as a weightless sensation filled his stomach. A few shallow pants ensued that were followed sharply by a shaky deep breath that he wanted to hold for some reason. Then the air shook out of him as a warm wet feeling started to flow around his elbow on the asphalt.

That was when he realized there was something else trying to fight through the ringing in his ears. In a mild state of euphoria, he was drawn to listen and understand. He concentrated and first heard the laughter. Then he heard the ruckus. "Oh fuck man…where'd it go? That fucker's history…"

He blew out a short, powerful puff like a woman about to give birth as his nerves tried to bring his stomach up. As the tears began to flow, he saw the man with the shotgun step back over him and stare down.

There didn't seem to be any joy or pity in Jason's face—only disappointment. His eyes lost their focus as he looked down and quietly stated, "I'm sorry old friend. You're not the one." After one last sigh, he walked off.

The rapid loss of blood started to pull Mike's eyes back in his head, but he had to know before he lost consciousness. With the strain of a long, drawn out grunt, he pulled his head off the ground and rolled his cheek toward his left shoulder for confirmation.

~~~

Mike felt like the life had been drained out of him when he woke up bound to a wooden chair. At first he couldn't feel anything. Then he noticed a strange tingling sensation along the left side of his body.

Before knowing any better, he tried to jerk free. That was all it took. A grating pain shot up his forearm, hit the rest of his body and launched him into blood-curdling scream. Every ounce of flesh tensed up as he violently slung his head from side to side. "Dear God!" he cried out as tears trickled down his cheeks.

As he quickly sucked in several short gasps, he turned and looked at his left arm. It wasn't a nightmare. The only thing that remained was a stump wrapped in a dirty towel and duct tape. "No!" A few tense seconds later, he filled his lungs completely and opened his tear-filled eyes. That's when he saw Bill ten feet directly in front of him with both arms bandaged. They had taken his friend's other hand.

"You back among the living?"

Mike bit down to quench the pain as he looked over his shoulder. Jason was sitting in the leather wingback on the curb behind him. "What are you doing?" he gasped.

"Thought you might like a front row seat to watch us saw off crip's right foot. You missed the other hand. Mark worked that saw so slow and meticulously…the screams. It was incredible."

Mike sucked the snot dripping from his nose back in and screamed, "For the love of Christ! Just kill the poor bastard—no more torture!"

"You want me to go ahead and burn him, cleanse his soul?"

"Yes! Whatever you want to do—just put him out of his misery."

"I'll do that for you," Jason said as if granting a favor for a good friend. Then he got up and walked around to where he stood between Bill and Mike. "You know what I want in return."

Mike tried to wet his lips. But his mouth was so dry that each breath produced a harsh rasp.

Jason called out, "Mark! I need you again."

The thought of more suffering brought Mike to a panic. "No! Don't!"

"You're not the one, but you can stop this just the same."

Mark ran past Mike's chair with the saw, then the same guys that were there before ran by. One had a bucket that Mike thought was water until he caught the smell trailing it. They stopped at Bill and waited for Jason to give the signal. Jason gave Mike a second to tell him what he wanted to hear. When it didn't come he turned to the men and said, "Take his right foot." Two of the men jumped back laughing as the third dowsed Bill with the bucket of urine and excrement. Like a brutal slap

226

in the face, the splash brought Bill to a groggy, conscious state of mind.

Then the moans started, although with less life than before. Bill's face was a ghostly white from loss of blood. He could barely hold his head up for longer than a second. When he saw what remained of his arms, he still had the will to scream. Mike closed his eyes and turned away. But that couldn't silence Bill's cries. "Mike...Mike is that you? Please God make them stop." There was a pause then one loud scream for mercy. "Mike!"

Mike couldn't ignore him. He looked back and saw Bill's head hanging forward. He was out of it—driven drunk by the pain and loss of blood.

Bill managed to meet his eyes for a second and with a grotesque smile, stammered out, "Hey old friend...they got you too."

"Yeah," Mike answered, as he glanced at the bandages of his own arm. "They got me too."

"Don't know what they want, told them everything they asked me..."

Mike looked at Jason who freely admitted, "It's true. Crip told us while we were cutting off his right hand." He paused and turned back toward Bill and asked, "It was your right hand wasn't it?"

Bill looked down at his right, then his left, and then looked back at Jason with a blank look on his face.

Jason nodded and continued, "It was his right. Anyway, he told us there were a bunch of you held up down in Madison. He told us how many were in your tribe. And then he gave some bullshit line about you guys having electricity and running water and all that crap."

Mike cried, "If he told you...then why are you still doing that to him?"

"He told us, but I want to hear it from your lips. I know your loyalty. You don't give it easily but when you do—you stand behind it." Jason walked over and put his hand on Mike's shoulder. "You betrayed me. Now I want you to betray them."

Mike met his eyes with a look of disgust on his face.

"I'll kill crip if you do. There won't be any more torture for him. And I'll let you live."

Mike shut his eyes and shook his head as he sobbed, "I can't!"

A moment later he heard Jason snap his fingers and then Bill started screaming. Mike lasted less than one heart beat before he screamed out,

"Stop! I'll say it." He forced himself to look at his friend, crying and only half conscious. Mark was kneeling at Bill's feet with the blood covered blade of the saw caught in the middle of the first stroke of metal against bone.

Mike cried, "I'll do it. Don't torture him anymore." He dropped his chin to his chest in defeat and whimpered. "Oh God, please forgive me Bill." Then with his lips trembling and tears running down his face, he looked up at Jason's smiling face and cried, "What do you want me to say?"

Chapter 39

Five vehicles, freshly tuned and loaded with supplies, pulled out of Madison two days after the unanimous decision to leave. Boston was the target destination for the first stage of the trip. Jim Sinclair had been there a few years before the End, and from what he remembered it was a good bet for finding a schooner worthy of crossing the ocean. The idea was to take the lesser-traveled highways and avoid the danger rumored to be in the large cities. The journey began by taking state road 421 north out of Madison. They'd jump on US50 in Versailles and rode it east into Ohio.

Kyle Thomson and Cathy Ferguson volunteered to take the point while Andy insisted in bringing up the rear in his Toyota four-wheel drive. They kept their speed slow and their ears to the wind, and for the two hours that it took the convoy to travel the thirty miles to Versailles, everything went smoothly. Kyle and Cathy were already dreaming about a fresh start in Scotland. They pushed aside any thoughts about the difficulty in crossing an ocean in favor of talking about what it would be like in their new home. As they left the vast fields of open country and started to pass the houses and gas stations along the outer stretches of the small town, Kyle said, "You know I never thought I'd see anything outside of the states."

"Tell me about it," Cathy chimed in as she pointed to the intersection two blocks ahead, and added, "Take a right—there." Before Chuck offered her the peace and safety of Madison, she thought she would never think again about traditional matters such as marriage or raising a family. Yet as Kyle smiled and caressed her thigh, she found herself dreaming about starting a new life with him in a fresh place. She was about to say how excited she was to get the chance to see the beautiful cliffs and rolling hills of Scotland, when a rapid string of pops slapped against the windshield. She clutched Kyle's hand and gasped.

Jamie Ross was trailing by thirty feet in the second vehicle with Lori Wilson and Mike Donaldson when Kyle's truck suddenly veered off the road, accelerated, and slammed into a tree. Jamie locked up the brakes and started to gasp, "What the fu—" before the sound of metal pings spraying across their hood cut him off. Lori slammed against the dash as puffs of dust and chipped paint formed a flowing wave of gray over the hood like dust shaken from a rug. Then he saw a man run across to the right side of the street half a block ahead. A second later he saw a flash over the hood of a derelict car on the left side. Something smacked the windshield like a hammer and the rear view mirror suddenly disappeared into the back seat. Jamie flinched and yelled, "Duck!" as he pulled Lori down on the seat and covered her up.

The three vehicles trailing Jamie all locked up and skidded, one after another like a chain of dominos as Chuck screamed, "Everyone down!" In an instant he had the door open and the rifle from the rack behind the seat. Cindy hit the seat face-first as he jumped out behind the cover of the door. After an immediate short burst of distant gunfire, he popped his head up over the bed of the truck to make sure Robby and Teresa were keeping low. He saw the fear in their faces and said, "You two stay put and keep down. If you hear anyone coming—pull the supplies up around you and hide." He dropped back down and peaked around the door at Jamie's Impala fifty feet farther up. He heard the pings of bullets against metal and saw the car rock as the occupants shifted. Then he saw the windows blow out from another spray of bullets. "Jamie! Lori!"

"Still here!" Jamie screamed in response.

"Everyone!"

"Yeah! But Kyle and Cathy…"

A round pierced the front fender of Chuck's truck and forced him back behind the door. Just as he ducked, a hand came out of no where and grabbed his shoulder. Chuck's nerves lit up like the 4th of July as he spun around—ready to kill or die fighting. Thank God it's Andy. He blew out a sigh of relief and then motioned to the Impala. "They're still alive…but I don't know for how long…they're getting pelted."

Andy popped his head over the door for a second and watched the action. He dropped back down and said, "If you can keep them busy for a few minutes—I'll work my way around and come up from behind. I think there are only two of them. Probably just scouts."

"We don't have much time if they are."

Andy nodded and glanced again over the door.

"Did you check behind us? I don't want to get boxed in."

Andy glanced over his shoulder and grimaced, knowing full well that Chuck expected more out of him. "Sorry boss. I'll check behind us first then work my way around."

"Hold on…" Chuck dropped down to the asphalt and stretched out with his rifle under the door. He spotted the man in the crosshairs just in time to see the kick of his rifle. A bullet slapped the sheet metal a few inches above Chuck's head. The man ducked back behind the car as Chuck squeezed the trigger and fired a blistering response. "Go! Now!" The shot peeled a streak of paint across the hood of the derelict car and chipped off a white cloud of dust on the brick house behind the man. Chuck glanced over his shoulder while the dust settled. Andy was gone.

Lori erupted into a blood-curdling scream as another spray of bullets shredded the Impala. A second later Jamie yelled again for help. Chuck jumped back up to his feet, aimed his rifle over the door of the truck and spotted the man behind the car just as he ducked back down. That was his chance. Chuck skirted around the door and took off running for the Impala under a surge of adrenaline. His heart was pounding so hard that he barely heard Teresa scream behind him, "Don't leave us Chuck!"

He slammed against the Impala's trunk and rear bumper with his shoulder. A second later Jamie screamed, "Chuck? Is that you?"

"Yeah! Stay put, but see if you can push the driver's door open with your foot," Chuck huffed, as he got back to his feet and crouched behind the trunk. He heard the door swing open and started to inch his way to the corner of the bumper.

As he was about to swing around behind the cover of the door, he heard little Mike say, "Chuck! You came for us. I knew you would."

He glanced over the faded green paint of the trunk and saw him. Mike was up on his knees and looking at him through the blown out rear window. Chuck reached for him and then suddenly flinched as blood splattered across his face. The air left Chuck's lungs as he slid back behind the trunk with his rifle clutched to his chest. His feet slid out to the side and he sat there staring into space while the boy's blood dripped off his nose and chin. For a brief moment, nothing mattered anymore. It took the heart-wrenching sound of Lori's wailing to snap him out of it. He wiped the blood off his face and flexed his grip on the rifle. As he slowly rose up, he saw little Mike sprawled out on the trunk with the back of his scalp peeled forward and hanging over the front of his head like the brim of a baseball hat.

Chuck screamed, "Goddamn it! No!" and ran around to the front door as another shot pierced the air next to him. Shaking and on the verge of crying, he aimed the rifle at the derelict car and waited for the man to show himself again. First he saw the barrel come over the fender. Then he started to see the man's head as he felt the tickle of the forged steel trigger against the tip of his finger. But just as he was about to squeeze off the shot—the man's face blew apart like a balloon popping in slow motion. A second later the man fell back and vanished behind the fender. Chuck scanned the area behind the derelict car with his scope and caught the barrel of the hunting rifle he gave Andy dipping back behind a tree.

He glanced inside the Impala and saw Jamie and Lori trying to squeeze themselves between the seat and dash to get closer to the floorboard. Another spray of bullets riddled the car. After the exchange, Chuck cautiously looked over the hood and saw smoke drifting in the air above an overgrown privet hedge. Since there wasn't anything to aim at, he simply pointed the rifle and fired. Then he quickly reached in the car and pulled Jamie out by the waist of his shorts. "Get back to my truck!"

Jamie grabbed Chuck's shoulder as he crouched next to him. "Chuck!"

Without taking his eyes off the privet hedge, Chuck yanked Jamie's hand off his shoulder and demanded, "Now! Go!" and then fired another shot into the overgrown shrub. Jamie obeyed and shot off toward the pickup.

As soon as Chuck pulled the rifle back off the hood, he made eye contact with Lori and before he could say a word she was out the door and squatting next to him. "As soon as I fire you take off running—got it?"

Lori answered in a thankful voice, "You don't have to tell me twice."

He took a couple of quick breaths and then swung the rifle back up and fired. Lori took off running and as Chuck chambered another round the man hidden in the hedge began firing. The bullets pelted the opposite side of the car and all across the hood. The right front tire blew and then a round skipped off the asphalt under the car and grazed his calf. The entire exchange, which pumped over fifty holes in the car, lasted perhaps two seconds. It ended when Chuck heard another shot from Andy's hunting rifle.

He glanced at the blood trickling down his shin before popping back up on the hood with his rifle. There was enough smoke slowly drifting in front of the hedge that in a more peaceful time it could have been mistaken for a fog bank. Chuck kept his rifle aimed and his finger on the trigger as he watched the movement of a dark figure behind the smoke. As the sweat ran down his forehead and started to sting his eyes, the figure broke through the cloud and into the clear. It was the lean, tanned figure of Andy strutting victoriously toward the Impala while pumping his rifle in the air. As Chuck slowly stood from the cover of the car, Andy beat the rifle against his chest and then hoisted it high above his head and gave a savage scream of victory.

Chuck was about to yell his thanks when Cindy screamed behind him. It wasn't a scream of fear, but the kind of scream that you hope you never hear. It was a death scream. The hairs on his neck stood as he spun around and saw her. She was slouched over a body not more than ten feet from the truck. Chuck didn't think—he just ran as the nightmare started to play out in his mind. Before he saw the body he knew it was Teresa. He knew exactly what had happened as if he had seen the whole thing. She had screamed at him not to leave. When he did, she jumped out of the truck and started after him. He remembered the bullet shooting past him. He remembered Jamie trying to get his attention. He knew it all and yet he knew nothing.

He flung his rifle to the side and took off running. At the end of a full sprint, he went down on his knees and slid right into her. He pulled Cindy back and gasped as he saw Teresa in a semi-conscious state. She was alive, but blood was spilling from a bullet wound in her small, swollen thigh. He scooped her upper body off the asphalt in one arm while he applied pressure to the wound with his free hand. "You're going to be okay! We're going to take care of you." As he looked around for help, he saw Jim and Sara holding Robby back to where he couldn't see his sister. He looked at Jim and said, "Get the first-aid kit out of my truck. And then find some cloth to tear up—I'll need several strips."

Andy ran up on the other side and stood panting. Chuck looked at him and said, "Go check Kyle's truck—see if they're still alive!"

Jim dropped down to the asphalt next to Chuck with the first-aid kit and a sheet. Cindy snatched the sheet out of his hands and began to rip it into strips while he opened up the first-aid kit. He folded a wad of gauze and pressed it to the wound. "We've got to stop the bleeding!"

"Help me lift her leg—gently!" Chuck demanded, as they raised her leg to look for an exit wound. "Here! Bullet went clean through. I can't tell if it hit any bone or not, but all we can do right now is try to stop the bleeding." He grabbed another wad of gauze out of the kit and pressed it against the exit wound as he looked at Jim and Cindy. "These were scouts…I doubt Jason is too far behind. And I have a feeling he brought his entire tribe."

Cindy quickly handed them several strips of torn sheet and they began to bandage the wounds with as much pressure as they could without fear of cutting off the flow to the rest of her leg.

"Kyle is alive!" Andy huffed as he ran back up, "Cathy is dead."

"Both vehicles shot?" Chuck asked.

"To shit…they're not going anywhere," Andy replied with a shake of his head.

Chuck pushed Jim's hands away and took over the bandaging. "I've got Teresa. You go on and take care of Kyle." Jim grabbed the first-aid kit and took off running. While wrapping Teresa's leg, he spoke to Andy without looking at him. "We need to lay out Teresa…and probably Kyle too as we travel. We don't have room to do that in only three vehicles. I want you to run back there and find out what those scouts drove down in. Check their pockets for keys first. Find whatever they had and drive it back here as quickly as you can."

"Sure boss," Andy said, as he sprinted toward the fallen snipers.

Chuck tied the strips in a knot over one wound and then crossed the strip around to the back of Teresa's thigh and tied a knot over the exit wound. After he finished, Cindy slid over next to him and he put his arm around her. "She's going to make it. She didn't lose that much blood."

While Cindy buried her face against his shoulder and started crying again, Chuck addressed the others. "Jeff, I want you and Brandt to find a working car. I don't care what it is or what it looks like. I want you to drive it or push it or whatever you have to do to get it at least two or three blocks north of the intersection of US50." He lowered his eyes and tried to detach his feelings from what he was about to say. "Then I want you to take Cathy and Mike—" his emotions started to boil up and close off his throat. He took several quick breaths and then said with as

234

much control as he could muster, "I want you to put them in the car and then set it on fire."

"You want us to do what!" Jeff exclaimed in disbelief.

Chuck's eyes started to burn as he said, "Jason has to think that we continued on north."

Jeff just stood there and stared at him.

Chuck ignored the pain he felt inside and forced out with as much authority as he could, "It can't be empty or Jason will never buy it. Now do it!"

Jeff grabbed Brandt by the shoulder and with a growing look of contempt, headed off to find a car.

"Jeff!" Chuck yelled. Jeff stopped and turned around. "Then position Jason's men like they came out into the open to shoot as we drove by. Gather up some empty casings to scatter on the road around them. Make it look like they were firing north."

"I got it!" Jeff snapped back, without any concern for how it sounded.

Chuck turned to Cindy for understanding. "You know I wouldn't do this if I thought there was any other way."

Cindy had no emotions left. She had cried herself out. Her face was flushed except for a pale, clamminess around her eyes. "I know… we have to do it this way."

"Hopefully it will buy us enough time to dress Teresa's wound properly. We'll disinfect it and then stitch her up. I don't know what else to do…except pray."

Cindy rubbed his back. "I know." A moment later she asked, "Do you really think Jason is out there…that these guys were scouts of his?"

"No doubt in my mind. And the fact that they were sitting and waiting for us makes me think that he probably had scouts set up on every road out of Madison. I bet their job was to keep us pinned down until Jason and the rest of the tribe could get here." He leaned over to where he could whisper without being heard by the others. "There were three men posted here…I'm sure of it."

Cindy glanced at the houses along the road and then tilted her head back toward Chuck. "Where is he?"

"I bet he took off to get Jason as soon as they saw us coming."

"But how? Why would you think that?"

"I don't know how. But I'm sure that's what happened. But don't worry. We'll be gone before they get here."

Chapter 40

The convoy was traveling northeast on State Road 42 in Ohio when Chuck heard the horn of the Avalon behind them. It was Jim and Sara. Teresa was laid out across the back seat of the car and Jim was signaling that she couldn't go much farther. Chuck pulled the road atlas off the dash and handed it to Cindy. "See if you can find a small town up ahead where we could spend a day or two."

Cindy flipped it open to the dog-eared page and traced their route with her finger. "We're coming up on Spring Valley. It looks pretty small, and it's close to Dayton."

He glanced at the odometer. Versailles was a hundred miles behind them. After a second of thought he nodded. "That should be far enough. We'll stop up ahead and take care of Teresa and Kyle." He stuck his hand out the window and signaled to Jim that he understood.

The Cadillac they took from the two dead scouts was directly behind the Avalon. Jeff drove while Julie rode in the back seat with Kyle and did what little she could for him. He had taken two rounds—one to the face and one to the chest.

Andy was still bringing up the rear in his Toyota four-wheel drive. Lori rode in the cab with him while Brandt rode in the bed with the supplies.

Plenty of daylight remained as they pulled into the small town of Spring Valley. From all appearances it looked like an older farming community that never grew to more than a few dozen houses along the state road. It was exactly what they were looking for. They were less than 30 minutes from Dayton. Close enough to run for medical supplies, but far enough away that they didn't have to worry about the violence of the city. Another nice benefit was that Spring Valley didn't have the telltale signs of rioting and destruction that came with the fall of civilization.

Chuck pulled onto the gravel lot of the only gas station in town and parked next to the pumps. As the other cars pulled off and parked behind him, he got out and hurried back to the Avalon to check on Teresa. Sara was stretched over the front seat and holding a wad of blood-soaked gauze against Teresa's thigh. "Jesus Christ…she's still bleeding."

Sara pleaded, "I can't get it to stop. The jarring of the road keeps opening it up. We had to stop."

"I know," Chuck replied, as he quickly pulled back out of the car to scan the area. Jim looked like a man who had already conceded the battle. He was leaning with his rear against the front fender and his face lowered. Chuck pointed at the houses along the street and said, "I want you to find a suitable place for us to use as a makeshift hospital. Make sure it's one with a propane tank outside and that it has enough gas for us to use the stove. It also needs to be big enough for two beds on the first floor. Then take the generator out of the Toyota and tie it into the electrical system."

Jim renewed his resilience with one deep breath and said, "Will do!" as he took off running for the houses.

Chuck called Andy and Jamie over. "I want you two to unload the Toyota and then drive up to Dayton. Find a hospital and grab as much as you can carry back in the truck. Get things like dressings, antibiotics, supplies for transfusions, whatever they have for stitching up wounds, gloves, sheets—"

"I got the idea," Andy interrupted, "we'll fill the truck—"

"Get a stretcher too in case we have to move them."

"We're on it," Andy said, as he grabbed Jamie by the arm.

Brandt ran up with Robby. "What can we do, Chuck?"

"I want you guys to search for a well. We're going to need water. After you find one, grab buckets or whatever you can find in the houses and fill them up, and then take them to whichever house Jim finds for us to use. After you've done that…" he walked the boys over to the exposed caps of the storage tanks buried under the gravel, "pop these caps off and test the gasoline. If it looks good, fill up all the vehicles and then start searching for any food that might still be good."

Brandt pointed out toward the overgrown fields. "Do you want us to search out there in case there's corn or anything still growing?"

Chuck squeezed his shoulder and said, "That's some good thinking, son." Then he gave Brandt a slap on the back and said, "Now go on."

Cindy and Lori met him half way back to the car. "What do you want us to do?"

"You guys go with Jim and help him find a house. As soon as you do, start getting it ready for Teresa and Kyle. Have Jim move two beds into one room and then find some lighting that we can move around." He put his hand on Cindy's shoulder. "I want you to supervise it all and make sure it's done quickly and right."

She met his eyes for a second and realized that he was focused solely on trying to save the lives of Teresa and Kyle. "We'll be ready," she said, as they took off after Jim.

With a heavy weight on his chest, he walked back to the Cadillac where Jeff and Julie were tending to Kyle's injuries. He kept his emotions in check as he looked in the back door and asked with controlled concern, "How's he doing?"

Julie looked at him and her expression said it all. He was alive, but the prognosis wasn't good. As nasty as the wound was to his face, it wasn't their primary concern. It was the chest wound that scared them. The round hit just below the collarbone on the right side of his chest and they could tell by the rasping sound of each breath that it hit a lung. Chuck wouldn't have hesitated to open him up if it were only a minor operation that Kyle needed. But something this severe, they would do more damage than good. The only thing they could do was dress it, keep the fluid pumped out of his lungs and hope.

Jeff turned toward the back seat and stared at Chuck for a moment before flinging the door open and getting out. There was no mistaking the tension as Jeff walked around behind him. Chuck could even see the change in Julie's face. Her concern for Kyle quickly grew into a look of apprehension as she followed Jeff's movements.

Jeff's voice was full of hatred and sarcasm as he stood behind Chuck and said, "What do you want me to do."

Chuck watched Julie eye the man standing behind him. After a second, he got her attention and said, "Stay here. Once we have a house ready you can help me move him and Teresa." He pulled his head out of the back of the car and, trying to be as non-threatening as possible, slowly took Jeff by the arm and walked him over to the edge of the gravel lot. He looked south on State Road 42 for a few seconds and confided, "I know you don't agree with what I did back in Versailles."

"You're damn right I don't! They weren't strangers. That was Cathy and Mike you had me set fire to."

"Look...if there had been another way, I would have taken it. But as hard as that decision was, I'd make it again if I thought it would increase the chances of everyone else living. Don't you think they would have felt the same way?"

"But you based it on the assumption that Jason was coming. And you really don't have any fucking idea if he is or not."

"You're right. I don't know for sure that Jason is coming. But would you have taken that chance? Putting respect aside for the moment... would you have let Julie die so that we could give the dead a proper burial?"

Jeff turned around and watched Julie tend to Kyle.

"Well?" Chuck prompted.

Jeff looked past him as he asked with a stiff jaw, "What do you want me to do?"

"After we move Teresa and Kyle...I'd like you to go back down the road a mile or so, and keep watch just in case Jason IS following."

"Alright," Jeff conceded with a nod. "You want me to fire off a round if I see him?"

Chuck grimaced at the implications. A shot would give away Jeff's position, and it probably wouldn't provide a long enough warning to make any real difference for the rest of them. Even so it was better than nothing. "Yeah, that'll be good."

After Andy and Jamie got back from Dayton, they stitched up Teresa, dressed her wounds, and immobilized her leg in an air splint.

Robby didn't want to leave his older sister's side, so Chuck pulled a chair between the two beds and hoisted Robby up onto his lap. "We'll wait up together if that's okay with you?"

Robby held Chuck's arms around him so that he couldn't let go and nodded as he stared at his unconscious sister.

Chuck wouldn't let go, and he had no intention of sleeping that night. He felt too responsible to sleep. The very least he could do was make sure that Kyle wasn't alone in his fight to live.

Flames shot from the windows and engulfed the car. The paint along the roof swelled into boils and then burst, forming small, charred craters spotted across the sheet metal. He was close enough to feel the searing heat as his muscles tensed up. Still, he couldn't turn away. Even as he began to hyperventilate, he continued to stare—waiting for something. A shiver of dread passed over his skin that stole his breath. Then the icy finger of death touched his back and he screamed. Except that it wasn't his scream—it came from inside the burning car. It was Cathy and little Mike—

Chuck flinched in the chair and would have fallen over if not for the weight of Robby sleeping on his lap. The tension of the nightmare slowly drained from his body as he wiped the sweat off his face. He checked on Teresa and Kyle. No change—both were still unconscious. He took a moment to close his eyes and pray. When he finished, he got up and carried the small boy to the other bedroom and laid him down on the bed next to Cindy. A few seconds later he was back on the chair between the beds.

Chuck gathered everyone into the living room the following morning. He led off with the news that Teresa was still unconscious. Then as his lower lip started to quiver, he told them that Kyle passed away during the night. The room grew silent and he could feel everyone beginning to give up. He knew it because he was beginning to feel the same way. Just as he started to lower his head, he suddenly caught the smell of saltwater blowing in off the ocean. It was from his dream. He closed his eyes and saw Cindy and the boy standing on the cliff. For the flicker of an instant he was there with them, watching the sun set over the ocean. He filled his lungs with the fresh air of hope and opened his eyes. He wouldn't let them give up. He looked around the room and settled on Brandt. "Where do we stand with gasoline, water and food?"

The question caught Brandt off guard. He stuttered for a second as he connected the question to his activity from the day before. "The gas still looks good. I don't think anyone has opened the tank since before the End." He paused for a second as he counted silently with his fingers. "We found…two…no three wells. They're deep and full of water. We couldn't find any food that wasn't spoiled. Packaged food I mean. We did find some corn out in the fields growing on their own. There wasn't a lot, but there was some at least."

"Good work! You and Robby did a real fine job." He started clapping his hands. Cindy grabbed onto his lead and followed suit. Slowly the others began to join in. The enthusiasm was low to start with, but continued to build as people pushed the morning news out of their minds. Chuck looked around the living room. Everyone had a place to sit. The generator was wired up, jugs of water were sitting in the kitchen, everything was unpacked and they had all the medical supplies they could use. "You all did a fantastic job yesterday in getting this place ready." He watched the nods and smiles. "I take it, Jeff, that there were no signs of Jason following us."

Jeff shook his head. "Not a damn thing. No one is following us."

Chuck rubbed his chin as he glanced at Cindy sitting on the sofa to his left. The color was fading from her face and she didn't look like she felt very good. He said to the others, "I don't want to take the chance on losing Teresa. I don't think we should move her for at least a couple of weeks. As long as we're not being followed, how does everyone feel about staying here for a while?"

Jim raised his hand.

Chuck grinned and said, "You don't have to raise your hand."

Jim flashed a smile along with everyone else, then his mood changed. "It doesn't look like there's any food here."

"I can make another run into Dayton," Andy announced. "I did see signs…you know of the rumors we heard. But I can get in and out without being seen. I can find us food." He smiled and added, "It may not be like we were used to in Madison," he paused to recognize a few chuckles in the group before finishing with, "but at least we won't go hungry."

"Okay," Chuck said, "as long as we can get the food…what's everybody say?"

Jim opened the floor. "Food was my only concern. This place seems like a nice little town." After a few others echoed his assessment, he added, "There are some nice little homes that seem to be in pretty good shape." He discreetly reached over and took Sara's hand and said, "I think we'd be fine here," while she smiled and nodded.

Everyone knew Jim and Sara's little secret wasn't really a secret at all.

Chuck heard Cindy start to gag and saw her throw her hand over her mouth. He stepped over quickly and asked, "Are you okay?"

Cindy nodded and indicated for him to go on.

"If anyone is against staying—at least until Teresa is safe to travel, speak now or forever hold your peace."

The consensus was evident as no one even looked around to see if anyone else was going to raise an objection. No one wanted to risk Teresa's health if they didn't need to. Chuck started to say that it was settled, when Cindy jumped up and pushed by him. He caught his heels on the bottom of the sofa and fell back into the overstuffed cushion as she ran into the bathroom and slammed the door.

He jumped up and started to follow her, when Sara grabbed his arm. "You don't want to see her get sick now, do you?"

"What do you mean? I don't mind…what?" He looked at the pale expression on Sara's face and asked, "What's going on?"

She bit her lower lip. "Cindy told me."

"Told you what?"

"You…and her…" Chuck stared at her like she was speaking some kind of code that he couldn't break. A second later she helped him out and said, "I'm guessing that it's morning sickness." She shook her head and continued, "Cindy said that you and her…you haven't forgotten what's happened with every pregnancy have you?"

"You mean…Cindy's pregnant?"

Sara nodded.

A warm feeling flushed over Chuck and a smile spread across his face as he felt the truth of his dream. He squeezed Sara's hands. The boy on the cliff was his son! Then just as quickly that dreadful sliver of darkness, the reality of the death Sara warned of, crept into his thoughts. No woman had given birth to a live baby since the End. He tried to hold on to the image of his dream, yet his face started twitching anyway.

Sara squeezed his hands. "First things first. You wait here and let me see if I can figure out what we have." Chuck couldn't muster anything more than a nod. "If it is morning sickness then you need to be strong for her. You need to be strong together. Remember she's already lost one baby."

He had never considered the possibility of having a child since he and Becky found out that she was medically unable to get pregnant. It didn't even cross his mind when he and Cindy were together. He started to picture Cindy with her stomach showing full term, and as he did, he remembered Becky crying on his shoulder when they received the news that she couldn't have children. The blood started to leave his head and he began to teeter. Sara grabbed his arm and helped him back on the sofa. She gave him a pat on the knee to keep his spirits high as she went to check on Cindy.

Andy walked over and kneeled in front of him. He grabbed Chuck's shoulder and tried to sound as optimistic as he could. "Big news!"

Chuck looked at him and for once in his life, he was speechless.

"You sit here and rest. I'll have the guys dig a grave for…" the forced smile faded from Andy's face, "…we'll take care of Kyle."

Chuck was still numb from the news as he nodded. "Okay…but I want to say a few words. When you're ready, you come back in and let me know. We'll get everyone out there." Andy started to get up, but Chuck grabbed his hand and said, "Thanks!"

"No problem, boss."

Chapter 41

Chuck maintained his bedside vigil with Teresa into the second night. He cupped her hand between his and while he waited for any sign of improvement, he replayed the events that led to her injury at Versailles. Could he have done something different to prevent it? By the third day he was beginning to concede that her injuries were more severe than he originally anticipated and that Spring Valley would be their home for more than just a few weeks. Robby still wanted to be by his sister's side, and since Chuck saw the boy's presence as only beneficial to her recovery, they made the necessary changes to the makeshift hospital room and Robby moved in.

Jim and Sara kept trying to relieve Chuck as the hours rolled into days. They insisted that they could watch over Teresa and Robby. They pressed the matter further by moving into the house. Finally after four sleepless days of watching over the injured girl, Chuck heeded the pleas from Cindy and the others and moved into the house across the street with her and Brandt.

Jeff and Julie took their own home, while Lori welcomed the role of mother figure to the independent duo of Andy and Jamie in another house. After a few days of rest, Chuck was ready to lead the group again. He established a rotational chain of daily chores and before long they were in a routine not too dissimilar from what they had in Madison.

The one chore not put on a roster was the weekly supply run to Dayton. Because of the experience they gained in Indianapolis, Chuck kept that responsibility on the capable shoulders of Andy and Jamie. The first run went smoothly and without incident. They were able to gather enough edible food along the outskirts of Dayton. On the second trip, they had to venture farther into the city and even then they came back light. Their third excursion, though, brought an unexpected bounty.

They were deep within city limits when a Ford Taurus sped through the intersection two blocks away. For a second they weren't sure if they were spotted. When they heard the screech of tires as the Taurus locked up the brakes, they relied on the evasive maneuvers learned in Indianapolis and their instincts to get them to safety. They accelerated down an alley and weaved their way out toward the suburbs. By the time they stopped to see if they were being followed, they were across the street from a large urban renewal project. An eight foot chain link fence enclosed the entire city block. A metal sign on the fence read 'Future home of Flowing Meadows—luxury condo's from the mid $300,000'. Andy looked over the sight which was still home to an old, dilapidated warehouse that the city never got the chance to raze. That was when Jamie spotted the small, secured metal shed with the sign that read 'Caution—Explosives'. A few minutes later, Andy popped the lock off the shed and they uncovered three dusty cases of dynamite along with a dozen walkie-talkies sitting in their recharging holsters.

Seven of the walkie-talkies were beyond repair, the other five were salvageable. They cleaned the dust out of the holsters, hooked them up to a generator and managed to get the walkie-talkies to hold enough charge to provide anywhere from thirty seconds to just over five minutes worth of air time. The immediate beneficiaries of the find were those on sentry duty.

Guard duty was a daily task just like everything else. Chuck kept a sentry posted from dawn to dusk, two miles down the state road on both the north and south ends of town. Everyone except for Jim took a turn at guard duty. Since he was the only one capable of sailing a ship he was too valuable to risk. They worked four-hour shifts and each person coming in relief carried a freshly charged walkie-talkie. They were instructed only to use it for the gravest of emergencies. Now they had a means of communicating without giving away their position.

As much as Chuck was against any aggressive behavior, Andy was somewhat surprised by his suggestion that they keep the dynamite. But that wasn't the only thing Chuck did out of character. Every once in a while he would disappear. No one knew where he went. One day Andy found out. There was a dispute over chores and no one could find Chuck to settle it. Everyone spread out and started searching. Five minutes into it Andy wandered to the back of the gas station and saw Chuck standing by himself, out toward the middle of the overgrown corn field. He was standing in the small clearing where they buried Kyle.

Andy walked over to the edge of the field, stopping just short of pushing through the weed-like crops. He peered down the overgrown path that was once a plowed row in the field, and saw Chuck standing perfectly still with his hands clasped together in front of his waist and his head lowered. Andy watched in silence until he started to feel a weight pressing against his chest. Whether it was sympathy, remorse or guilt, he quietly walked back to the others and settled the dispute himself.

Chuck couldn't have been more excited when Teresa finally regained consciousness during the second week. It was a cause for celebration. That night they danced under the stars to the rhythm in their heads. The next day, Teresa's painful recovery began and continued past the long daylight hours of summer and into the brisk northern winds of autumn. The warmth of summer left without much notice. The group was becoming complacent in their new home and winter only amplified their content. Spring Valley was made up of quaint, older little farmhouses—each with its own propane tank in the yard. The shared excitement that swept through the group when they first felt the unmistakable warm blast of the furnace. They took turns standing in front of the vent and feeling the heat against their backs. Even Chuck didn't want to leave. A working furnace brought back so many wonderful memories of what life used to be like. It was the edge they needed to keep their spirits high and represented far too much to simply walk away from. With plenty of propane available, all they needed to do was hook up the thermostats and electronic pilot lights to a 12volt car battery. Each household had its own generator so keeping the battery charged and the furnace working wasn't an issue.

Teresa's rehabilitation was painful. The bullet that pierced her thigh, not only shredded muscle tissue, it also produced multiple fractures along her femur. To help strengthen the bond of the group, Chuck setup a rotation for everyone to work with her each day in stretching and strengthening her leg. Everyone would share in the joy of her recovery. That's not to say that it was a pleasant task in the beginning. The screams and cries that echoed from her room each morning during the first few months were unbearable. As the frequency and intensity of her cries diminished, her mobility increased. The leaves were full of autumn color and still on the limb when Teresa first ventured outside with only a crutch for assistance. She knew she would always walk with a limp, but at least she could walk.

The furnaces were in full use by the time Teresa requested Chuck's attendance late one day. Chuck figured a surprise was coming as he and Cindy walked through the cold to Jim and Sara's house. When Sara opened the door, her smile left no doubt about it. He followed Cindy inside, helped her off with her coat, put his arm around her and then rubbed her belly. "You staying warm in there?"

Cindy laughed and pushed his hand away. "Quit doing that. You're making me feel fat."

"Oh…you can barely tell," he consoled her, as Jim walked over. He looked around the room and asked, "Where's that little pistol, Robby?"

Jim slid his arm around Sara and said, "He's waiting in the other room."

"Has he got a surprise for us?" Cindy asked.

Both Sara and Jim fought to keep their joy hidden behind their smile. Jim cleared his throat and said, "Come on back…they're waiting."

The four of them headed to the bedroom that was originally the makeshift hospital room. As Jim opened the door the sound of a hush escaped. They walked in and Chuck saw Robby and Teresa sitting fully dressed on the sides of their beds facing each other. Everyone else was seated on folding metal chairs around the parameter of the room. He looked at Teresa's crutches resting upright at the foot of the bed, and then glanced around at the excitement in everyone's eyes. At the center of it all, was a single chair setting in the middle of the room, ten feet from the foot of the beds.

He glanced back at Cindy as she cracked a smile. Then she nudged him out toward the center of the room as Robby slid off the bed. The boy ran over, grabbed Chuck's hand and led him to the chair. Chuck's heart was racing as he glanced around at the smiling faces and slowly sat down. As he settled on the sparkle in Teresa's eyes, he grabbed her little brother and hoisted him up on his lap. He needed Robby. He needed the strength of someone else to keep his nervous excitement under control. For the first time in his life he finally understood how a new father feels when he sees the doctor walking toward him with news of whether it was a boy or a girl.

He was already trembling so much that he could barely hold a straight smile, and that was before he watched Teresa slowly ease off the bed and put her weight over her right foot. His stomach knotted up as he felt the slight grimace on her face. He hugged Robby as Teresa took her first step without crutches. The butterflies swarmed in his stomach and the tears of joy flowed as she looked at him and smiled. He let Robby go and threw his arms out for her as she crossed the ten-foot span on her own. Like a baby taking her first steps, she reached out and fell into the arms of the man who had twice saved her life.

Chuck clutched her to his chest in a way that only a parent could understand as cheers erupted around the room. He kissed her cheek and whispered as the tears continued to flow, "I'm so proud of you."

Teresa hugged him and said, "I wanted to surprise you. Did you know I could walk?"

Chuck freed one hand to wipe his face as Cindy walked over and kneeled beside them. "No I didn't. It was just about the best surprise I ever had." He slid his free arm around Cindy. "You knew about his didn't you?"

She smiled and started to cry herself. "We all did. We knew how much it would mean to you and—"

"You wanted to see my cry, didn't you."

"No," Cindy said with a laugh, as she wiped her eyes. "We just wanted to repay you for all you've done for us."

Chuck smiled, but his thoughts were suddenly far from the joyous celebration at hand. He knew Cindy's intentions were good, yet deep down he also knew the compliment wasn't true. How could it be? They weren't all there.

Cindy leaned forward until her forehead touched his. "You gave us a home, a place safe from all that was going wrong in the world…a place that gave us meaning and love."

Chuck heard her kind words, but couldn't stop thinking about Cathy and Mike. They wouldn't have been so thankful. He remembered his dream—watching them twist and scream in the fire. They sacrificed their lives following his leadership and how did he repay their loyalty? What did he do to show them how much they meant to him? He pictured the makeshift grave in the overgrown corn field. Would Kyle be the last to die?

Robby joined Cindy and Teresa in throwing their arms around him in one loving hug. While they conveyed their appreciation, Chuck felt the defiant stare from the one man who wasn't celebrating. Jeff stood against the wall with his arms crossed over his chest.

Chuck's heart wasn't in it either. But the others were. They needed it and he owed it to them. So he closed his eyes and remembered the three souls that weren't there, while Cindy and the children had their way with him.

Chapter 42

As winter set in, Cindy continued to fight Chuck's assertion that a woman in her condition should be excused from guard duty. Five months into her pregnancy, she was still insisting that she hike through the bitter cold to take her turn at the post. It wasn't until the ice started to melt in the spring, that she finally gave in to her limitations and accepted the less physically demanding chores around the camp.

Except for a slight limp, Teresa recovered fully from her leg wound. Jeff appeared to let go of the contempt he held for Chuck. But the biggest news was that they had gone the entire winter without any sign of Jason. It was a period of relaxation unlike any before. For the first time in several years, they had the soothing heat of a forced air furnace to help fight off the cold of winter. Water wasn't an issue, nor was food, and since they kept to themselves, there was no anxiety about the possibility of getting caught while looking for survivors. For most of them, it was the first time since the End that they truly felt relaxed. But as so often happens with relaxation, they began to misjudge the danger around them.

It was a brisk, overcast day in early spring when Chuck tried to maneuver around Cindy and her seven-months belly as they both worked at the stove to prepare lunch. Cindy huffed as Chuck squeezed around her. Despite the posturing and sighs about the other always being in the way, they really enjoyed doing things together even if it was a little cramped.

Chuck saw Brandt waiting patiently at the kitchen table. Cindy reached across and bumped his arm as she dropped a pinch of Italian seasoning into the small pot of ketchup. He grinned and slipped the spoon into his left hand so that he could still stir the noodles while he slid his right hand down to her lower back. It felt like it was one of those sweet moments when a man softly whispers his love for the woman at his side.

He leaned over and gave her a quick peck on the cheek. He rubbed his face in her hair and said, "I love you."

She looked up at him and smiled. "I love you too."

That was the extent of the moment. It was brief, but it was exactly what he needed after the dream he had last night. Not that the dream was anything horrible. The entire sequence was nothing more than Becky opening the front door of the Victorian back in Madison. It was like she was welcoming him home after a night at the antique store. That's it. She opened the door and smiled at him. Then it was over. The part he couldn't shake—was that in the dream it felt like she had never died, like they were still together.

"What are you thinking about?"

Chuck shook it off. "What's that?"

"You've got some giddy smile across your face."

"Oh..." he shook his head, "it was nothing. Just spacing out I guess."

"Well your spaghetti is done. Why don't you pour it in the colander and take a seat. I can manage the rest."

Chuck dumped the noodles into the strainer and was about to join Brandt at the table, when someone started pounding on the front door.

It was his good friends Andy and Jim. But the smile faded from Chuck's face when he saw the look in their eyes. It was a look he hadn't seen since Versailles.

"What is it guys?"

Andy took the lead. "We may have a problem."

Chuck felt his chest constrict. "What's wrong?" he asked cautiously, as he stepped out of the way so that they could come in out of the chilly breeze.

Andy waited for Cindy to start setting the plates on the table before turning to Chuck and whispering, "Julie had the south post this morning." He paused and made sure that neither Cindy nor Brandt were within earshot. "She hasn't checked back in yet."

Jim put his arm around Chuck and pulled in close. "Robby went out to relieve her at ten...and we haven't been able to raise him."

Chuck wasn't prepared for the implications of what his friends were telling him. With a gasp, he lashed out for Jim's arm just as he started to fall. Their words were like daggers assaulting his will. It couldn't be—not

Robby. An uncontrollable shiver buckled his legs.

Andy grabbed Chuck's other arm, and with Jim's help they were able to keep him upright as he came to grips with the situation. Andy slipped under his arm, grabbed him by the waist and asked, "What are we supposed to do?"

Chuck could barely keep his head upright. His tongue swam in his mouth and his nostrils flared as he struggled to find the voice of reason. That was the one thing that had saved him from hysteria so many times. He closed his eyes and told himself that they didn't know anything for sure. A few seconds later he opened his eyes and stood on his own. He took another deep breath and the authority started to return to his voice. "We need to try to raise him again."

Without saying a word to Cindy, Chuck grabbed his coat and they were out the door, headed toward the command post that was set up in the gas station. The recharging holsters and walkie-talkies were there along with a base receiver that was hardwired to a generator. The receiver was kept on and monitored for transmissions whenever anyone was stationed at the guard posts.

The bell mounted over the old wooden door clanged as they rushed inside. Chuck shot past the pyramid of motor oil stacked in front of the dirty plate glass window and plopped down on the swivel chair behind the heavy metal desk. Trailing by less than a step, Jim and Andy flanked him as he keyed the mike and said, "South post...come in. South post... if you're there, pick up." He waited as dead air filled the room. He glanced up at Jim and Andy and then keyed it again. "South post...come in." He started rubbing his chin as the silence from the speaker picked at his stomach. Ten seconds of torment later he pressed the switch down and said, "North post...come in."

He barely had his finger off the switch before the speaker sounded, "This is north post. Come in home base."

Chuck was hoping that the mike was faulty, but the sound of Jeff's voice put an end to that. He poised his finger over the mike as he tried to decide how much to tell Jeff. He had a right to know. After all it was his Julie. But more often than not, Jeff let his emotions get the better of him.

Chuck teased the mike switch as he thought. Jeff surely would have heard them trying to raise the south post. He also knew that Julie's shift ended at ten. With a grimace, he decisively keyed the mike and said,

"North post return to base. North post return to base immediately."

"Copy that. North post returning to base. Is something wrong?"

Chuck pushed back from the mike without answering. He rocked back in the swivel chair and covered his face for a second to let the tension escape. He said, "Get everyone packed up. I want everyone ready to leave in fifteen minutes. I don't care what you have to leave behind. Fifteen minutes…that's it…am I clear?"

Andy understood and nodded. Jim asked, "What about Julie and Robby?"

Chuck clamped his jaws down tight as he hated to have to speak the thought out loud. "We're not looking for them. They're on their own if they're still alive."

Jim's face turned pale as he fought hard to swallow. "You think they're dead don't you. You think Jason is coming."

Chuck didn't need to say anything, his numb stare answered the question.

Andy grabbed Jim and pulled him through the door. "Come on! We've got to get the word out."

Chuck sat, pretending to watch his friends sprint across the street to warn the others. The decision cut deep. Chuck started to lose his composure as his eyes began to moisten. Robby…he could still remember the day he found him in Indianapolis, but he couldn't recall how skinny and close to death the boy was. Those images had been pushed out and buried so long ago that no matter what memory he conjured, he always saw Robby healthy and with that wonderful smile on his face. He thought about the times he and Cindy sat on the porch and watched him play with the other kids—the laughing and the teasing. He looked down and remembered how Robby fell asleep on his lap back when Teresa was hurt.

Chuck buried his face in his hands. Lord…how could he just leave him? How could he not even try to find out what happened? He thought about what Jeff said after they left Versailles—that he should have given Cathy and Mike a proper burial. Jeff could have been right back then. Chuck swallowed as he thought about how Jeff would react this time. After all he didn't know for sure that it was Jason. It could be anything. It could be that Julie fell and hurt herself, and that Robby's walkie-talkie lost its charge.

Tears trickled down his face as he fought the decision at hand.

What would he tell Teresa? How could he tell Teresa? He shook his head as he lowered his face and let his nose drip onto his jeans. As if a trembler was working down his body, his shoulders began to heave as he suddenly lost all ability to hold his emotions in check. In truth, no one wanted to search for them more than he did. There were a thousand scenarios that could account for the radio outage and only one of them meant any danger to the group. All it took, though, was that one in a thousand. He couldn't risk it and the rest of them couldn't risk it either even if they didn't know it.

He took a deep, shaky breath and then slowly pushed himself out of the chair. Jeff would get back as quickly as he could. Fact is he would probably run most of the way and be back in less than twenty minutes. First thing Jeff would do is head to the house to check on Julie. Chuck had to get there before he did.

~~~

Jeff was jogging when he rounded the curve and saw everyone scurrying to load up the vehicles as fast as they could. His pulse picked up as adrenaline fueled his speed to a full sprint. He saw Jim carrying Teresa, crying and kicking, out to the back seat of their car as he ran past their house. Where was Robby?

He thought about the south post not answering Chuck's call. He sprinted through the grass and leaped up onto the porch of his house as a tingling sensation overcame him. Julie had to be waiting for him inside. But as much as he needed that to be, he had a horrible feeling that she wasn't.

He burst through the front door and was already starting to scream out for her when he saw Chuck standing in the living room. Both mind and body locked up as he crashed into the wall. Without any attempt to brace against the fall, he hit the floor hard as Chuck came running over to help. He didn't even notice the impact. All he felt was the numbing sensation of the tingling all over his body. It was a nightmare that he had to wake up from. He pushed Chuck off and screamed, "No! No! It can't be her!" as he scrambled off the floor. He fought through Chuck's hands and made a run for it. Just before he got to the door, Chuck grabbed him from behind and wrapped him up in his arms.

He tried to fight. Then the strength left his arms as he began to sob. As he did, he stopped trying to pry himself free of Chuck's grip and clutched him for support instead. As if someone suddenly pulled the plug to Jeff's life support, his legs buckled and they both fell to the ground.

Chuck pinned him to the floor and cried, "I'm so sorry! We lost Robby too."

All Jeff could do was tremble as the emotions poured out of him.

"I know, I know," Chuck panted, as he wrapped his arms around him.

As soon as Chuck began to ease his hold, Jeff erupted again. He started kicking with his knees and feet as he cried out, "No!" As Chuck fought to stay on top of him, he gathered the last remnants of his strength and connected with a round-house right. In the split second that it took for Chuck to recover from the punch to his jaw, Jeff was out the door and scrambling to escape what he couldn't accept. He made it halfway across the yard before a weight hit him from behind and everything went dark.

When he woke, he was face down in the weeds and grass with Chuck back on top of him. In desperation he cried out, "No! Somebody help me!"

Jim and Andy ran over, but instead of helping him, they helped Chuck hold him down.

~~~

Chuck barked out, "Get me some rope—Fast!" and Andy took off running.

The vehicles were lined up and ready to head out when Chuck climbed back out of the Chevy without saying a word to Cindy. She was staring straight ahead with bloodshot eyes and a wet, clammy face that left no room for mistaking her position. She thought it was wrong to leave without searching for them.

The fifteen minutes had turned into half an hour, and Andy and Jim were still standing outside the Toyota at the rear of the line and talking. Chuck ran back to the two of them and asked, "What's the delay? We should have been on the road already."

Andy turned and expressed his concern. "Are you sure? You don't want to look for them?"

"We can't take the chance."

Jeff twisted and pushed himself up to a sitting position in the bed of Andy's Toyota. "What are you guys talking about?"

Jim reached in the bed and tested the ropes around Jeff's ankles and wrists, saying nothing. He turned to Chuck, "Remember who you're talking about. That's Robby out there."

Chuck closed his eyes. He couldn't fight this now.

Andy added, "They might just be hurt…or their walkie-talkies might not be working."

Jeff banged his feet on the steel bed of the truck and yelled, "You mean you don't know if they're dead?" as he fought to free himself.

Jim glanced at him but ignored the question.

"Goddamn it! Does anyone know if Julie is actually dead?"

This time Jim did answer. "Chuck feels it's too dangerous to go back and look."

Chuck dropped his head. *Do I have to bear all this guilt myself?*

"Chuck!" Jamie shouted, as he ran up. "Let me go. I can be there in fifteen minutes, tops, and find out for sure."

Jim jumped in. "Let him go, Chuck. He's run with Jason. If it is him, he'll know how to hide and stay out of Jason's way."

Chuck looked at Andy. "What do you think?"

"I don't know, boss. I'll go whatever way you say to go."

"I'm not questioning your loyalty, I'm asking for your honest opinion because I value it."

Andy lowered his eyes. He wasn't ready to voice that kind of decision yet, but it was fairly clear that he thought they should search for them.

"Remember what that mother-fucker did with Cathy and Mike back at Versailles," Jeff spewed from the bed of the truck, as he raised his head high enough to glare at Chuck. "That son-of-a-bitch doesn't care about anyone but himself. If he's too scared to go—cut me lose and I'll go find them!"

Chuck walked over to the bed and said with a stare that put Jeff back in his place, "You're not going anywhere! You're way too emotional for this. It's that kind of emotion that will get us all killed." He returned his attention to Jamie. "You're sure you want to do this?"

"I can do it, Chuck. Fifteen minutes is all I ask. Then we'll know for sure."

Chuck thought hard. Then he directed Andy, "Go grab a few sticks of the dynamite out of the back of my truck and four of the walkie-talkies." Andy took off for the front of the line while Chuck turned to Jamie. "I'm not going to send you back there naked. You get in trouble—you use that dynamite."

Jamie nodded "And your shotgun is the wrong tool for this job." He pulled Jim over. "Get Jamie one of your rifles and a pistol and plenty of rounds for both." Jim took off running for his Avalon while Chuck took Jamie by the arm. "There's no need for you to take any chances. You see anyone—and I mean anyone—whether or not it's Jason's men…then you head right back here."

"What if I haven't found Julie or Robby yet? They could still be alive."

"Don't be a hero now, son. If there are others back there and they hear you shoot one of their men, they're going to come running."

Andy ran back with the radios and the dynamite. While Andy pushed a fuse into the end of each of the three sticks, Chuck gave Jamie two of the walkie-talkies. "You take two: one as a backup in case the charge is gone in the other. You notify us when you get there, what you find, and when you're heading back."

Jamie asked, "Are you guys going to pull out?"

"No. We're going to wait for you to come back." He grabbed Jamie by the back of the neck. "You're coming back right!"

"I'll make it."

Jim ran up carting a rifle and one of his pistols. Jamie shoved the pistol in his front pocket, slung the rifle over his shoulder, and stuck the dynamite under his belt before tightening up the slack in it.

Chuck held him by the arms for a second as he tensed up in thought. He clamped his teeth together and inhaled, then he let go. With his jaws so tense that it was hard to talk, he said, "Go!" and Jamie took off running.

He, Jim and Andy watched Jamie round the bend of the road and disappear behind the tree line. Chuck grabbed Jim by the arm. "Go back to your car. I want you to drive my truck, have Sara drive your car. I want you guys to head on out. Cindy has a map and knows where to go. We'll meet up with you as soon as we can."

"You sure you want to split us up?"

"No, but I don't want to take a chance on none of us making it.

Now go on!"

Jim took off running and a few seconds later the Chevy and Avalon pulled away. From the bed of the truck, Jeff spit out, "Don't think you're some kind of hero...I can't believe you were just going to leave them here."

Andy stepped over next to Chuck. "You want me to gag his mouth?"

Chuck kept his eyes on the bend in the road where Jamie disappeared. "No, he's got a right to his opinion."

Their wait felt like an eternity. Finally the mike keyed up on one of the walkie-talkies. In a soft whisper they heard Jamie say, "At the post. No sign of J or R yet. Wait—" There was dead air for ten seconds before Jamie's whisper came back. "Somebody's here. There's movement all around me!"

Chuck jerked alive and keyed the mike, "Return...repeat...return."

For almost a minute the air was quiet as Chuck and Andy huddled around the walkie-talkie. They were about to key up again when they heard the first shot in the distance. Chuck flinched and jerked back against the side of the truck. "Fuck!"

Andy started for the cab of the Toyota when two more distant shots rang out and stopped him in his tracks. He turned and looked at Chuck still standing against the bed and staring at the walkie-talkie. That's when they heard Jamie's last transmission. The short transmission was rushed, forced out before it was too late, "Its Jason...repeat, its Jason...Go! Go! Go!"

There were two more shots as Chuck and Andy looked at each other. Before they had a chance to say anything, a flash lit up the overcast sky. A second later they felt a tremor rumble through the ground beneath them as a distant thunder rolled in—it was the dynamite.

Chuck was in shock. He had let a man go to his death. He turned around and leaned against the bed of the truck for support. As he swallowed and opened his eyes, he saw Jeff staring at him with his mouth gaping open. For that moment they both shared the same terrible feeling. Then Andy yelled, "Come on! Let's go! They're coming!"

Chuck left Jeff staring in utter loss at the dark sky overhead as he ran up and jumped behind the wheel of the Cadillac.

Chapter 43

Cindy guided them east along State Road 42 until they reached London, a small town southwest of Columbus, Ohio, that Chuck had circled on the map. That's where they would wait for the others.

Jim pulled off at the first gas station they came to and parked under the canopy next to the pumps closest to the road. While Cindy slowly eased herself out of the truck, he grabbed the tool pouch out of the back and headed over to pop the caps off the buried tanks.

Cindy tried to keep a stiff upper lip as the face in the rear window of the Avalon pulled even with her and stopped. It was Teresa, or at least what was left of her. There didn't seem to be any life behind those young eyes staring out the window. Cindy felt her throat start to swell up as she reached over to open the door. She never got the chance as Teresa suddenly came to life and got out. Without saying a word, she hurried across the lot with her head lowered and disappeared around the side of the building. Cindy didn't follow her or try to stop her. Teresa wanted some time to be alone. The only thing they could do was be there for her if and when, she needed them.

Sara glanced over to the side of the building. "It'll take a while."

Cindy sighed, "I just can't believe it."

Sara looked over her shoulder and watched Jim snap the cap off one of the buried gas tanks as she walked on over to Cindy. "Do you think we did the right thing?"

"What do you mean?"

"You know...leave without looking for them."

Cindy fired back, "They are looking."

"But Chuck—"

"But Chuck nothing," Cindy interrupted, as she started to get mad. "He did what he thought was best. Don't get me started. I've watched that man suffer with decisions that no one else had the balls to make."

She pinched her lips together and shook her head. "No...don't get me started. You don't have the right to criticize my man until you've walked in his shoes."

"I'm sorry...I didn't mean—"

Cindy raised a hand and turned her attention back to the stretch of State Road 42 from which they came. In truth, she knew her staunch defense of Chuck's position was at least in part motivated by her own fear that he had made the wrong initial decision. As Jim worked from one cap to the next, she and Sara leaned against the truck and waited.

~~~

Chuck was drained. Even the sight of the Chevy and Avalon parked under the canopy did little to spark his energy. The deaths of three friends were weighing heavily on his conscience. It didn't help that Brandt kept asking about the ground tremor for a good ten minutes after they took off. When the boy finally accepted that no answer was coming, he quit trying and adopted Chuck's absent stare out the windshield.

Chuck pulled off and parked the Cadillac along the left side of the Chevy, while Andy pulled in behind him. Chuck opened the door but had to wait a few seconds before he had the strength to pull himself out. When he finally got out and raised his face to Cindy and Sara, it was clear he needn't say a word. Sara covered her mouth and looked away while Cindy dropped her head and ran over to him. They wrapped their arms around each other, and as he felt the beat of her heart against his chest he saw Lori shaking her head in the Avalon. A moment later he spotted Teresa peering around the corner of the building. He saw the initial hope in her eyes fade right before she ducked back behind the cinder block wall.

Andy walked over and asked with the most energy of anyone there, "What do you want me to do with Jeff?"

Chuck didn't respond immediately. He felt like he had to gather his strength before he could. He put his hand on Andy's shoulder and said, "We need to untie him. The poor man has been through enough."

Chuck didn't really know what to expect from Jeff. But any concerns of hostility were quickly laid to rest when he looked in the bed and saw Jeff's state. Like all of them, Jeff was simply trying to deal with the loss. Chuck reached in and untied his hands and feet while barely making eye contact. Jeff was in no hurry to get up. He waited for Chuck to lean back out of the way before slowly climbing out and walking off to be alone.

As the journey got back underway and they continued through Ohio, Chuck started thinking about the joy and celebration they originally shared back in Madison when it was decided they were leaving. It all seemed so incredibly long ago. The more he lingered on the memory, the more it left him longing for the peaceful times along the river. Maybe they would have been better off if they had stayed—but he knew that was no longer an option.

He and Cindy talked very little as they drove. It was an uncomfortable time, compounded by the fact that he could feel them falling into the same trap of non-communication that he and Becky had spiraled down. But this isolation bothered him even more because deep down he needed to talk to her. He needed the comfort of sharing his thoughts. He needed to unburden himself of the dread filling his mind. He needed to share the awful feeling that the light at the end of the tunnel was slowly being snuffed out as Jason closed in around them. His fear was that they were being played with, teased the way a cat does with a mouse right before eating it. He wanted to tell her these things, but he didn't. He would shoulder their weight alone as long as he could. That was his job. Everyone was down already and they didn't need any unfounded concerns adding to their anxiety.

Teresa was in the worst shape. She looked at him differently, looked at everyone differently. She was going through the motions of living, but her heart wasn't in it. She had undoubtedly watched the painful death of her parents, been shot in the leg, and now had lost the last member of her family—the younger brother that she felt responsible to keep alive and safe.

He looked for the sparkle in her eyes, the look that always made him smile. But it was no longer there. Perhaps not seeing it was best. It prepared him for what happened when they stopped for gasoline outside Franklin, Pennsylvania.

~~~

Andy popped the cap off the premium unleaded tank while Jim grabbed the transfer pump out of the Chevy. Chuck picked a spot along the shoulder of the road and kept watch on the line of trees across the street. He could sense Jason's men all around them. He could feel them hiding in wait. With that feeling came the dreadful knowledge that the game wasn't going to last much longer—the cat was finally getting hungry.

The sound of a car door shutting spun him around in time to see Teresa walking toward the side of the building. "Teresa!" She didn't acknowledge his yell. He looked over at the corner of the building and saw the words 'Women's Bathroom' painted six feet up on the whitewashed cinder block. Since he figured she was going to the bathroom, he continued his watch of the trees.

Twenty minutes later the cars and the two portable generators in the back of the Chevy were full of gasoline. Andy walked over and kicked open the door to the station, went inside and returned a few seconds later cradling as much octane booster and stabilizer as he could carry in his arms. Even the premium gasoline had degraded to the point that it was almost useless. Their only hope was that their engines wouldn't foul up before they made it to Boston.

Everyone filed back into the cars as Chuck slid behind the wheel of the Chevy. Just as he was about to turn the key, he stopped and jumped out. He hurried back to the Cadillac as Jeff opened the driver's door. "Have you seen Teresa?"

Jeff looked at him with a blank face. "She's not in the Avalon with Jim and Sara?"

Chuck ran up to the rear window and scanned the backseat of the Avalon. She wasn't there. The bathroom. He sprinted around to the side of the building. Jeff caught up to him as he slammed the metal door shut in disgust. Teresa wasn't in it.

They looked at each other for a second as the others came running. Then everyone split up and started searching the derelict cars and overgrowth surrounding the station. Within minutes they were fanning out from the building.

That was when a shiver hit Chuck that stopped him dead in his tracks. He looked at the others. Andy was out a few hundred feet by himself. Jim and Sara kept disappearing behind cars and trees. Brandt had hopped a barbwire fence and was plowing through the high growth of an old field. Chuck slowly turned around and looked at the woods across the street. As he stared at the shadows lurking behind the trees, a fear started to grow in him that none of them were going to make it. In a moment of desperation he tried to picture his dream of Cindy and their son watching the sunset from the high cliffs of Scotland. But he couldn't! He couldn't get himself to visualize what had become his driving force. He flinched and yelled, "Stop!"

The rustling sounds of the search came to stop as everyone stood and turned to see what he wanted.

"Back in the cars—NOW!" he demanded with urgency. All but Andy and Jim started back toward the cars. Those two lingered where they were, trying to catch one last glimpse before giving up the search. Chuck yelled, "Get back here now goddamn it!"

That got their attention. As they ran back, Cindy grabbed Chuck's arm. "What is it?"

He couldn't hold it in any longer. "They're all around us…I can feel it. We've got to get out of here right now."

Cindy's concern was evident in her face as she put her hand on his shoulder and asked, "Are you okay, honey?"

Chuck grimaced and squeezed her hand. "I'm not losing it. You may think I am, but I'm not—I promise." He looked back over at the line of trees. "Jason is playing some sick game with us. I can feel it. He wants us to separate so that he can take us one at a time…make the rest sweat it out."

No matter what Chuck said or where he looked, Cindy never took her eyes off his face. "You think he's still behind us?"

Chuck wanted her to confirm that she felt Jason's presence too, but when he looked in her eyes and saw her fear he recognized it immediately for what it was. Her fear wasn't that Jason was lurking in the shadows, her concern was about him. He knew when to shut up and now was that time. "Never mind. Just get in the car. We need to go."

"What about Teresa? We can't leave her."

His look gave her an answer that she couldn't bear.

"Like hell we are!" she huffed, as she pushed past him and tried to burst into an all out sprint for the field behind the station. He wrapped his arms around her and pulled her back before she could. "No!" she cried out, as he dragged her kicking and screaming back to the truck. "Not her! You can't leave her!"

The others stood around the cars and watched as Chuck swore. "She's gone, baby…I thought I saw her going to the bathroom…but she was really running away."

Cindy screamed and clawed his arms as he jerked her around the front of the truck. "I hate you!" she screamed once and then cried a second time as he forced her in the truck and shut the door. He ran around and jumped in before she could pull herself together and get back out.

Half an hour later Chuck pulled to a stop in the middle of the road, took the keys out of the ignition, got out, and walked back to Andy's Toyota.

"What's going on?" Andy asked.

"I've got a big favor to ask."

"What you need boss?"

Chuck reached in through the window and put his hand on Andy's shoulder. "I think we're being followed." Andy turned and looked behind the cab. "You can't see them. I think they're staying back far enough to keep out of sight, but close enough to keep tabs on us."

Andy looked Chuck in the eyes and asked, "You want me to lay back with a rifle and some dynamite and provide a little deterrence for them?"

That actually sounded like a really good idea, but Chuck wasn't going to let Jason or his men take one more soul from his group. "No, but I would like you to fall back about a mile and see if I'm right. Can you do that for me?"

"What about Brandt?" Andy asked, as he motioned toward Brandt listening from the passenger seat.

Chuck dropped down to where he could see Brandt through the window. "Why don't you go up and ride with Jeff in the Cadillac."

"Sure, Chuck," Brandt said, as he opened the door and jumped out.

"You want to stay in touch with a couple of the radios?" Andy asked, as he gestured to the two walkie-talkies sitting between the seats.

"Those the ones we got for Jamie?"

"Yeah."

"Good idea. You keep them. I'll grab the other one. Give me a click before you take off to make sure they're working."

"Sure thing boss."

As Chuck walked past the others waiting in the Cadillac and Avalon, he felt their discerning looks falling on his back. It made him feel like they could be a group without a leader before too long. He grabbed the last radio out of the back of the truck, turned it on, and signaled to

Andy. A second later he heard test clicks from both of Andy's radios. He held up his hand, and then clicked the mike button on his. Andy signaled out the window that it was received. Chuck gave him a nod and turned around to climb in the truck, but then froze with the door half open.

In the split second that it takes to blink, he saw her. Not Cindy—but Becky. She was sitting on the passenger side, waiting for him. She smiled and for that instant, all the stress and exhaustion simply melted from his body. For that same second he was filled with the kind of warmth that gives strength. As if none of it were real, he blinked and Becky was gone. Cindy was staring out the windshield, still stewing in her anger and refusing to look at him. The pull of gravity brought back the burden of his weight and forced an exhaustive effort for him just to climb in the truck.

Chuck's fear was confirmed in less than two miles. He and Cindy heard Andy key the mike and say, "You're right boss. I can see reflections off the glass and steel of several cars. I also see exhaust smoke every once in a while. By the looks of it, I think there's quite a few of them." Chuck saw a confused mix of regret and fear in Cindy's eyes when she jerked around toward him. Andy said, "What do you want me to do boss?"

Cindy scooted across the bench seat toward him as he keyed the mike. "Do you think they've seen you?"

"I'm afraid so, boss."

Cindy grabbed his arm as he considered their situation. "Do they seem to be staying back or do you think they're going to make a run at you?"

"Strange as it sounds…they seem to be satisfied just hanging back. But they're not making any effort to conceal themselves either."

Cindy squirmed as she dug her nails into Chuck's arm. "Why? Why are they doing this? Why won't they leave us alone?"

Chuck kept his thumb off the mike button and said, "I can't say for sure. You ran with them, what do you think?"

She didn't respond. Instead she slid both hands along the ripe shape of her belly as she fought back a slow, but steady stream of tears.

Chuck hit the mike. "Can you stay back there so that we know what they're doing?"

"Sure can boss."

"If they do make a run at you…you get your ass up to us as fast as you can. You hear that—we need you too much for you to do something stupid."

"Got that boss. Keep you appraised. Out."

Cindy pressed in closer and put her arm around him. Then, as if his touch gave her strength, she stopped crying and asked again, "Why don't they attack? They have so many and we have so few?"

Chuck rubbed her leg and said, "I think that question will be answered soon enough."

After a moment of silence she said, "I'm sorry."

"Sorry about what?"

"You know…back there…"

Chuck shook his head. "There's nothing to be sorry for. You had no reason to think that Jason was following us."

"But how did you know?"

Chuck didn't answer as he thought about the dream he had of Cindy and their son standing on the cliff. He knew about Jason in the same manner that he knew their baby would defy the odds and live when no other baby had. He thought about his dream of Becky waiting for him at the door to the Victorian in Madison, and then seeing her just moments ago in the truck. He thought about how peaceful he felt when he saw her. As he began to wonder about the meaning behind the things he saw and felt, he said, "I don't know how I know…I just do."

"Do you think we should tell the others…about Jason I mean?"

The words came out of his mouth before he even thought about it. "Tomorrow, wait till tomorrow."

Andy checked in periodically as Jason and his men followed the group across the state line into New York. It was getting too dark to drive on unfamiliar roads. They didn't want to crash into a derelict car, or find out a second too late that a bridge had been blown up in the madness of the End.

A few minutes later they pulled into Jamestown. Chuck slowed for a look as they drove through downtown. As the Cadillac and Avalon pulled alongside him, he had a second thought about stopping. Something didn't feel right. He gave the Chevy some gas and veered on to a tiny two-lane road into the surrounding hills. A few miles out of town he came upon a gravel drive. An old farmhouse was waiting for them a hundred yards up the hill.

Chuck and Cindy got out of the truck and stretched in the night air.

As the others made their way up the gravel drive, he reminded her not to say anything about Jason following them.

Jim and Sara got out of the Avalon and as they walked over, Jim asked, "What happened to Andy? Where'd he go to?"

"I asked him to check on something. He's been in radio contact and right behind us the entire time," Chuck said, as he looked for any sign of the Toyota's headlights through the dark of night. "Should be—" then he saw the high beams of the Toyota and pointed, "should be him right there."

Sara asked, "Why'd we come out here? That little town looked like a good spot."

Chuck glanced at Cindy to make sure that she wasn't going to say anything, and said, "Just didn't get a good feeling about that place."

Jim shot Chuck a quick look that questioned his choice of lodging for the night as Jeff trudged by with his head hung low. That was as far as Jim took it. He grabbed a lantern out of the back of the Chevy and then took Sara by the waist and said, "I guess we might as well go see what we got here."

Brandt loitered for a moment and then chased after them.

As Andy killed his headlights and drove the last hundred yards with his running lights, Cindy asked, "Why don't you want to say anything?"

"They need to get a good night's sleep and that won't happen if they know Jason is right behind us."

Andy parked and ran up to them. "It looks like they're stopping in that town back there."

Chuck slapped him on the back. "You did a real good job."

"No problem, boss."

"One other thing. Don't say anything to the others about Jason."

"Gotya," Andy replied. "Don't want to panic them."

"That's right. Now go on and help the others settle in." Andy lowered his shoulders and sprinted over to the steps.

Chuck continued to stand and stare through the darkness like he was waiting on something. Cindy walked over to his side, put her arm around him and matched his stare. It was almost cool enough to see the fog of their breath as they huddled closer together. A few minutes later the chill was about to chase Cindy inside when Chuck pointed. "There." It started as the faintest of glows, but quickly grew until it lit up the distant sky.

"Is that Jamestown?"

"Yeah, they're burning it." They heard the slight echo of distant gunfire. "That's them," Chuck said. "They're getting drunk and firing their guns into the air."

"Like they're celebrating?"

"Yep."

"What are they celebrating?"

Chuck turned her from the fire and started walking her up the hill to the house. "It doesn't matter."

Chapter 44

Chuck glanced around as they stepped inside the dilapidated old farmhouse. Other than an old couch that looked like someone dragged out of a trash pile, there wasn't any furniture at all in the place. But it wasn't completely empty. There were several dozen crumpled beer cans and broken bottles catching the light from the lanterns in the far corner, as well as a few makeshift ashtrays setting on the floor around the couch. In the middle of everything was the cover to an old barbeque grill. It was held firmly upside down on the floor by a couple of bricks and surrounded by scorch marks. It looked like the local kids had used the abandoned house as a party place before the End.

As he helped Cindy to a spot on the couch next to Sara, Jim spoke up from across the room. "It looks like there's a fire back in that small town."

Chuck gave Cindy a heart-felt look and joined Jim and Andy at the window. "It does? I guess there must have been a survivor back there."

"What do you suppose he's doing?" Jim asked.

Andy piped in. "He probably saw us drive through and is trying to signal us…let us know that he's back there."

Chuck nodded as he watched Jim eyeing the glow in the distance. He added, "Yeah, but we can't take a chance on picking anyone else up right now."

Jim looked at Chuck for a long second and slowly turned and walked away. "Yeah, I guess you're right." He stopped at the couch and took a tired seat on the floor between Sara and Lori's feet as Brandt and Jeff joined him. It had been a long, stressful day—one they wouldn't soon forget, and one that made unnecessary conversation both painful and uncomfortable. Jim leaned against the edge of the sofa, lowered his head and closed his eyes. Within minutes, all but Andy and Chuck were beginning to drift off.

Andy leaned closer to Chuck as they continued to stare through the torn screen and cracked glass of the window. "You know…I bet Jason probably knows exactly where we are."

Chuck nodded and asked, "You have any better feel for how many are with him?"

"I counted eight vehicles, but there's probably more. If you figure at least three men per car, then we're looking at twenty-four men—minimum."

They glanced at each other and then looked back at the glow. Chuck was thankful that the walls and glass provided enough insulation that the others couldn't hear the sounds of the distant gunfire. He squeezed Andy's shoulder and said, "You go grab some sleep with the others. I'll take first watch."

"What are we going to do? I think Jason's figuring on making a run at us tomorrow." Andy shook his head, "There's no way we can fight off that many."

"Tomorrow's a long way off. Go get some sleep. It's going to be a big day and I need you to be fresh and alert."

"Sure boss."

As Andy joined the others, his words lingered in Chuck's mind. Andy was right on both counts. Jason was going to make a run at them tomorrow and they couldn't fight off that many. But then perhaps they didn't need to. Chuck thought back to his worries about losing the leadership of the group. His concern hadn't been about any personal loss of power—it was about what would happen if Andy didn't step up and take charge. Without a leader, the group would lose their direction and will to finish what they had started. Every group needed a leader to hold them together; without one, personal feelings and motives would take control and it would quickly become a chaotic mob where everyone was only interested in looking out for themselves.

He rubbed his chin and thought about Jason's men. They were probably guzzling down all the alcohol they could find. In a few hours he could see most of them either passing out or simply falling asleep. Chuck thought about his deer hunting skills. He could slip back in town under the cover of night, and cut the head off the snake. Kill Jason and you kill the threat. He looked over his shoulder at Cindy and the others falling asleep behind him. It was too late for those he had already lost—but not for those seven.

He thought of his dream where Cindy stood on the cliff with their son. Now he knew why he never saw himself standing there with them.

He looked back at the sky glowing in the distance and it hit him. He had seen the distant glow of that town burning before. It was way back, back before the End. It slowly started to come to him. He had the passenger side of the Chevy up on the sidewalk and was speeding toward a newspaper machine. It was the day he realized that the bug wasn't contained.

He looked back at the distant glow and slowly started nodding. Perhaps somewhere deep down, he knew it would come to this all along.

Chapter 45

As the distant glow over Jamestown slowly burned itself out, Chuck thought about how much his life had changed since the End. Perhaps he would never know why Cindy and the others followed him, or in what they based their faith in his leadership. Perhaps sometimes you just had to live and not worry about the reasons that explained why.

Chuck maintained his watch until the calm of night settled in over the echo of distant gunfire. He quietly walked over to those sleeping on the floor around the couch and paused briefly in front of Cindy. She was resting peacefully with her head on Sara's shoulder. But what he saw was her smile and laughter as they sat on the porch swing back at the Victorian and watched the children play. He remembered the feel of her hand in his as they walked the streets in Madison, and how it felt to be close to her when she whispered that she loved him. He smiled as he thought about the man his son would grow to be. He looked at her stomach and then back at her face. Cindy was a good woman. She would tell their son about him. She would tell their son how proud his father was of him, and that his father loved them both deeply. He closed his eyes and burned her image into his memory. After a moment for himself, he kneeled next to Andy and gave him a slight nudge.

That was all it took for the ever alert young man. After a quick yawn, Andy got up and followed Chuck out the front door without disturbing those sleeping around him.

Chuck walked down the steps and out onto the gravel drive before he finally turned around to face Andy. He wasn't sure how to start off what needed to be said, but knew it would come to him once he got going. He extended his hand with an open palm. Andy reciprocated, and as Chuck shook the young man's hand, he said, "You know you've done well." But instead of releasing Andy's hand after the compliment, he continued to hold on to it as he said, "The others look up to you.

I look up to you." Andy tried to let go and pull away, but Chuck kept a firm hold of his hand. "You've really shown your courage by what you did back there in Versailles. No one has ever doubted that. Time and time again you've shown there's no need to. Your runs to Indy for survivors...the way you laid back behind us when I asked you to. All of that goes a long way in a man's book. At least it sure does in mine."

Andy tensed up and re-gripped Chuck's hand. "You're not going any farther are you?"

Chuck studied the dark silhouette of Andy's face under the night sky and said, "No son...I'm not. It's time for you to lead the others. Time for you to make sure they reach their destination."

"I don't know if I can."

Chuck pulled Andy over to him and wrapped his arms around him in a heart-felt hug. "You can," he said with a squeeze. He pulled back and said, "I don't know if anyone else could...but I know you can. This is what you were born for. This is your destiny."

"But I don't know if I could make the decisions you've had to make."

"You can. It won't be easy...it never is. But you'll make the decisions that need to be made and they'll follow you. Just like me, the others have seen how much you care for them and their safety. They've seen how much it tears you apart when we've lost someone."

"It tears us all apart."

"I know it does. But it's how you handle it and what you do afterwards that sets you apart from the rest. I don't think Jim could ever make a decision that might put others in danger. If it were up to him we would have turned around long ago. And Jeff...he'll make a decision alright, but he can't separate the emotion from the logic of what needs to be done. You have. Besides, Cindy will be there to help you. She's got a good head on her shoulders. You need to listen to her and learn. But in the end, it will be you that has to decide what to do next." Once he saw that Andy was nodding, he pulled the young man over to his side and draped his arm over Andy's shoulders. "I know it's a little scary, but you have it in you. I've seen it. So has everyone else. They'll all support you as leader...you watch and see."

"Okay," Andy said softly, "I'll do it." He put his hand on Chuck's back and said with growing confidence, "I'll make sure they get to Boston."

"Good, I don't have any doubt that you will."

After a brief period of silence, Andy asked, "You're going after Jason, aren't you."

Chuck pointed toward the faint glow in the distant sky. "I've been watching their fires die out. Most of his men are asleep or passed out. It won't be any problem to get in close enough to line the bastard up in my crosshairs. I'll take him out and then the rest will lose interest."

"After you're dead they might! You know they'll rush you with everything they have at first."

"I figure as much. If they do, I'll take a few of them with me."

"You know you would stand a much better chance of getting out of there alive if I went with you."

Chuck reached up and grabbed Andy by the back of the neck. "No—that would mean Cindy and the others would be left without a leader. Your job is to make sure she gets to Scotland. Period! Our baby is going to live. Everyone needs to see that. The world needs to believe that there's still hope." Chuck squeezed his neck. "And you're going to make sure that happens, aren't you?"

"Yes sir, boss."

Chuck let go of his neck. "Good!"

Andy rubbed the back of his neck and said, "You know several of us talked about you and Jason one night back in Madison."

"So what'd you have to say?"

"It was around the fire pit after one of our meetings. Big Mike and Julie were talking about how they'd seen Jason ask this guy if he was the one that was going to stop him."

"And?"

"The guy said that he was and then Jason gave him a gun. According to Mike and Julie, the man stood not more than ten feet from Jason and pulled the trigger. Somehow the guy missed."

"What's your point, Andy?"

"I'm saying that no one knows why Jason does that, but every time someone has tried to kill him, they've failed. Some people actually believe he is doing God's work. They believe that's why he can't be killed."

"That doesn't change my mind. I'm still going to try."

"That's not what I'm saying."

"Well what are you trying to say?" Chuck said in frustration.

"Afterwards we got talking about who could kill Jason." Andy stressed the 'who' as he turned from the fading glow over Jamestown and faced the only man he'd ever truly placed his trust in. "We all thought that you could. Every last one of us."

A chill shot up Chuck's back that made him step away from Andy.

"There's something about you. I felt it when we first met in Indy. We've all felt it."

Suddenly Chuck was back in Indianapolis behind the derelict car, sighting up the woman he shot in the crosshairs of his scope. Once again he watched her mouth the words. This time as he watched her in his mind's eye, he heard the words spoken on his own lips. "You're the one." For the first time in his life, Chuck knew the man staring back at him from the mirror.

"I'm serious, boss!"

"I know you are," Chuck said, as he stared at the moonlit gravel around his feet. He filled his lungs and turned Andy back toward the old farmhouse. "But let's get back to what needs to be done. The most important thing is to keep everyone quiet. If Jason has any scouts posted around us, let's hope they're asleep, and do our best not to wake them. Get the vehicles loaded back up and then you guys are going to head out. Cindy has the map."

"This is going to be real hard on her. She may refuse to go."

"She'll go. She knows it's the right thing to do. I'll wake her up and ease her into it. But if later on she tries to get you guys to turn around—"

"Don't worry boss. I won't let that happen."

Chapter 46

Chuck stood with his hunting rifle slung over his right shoulder and his pistol wedged into the front pocket of his pants as he watched the taillights of Andy's Toyota fade into the night. The situation felt peculiar. But the feeling wasn't fear. It was the strange sensation of standing on unfamiliar ground without the added weight of his missing backpack. Not having it left him feeling awkward and unbalanced. He knew it was in good hands. He had given it to Andy when he said goodbye. As the last visible sign of the four-car convoy disappeared into the dark, Chuck turned and started the trek back to Jamestown.

A mile into it a rustling sound stopped Chuck dead in his tracks. He spun around and scanned the road behind him. The old asphalt reflected a soft glow from the stars and moon, but the ditch and trees that ran along the west side formed a solid curtain of darkness. Anyone could have been hiding in those trees.

He thought of Jason's sentries as he slung the rifle off his shoulder and dropped down to his stomach and elbows in the ditch. He chambered a round as he peered back at the shadows along the moonlit road. The scope was useless in the dark, in fact downright dangerous when you didn't know where your target was coming from. Instead he sighted along the barrel and looked for movement. Years of hunting had prepared him for this.

His palms were dry as he ran his finger along the steel curve of the trigger. But that didn't mean that his heart wasn't pounding. Preparation couldn't eliminate instinct. It could only help him control it. He started to force a hard swallow and that's when the hand grabbed his shoulder. Chuck flipped over onto his back but a foot pinned his rifle down against the ditch before he could swing it around. He tried to snatch the pistol out of his pocket, but the shadow standing over him grabbed his hand and whispered, "It's me boss!"

Chuck let go of the rifle, grabbed the shirt of the man hunched over him and yanked him down to where he could make out his face. "Damn it, Andy!" he hissed through a grimace. "You just about gave me a heart attack." He let go of Andy's shirt and scrambled to where they were both squatting in the cover of the trees and weeds. "What are you doing here?"

"Cindy made me—"

"She's not around here is she?"

"No. She's with the others a few miles on past the farmhouse. She had me stop and then she jumped out and refused to get back in unless I agreed to bring you these," Andy said, as he pulled Chuck's backpack off his shoulder.

"I don't need that."

"It's not your stuff," Andy fired back, as he pulled out something about a foot long and handed it to Chuck. "She said that you had to have something and this is what we came up with."

Chuck had a good idea of what it was from the weight alone. When he stuck it out into the moonlight, it still brought a smile to his face. It was three sticks of dynamite taped around a road flare. "How's it work?"

"Just like a match—scratch the tip of the flare across asphalt or rough cement and then get the hell out of Dodge. The way I have it figured, you've got about three or four seconds before that sucker explodes."

"Any more?"

"There's two more," Andy whispered, as he shook the backpack to give a sense of the weight inside. "That was all the road flares we had."

"Three's great!" Chuck said, as he took the backpack, arranged the three bombs, and then slung the canvas bag over his shoulder. "They'll definitely help. That is, as long as I don't let anyone else sneak up on me."

Andy let out a long, raspy, "Ahh…" to discount any validity in Chuck's statement. With a grin he quickly added, "You just taught me too well."

Chuck feigned a smile at the thought and then asked, "What about Cindy, is she doing okay?"

"Pretty much the same as when you put her in the truck. She's still crying. Not bawling or anything. She's keeping a stiff upper lip so that it's not real obvious to the others. But I see the tears." Andy then performed his first act as the group's new leader. He reached over and squeezed Chuck's shoulder. "She'll never forget you—none of us will."

Chuck nodded but didn't say anything.

"You still want to do this?"

Chuck took a deep breath and said, "Yeah."

As Andy helped Chuck up to his feet, he said, "It'll take me about twenty minutes to get back to the others."

"No problem. I won't do anything until I'm sure you guys have gotten away and are safe."

Then Andy offered his hand as one leader to another.

Chuck took it and said, "When my son is old enough to understand what happened, make sure that he knows why I did this."

Andy covered their handshake with his other hand and said, "Sure thing, boss." There was one last squeeze before he disappeared behind the tree line as stealthily as he came.

Chuck's empty right hand was still extended as he stared at the darkness where Andy disappeared. A moment later he made his own tracks in the opposite direction. Jamestown lay just down the road.

~~~

Chuck was beginning to wonder if anyone at all was still awake. He had worked his way in close to the heart of Jamestown and he hadn't seen any guards yet. The flicker of fires still danced across the faces of the buildings at the next cross street, but he saw no shadows or movement in them. He pressed against the brick façade of on old store and inched closer to the intersection. There was a shell of a burnt out four-door sitting along the curb, not more than fifteen feet from the corner of the building. From there he would be able to see the fires and any activity around them.

He took a sweeping scan of the surrounding roof tops and streets. No one was watching. He crouched low to the ground and shuttled past the corner of the building, out into the open for a second, and then found the pavement behind the scorched sedan. With his back to what remained of the rear bumper, he slowly pushed himself up. As the back of his head followed the curve of the trunk, he looked over his shoulder and saw the bonfires down the street. The closest one was about half-a-block down. The fires were still going strong, but not raging like they had been earlier in the night.

There were two guards sitting on the curb in front of an old two-story brick building. The first floor of the building was dark, but the second floor was lit up from a torch or lantern. Chuck squinted as he looked at the dark sign hanging ten feet over the heads of the two guards posted outside. It was an old neon type with a black background that made it nearly impossible to make out, but it looked like it read 'The Vault'. He lowered back down behind the car.

It was probably an old bank that someone converted to a bar or restaurant before the End. Based on the light it looked like someone was upstairs. But where was everyone else?

Chuck rose back up and looked at the buildings on each side of The Vault. There was an old, three-story hotel on the side closest to him. By the looks of it, it was probably big enough to house forty or so men if sleeping three or four to a room.

He caught the fire's reflection off some broken glass in front of a building a half block farther down on the other side of the street. It looked like another bar, one that they had trashed. That meant some men could still be in there. Passed out or not, they would come running if they heard gunshots.

He was about to ease back down behind the car when a man walked out of the trashed bar. Actually calling it a man wasn't as accurate as calling it a mountain that moved on two legs. He was a big, strapping redhead that walked with a heavy gait. The man walked up to one of the guards sitting on the curb in front of The Vault and sneered at him. A second later he raised his foot and rammed the heel of his boot into the side of the man's head. The guard's rifle slid across the sidewalk as he flipped shoulder over shoulder in a painful roll along the cement. The second guard jumped up from his sleep as the big redhead snatched the guard he kicked by the throat. Chuck watched in disbelief as the burly man shook the helpless guard like a rag doll. Then he yelled something at the man. The volume was easily audible, but the man's words slurred into one continuous triad of fury. Whatever he said, both guards must have understood, because when he let go of the one, they both ran back to the exact spots where they were sleeping before, except this time they stood at rigid attention.

Chuck ducked down as the big redhead took a sweeping scan of the street. By the time he raised himself back up, the man was clearing his throat and spitting onto the street. The man turned around and headed back for the bar with the shattered window. It couldn't have been more than a few seconds after he disappeared through the door of the establishment, that a man flew out the broken window, hit the sidewalk, and rolled onto the street.

Chuck eased down again and took a seat behind the car. He opened the backpack sitting on the ground next to him and looked at the three bundles of dynamite. Not yet. He pulled his rifle against his chest and closed his eyes. Every second he could wait gave Cindy and Andy a little more time to get away.

Cindy. When he closed his eyes he could picture the tears in her eyes as she nodded that she understood why he had to do what he was going to do. He could still feel how hard she pulled him to her body. The fact that he had to practically pry himself free of her loving hug brought a smile to his face. He could still taste her lips from their last kiss. He remembered the weight of her body as he kept her from collapsing on the way to the truck, and then his smile faded. That brought back the look in her eyes as he shut the door. They stared through the window at each other for a long moment—both knowing that it would have to last them the rest of their lives.

Chuck pulled in another deep breath as he opened his eyes and rubbed the blood back into his face. If there had been another way—he would have jumped at it. But there wasn't. He knew it, and so did she.

He pulled the pistol out of his pocket, checked the clip and then laid it on the road next to the backpack. The wait was starting to take its toll on his nerves. Anxiety was beginning to show in the jerkiness of his movements. He had to relax, become smooth and fluid like the wind.

Then a man yelled, "Mark!"

He looked over the scorched trunk to a set of French doors that opened up to a small balcony on the second floor of The Vault. Standing there with his hands planted on the wrought iron railing was the man in the canvas duster. It was Jason.

The big redhead came lumbering up from the bar down the street. He stopped under the balcony, and between pants yelled up, "Yes Sir... What can I...do you for?"

Jason yelled down, "Bring me the gimp!"

The big redhead trotted to the door of the hotel.

About a minute later Chuck heard the screams of a young girl, screams that he recognized deep in his soul. Everything else took a back seat as he popped up over the trunk and stared at the entrance to the building. The door swung back open in the middle of his next breath and his world stopped for a brief instant. He saw her. The strength left his muscles and he slid back to the ground behind the car. It was Teresa! They had her bound at the wrists. She wasn't dead. But by the looks of the torn clothes, bruises, and blood-covered jeans, death would have been more humane.

Chuck shut his eyes and clenched his fists as the images of what they had done to her plagued his mind. His anger started to build as the tension swept down from his shoulder and into his chest. He fought down a swallow and then pushed himself back up the trunk to where he could see.

Mark dragged Teresa kicking and clawing through the front door of The Vault. A minute later he came out alone, paused between the two rigid guards, and looked around before heading back for the trashed bar.

Jason walked out on to the balcony with Teresa held firmly at his side. He walked her out to the end and then shoved her out in front of him and started moving her from side to side like he was displaying her for someone to see. But other than the two guards, there wasn't anyone else around.

Jason slowly scanned the street and buildings as he grabbed a fistful of Teresa's hair. When he finished, he bent over and whispered something that immediately got her crying and pleading as she squirmed to get free. As Chuck shifted his weight over his toes, Jason yanked her around in front of him and shoved his hand down the front of her jeans. Her scream came instantly.

Chucked winced as he snapped up the rifle, slung it over the trunk of the car and took aim on Jason. His lower jaw continued to tremble, as he heard her scream even louder while he positioned the crosshairs on Jason's head. He felt the sharp curve of the trigger as he focused on Jason's temple, but then his vision blurred. For a second he no longer saw Jason's head through the scope, instead he saw the buck from his first hunt with his dad. He felt his dad's whisper against his ear, "You don't want the creature to suffer."

Chuck blinked as he pulled his thoughts back to the present. Before he could pull the trigger, Jason turned and walked back inside with Teresa.

He hammered his fist against his thigh as he dropped back behind the car. As he did, he found strength in the man staring back at him from the mirror, and remembered Andy's words. 'We all thought that you could kill Jason—every last one of us'. He peeked over the trunk at the closed French doors and twisted as Teresa's blood curdling pleas for Jason to stop ate at the pit of his stomach.

He was beginning to shake all over as he pushed the pistol under the waistband of his jeans. He remembered swearing that Jason wouldn't take another soul from him. He looked at the backpack and then at the hotel next to The Vault. Most of the men were in there. Before he could plan his next move, Teresa screamed again and all reason left his mind.

He slung the rifle back over the trunk, targeted one guard's bobbing chest under his shaky aim, and pulled the trigger. Before the slight kick of the rifle could find his shoulder, he grabbed the backpack and ran.

The guard went down as Chuck struggled to grab the dynamite in the backpack while sprinting at full speed. At the last second he had to come to a complete stop in front of the hotel.

The other guard screamed, "Intruder!"

Chuck latched onto one of the bundles at the same time the guard drew aim on him and fired. The bullet passed overhead as he bent over, lit the flare, and hurled the bundle through the door of the hotel in one sweeping motion. He shoved his hand back into the bag and managed one stride toward The Vault before the flash. In the blink of an eye, he found himself on his back several feet from where he last stood. For a second, he was dazed and didn't know what happened. Then the adrenaline sparked him back to life. He ignored the pain and blood trickling from his ears, jumped back to his feet, picked up the backpack lying next to the curb, and ran for The Vault. As he fumbled in mid-stride for the second bundle, something slapped his left shoulder and spun him around.

As soon as he hit the asphalt he tried to jump back up, but his left arm buckled and he dropped back to the street face first. He rolled onto his side and saw his left arm covered in blood. Then movement caught his attention and he jerked around in time to see the big redhead standing over him. Mark said something as he straightened his arm out to where the barrel of his rifle hovered just over Chuck's face. But Chuck couldn't hear it. He couldn't hear anything.

Just when it looked like Mark was going to pull the trigger, Chuck saw the middle of the redhead's T-shirt flap out from his body as if it were caught by a gust of wind. Mark rocked and instead of pulling the trigger, he pressed his hand against a small red patch soaking through the white cotton of his shirt.

Their eyes met for a split second and then anger filled Mark's face as he said something and turned around.

Chuck tilted his head back and saw another man standing two buildings down on the sidewalk with a rifle across his forearm. Then he saw a flash and a small puff of smoke. He looked up in time to see blood spray from the top of Mark's shoulder where the round ripped out a chunk of flesh and shirt. He glanced back at the man who fired the shot. The first thing he noticed was that the man was missing his left hand. As the flicker of the flames from the burning hotel and bonfire illuminated his face, he saw who it was. It was Mike Cameron. He wasn't dead.

Chuck's hope was short-lived as a flash lit the night air directly over him. He saw the look of surprise on Mike's face as he staggered back and slowly lowered the rifle as if it were too heavy for him to hold. A moment later the rifle slipped from his grasp and Mike collapsed.

The whole exchange lasted only a few seconds, but it was all the distraction Chuck needed. He snatched the pistol out of his pocket, rolled onto his back and started firing as Mark swung back toward him. For close to five seconds a constant flame shot from the tip of its barrel as Chuck emptied all fifteen rounds from the clip. Mark bounced on the balls of his feet as shot after silent shot struck him in the stomach, chest and neck. It wasn't until the flame at the end of the barrel stopped, that the weight of the big redhead came back down hard on his heels. Chuck saw him falling and rolled out just before the man's knees buckled and he crashed down on the street.

Deaf to any screams and gunshots from those running out of the ransacked bar, Chuck grabbed his backpack and yanked out another bundle of dynamite. As he struck the flare across the asphalt he looked up at the second floor of The Vault. Jason was back out on the balcony with Teresa, holding her flaccid body upright with one arm. The bastard knew it was coming and he wasn't even trying to get away.

Chuck hurled the dynamite, and while Jason reached out to welcome his salvation, Chuck saw Teresa open her eyes and recognize him. For that brief instant he could feel her in his arms again. He was her father and she was his daughter. Chuck didn't try to run or duck. He held her stare and returned her smile for that moment of peace before the sun lit up the night.

Chuck didn't feel anything until he woke on the curb across the street. Even then he didn't really feel any pain. Instead he felt strangely warm and relaxed. Laying face down in a warm puddle on the sidewalk, he watched as the few men and women still alive ran around looking for answers. He saw their screams and cries but heard nothing. A few even ran right past him, apparently believing he was already dead.

He could have been. All he could think about was Cindy and their son standing at the cliff. As he started to picture her, it was different this time. He felt that as she pointed toward the setting sun, he could hear her tell their son that his father came from over there. That's the dream he hoped to fall asleep with.

Just as he knew that Jason was dead, he knew that Andy would lead Cindy and the others safely to Scotland. Yet there was still something that wouldn't allow Chuck to rest. Something still tugged at his heart that he had to make right. As he slowly opened his eyes, he saw Becky and he reached out for her. She was silently weaving her way through the people clamoring on the street. As each rise of his chest came weaker than the last, he knew that she was coming to take him back. He would fall into her arms and feel the same warmth and relaxation he felt when he saw her in his dreams. She would bring him rest. Just as he was about to close his eyes and welcome her, she smiled and he pulled his next breath in deeper.

Chapter 47

Summer came and went three more times before the story started circulating around the villages about a farmer who claimed to have seen a bird. At first, people nervously laughed it off. But then a woman living in Duns Castle in Berwickshire said that she almost fainted when she saw a bird flying overhead too.

A year later, a young boy playing in the shallow waters along the rocky coast suddenly jumped out of the water and started screaming as he ran back to the village. When the elders asked him what was wrong, he said, "Something moved in the water…it touched my leg."

Not all species were entirely wiped out by the bug. As time went on, the New World came to understand and teach about the End. All living creatures that existed prior to the End could be grouped into one of four categories. The first category contained those creatures unaffected by the disease—like most of the insects. The second covered those species that were completely wiped out from the outbreak—where none were resistant to the disease. The third category covered those species where some initially survived the outbreak, but died off later due to the break in the food chain—this category was more speculation than fact—it was based on the collected observations that humans appeared to be the only carnivores that survived. The theory was that undoubtedly a few other species initially survived the outbreak, but then starved into extinction because they couldn't adapt to the scarcity of food.

The fourth category comprised the New World. It included humans and a few other species. Like Andy's group, the New World not only initially survived the outbreak, but also learned how to adapt their life to the resources available to them. At last count this category had comprised roughly three dozen species. The most exciting aspect of this last category was that just about the time that everyone thought the count was firm, another species would be seen.

It reinforced the first lesson that Cindy taught her son. She told him that nature has a resilient backbone—as long as those selected to bear the burden have the will to keep hope alive.

Chapter 48

The gears produced a soft whine as the convoy of electric cars passed the 'Welcome' sign on State Road 7. Cindy didn't say anything and neither did Andy, but she knew he saw it too. Someone had whited-out the old town name of 'Madison' on the welcome sign. It now read 'Ferryman'.

She thought of the rotten backpack they found in Jamestown. It wasn't close to any of the three dozen skeletal remains scattered about the street. Instead, it was lying on an open spot of asphalt along a line of parked cars. Unlike most of the other cars around town, the cars in that line weren't burned out. They had been sitting there for nearly eight years, right where Jason and his men had left them.

So when she saw the 'Welcome to Ferryman' sign it made her heart jump. Chuck had made it out of Jamestown—it was the only reasonable conclusion. She bit her lower lip and tightened her grip around Charles. The thought of her son finally meeting his father held an emotional grip on her heart.

No one said a word as they crossed over State Road 62 and headed down the bluff toward the Victorian they called home so long ago. She stroked the hair of her son as she looked at Andy behind the wheel. He had grown into a fine man, a real leader. Andy was the one that finally brought unity to all the villages in Scotland. Chuck had been right about him, and about finding more survivors there. The fatality rate among the Scottish was much lower than that of other nationalities. The latest estimate indicated that roughly one out of every seventy-three Scotts survived the End. That was nearly five-hundred times better than the numbers shown for the States.

Andy finally cracked a smile as the car rounded a curve overlooking the town below. "There it is."

Their eyes met for a second and she could tell that he was as excited about seeing Chuck as she was. She asked, "Do you think about him much?"

Andy's eyes lost their focus as he smiled. "It's not like I'm actually thinking of him…it's more like I feel his influence in my subconscious. You know what I mean?"

"Yeah."

Charles asked, "Is this the place you told me about?"

Cindy squeezed him. "Yes! This is where your father and I lived before you were born."

Charles stretched his neck out so that he could get a better view over the dash as they took a left on Main Street at the bottom of the hill. The experience of driving along the street after so many years felt dreamlike to her. Everything looked the same as she remembered—yet different. Young trees had sprouted up in clusters around the older trees that lined the street. Vines had completely overtaken some of the smaller houses, and knee-high weeds highlighted every crack in the street and sidewalk. It appeared that the town of Madison was slowly being reclaimed by nature. Cindy pulled back into the cushion of the seat. Chuck wouldn't have let that happen.

Just as her hope was starting to fade, she saw the corn, neatly tended and growing in the same field that Jim and Sara had worked so long ago. Her pulse quickened as the old Victorian came into view. She looked over at Andy and saw his excitement as well.

Andy pulled up along the curb, jumped out and was running up the path through the weeds before Cindy even had Charles out of the car. Andy called out, "Boss!" and ran into the house.

Cindy took her son's hand, and then with her chin held high and chest pushed out in pride, she slowly led him along the path to meet his father. They passed the old fire pit on their right, and then walked up to the wooden platform where Chuck would address the group. The bell was missing from the post, and the platform was rotting and falling apart, but it was still there after all these years. A few steps farther and she heard the commotion of voices in the house. Nothing could take away from the joy she was feeling—not even if he had taken another wife.

The voices worked their way toward the door and a few seconds later Andy stepped out. He looked lost for a second as his eyes darted back and forth, then he stepped aside and Cindy saw the older couple standing behind him. For the briefest of instances she still held on to the hope, but then she saw that it wasn't Chuck.

She looked at Andy, as he shook his head and started to say, "This is—"

The old man helped Andy out and introduced himself. "I'm Robert Weiss and this is my wife Vivian."

Cindy stood with her son, five feet from the couple with her mouth hanging open. Charles pointed to the man and asked, "Are you my father?"

Robert smiled as he bent down to where he and Charles could see eye-to-eye, "No, son, I'm not your father. Are you looking for him?"

Charles nodded empathetically.

"What's your father's name?"

"Chuck Bain. He has the same name as me."

Robert straightened up with a speed uncharacteristic for a man his age and stared at Cindy. "Chuck Bain?" he asked with a drawn face.

Cindy nodded and then asked with hope, "Does he still live here?"

The man continued to stare in amazement at her. "Might you be Cindy McKay?"

Cindy reared back slightly as she cocked her head toward Andy and nodded.

The old man pushed his face out farther and turned toward Andy. "Then can I assume that you must be Andy Jones?"

Andy said, "What's going on, old man?"

Robert slowly grew a smile that stretched across his face. He reached back and pulled his wife forward as he said, "It's them!" Vivian reflected her husband's smile as he probed for clarification. "The stories we've heard are true...aren't they?"

"What stories are you talking about?" Cindy asked.

"You," Robert said, as he pointed at Cindy and then Andy, "him... and the Ferryman."

Andy piped in, "What kind of story?"

Robert cleared his wife out of the way as he gestured toward the door. "Come in and sit. I'll tell you everything I know."

Andy broke from the discussion and yelled out orders to the men in the other two cars. He told them to look around and help wherever they could while the batteries recharged. He swung back around and accepted the hospitality of the older couple.

Cindy studied the kitchen table as Vivian brought tea for everyone. She felt the worn lip of the wood and ran her hand across the top, but wasn't sure if it was the same table that she and Chuck ate at every night.

Andy asked, "There are others here, aren't there?"

Robert nodded. "We've got two boys and a girl out taking care of the crops. And another boy and girl over at the library down the street—and they have a little girl about half your boy's age." Both Cindy and Andy stared at him for a moment, before he understood the basis of their shock, and said, "Not really our children you know, but we've all kind of taken a liking to sticking together. You might say that we adopted each other."

She and Andy exchanged glances of understanding.

Then Robert cleared his throat and said, "What I can tell you folks is what was told to me. See this place is kind of like a staging ground. Folks come and stay here for a couple of years, learn how to farm and see how the windmills work and things like that. Then as more people come, the first group takes off." He paused and nodded to himself as Vivian pulled up a chair next to him. "Come next spring we'll take off."

Vivian put her arm around her husband as Andy asked, "Why would you take off?"

"That's just the way it's been done. Our responsibility is to go out and teach what we've learned here to any others we come across as well as spread the word about this place. That way more people will come and the process continues."

"Who told you to do that?"

"The man who led the group here before us. His name was…" Robert tipped back in the chair and searched his memory as both Cindy and Andy leaned closer. A second later he slapped his hand down on the table and said, "Terry Walton was his name. Group before him told him just like he told me." Andy nodded. "Along with telling us what to do…they passed on the story of…" Robert lost himself as he stared at Cindy and Andy again. "They pass on the story of you guys. To tell you the truth I always thought it was just a fairytale used to motivate the younger folk."

Cindy lifted Charles onto her lap and then for the next twenty minutes the three of them listened to the old man recount the story of their battle with Jason. Whether it was the story itself, or just the way the old man told it, listening to it after all these years made it sound somewhat biblical. Andy blushed when Robert told the stories of his heroic ventures to save the unfortunate from Jason's tyranny. But it wasn't until the old man spoke with reverence about the battles of Versailles and Jamestown that their emotions nearly got the better of both of them. It was the first time Cindy heard what Chuck went through in Jamestown to buy their freedom. She knew how much he loved Teresa, and she knew how hard it must have been for him to throw the dynamite. She pushed back from the table as tears silently trickled down her face.

After a couple of minutes for Cindy to collect herself, Robert told them that it was the few men and women that survived the Battle of Jamestown that started spreading the story of the Ferryman. It was the Ferryman who showed them that Jason wasn't doing God's work. People also started talking about what the Ferryman had done in this town. "As the stories I just told you started to spread, they gave people the strength to start believing again." Robert put his arm around his wife and said, "For us...this was kind of a pilgrimage."

Cindy leaned across the table. "Do you know whatever happened to Chuck?"

Robert shook his head. "Sorry Miss, I sure don't."

Vivian nudged him and said, "Tell them about the flowers!"

Cindy's eyes shot back to Robert, "What flowers!"

"Well I can't really say for sure what it means...if anything, but..." he pushed his chair back and got up, "...if you all want to follow me outside, I'll show you what we got."

Cindy took Charles by the hand and followed the old couple out the front door and around to the side of the house to a neatly kept flower garden bordered by railroad ties.

Robert pointed to it and said, "Don't really know what it means, but Terry told me to keep it free of weeds and full of flowers. Told me to make sure that whoever comes after me does the same." He pointed to the tulips blooming in the corner. "My Vivian put those bulbs down herself. Everyone that comes through here adds a little bit of themselves to it."

Cindy looked over the bed of mixed flowers and roses as she remembered what Chuck told her. During the life she shared with him, he mentioned several times how much his wife had loved this house. It was never said with a passing casualness—he would say it and then stand back and look at the house. He said that she thought the house was perfect, except that it needed a flower garden.

Cindy studied the flowers—so much color, so much beauty. That was when she knew she was right about the rotten backpack. Chuck discarded it when he took one of the cars. He didn't die at the battle of Jamestown. He made it back here. He came back to build this flower garden for his dead wife—his one true love.

A sense of calm suddenly spread through her as she realized where Chuck was. She squeezed Charles' hand, and said to Andy, "We need to go to the river."

As Andy took her hand and started to lead her and Charles back to the street, Mr. Weiss yelled, "Is it okay for us to continue staying here?"

Andy turned and looked at the old couple standing arm-in-arm. He said, "Of course it is! That's what this place is for. That was Chuck's dream. He wanted a place where people could come and feel safe and loved; a place where hope would never die. All we ask is that you keep the tradition alive and pass it on to those who come after you."

~~~

Cindy wasn't sure how she would react as they started walking down the boat ramp. She thought she might lose it and collapse, but as she put one foot in front of the other and came upon the rippling waters of the Ohio, she didn't feel like breaking down—she felt proud. She pulled Charles around and held him in front of her as she looked out to the muddy waters.

"You think?" Andy asked.

Cindy slowly nodded her head. "I think he got hurt in Jamestown and came back here to die. He wanted to be with his wife. You know he never stopped loving her." She smiled and looked down at the curly black flocks of hair on her son's head. Without realizing it, she inched forward until the cold waters were flowing over her and her son's feet.

Andy bent down and scooped up Charles in his right arm. As he stood up, he pulled Cindy back from the water's edge and slid his left arm around her. For a couple of minutes they simply stood there in silence and stared out over the Ohio. Then Cindy took a deep breath and laid her head against his shoulder.

Charles pointed and asked, "Did my father drown in the river?"

Andy raised his eyebrows and said, "That's where he's buried, but he didn't drown. He died saving all of us."

"Even me?"

Andy smiled. "Yes…you too. You weren't born yet, but he saved you just the same." He waited for the boy to look at him before he said, "You know your daddy always knew that you would live."

The boy scratched his nose and said, "I was the first one!"

"Yes you were. You know how your daddy knew that you'd live?" The boy shook his head. "Because he loved you so much that he could see you in his dreams." The boy smiled and looked back out over the water.

Andy pulled Cindy closer as she slid her arm around his waist. As they stood and watched the rippling waters of the Ohio River flow by, he whispered softly, "He was a father to more than he knew."

Made in the USA
Charleston, SC
01 February 2012